TQB JUL 2 6 2000

D1441331

Island Flame

**Center Point
Large Print**

**This Large Print Book carries the
Seal of Approval of N.A.V.H.**

ॐ श्री गणेशाय नमः

Island Flame

Karen Robards

Center Point Publishing
Thorndike, Maine

This Center Point Large Print edition
is published in the year 2000 by arrangement with
Bantam Dell Publishing Group, a division of
Random House, Inc.

Copyright © 1981 by Karen Robards.

All rights reserved.

The text of this Large Print edition is unabridged.
In other aspects, this book may vary from the original
edition. Printed in Thailand. Set in 16-point Plantin type
by Bill Coskrey.

ISBN 1-58547-025-2

Library of Congress Cataloging-in-Publication Data

Robards, Karen.
    Island Flame / Karen Robards.
        p. cm.
    ISBN 1-58547-025-2 (lib. bdg. : alk. paper)
        1. Large type books. I. Title.

PS3568.O196 I8 2000
813'.54--dc21

99-089395

To Doug, with love.

One

Lady Catherine Aldley was beautiful, and she knew it. She was very much aware of the picture she made as she stood bracing herself against the rail on the deck of the "Anna Greer," a light wind ruffling her hair and the setting sun turning its red-gold splendor to a vivid flame. The brisk sea air had whipped into her cheeks, and her blue eyes sparkled.

She was only seventeen, and had been pampered and protected all her short life. Since her mother's death ten years before, she had been raised by a nanny and a succession of governesses whose duty in life had been to teach their young charge the things that were important for a lady to know in 1842: to play the harp and the pianoforte, to execute insipid watercolors, to speak the French tongue like a native, and to appear sweetly mindless and childlike at all times. In this last, the good ladies were only partially successful. Cathy could assume the role of a gentle, well-bred young lady very well when it suited her, but when it did not, she was a termagant. Her explosions of rage had sent more than one governess running from the house in tears, vowing never to return. Which, in Cathy's opinion, was just as well. She had no desire to learn anything that was contained between the covers of a book. She wanted to live life, not read about it!

"The girl's plain ignorant!" her father snorted indignantly on one occasion, and it was perfectly true. Although her various governesses had labored long

7

and hard, trying to instill the rudiments of education into her saucy head, Cathy remained sublimely indifferent. When it was discovered that the only use she had made of her learning was to read racy novels, her long-suffering father gave up. Cathy was allowed to dispense with the tiresome business of being educated.

Instead, she learned to dance, and her step was the lightest for miles around. She learned to walk with her toes turned slightly inward so that her flounced skirts swayed like a bell. She learned to smile entrancingly through her lashes, and to laugh, like a tinkling, silver bell, at the men who begged her for a kind word, or, more daringly, a kiss.

Most important of all, she learned to hide her true nature from the men who swarmed around. In company, especially the company of eligible young men, her actions matched the sweetness of her face. Her keen intelligence and hot temper were known only to her nanny, who fervently exhorted her charge to keep that one fault hidden until she found herself a husband.

Cathy's father, Sir Thomas Aldley, ninth Earl of Badstoke and the Queen's Ambassador to Portugal, loved his only child dearly. He saw very little of her, however, and had no idea of how headstrong and selfish she really was. He only knew that she was beautiful and charming, and a great credit to him in his position. It was unfortunate that she had inherited his own wildness of temperament, but she seemed to keep it carefully under control. It was a good thing, anyway, for a woman to have a bit of spirit. Kept a man on his toes. She was really a very good child on the whole, and it was only recently that she had ever given him cause for concern. But during the past six months it seemed like every young puppy in Lisbon had been making up to her, and his daughter's marriage to a foreigner could not in any way help his political career. Sir Thomas began to toy with the idea of removing his daughter from harm's way by sending her, say, on a visit to his sister in England. He could join her there himself next year when his term as ambassador would be ended. In the meantime, he was confident, Cathy would become so caught up in the whirl of a London Season that she would have no time to miss her Portuguese beaus. And sister Elizabeth could be counted on to screen her niece's new friends very thoroughly. Yes, sending Cathy to England was the best thing to do.

Cathy herself had stormed and cried when she was informed of these plans, but her father, once he had made up his mind, could be as stubborn as she was. In the end he wore her down, and, together with her nanny, was able to convince her of the wisdom of his scheme. It was true that she would enjoy being presented to Queen Victoria, who, in the fifth year of her reign, at age twenty-three, was not much older than Cathy herself. But England was so far away, and it had been almost seven years since they had lived there. What if the men did not find her attractive? Perhaps the fashion was for dark ladies in London, instead of for charming blondes. But her father and nanny both assured her, in their different ways, that her unusual beauty would stand out in any company, and Cathy allowed herself to be convinced. She had been an acknowledged beauty since before she entered her teens, and she could not seriously entertain the thought that any man might not admire her.

When the storm of her objections was safely weathered, the Earl heaved a sigh of profound relief, and told himself that he would have to take steps to correct Cathy's wilfullness when he joined her in England. He then turned his attention to making arrangements for her safe transportation there—no easy task in such turbulent times. Lately there had been much talk of a band of pirates cruising in Portugese waters and preying on unarmed ships. The Earl shuddered at the thought of his daughter falling into the hands of men who would have no regard for her innocence or high estate.

When the Earl heard through a friend that the "Anna Greer" was soon to sail for England, it seemed like the answer to a prayer. On loan from England to the Portuguese navy, the "Anna Greer" was outfitted with an awesome array of armor and cannon. No pirate would dare to attack such a formidable ship!

It had been surprisingly easy to arrange for Cathy to be taken on board. She joined a small group of passengers on a ship that had, until this voyage, been confined solely to military operations. Neither the Earl nor his daughter thought to wonder why the "Anna Greer" had so suddenly been permitted to carry civilians.

When the time came, Cathy parted from her father with scarcely a qualm. By then she was far too excited at the idea of taking London society by storm to feel sad about leaving a father of whom she really saw very little anyway. Besides, he would be joining her in England shortly, and he had assured her that she would love her Aunt Elizabeth on sight.

It had been understood from the start that Martha would accompany her young mistress. With Martha along, Cathy could not possibly feel homesick, and the Earl would be certain that his daughter was in good hands.

Two weeks later, with the "Anna Greer" well out to sea, Cathy was cursing the day she had ever consented to make the voyage. She was bored almost to the point of tears. The other passengers were all old enough to be stuffed and put on display in a museum, and the captain was more interested in sailing his ship than in entering into a light flirtation with the loveliest lady on board. She had attempted to try her charms on various members of the crew, some of whom were attractive in a rough sort of way, but Martha was always hovering nearby to spoil such sport.

Cathy sighed, leaning her chin on her hands and staring out over the rail disconsolately. If only something, anything, would happen to relieve the awful boredom!

11

The sun glinted on a thread in her peacock blue brocade gown, and Cathy looked down at it absent-mindedly. It really was a beautiful dress, she thought, as she smoothed the sleeve and admired the elegant way the cascade of lace at her wrists fell over her hands. It was, in fact, one of her favorites. The deep green-blue of the material made her eyes seem as dark and mysterious as the sea itself, and the tight-fitting bodice accentuated her tiny waist and rounded breasts. It was no wonder that she was attracting the attention of a good many of the sailors who were busy with chores about the deck.

Cathy tapped her foot against the deck impatiently, and her bottom, clearly outlined as she leaned over the rail, bobbed up and down in time to her tapping. A husky blond sailor who had been coiling rope nearby stopped what he was doing to stare openmouthed at the befuddling sight. Cathy saw his absorption out of the corner of her eye, and, with a little gurgling laugh turned around. She smiled at the man, her blue eyes sparkling provocatively, and started to speak. But before she could say a word a plump hand tugged at her sleeve.

"Don't you be talkin' to them rough sailors, now, Miss Cathy." Martha had crept up behind her as quietly as a cat. "What would your papa say? Besides, you know yourself that you don't want to have anything to do with 'em. You're goin' to be marryin' some rich Duke or Count or somethin', when we get to England."

"Oh, hush up, Martha!" Cathy scowled at the

gray-haired little woman who was clinging so doggedly to her sleeve. "I shall talk to whomever I please. Besides, I was just going to ask this fellow how long it will be before we reach England."

"Be at least another week ma'am," the sailor said, grinning at Cathy and cheerfully ignoring the frown that Martha directed at him.

"Another week!" sighed Cathy, demurely lowering her dark lashes and allowing her dimples to come into play. "It sounds like forever! And sea voyages are so deadly dull! I wish there was something to do to occupy the time." She smiled at the sailor, who flashed another of his impudent grins at her.

"Now, Miss Cathy, you hush talkin' like that!" Martha said, scandalized by her charge's bold behavior. She grasped Cathy firmly by the arm and attempted to drag her away. Cathy resisted indignantly, and, in desperation, Martha turned on the grinning sailor.

"And you, sailor, if you don't get on about your business and stop annoying innocent young ladies, I'll report you to the Captain. That I will!"

The sailor made a face at her, and opened his mouth to give voice to what Cathy was certain would be a very pithy reply. Fortunately, a cry from overhead cut him off.

"Sail ho!" The words came echoing down from a man high aloft.

"Where away?" a chorus of voices demanded at once.

"Off the port bow!" boomed the reply, and immediately everyone on deck peered to the left, across the open sea.

Cathy stood on tiptoe, straining her eyes for a glimpse of the approaching ship. She could see nothing but an endless expanse of water, broken only by tips of white, as gentle waves broke into the sea. The horizon was a fiery orange as the sun sank beneath it, and Cathy was certain that there was no ship anywhere near at hand.

"It's just a mistake," she said to Martha, disappointed. "There's nothing out there. I can see clear to the horizon, and there's not a thing."

The blond sailor turned from the rail to smile at her. "It's not likely that you could see anything, ma'am. That ship is pretty far away. But there's a ship out there if Dave says so. He's up a lot higher than we are, and he has a spyglass. Likely we won't be able to see her until tomorrow morning at the earliest. That is, if she's coming this way."

It seemed as though he was right. Cathy stayed out on deck until long after dark, hoping for a glimpse of the ship, but she could see nothing. Finally, the cold and Martha's repeated admonishments drove her to her cabin. Once there, she wrapped a blanket around herself and huddled, shivering, on the edge of her bunk while Martha prepared her bath. Under the old woman's disapproving eye she sprinkled rose bath salts liberally in the water, and then lay back, luxuriously to soak the chill away.

As she bathed, Martha bustled about the cabin,

picking up Cathy's discarded clothing and putting it neatly away. She grumbled loudly as she did so, scolding Cathy for her boldness in speaking to a common sailor in such a familiar way. And as for putting scent in her bath water, well, it was all of a piece. They both knew that only one kind of woman acted that way. Martha sighed and said that Miss Cathy's poor mother must be turning in her grave to see her daughter acting so common.

Cathy smiled faintly at the tirade, closing her eyes and sinking deep into the water. Martha's scolds didn't upset her in the least—she was used to them. She ignored the angry muttering and turned her thoughts to what she would wear the next day. She wanted to look her best. She had enjoyed talking to that sailor today, and seeing the admiration in his eyes. Tomorrow she intended to thoroughly bewitch him. Perhaps the primrose silk. . . . She went on making plans until she fell asleep.

Dressed in pale-yellow silk, with her red-gold curls piled high on her head, Cathy was a vision to rival the sun the next morning. As soon as she had completed her toilette she rushed up on deck to see if she could catch a glimpse of the approaching ship. She saw it as soon as she reached the rail. It looked like a beautiful ship, far different from the flat, military vessel on which she was traveling. Under full sail, the other ship was as graceful as a bird, and its proud, high prow rode the waves with ease. It grew larger as Cathy watched, entranced, and she realized that it was closing on the "Anna Greer" with

15

amazing speed.

"It . . . it's so beautiful!" she murmured aloud, as the blond sailor she'd met the night before came up beside her.

"She is that," he said. "But Captain Hogg. . . . Well, he don't remember that the Frogs had a ship like that under sail, and she's flying a French flag. She looks more like one of them new clipper ships, from New England out in the colonies. Until we find out for sure, the Captain requests that you ladies retire to your cabin. Just in case, you know." He squirmed uncomfortably as Cathy turned to look at him.

"What do you mean, in case? What does Captain Hogg think it is? Not . . . surely not . . . pirates!" Her voice rose on the last word, and the sailor stared down at her, alarmed. The last thing they needed, with a possible pirate ship closing in, was an hysterical woman. He swallowed, and spoke up hastily.

"No, ma'am, probably not. The Captain just wants to make sure . . . just in case, you know. Most likely she's just a new ship we've not seen before. But until we find out, it'd be healthier for you ladies in your cabin." He turned to Martha, who had just come up on deck, and repeated the warning. Then, in response to a hail from the quartermaster, he hurried away.

"Miss Cathy, we must go below at once!" Martha said, clutching at Cathy's arm and attempting to drag her away from the rail by main force.

"I'm not going anywhere, Martha, so you can just

16

let go of me!" Cathy cried, and shook off Martha's hand with determination. "I want to be up on deck where I can see whatever happens. You know yourself we'd both go crazy down in the cabin, not knowing what was happening or if it was a pirate ship. No, there will be time enough to go below if trouble starts." She shook her head decidedly, and Martha, long familiar with the stubbornness of her charge, gave up arguing. Sir Thomas should really have done something about Miss Cathy's willfulness years ago. Now it looked as though it might get them both killed! Angrily muttering, Martha remained at Cathy's side.

The ship drew steadily closer until Cathy was able to make out the name, "Margarita," painted in bold black letters across its prow. She could see men, looking no bigger than ants, scurrying about the deck. On the quarterdeck a lone figure motionless, staring across at the "Anna Greer'" through a spyglass.

As Cathy watched, the fluttering square of silk that had been flying at the "Margarita's" flag pole was slowly lowered. In its place rose a black flag which was all too obviously the emblem that had been described to her at sedate afternoon teas. When she had heard about the black flag and what it stood for, Cathy had said proudly that she would never be afraid of any pirate, and that, indeed, she would quite like to meet one. Now her fear was like an iron band closing around her throat, cutting off her breath.

"Miss Cathy, it's pirates! Pirates! Oh, my land, Jesus and his saints preserve us! What shall we do?" Martha's hand was cold with fear as she pulled on Cathy's wrist. "We must go below, Miss Cathy! There's going to be fighting up here!"

"Wait a minute, Martha. I must see . . . maybe they won't fight."

Even as she spoke, a cannon roared, a round black missile soared high in the air and then arched back until it hit the water with a loud splash.

"They want us to surrender!" came the cry from the crow's nest.

"May the fishes feast on my bones if we do!" roared Captain Hogg. "If they want a fight, we'll give 'em a fight!"

He clambered down from the quarterdeck and strode furiously toward the forward cannoneer, bellowing urgent directions to his men.

"Take your positions! Load that cannon! The bastards'll wish they'd stayed home planting crops after this fight, I fancy!"

The captain caught sight of Cathy and Martha standing as though frozen to the deck, and swore roundly. He stamped across to them and looked them over for a moment in silence. When at last he spoke, he made an obvious effort to be courteous.

"Lady Catherine, Miss Jameson, you must go below at once!" His control deserted him abruptly. "Damn it, there's going to be fighting up here! With real guns and ammunition! Don't you women have any sense? Get below, and lock yourselves in your cabin!"

He turned on his heel and marched away, not trusting himself to say more. Martha tugged frantically at Cathy's hand as another cannon roared from the pirate ship.

"Miss Cathy, we've got to get below! You heard Captain Hogg! And they've started shooting! Please, Miss Cathy!"

Martha sounded terrified, and Cathy didn't blame her. She was frightened half to death herself, and she allowed Martha to drag her toward the open hatch. Just as they reached the opening the cannon from both ships boomed simultaneously. Cathy swallowed a sob. This would be a wonderful tale to tell in a London drawing room, modestly downplaying her own heroic bravery, but what if the pirates should actually succeed in capturing the ship? Would they all be murdered, or worse?

Of late, the sadistic cruelty of pirates towards passengers and crew members of captured ships had been a favorite topic of conversation among the ladies of Portuguese society. They whispered of women being stripped naked, searched for loot, and then raped by entire pirate crews. If the women were young, and pretty, the pirates might let them live until they reached some port and let them go. Or they might throw them over the side to drown after having had their way with them. Listening to these tales, Cathy had felt a pleasant shiver of excitement go down her spine. But now . . . now it might happen to her! Suddenly the prospect did not seem exciting—it was terrifying.

"Dear God," she prayed. "Please help me. I'll be so good, if only you'll help me."

"But of course they won't win," she comforted herself, thankful for the first time that her father had insisted on putting her aboard a military ship like the "Anna Greer." It would certainly be impossible for a motley crew of pirates to capture such a heavily armed vessel!

Martha, nervously clucking, herded Cathy inside the small cabin that they shared. Cathy crossed to one of the narrow bunks and sank down upon it while Martha bustled about, first bolting the door, then piling all the movable furniture in the room up against it. Cathy laughed out loud. The furniture looked so funny, piled up against the door that way! Martha looked at her sharply.

"You'll not be gettin' hysterical on me, will you, Miss Cathy? There's no need to be frightened. Like as not, them devils will never even set foot on this ship."

But even as Martha spoke, the harsh shriek of wood scraping on wood told a different tale. The pirates were trying to board the ship! Hoarse cries and the clang of steel against steel rang out loud as the pirates threw grappling hooks to hold their prey, then rushed the crew of the "Anna Greer" in a body. The roar of the cannon shook both ships and Cathy felt the "Anna Greer" heel sharply to port as a cannon ball found its mark in her side. Then came a sound like rain against a tin roof as bits of metal from a cannon ball raked the deck of the "Anna

Greer" like hail. Screams of men in mortal agony made Cathy turn white, and Martha quickly clapped her hands over the girls ears.

"Don't you listen now, my lovely. Don't you listen," she crooned, rocking the terrified girl back and forth in her arms.

The sounds of the battle raging above them grew more terrible. Cathy broke into tears and clutched at Martha frantically, pressing her head into the woman's ample bosom and sobbing as though she were seven instead of seventeen. Martha held her tightly, and Cathy took absurd comfort in the childish conviction that if Martha were there nothing bad could happen to her.

The fighting continued for what seemed like hours. In the close confines of the cabin Cathy and Martha lost all track of time. Hoarse screams and the rattle of gunfire made them hide their heads under their pillows. But finally, and abruptly, there was silence.

After a long, agonized moment in which both women strained to hear any sounds that would tell them the outcome of the battle, Cathy sprang to her feet, clenching and unclenching her fists. She had to know. She couldn't bear not knowing. She began to walk towards the door like a sleepwalker. Martha scrambled after her, catching her around the waist and attempting to pull her back to the safety of the bunk.

"Let me go!" Cathy cried. "I have to get out of here! I can't stand it! Please let me go!"

She tried to wrench herself free but Martha hung on grimly.

Footsteps sounded in the hallway outside the cabin. They both froze, eyes and ears trained on the door. The same question burned in both their minds. Who had won, the crew of the "Anna Greer," or the pirates?

The bolt rattled as someone on the outside tried to get in.

"Hey, Quincy, it's locked! Over here!" The voice was hoarse with excitement.

Cathy swallowed convulsively, her knees suddenly weak. She sank back down upon the bunk, clinging to Martha for support. That voice, with its strange, twangy accent, certainly did not belong to a member of the "Anna Greer's" crew. The pirates had taken over the ship!

"Everything's going to be all right, Miss Cathy," Martha whispered fiercely. "The good Lord will see to that. Just you be quiet now and hide yourself in that wardrobe. Martha'll keep 'em off."

Cathy protested tearfully, but Martha dragged her over to the tall oak wardrobe and thrust her firmly inside. Cathy stumbled, half-falling in the suffocating darkness. There was barely enough room for her to stand upright. Martha closed the wardrobe door without a sound and Cathy heard the click of the latch as it slid into place. She whimpered, like a small, frightened animal. Martha whispered to her reassuringly through the thin panel.

"Everything'll be all right, my lovely. You'll see.

Just you be quiet in there and look to yourself. Martha'll take care of you."

Cathy could hear Martha's footsteps receding as she moved away from the wardrobe. Left alone in that small space, Cathy was terrified. She shook with fear, and had to press both hands tightly against her mouth to stifle her sobs. Her heart was beating so loudly that she was certain it would burst through her chest, at any moment. She could hear the pirates, outside in the hallway, as they began to hammer on the door.

"Open up in there!" the thickly accented voice ordered.

"Open up in there or we'll set fire to the door!"

A heavy crash shook the entire cabin, and Cathy's heart lurched sickeningly. The pirates were going to break down the door!

She sank abruptly to her knees. Her legs felt like they had suddenly turned to water. Her teeth chattered with fright.

"Please, God," she prayed mindlessly. "Please, oh, please!"

Another crash shook the cabin. Then another. And another. When a last splitting sound announced the surrender of the door, Cathy thought she was going to faint. Only the thought of being helpless in the hands of savages kept her conscious. Tears ran down her cheeks, and she had to stuff her skirt into her mouth to muffle the sound of her ragged breathing.

"I must stay calm," she told herself firmly. "If I

23

make a sound, they will surely find me."

From the other side of the partition, Cathy heard grunts and the tramp of heavy feet as the pirates surged into the room. She heard Martha's voice, shrill now with fright, as she berated the invaders.

"Get ye gone, ye heathens!" Martha shrieked. "The good Lord will smite ye with his sword for this day's work!"

Martha's words ended with a gurgle. There was the sound of a blow, and then a thud as though something heavy had fallen to the floor.

"Oh, dear God, no!" moaned Cathy, wanting to rush to Martha's defense but knowing that it would be worse than useless.

Although she strained to hear, there was no further sound from Martha. Cathy listened with helpless terror as the pirates tore the cabin apart. They left nothing undisturbed in their search for valuables, and Cathy knew it was just a matter of moments before they looked into the wardrobe. She hid herself as well as she could amidst the clothes that hung there, but she knew she would be immediately visible to anyone who chanced to open the door.

She heard footsteps approaching and braced herself. This was it.

The door to the wardrobe was jerked open. Light flooded in. The flushed, bewhiskered face of a man old enough to be her grandfather blinked at Cathy bemusedly. His teeth, exposed in a wide grin, had rotted to black stubs. Cathy shuddered, straining as far back into the recesses of the wardrobe as she could. She screamed as the pirate closed one grimy hand over her arm and dragged her from her hiding place.

The old man chuckled at her screams, and pulled her tightly against him, attempting to press his wet mouth to her lips. His breath was fetid and Cathy's stomach heaved with revulsion. She fought him fiercely, silently, too sick with fright to force enough air into her lungs for a scream. He sniggered, dearly enjoying her struggles, and held her out at arm's length while he lewdly ogled her from head to toe.

"Ain't she a beauty?" he marveled over his shoulder, and Cathy saw that there was another man who was bending over Martha's crumpled form. The second man straightened at his companion's words, and stared at Cathy with undisguised desire.

"By God, Quincy, she is that! We best hurry up and take a turn on her before the Cap'n gets a gander at her! We likely won't get another chance!"

"My thoughts exac'ly!" chortled Quincy, and he released his hold on Cathy's arm only to lock his hand over the neck of her gown and jerk downwards with all his might.

The thin silk gave with a loud rip, and Cathy's muslin chemise ripped with it. She stood exposed almost to the waist. She looked at the two leering men with dawning horror. It was true, then, about what happened to ladies taken prisoner by pirates! Her reflections were cut short abruptly as Quincy reached out a hand to fondle her breasts. At his touch Cathy screamed like a demented creature, and tried frantically to pull away. The man giggled, on fire for the wench already, and his companion laughed out loud, adjuring him to be quick about it.

Quincy jerked her up against his chest, locking her hands behind her back as he pawed at her breasts. He tried again to kiss her, his slimy tongue leaving a wet trail across her face. She felt as though she would vomit.

"For God's sake, get on with it!" the other man urged hoarsely, wetting his lips as he stared at Cathy's naked bosom.

Quincy began to force her down on the bunk, and Cathy fought him with a strength born of terror. She bit him, her teeth sinking deep into his hand, and when he jumped back she managed to free one hand and rake her nails viciously across his face. He swore, and balled his fist, ready to knock her unconscious and have done with the fight. Cathy screamed desperately one last time.

"What in sweet Hell is going on down here?" a man's voice demanded harshly.

"God, Quincy, it's the Cap'n!" gasped the watcher, and the old man dropped Cathy as though her flesh had suddenly burned him.

She caught her breath in an outraged sob, and swung her hand in a wide arc that found its mark below Quincy's ear. He yelped, jumping back, and Cathy stormed after him to press home the attack. But she found her hands caught from behind in a grip like iron, and kicked and fought in a blind panic against her new captor.

"That's enough!" the unseen man said sharply, and the hands that held her shook her until she thought her head would fly from her shoulders. When at last she was still, the shaking stopped, and she looked up to meet the coldest, most merciless eyes she had ever seen in her life. They were gray, as hard as the granite they resembled, and their expression was distinctly menacing. The face that went with them was no less so, and Cathy trembled under its stern regard. When the man saw that she meant to stand quietly, he transferred that unnerving gaze to the two men. Cathy still stared at him, transfixed.

His hair was coal black and wavy, and his skin was dark too, in odd contrast to those icy gray eyes. His nose was long and arrogant, and his mouth was a thin, cruel line. He looked at least thirty, and Cathy could feel enormous strength in the grip he kept on her hands. His arms and shoulders were thick with muscles, and he was very tall. He was also one of the handsomest men she had ever seen in her life.

The two sailors cowered under his gaze, and he contemplated them with a frightening calm. Quincy started to speak, then fell silent as the captain's face darkened ominously. After a moment, his hard gray eyes swung back towards her, and Cathy hastily lowered her gaze. His eyes narrowed slightly as they took in for the first time her beauty, and lingered on the display made by her heaving bare breasts. Cathy colored hotly when she realized where his eyes rested, but she had no means of covering herself and was forced to remain passive under his regard. After a long moment he took his eyes away.

"Quincy, O'Halloran, I gave orders that all prisoners were to be treated with consideration. 'Consideration' does not include forcible rape. Nor does it include physical violence against an old woman," he added, seeing Martha for the first time as she groaned. Cathy pulled away from his hands and ran to Martha at the sound. He looked after her briefly, then returned his attention to his men.

"But, Cap'n, we was only. . . ." Quincy whined, then fell back a pace at the naked fury in his captain's eyes.

"Be quiet!" he said coldly, and then shouted a new command. "Harry!"

A young man, impeccably dressed in the garb of a second officer in the British navy, hurried through the door and saluted smartly.

"Yes, sir?"

"Escort these men back to the "Margarita." I'll decide what to do with them later."

"Yes, sir!" Harry saluted again, then gestured to Quincy and O'Halloran, who followed him glumly through the shattered door.

Cathy listened to their retreating footsteps with mixed feelings. She was glad of course, to be free of Quincy and his friend, but she didn't like being left at this man's mercy. There was an air of ruthlessness about him that told her plainly that if he'd been her attacker, nothing and nobody could have

28

stopped him.

"I must apologize to you for the conduct of my men," he said, turning to her as she knelt beside Martha and bowing with what seemed like great politeness. "Captain Jonathan Hale, entirely at your service."

"Your apology is accepted, Captain," Cathy replied with dignity, pulling the front of her gown together and getting to her feet as she spoke. She looked at the man distrustfully. His unexpected courtesy was vaguely alarming. She felt as though he was testing her in some way. She decided that her best course of action was to simply follow his lead, and extended one small hand to him accordingly.

"I am Lady Catherine Aldley, daughter of the Earl of Badstoke."

"I am honored to make your acquaintance, ma'am." He took her hand with just the right degree of gallantry and pressed it to his lips. The feel of his hard mouth on the back of her hand made her skin tingle. At his apparent gentlemanliness her fright and wrath ebbed somewhat, and she felt safe enough to dare a faintly imperious tone.

"My maid has been injured by your ruffians. She needs immediate attention."

"I will see to it at once, ma'am," he promised gravely, then laughed out loud, flinging her hand back at her.

"So it's 'my lady,' is it?" he grinned, surveying her from head to toe. He strolled toward her until he stood directly in front of her. She had to tilt her head way back to see his eyes.

"And just how old are you, my lady?"

He flicked her chin playfully with one finger. Her eyes shot bullets of blue fire at him, and he laughed again, as though she was the most amusing thing he had ever encountered.

"Best answer me, sweeting, before I begin to wonder if perhaps you're older than you look, and act accordingly."

His mocking words enraged her, and she kicked out at him, her daintily shod foot coming in contact with the hard muscles of his lower leg. He winced, caught her by the shoulders, and pulled her hard up against him. When she tried to claw his face, he easily caught both of her flailing hands in one of his and held them pinioned behind her back. He smiled lazily down into her contorted face, then lifted his free hand and ran it casually over the soft mounds of her breasts.

Her skin felt as though it were on fire! The nipples hardened abruptly under the intimate caress, and the physical sensation made Cathy gasp. She writhed, trying with all her strength to break free, but he held her easily. He continued to caress her breasts, looking down at her with something that was not quite a smile in his eyes.

"How old are you, sweeting?" he asked again. His voice was very soft, but the grooves in his face had deepened with amusement. At her continued silence, he brushed the tips of his fingers ever so gently across her nipples. Cathy felt what was al-

30

most a pain deep in her belly. She was horrified by what was happening to her. She was a lady, a virgin, daughter of one of England's most distinguished families. And when this animal, this canaille, dared to put his hands on her bare flesh, instead of screaming or fainting dead away as a lady should, she was actually standing quietly in front of him while he did it! A wave of fury and shame, stronger than anything she had ever felt before, swept over her, and, before thinking further, she spat into his mocking face.

After a stunned instant his brows rushed together ominously and his eyes began to glitter in a way that frightened her. He wiped the spittle very deliberately from his face. Cathy was truly terrified by the look in his eyes, and was almost as startled by her action as he was.

"Oh, dear God, he will surely murder me now!" she thought.

He looked at her for a long moment without speaking, and Cathy felt what little courage she had managed to hang on to leave her. She began to tremble with fright. At her obvious terror, the tense muscles around his mouth relaxed slightly and some of the anger left his face.

"What you need is schooling, my lady," he drawled, and pulled her roughly into his arms. His mouth came down over hers, hard and hot and demanding, and he kissed her as she had never been kissed before. The chaste pecks she had had bestowed on her once or twice in the past had been

31

nothing like this, and had in fact left her feeling faintly contemptuous of the boys who had been reduced to trembling incoherence because of them. But she was being kissed now by a man, not a boy, and it was she who was on the verge of trembling incoherence.

His tongue parted her lips and probed deeply inside. Cathy nearly swooned as she felt its scalding heat enter her mouth. She pushed vainly at his chest, feeling both hot and cold at the same time. He twined one hand in her long hair and held her, tugging cruelly at the roots when she moved. At last she lay against him quietly, submitting to his embrace. He caressed her trembling breasts with expert hands, gently titillating the nipples, and Cathy felt a scalding heat pulsating upwards from the very center of her being. Horrified, she made one last convulsive effort to escape. He jerked on her hair so viciously she cried out.

His mouth was stopping her breath and she felt as though she would faint. The cabin swam before her eyes in a sickening swirl. She closed them, leaning heavily against him as the only solid thing in a swaying, unsteady world. She could feel the hardness between his legs as he pressed her closely against him.

His touch, his primitive male nearness, awoke something equally primitive in her. She felt strange, unlike herself. She hated and feared him, but his hands on her body made her burn as though she had a fever. She shivered, and without conscious

32

thought her arms slid up around his neck. She was kissing him back.

When he drew away at last, she was shaking so badly she could hardly stand. He stared down at her, his expression unreadable. Cathy blushed hotly under his steady gaze, and hastily dropped her eyes.

"So you're not quite as young as I thought," he said slowly, and her whole body felt on fire with embarrassment.

"I hate him, I hate him," she thought wretchedly. "Whatever possessed me to behave like that?"

He stood looking down at her a moment longer, then swooped her up in his arms. The movement was so unexpected that she was temporarily shocked into silence. He held her cradled against his chest as he stepped through what was left of the cabin door. Outside in the hallway, Cathy saw the still body of what had once been a member of the "Anna Greer's" crew. His head had been cleanly separated from his shoulders, and he lay in a pool of drying blood. Cathy shuddered, and turned her face away from the horrible sight. The captain's arms around her were oddly comforting.

"He did this!" she thought, stiffening. "And now he's carrying me away to do God knows what with me!"

She wriggled violently in his grasp.

"You put me down, you murderer!" she hissed, trying vainly to throw herself from his arms. He ignored her struggles, which did not seem to hamper him in the slightest. Desperately, Cathy raked her long fingernails down the side of his face, drawing tiny drops of blood. The raw anger that blazed in his eyes made her suddenly go limp, but he made no attempt to avenge her violence. Instead, he swung her up over his shoulder where she was left to dangle head down like a sack of meal. This ignominious position infuriated her, and she screamed at the top of her lungs. His hand came down in a hard wallop against her conveniently placed backside. Cathy gasped with pain and shock. No one had ever dared to hit her before!

She kicked at him viciously. The hard toe of her pointed little shoe caught him squarely in the stomach, and she smiled with satisfaction when he grunted. The next instant his hand whacked down against her bottom with a stinging slap that made the first seem like a mere love-pat.

A whimper of pain escaped her. She writhed, trying to throw herself to the floor. He smacked her bottom again, and she screamed with fury and pain, calling him all the filthy names she had ever heard. When at last she ran out of breath, she pounded her fists against his back for emphasis. He spanked her bottom again, hard, and continued spanking as he climbed the narrow stairs.

By the time they reached the main deck, Cathy was lying across his shoulder quietly. Tears poured down her cheeks and her bottom felt as though it were on fire. She closed her eyes at the sight of mutilated bodies sprawled where they had fallen, and, with a supreme effort of will, managed to bite back a sob. With all the strength that was left in her she hated the man who had done this to her, to all of them. Her mind seethed with impotent hatred and rage and shame.

Two

Jonathan Hale carried his burden easily. He took the narrow stairs two at a time, and then strode along the deck to where half-a-dozen of his men were standing guard over the assembled passengers and crew of the "Anna Greer." The girl was a dead weight over his shoulder. She seemed to be subdued at last. Jon grinned to himself with wry amusement. He wanted her more than he cared to admit, even to himself. If circumstances had been different he would have greatly enjoyed taming her. But he had managed to elude capture during his eight years under the black flag partly by following one guiding principle: never take prisoners. They were more trouble than they were worth. Maybe, though, he would make an exception regarding this girl.

Jon stopped abruptly, heaving the slight body off his shoulder and dumping it unceremoniously on the hard boards of the deck. She struggled to a sitting position, raising her tear-drenched eyes to his face and glaring at him defiantly. Her hair was dishevelled from the rough treatment she had endured, and hung in a coppery tangle down her back. Tears had traced dirty paths down either side of her face, and she pressed her lips tightly together to keep them from trembling. The lush swell of her breasts was clearly visible even though she was clutching the torn front of her dress together with both hands. Jon thought he had never seen a woman look more desirable.

"Watch her," he said briefly to a sailor standing nearby, then crossed the deck to supervise the transfer of the "Anna Greer's" cargo into the hold of the "Margarita."

That cargo consisted of thousands of dollars worth of silver ore, partial payment from the Portuguese government to England for six English-built frigates. Jon had learned of the proposed shipment through a paid informant who worked as a clerk in the Portuguese embassy in England. The interesting part of the information was that the silver was to travel virtually unguarded. Although it would be carried on a military vessel, the ship would sail alone. The customary flotilla of guardian ships would be left behind.

Jon had been incredulous when this news was passed on to him. He could not believe that any government would be foolhardy enough to send so much silver out unprotected. But he had the story checked out carefully and could find nothing to contradict it. The reasoning of the Portuguese government, as they had gradually pieced it together, had been that less attention drawn to the shipment would mean greater safety from attack. The original idea had been to place the silver on board a passenger ship with no heavy guns at all. But this had been deemed too risky, and a compromise had been reached: the silver would be shipped out on a lone military vessel, unguarded, as though the ship was making a routine voyage. The "Anna Greer" had been selected as the carrier ship, and had even been instructed to take on a few passengers to make the voyage seem as innocuous as possible.

Taking the "Anna Greer" had been a dangerous piece of business. The "Margarita" had tailed her for days, watching for anything unusual. They had spotted nothing. It seemed as though his information was correct, but Jon still felt uneasy. Something about the situation just did not feel right.

He had come to a decision only that morning. They would take the "Anna Greer." Late afternoon would be the best time, when the lulling effects of the sun and water had dulled the senses of the "Anna Greer's" crew. The whole operation should take less than an hour, and the "Margarita" would be away. With luck, none of the "Anna Greer's" passengers, and few of her crew, would be harmed.

So far, the operation had gone without a hitch. Of course, it was unfortunate that the "Anna Greer" had not surrendered at the outset, but then he had not really expected her to. The "Margarita's" own losses had been minimal, and at this moment most of the men were happily engaged in gathering up all the plunder they could carry. It would be divided among them all as soon as they reached port safely, with each member of the crew receiving an equal share. As captain, he was entitled to one-fifth of the whole. The taking of the "Anna Greer" would make this voyage extremely profitable for him.

"Get a move on it, Harley, Thomeon!" he roared, annoyed at the slowness of their efforts. The two men, who were carrying a load of silver across a makeshift bridge between the "Margarita" and her prey, almost fell overboard in their haste to obey his command. Jon watched the loading crew at work for a while, then turned to survey the passengers who had been segregated from the crew and were being loosely guarded by two of his men.

Except for the girl, they were an unattractive lot. There was a middle-aged man and his fat, sobbing wife, who were obviously members of the wealthy merchant class; a foppish English lord and his poker-faced valet, the girl's stout nursemaid, who had come around and was peering anxiously at her charge; and an elderly woman in an ugly lavender gown that had been in fashion twenty years before.

"Not much to look at, certainly," thought Jon, making a mental exception of the girl. But each and every one of them had to have money, or be in some way connected with it.

"They'd bring a fat ransom," he thought, regretting as he sometimes did his iron-clad rule concerning prisoners. He shook his head thoughtfully. They were just too much trouble, especially if they were female. Liable to cause trouble among the crew. It was a pity, though. He would have liked to have had a little time with the girl.

"God, Cap'n, look to starboard!" a seaman

gasped. "It's a bleedin' navy!"

Jon whirled, staring out to sea. Ship after ship appeared on the horizon, heading grimly for the "Anna Greer." Jon mentally cursed himself for being every kind of a fool. He had ignored the tiny inner voice that had tried to warn him, and so walked right into a trap. It was painfully obvious that the "Anna Greer" had been a carefully thought-out lure.

"To catch some damn fool who couldn't resist the honeypot!" Jon thought angrily, then turned to issue sharp orders to his crew.

"Finish loading that silver! Fast! For your lives!" His voice was grim with determination, and the men rushed to do his bidding. Jon turned to Harry, who had come up beside him and was looking at him anxiously.

"Find the 'Anna Greer's' captain and bring him to me!"

Jon's mind worked furiously as he waited for the captain of the captured ship to be brought before him. The "Margarita" could undoubtedly outrun the frigates if she could only get enough of a start. But they were less than an hour away, and closing rapidly. And it would only take one of the mighty ships to blow the pirate vessel clean out of the water. Guile was what was needed to bring them all through safely. Jon came to a decision abruptly, just as Harry approached with the captain of the "Anna Greer."

"Harry, get that fat couple over there, the old lady, and the girl. Put them on board the 'Margarita.' They'll be hostages for the good behavior of the frigates!"

"Aye, aye, Captain!" Harry saluted smartly, then grinned. Jon would bring them through. He had never failed them yet!

"Sir," Jon said politely to the spluttering captain. "I very much regret the necessity of taking any of your passengers as hostages. However, they will not be harmed as long as the frigates keep their distance and their guns remain covered. If not—well, you have my word that the hostages will be executed immediately if one shot is fired. One shot. I depend on you to carry this message to the captain of the frigates."

The captain of the "Anna Greer" looked appalled.

"Sir, you cannot hope to escape with such hostages! The elderly lady is the Duchess of Kent, and the young lady is the daughter of the ambassador to Portugal! I implore you not to take them! Take myself, and my crew, instead!"

Jon laughed, turning away.

"Carry my message, Captain!"

He gave low-voiced orders to another crew member and within minutes the "Anna Greer's" outraged captain was being lowered in a gig with a crew of six to row.

"Pull! Pull for the frigates!" Jon bellowed over the side at them. "Pull, damn your eyes, or I'll blow you out of the water!"

Thus admonished, the oarsmen fell to with a will.

The little boat fairly skimmed through the water towards the frigates.

Jon leaped on board the "Margarita" just as the last of the hostages was escorted over the makeshift bridge.

"Cast off!"

The ropes that tethered the two ships together were axed, and they began to drift slowly apart.

"Square the yards!"

The huge main sail was hoisted up the mast and flapped wildly for a moment before filling with wind.

"Lie to windward!"

The "Margarita" seemed to take on wings as the wind sent her clipping through the waves.

On deck, Cathy held back frightened sobs as the "Margarita" picked up speed. A hard knot of unshed tears formed in her throat. She had never felt so helpless, or so alone.

The hostages had been herded into a compact group directly under the main sail, and a rope had been twined loosely about their waists and legs to keep them in place.

"So we can get to ye quick," the man who tied the ropes told them, and his sly grin left them with little doubt as to his meaning. If the frigates misbehaved their lives would serve as forfeit.

"We won't be harmed. The frigates will never open fire as long as we are on board," said the Duchess in a clear, strong voice. She took pity on Cathy's obvious fright and patted her hand reassuringly. The merchant was too busy coping with his fat

41

wife's hysterics to argue with this statement, as he seemed to want to do.

The deck of the pirate ship was a swarm of activity. Men darted about, obviously in their element. The mongrel band of pirates turned before their eyes into experienced, disciplined seamen. Cathy caught an occasional glimpse of the captain, who seemed to be everywhere at once, shouting orders and lending a hand where needed. His men appeared to hold him in considerable respect. From all sides Cathy heard mutters of "Cap'n will get us out of this. He ain't never let us down yet!"

The "Margarita" was built for speed, and fairly flew through the water. The frigates lost ground behind her, but they were always there, just a little further in the distance. The sun went down and a stiff wind began to blow. Cathy was shivering with cold in her place underneath the mast, and the old Duchess was turning blue around the lips. The merchant couple apparently had enough layers of fat to keep them warm.

The moon was a pale ghost floating high overhead when the captain came to stand before them. He looked them over in silence, a grim expression on his face. Cathy's heart began to pound uncomfortably.

"You can all thank whatever God you believe in that the frigates didn't open fire. It looks like they value your lives more than silver. If I were you, I'd pray that they don't change their minds."

He called sharply across the deck to Harry, who hastened to his side.

"Have a couple of the men take them below and lock them up. In the hold, I think. Tell them to make sure the man is chained—we have enough problems without him taking it into his head to be a hero."

The hard, gray eyes rested for a moment on Cathy, who hastily looked away. She blushed hotly under his regard. He hesitated, staring at her as though he had something on his mind. Finally he spoke in a low voice to Harry.

"Take the girl to my cabin."

"Sir?" Harry squeaked in surprise, unable to suppress his astonishment. Jon's voice was rough when he answered.

"You heard me. Take her to my cabin. And see that she's locked in."

"Yes, sir!" Harry said woodenly, flustered by his own loss of control. The captain scowled blackly at him before striding away.

Harry carried out his orders quickly, unable to keep from wondering what was going on in Jon's head. Jon liked women, but it wasn't like him to resort to rape. And rape it would have to be with a girl as obviously innocent as this one was. In spite of her lovely face and seductive figure, she was little more than a child, and a frightened one at that. Besides, she was a lady! She wasn't the type Jon could tumble casually, then just as casually dismiss when he tired of her. Her family would be out for blood!

Harry shuddered to think of what would happen to Jon if the "Margarita" were captured, the hostages rescued, and the girl were found to have been ravished! He doubted they would even wait to hang Jon properly. More likely shoot him down on the spot. Harry shook his head in disbelief. The girl was a beauty, no doubt about it, but, hell—no woman was worth *dying* for! As Jon would have been the first to agree less than twenty-four hours ago! But as Harry knew from experience, there was no stopping Jon once he had made up his mind to do something. And it certainly wasn't for a member of the crew like himself to attempt to tell the captain what to do!

Still vaguely troubled, he saw to the safe movement of the other prisoners before returning to untie the girl. She was as cold and still as a piece of white marble, and his conscience smote him as he had to practically drag her to where the captain's cabin nestled under the quarterdeck. She stopped stock still in the doorway, and Harry could feel her arm shaking under his hand.

"Don't do this," she breathed, her eyes wide as she looked at him.

"Captain's orders, ma'am," Harry replied uncomfortably, wishing the deck would miraculously open up and swallow him. He started as she placed one small hand on his arm entreatingly.

"Please put me in with the others. Please. My father is a rich man, he will pay well to have me back . . . unharmed. Or if I could just be lowered in one of those little boats. . . ." Her voice trailed off. Harry swallowed, unable to meet that beseeching gaze.

"There's nothing I can do, ma'am. I'm sorry.

ld not understand herself or this partly sup-
ssed longing for what she did not know.

Hastily she forced her thoughts away from such
indelicate subject, and turned them severely to
ming up with a plan of escape. Try as she would,
e could think of nothing that had the least chance
success. At last, her head dropped wearily on the
llow and she nodded off to sleep.

She awoke with a start, almost thrown from her
akeshift bed by a violent pitch of the ship. She
eered around the cabin groggily, uncertain for the
oment of where she was. The candle was guttering
its own tallow, and cast only a feeble glow over the
oom. A movement in one corner of the room
aught her eye, and she stiffened with dismay. A tall,
masculine form knelt with its back to her, rum-
maging through one of the sea chests. The captain!
His hair was plastered to his skull with water, and
his clothes were soaking wet. He looked as though
he had fallen overboard. Another violent heave of
the ship, followed closely by a muffled crash of
thunder, enlightened her. There was a storm, and he
had been out in it. Cathy breathed a silent prayer of
gratitude. With a storm to battle, at least he
wouldn't have time for her.

Jon found what he was looking for in the chest
and slammed the lid shut. He turned partially towards her and began stripping off his wet clothes,
not even so much as glancing in her direction. It was
as though he had forgotten her very existence.
Cathy watched him through her lashes, carefully

Cap'n would have me clapped in the brig, or worse,
if I was to disobey an order."

He put a hand to the small of her back, urging her
gently inside. She took a few reluctant steps into the
room, then turned to face him. Harry was touched
by the fright in those huge eyes.

"Look, ma'am," he said almost desperately. "Captain Hale is no saint, but he's not a fiend either. I've
been with him for eight years, and I've never known
him to hurt a woman. You'll be all right."

"No thanks to you," she said, suddenly bitter, and
turned her back, obviously waiting for him to go.
Harry looked at her helplessly, then stepped back,
closing the door and bolting it from the outside.

Cathy listened numbly as the bolt slid into place.
She could not believe that this nightmare was really
happening. She sobbed, a hoarse dry sound deep in
her throat. But tears would not help her where there
was no one to hear or care, she reminded herself
grimly. Squaring her shoulders, she turned to ex-
amine the room for a possible means of escape. It
was very dark and she could barely make out the
outline of a box of matches on the table. Striking
one with shaking hands, she lit a candle.

The cabin was small, so as to take up less of the
precious cargo space. The walls were panelled in
dark pine and had bookshelves built right into them.
The shelves were fronted with glass, to keep, Cathy
supposed, the books from flying about in case of
rough seas. A bunk bed was neatly made up against
one wall. Besides the bed, there was the round table

and two chairs, a wardrobe, a coal stove, and a couple of sea chests pushed against the wall.

The only possible exit was a small, glass-paned window. Cathy rushed over to it, fumbling with the latch and then flinging it wide. Cold salt spray struck her in the face, and she saw to her disappointment that she was leaning out directly over the dark sea. The wind had whipped the water into tall, angry waves that pounded viciously against the hull. Cathy shuddered, drawing back a little. She was not that desperate yet.

In the distance she could see a dozen or so small lights bobbing up and down. The frigates! They were still out there, not daring to come too close. Cathy drew a relieved breath. If she could only hold on for a little while she would surely be rescued. The pirate ship could not outrun her pursuers forever!

The spray dampened her dress, and she drew back from the window, thoroughly chilled by the cold, moist air. She longed to undress and sooth her abused body in a hot bath, then put on a dry nightdress and crawl into bed. But there was no bath in sight, and no nightdress either. And even if both had been set before her she would have been hesitant about using them. She had no doubt of the captain's purpose in having her locked in his cabin, and she hoped to keep him at arm's length until the frigates came to her rescue. But if he were to come in and find her freshly bathed and tucked up cozily in his bed, she had no doubt about her fate. Innocent as she was, she knew that.

Cathy compromised, slipping off her w   co
and hanging it over a chair to dry. She would   pre
there overnight and put it on again first thin
morning, doing up the torn bodice with   an
straight pins she had found in a shallow dish   co
the box of matches. She shivered in the   sh
chemise, and crossed hastily to the bed, draggi   of
heavy quilt from it and wrapping it around h   pi
for warmth. Her eyes searched the room for a
place to sleep, coming to rest on the cushione   m
cove beneath the window. She took a pillow fron   p
bed and settled herself as comfortably as possib   m
that small space. It was cramped, but that was a   i
the good. She had no intention of being fast asl   n
when the captain returned to his cabin.

Cathy twisted and turned in her nest, trying d
perately to stay awake. Her mind went over t
events of the day, and turned at last to the frigh
ening man who held her prisoner. Unwillingly, sh
remembered his handsome face and broad shoul
ders and the way he had held and kissed her. O
course, the man was a pirate and a criminal and not
fit to associate with a lady like herself But still. . . .
His kiss had roused something deep inside her,
something that made her wonder, with a kind of
shivery fear, what would happen if he took her in his
arms again, and kissed her, or did even more. Cathy
was not certain exactly what "more" was, but she
knew that it had something to do with the way the
captain had stroked her breasts. The memory of that
intimate caress both excited and shamed her. She

46

47

feigning sleep.

His chest gleamed in the light of the candle, the dark mat of hair glistening with moisture. The muscles of his arms and chest rippled in the dim light as he tossed aside his shirt, and then he half turned away as he began to peel off his sopping breeches.

Cathy felt hot color wash into her cheeks as she watched him undress, pick up a rough towel from the bed, and briskly rub himself dry. Seen from the back, he looked like a magnificent male animal with his broad shoulders, narrow hips, and long, muscular legs. His back and shoulders were deeply tanned. The contrast between them and the skin lower down was startling. Blushing furiously, Cathy let her eyes wander downwards to stare with fascination at his buttocks. They were well-muscled and taut looking, completely unlike her own rounded posterior. She imagined that they would be hard to the touch . . . Cathy quickly shut her eyes, shamed to the bone by her own thoughts. She had never seen a naked man before, and that she could even look at one without swooning from the shock both frightened and amazed her. There had to be something wrong with her. A true lady would have fainted dead away at the sight.

Jon stepped into a dry pair of breeches, fastened them, then turned, pulling on his shirt. He looked directly across the room at her still form huddled on the window seat. He grinned, and moved towards her unhurriedly. The wench was trying to make him think she was asleep.

Cathy saw him move in her direction, and hastily closed her eyes. She tried to make her breathing regular and deep as he bent over her. Her heart was pounding so loudly she was sure he must hear it, and know she wasn't asleep. She concentrated on her breathing, then started violently as she felt his arms slide around her. He swung her up in his arms, and she forced herself to go limp, desperately feigning sleep.

Jon chuckled at her play, and carried her across the cabin to the bed. He lowered her gently to the mattress and stood looking at her. She looked so young and defenseless, with her eyes shut tight against him and her copper hair tumbling across the pillow. Her lips were parted and slightly moist, and the alluring curves of her body were clearly visible through the torn chemise which was all she had on. Staring down at her, he felt desire, such as he had not known in a long time, rage through his body. His mouth went dry as he imagined crawling into bed with her and easing his lust in her soft flesh. A crash of thunder sobered him as he reluctantly remembered the storm and the lives that depended on his skill. He reached down and pulled the covers over her, then straightened.

"Another time, my lady," he said softly, and Cathy's ears burned. Had he known she was not asleep, then? If so, why had he left her alone, and unmolested, in his bed? Cathy pondered these questions, and the man who caused them, for some time. Dawn was streaking the sky before she finally fell asleep.

When Cathy awoke hours later, the cabin was still almost as dark as it had been during the night. Briefly she wondered at it, then remembered. The storm. It must be very bad, then. The ship was tossing and pitching wildly, and Cathy had a hard time getting to her feet. She had to hold on to a bedpost to steady herself. Someone had evidently already been in the cabin, for there was fresh water in a covered jug, a basket of rolls and honey, and a pot of tea. Her gown had been neatly folded and lay across the foot of the bed. Cathy donned it hastily, clumsily pinning the torn front together. She seated herself at the table, wondering at her lack of hunger. After all, it had been many hours since she had eaten, and she had had no supper at all the night before.

The sweet scent of the rolls wafted up to her and she turned her head away, feeling suddenly queasy. A sidelong roll of the ship made her clutch at her stomach, then get up from the table and run headlong for the window. She barely got it open in time. Mountains of angry dark waves threatened her as she leaned out, emptying her stomach into the sea.

Cathy spent the next three days in bed, alternating between an uneasy sleep and emptying her insides into the slop jar provided for her convenience. She thought that she was going to die, and towards the end of the first day prayed fervently that she might. Anything to escape this misery! The captain laughed unfeelingly when made aware of her state, and instructed his valet, Petersham, to see to her needs.

Petersham was a thin, wiry little man, well into middle age, who had known the captain since he was a mere lad. He had been a groom for the captain's father at Woodham, he told Cathy, the Hale family home in South Carolina. When young Jon had quarreled with his father and run away to sea, Petersham had been dispatched by the infuriated gentleman to fetch his son back. One thing led to another, however, and Petersham had ended up going to sea with his young charge. He had been with Master Jon ever since, and the things he had seen. . . . They were enough to curl a person's hair! All in all, though, he liked the life, and there was no dragging the captain away from it.

Cathy was very much interested in what Petersham told her. So Captain Hale was an American, was he? That explained much. Cathy had heard that the people who lived in the colonies were all wild, heedless savages, and Jonathan Hale certainly bore this out. He was no better than a savage—plundering, murdering, and stealing women at will.

The captain entered his cabin infrequently, always to snatch a quick meal, or a few hours of badly needed rest. The first night she had been asleep when he came in, and had awakened to find him stretched out in exhausted slumber beside her. He was completely naked, and Cathy could feel his skin burning her where he touched her, even through the material of her dress. She tried to edge cautiously away from him, but his arm was resting on her hair and she could not free herself without waking him. She lay back against the pillows uneasily, watching him with wariness in her eyes. As he continued to sleep, she gradually relaxed, and finally dozed off beside him.

He was still sleeping when she awoke, one of his hands cupped casually around her breast and his knee resting between her thighs. Cathy gasped at the intimacy of their position, and tried frantically to free herself, waking him with her frenzied movements.

"Be still!" he growled, scowling at her through red-rimmed eyes. Cathy subsided weakly, frightened of what he might do if she disobeyed, and he closed his eyes again. But a few minutes later he got up and stretched, casually displaying his male nudity. This time Cathy shut her eyes in real horror. His front view was far more terrifying than his back.

Thunder rolled, and the ship rolled with it. The captain cursed, and dressed himself hastily. His shoulders drooped and his eyes were bloodshot from weariness. Cathy was surprised to find that she actually felt sorry for him. But her softer feelings were quickly dissipated by his next words.

"Next time I get into bed with you, I want you out of that dress. Get Petersham to find you a nightshirt of mine if your modesty is offended. It's like sleeping with a goddamn pincushion! I warn you, if you are not undressed by the time I return, I'll strip you myself. And believe me, it won't displeasure me in the slightest to do so!"

He leered at her, and she pulled the bedclothes high around her neck, not daring to look at him lest she provoke him to some violence. He slammed out of the cabin, in no very good humor, and she smiled gleefully to herself. So the high and mighty captain had been stabbed by the pins in her dress, had he? It was small vengeance for all she had suffered at his hands!

Despite her mirth, she did not dare disobey him. There was no sense in provoking a confrontation if she could avoid it. She rummaged through his seachests herself, found a neat pile of nightshirts, and dressed herself in one. It was many times too large for her, the sleeves hanging almost to her knees and the bottom dragging the floor by a good ten inches. But she had to admit that it was far more comfortable than her torn and filthy dress, and as long as she was careful to keep the bedcovers high around her chin when someone was in the cabin, there could be no objection to it. It was certainly far less revealing than her own filmy lawn nightdresses.

The captain did not return to his cabin until late that night, by which time Cathy had grown used to her unaccustomed attire. She was sitting up in bed, propped against a mountain of pillows, cautiously sipping a cup of tea. Her stomach had settled some-what, but it still went into violent rebellion if the ship pitched too hard. When the captain entered the room, reeling with fatigue, she stared up at him with wide, frightened eyes, and made a motion as though she would vacate the bed.

"If you step one foot out of that bed, I'll make you sorry you were ever born, my fine lady," he snarled. "Consider yourself reprieved until a later date."

Cathy stayed where she was, watching warily as he blew out the candle and then undressed. She could just make out his shadowy form through the gloom. She jumped when he crawled into bed beside her, and tried to pull away when he twined one hard arm around her waist. Then she felt him shiver with a chill. It was just possible that he had spoken the truth, and wanted her solely for her warmth. It was a chance she had to take. She allowed him to pull her close in the warm darkness, his limbs entwining themselves around her stiff body. When he did nothing more than hold her, she gradually relaxed. The nearness of his body was still frightening—and disturbing, in an odd sort of way—but as long as the storm raged she did not think that she had reason to fear him.

He fell asleep almost at once, his breathing deep and regular. Cathy raised herself on one elbow, peering down at the bronzed face nestled so cozily into her pillow. His eyelashes were ridiculously long for so masculine a man, and lay in dark crescents against his cheeks. His mouth was sensitive, his jaw lean and hard. She felt curiously drawn to him as he slept, and wondered idly how it would feel to run her lips across his sandpaper cheek. . . . Angry at the turn her thoughts had taken, she flounced back down upon the mattress, closing her eyes. Eventually she drifted off to sleep.

Cathy awoke to find the sun shining at last, and the bed empty beside her. She sprang to her feet, running to the window and leaning out. The sea sparkled like diamond-paned glass. The sun was warm upon her upturned face, and the air was balmy and sweet. Cathy longed to be out in all that freshness, and determined to beg Petersham to get permission for her to go up on deck. Even murderers were allowed some exercise, she thought rebelliously.

"But how can I?" she wondered as she splashed her face with cold water. Her once-beautiful gown had been reduced to a grimy rag, and her only alternative seemed to be one of the captain's nightshirts. The nightshirts were clean, and covered her after a fashion, but that was all that could be said of them. They were definitely not suitable for a promenade about the deck.

Disgruntled, Cathy settled herself in a chair with a book of plays in her hand. "Property of Jonathan Creighton Hale" was scrawled in a bold, masculine hand on the flyleaf, and she was contemplating that signature when Jonathan Creighton Hale himself strolled in. Looking at him now she could not understand the softening she had felt toward him as he slept. Awake, he was the same arrogant, disgusting monster who had abducted and abused her. She scowled blackly at him.

"You're looking pale today, my lady," he said, the hateful, mocking note back in his voice.

56

"It's no wonder, the way you keep me locked up here. Are you trying to kill me by suffocation or boredom?" Her tone was venomous.

"I'd watch my tongue if I were you, my sweet. There are worse fates, as you may quickly find out." He crossed to the bed, divesting himself of coat and shirt as he went. Cathy bit her lip in vexation, watching the muscles flex in his broad back. With the storm ended, she was again at his mercy. She controlled her temper with an effort, and tried a sweeter tone.

"I would very much like to go up on deck, Captain."

"What's stopping you? The door has been unlocked for the past two days. After all, we are on the high seas, and there's really no place for you to run even if you wanted to. Unless, of course, you prefer the somewhat rough advances of my men to my charming self." He grinned at her wolfishly, and Cathy nearly choked with rage.

"I would prefer the advances of anything to your vile presence!" she spat.

"Would you indeed, my lady? Then by all means, go up on deck. Flaunt yourself. I wonder how long you would last, with each of my men taking a turn on you? I wager you would be dead long before the 'Margarita' reached port." Anger darkened his eyes, and his words hit her like tiny stones. Cathy was prudently silent, slumping back in her chair and eyeing him with a smoldering resentment. He turned away, flopping full length upon the bed, and lay that way for some time. When he spoke at last, some of the anger had faded from his voice.

"I have no objection to you taking the air, provided you remain on the quarterdeck and stay away from the men. They've been at sea a long time, and with a woman like yourself around. . . . Well, there's no point in asking for trouble. I need every man I have. I don't want to have to kill one of them because you tempted him to madness."

"Heaven forbid!" she replied, her voice dripping sarcasm. "Which brings us to another slight problem. Just what am I to wear for the remainder of this delightful voyage? Your precious men, if you remember, tore the clothes from my back!"

He made no answer to this piece of impudence, and she ventured on, daring a little further.

"What exactly did your fine pirate laddies do with my trunks, Captain? Throw them overboard? Or are they using them as rags with which to scrub their decks?"

"Your trunks were taken on board, my lady, and were inventoried along with the rest of the 'Anna Greer's' cargo. You have a very nice wardrobe— dresses that cost enough to feed a family for a year, silk petticoats, even real Irish lace drawers. Valuable plunder, ma'am, whether you know it or not." He still lay on his back on the bed, seemingly unconcerned with her rising anger.

"Will you give me my clothes?" Her voice trembled with outrage, and it was all she could do to keep from hurling words of hate and abuse at him.

She burned all over at the thought of him going through her belongings.

"As I said, my lady, they are worth a great deal. And they belong not only to me, but to my men. I could not in good conscience give them away. Of course, if you were of a mind to buy them. . . ." His voice trailed off, and he swung himself into a sitting position on the edge of the bunk, surveying her mockingly.

"You know I have no money," she said bitterly.

"Who said anything about money? Perhaps we could arrange a trade, you and I. Say, for instance, a gown . . . for a kiss."

She stared at him, her temper rising. So he hoped to arrange a trade, did he? He must think that she was simple minded. A kiss was the very least of what he had in mind.

"Well, Cathy?" he said softly, watching her. "A gown for a kiss. That seems a fair enough arrangement."

Cathy stared at him, trying to divine the thoughts behind that dark, mocking smile. His expression was unreadable, but something flickered in the back of his eyes like a tiny raw flame. Cathy began to feel frightened. He looked so strong, so very male sitting there, and he was eyeing her as a hungry cat would eye a particularly appealing mouse. She swallowed, then met his gaze squarely, her chin high with defiance.

"I would sooner kiss a pig!"

He did not seem at all angry at her rude reply. On

59

the contrary, he gave a bark of delighted laughter.

"So you would sooner kiss a pig, would you, Lady Catherine? Are you sure? I doubt very much if, in the course of your peculiarly sheltered life, you've ever had the opportunity to kiss anything, much less a pig. So you really have no basis for comparison. What you should do is kiss me, then go out and kiss a pig. Then you could compare the two kisses and decide which you prefer."

He was mocking her, laughing at her, and she felt a murderous rage begin to burn in her veins. Never before in her whole life had anyone dared to laugh at her! And now this arrogant man had the temerity to make her the butt of his joke! Her eyes glittered with anger, and her lips parted in something closely resembling a snarl.

"I hate you!" she hissed at him, her blue eyes seeming to throw off sparks.

She looked very beautiful as she panted fire and defiance at him, and Jon found himself wanting her so badly that he ached. She reminded him of an angry red vixen at bay. . . . He stood up, and began to move toward her very slowly, stalking her.

Cathy jumped to her feet as he moved, leaving the sheet she had been clutching for modesty's sake behind. Her breasts were sharply outlined beneath the linen nightshirt. Jon smiled broadly, and she began to back away, dodging behind the table. He followed her relentlessly, smiling at her, coolly confident of the outcome of the game.

Cathy retreated as far as she could, and found

herself backed up against the wall. He snaked forward, his arms shooting out on either side of her to hold her in place. She looked up at him, her eyes widening with sudden realization. This, then, was to be the showdown. She felt tongues of fear lick at her insides. He was close, so close she could smell the warm musky odor of his body. His eyes glittered down at her dangerously, and his mouth curved in a wicked smile.

Cathy had never lacked courage, and it stiffened her spine as she glared at him.

"You let me go, you animal!" she spat at him, her eyes daring him to touch her.

"So I'm an animal, am I?" he drawled, his eyes glinting down at her. "But that should appeal to you, my lady. After all, you just admitted to an astonishing partiality for pigs. Now you can see how you like the kind of animal I am."

He bent over her deliberately, and Cathy closed her eyes, turning her face away and trying to push him back with both hands against his chest. Her efforts were futile. His mouth grazed her averted cheek, burning her, and then his hand was beneath her chin, forcing her head around until his mouth covered hers. His lips seared her mouth. She kept her own lips tightly clenched, rejecting his kiss utterly. She remembered the last time all too well. She would not disgrace herself in such a way again.

His arms slid around her, pulling her away from the wall and into his embrace. Cathy clawed at his face desperately, but he caught her hands before she

61

could inflict any damage, imprisoning them. His mouth closed over hers again, and this time his tongue succeeded in prying her shaking lips apart. She arched away from him in a hopeless quest for freedom, but the movement only made her more burningly aware of his hard male body as it pressed intimately against her softer female one. She felt his tongue touch hers, and the tremor that wracked his arms as he held her. A strange heat began to pulsate in her loin. His hands moved over her back and buttocks, warmly and seductively. Her knees felt suddenly weak, and she was forced to cling to his shoulders for support. He bent her backward over his arm, his mouth ravishing the slim white column of her throat before returning to devour her mouth. Cathy knew suddenly, helplessly, that she was lost. Her arms crept around his neck of their own volition, her fingers curling through his thick dark hair.

As he felt her response he groaned, then swung her off her feet and into his arms, carrying her on unsteady legs over to the bed. Cathy lay nestled like a small trusting kitten against the hard muscles of his bare chest, her arms twined around his neck. She could no more have resisted him than he could have stopped himself.

He laid her gently on the bed and stretched out beside her, drawing her up tightly against him and kissing her in that strange, animalistic way that drove her almost out of her mind. As his mouth twisted across hers, she shivered, and then she was kissing him back.

"This is wrong," a small voice inside her head warned. But Cathy was beyond heeding her own advice.

Jon's hands explored the curves of her body through the thin nightshirt, reveling in her budding womanliness. Her nipples grew rigid under his hands. He ripped aside the material covering them impatiently, then caught his breath as if the sight of her milky white, pink-tipped breasts caused him physical pain. He stretched out a finger and ran it reverently over the soft peaks, marveling at the velvety warmth of her skin.

He bent his head, gently kissing first one nipple and then the other, drawing the last one into his mouth and nibbling at it teasingly. Cathy gasped at the fiery sensation that stabbed her, and her eyes flew open. The sight of his black head nuzzling so intimately at her breast shocked her back to awareness. She went hot with shame. Her hands flew to his broad shoulders and she tried frantically to push him away.

"No! Please stop! Jon, please!" she panted, her nails digging into him.

"Hush, Cathy," he murmured in reply, his voice thick and his eyes glazed with passion. "Hush, now, Cathy love."

He reached up and gently removed her claws from his flesh, drawing her hands over her head and holding them pinioned. His lips returned to press hot kisses over her breasts. Cathy twisted, frightened now, and tried vainly to pull away.

"Just be still, sweetheart," he said against her ear. "I won't hurt you. Easy now. Just be still."

He held her hands pinned to the mattress with one of his, while the other stripped away the remnants of the torn nightshirt. In a few short moments, her body lay bare to his gaze. His eyes went over her slowly, possessively, seeming to scald her flesh. She sobbed with fear and embarrassment as he studied her from head to toe, and when his hand went to the buttons of his breeches, she renewed her frantic efforts to escape.

Naked, he held her with his leg across her body, stilling her harsh cries with his mouth. He kissed her in a leisurely fashion, his hands resuming their shameful wanderings. They roamed casually over the sensitive peaks of her breasts, then moved downward to caress her soft belly. She whimpered, her head thrashing from side to side on the pillow, her nails tearing at his shoulders. He continued with the gentle kneading of her belly, disregarding her struggles. Then his hand moved even lower and began to stroke the silken flesh of her inner thighs.

"No!" she gasped as his calloused palm ran gently across the place where her legs joined. Horrified, Cathy clamped her legs tightly together, crossing them against him, desperately resisting his attempts to pry them apart with his hands.

"Relax, Cathy. Relax, sweetheart," Jon murmured hoarsely. "Open your legs, Cathy love. I won't hurt you."

His words appalled her. Her body went rigid, then

wriggled and slid like a contortionist's, as she tried frantically to squirm out from under his hands. He was too strong, and finally, with a shuddering sob of surrender, she went limp. There was nothing else she could do.

Jon raised himself on one knee above her, wedging the other between her tightly crossed legs. He at last succeeded in parting her thighs. Cathy gave one last convulsive heave as he spread them wide, then lay sobbing quietly, not even trying to resist him any longer. She shuddered at the feel of his hardness against her as he probed between her thighs.

A flash of fire surged through her as he found the opening between her legs, entering slightly. Then with one quick thrust he was deep inside her. The knifelike pain was so intense that Cathy screamed. His lips closed over her mouth, silencing her, and he lay on top of her without moving, embedded in her soft flesh. His breath came in jagged bursts, as though he had run a long way. Cathy turned her head away, repulsed by its warmth upon her face. Finally, as if he could no longer help himself, he began to move, slowly at first so as not to hurt her more than he had to, and then harder and stronger.

Cathy lay unresisting beneath him, letting him do what he would with her body, numb with shock. She couldn't believe that this awful thing was really happening. She was being raped by a pirate, and there was nothing she could do about it. It was already too late. She was ruined, disgraced. She could never hold up her head again. And all because of this heaving, trembling animal who panted and plunged over her. . . . How she hated him!

She tried to force herself to think of something else, but it was impossible with his hard, hot flesh joined so intimately to hers. She moved a little, experimentally, hoping to at least ease the crush of his chest on her breasts. Her movement seemed to incite him to even greater frenzies. Unwillingly, Cathy felt herself begin to get caught up in his passion. With an instinctive movement she surged to meet his next thrust. He sucked in his breath sharply, then shuddered and went limp. Cathy felt an unreasoning pang of disappointment as his big body sprawled across hers.

After a moment, Jon rolled away and lay on his back, staring up at the ceiling. Cathy sidled over to the far edge of the bed and turned her back on him, feeling hot and sticky and thoroughly humiliated. She thought of the way her body had betrayed her at the last, when she could not stop its instinctive movement, and hot tears of rage and shame filled her eyes. She stifled a sob, but Jon heard the small, muffled sound and pulled her roughly against him. He stroked her hair absently, and at the careless tenderness of his gesture she forgot her pride and her hatred of him and sobbed like a baby. He continued to hold her, stroking her hair and murmuring comforting things into her ear. When her sobs were finally reduced to hiccuping gulps, he put her away from him and stood up, pulling on his clothes. He stood looking down at her for a moment, buckling his belt, a faint smile curving his lips. Cathy closed her eyes and refused to look at him.

"Don't let it worry you, sweet. It'll be better the next time, I promise," he said softly, and then chuckled at the exclamation of rage she gave as the full import of his statement sunk in. He actually expected her to submit to that disgusting performance again! She bounced furiously from the bed, dragging the sheet with her to protect her body from his gaze, murder blazing in her eyes. She looked around wildly for a weapon, but before she could find something hard enough and sharp enough he scooped her up in his arms and threw her back onto the middle of the bed. She floundered helplessly in a mad tangle of sheet and hair while he laughed uproariously. By the time she managed to get herself sorted out, he was gone. Cathy glared ferociously at the closed cabin door. Nobody could treat her like a doxy and get away with it! She made up her mind there and then that Captain Jonathan Hale was going to be taught a much needed lesson. He would soon find out that he had met his match in her!

Three

Cathy was left alone to fume for several hours. Which was a wise move on someone's part, she thought blackly, because she could have cheerfully scratched the eyes out of the first person who crossed her path. Without exception, they were all thieving, murdering cutthroats, and Captain Jonathan Hale was the worst of the lot. How she would enjoy seeing him hang, his long body twisting and turning at the end of a rope, his mocking face blue and swollen! Cathy smiled more sweetly than she had in days. Just imagining it made her feel better!

Oh, what she wouldn't give for a long, sharp knife! She would carry it with her constantly, hidden in the sleeve of a voluminous nightshirt, and the next time the brute tried to rape her, she'd plunge it deep into his back! She pictured his writhing agony with deep relish. But the cabin was bare of knives, or any other obvious weapons. So she rescoured the cabin for anything that could possibly be used as a weapon. When she stopped at last, exhausted, her arsenal was not impressive. A heavy brass candlestick was the most promising of the small collection. She thrust it beneath the mattress so that it would be handy for use as a head-basher. The porcelain chamber pot also had possibilities, but she was afraid that if the pot were nowhere to be found, her captor would undoubtedly become suspicious. Despite his villainy, Cathy knew that the pirate captain was far from stupid.

She flatly refused to dress again in another of the hated nightshirts. If she could help it, nothing of his would touch her skin again for as long as she lived. Instead, she wrapped herself mummy-fashion in a quilt, and settled down in one of the hard chairs to wait. Sooner or later Captain

Jonathan Hale would have to return to his cabin. When he did, Cathy wanted to be sure to make the occasion a memorable one.

It was Petersham, however, who next tapped on the door. The cabin was beginning to darken as the last of the day's brightness faded away, and Cathy's legs were growing cramped from sitting so long in one position. But she was determined not to be caught unprepared a second time. At the knock she stiffened, then relaxed. If there was anything certain in this suddenly mad world, it was that the arrogant scoundrel would not have the courtesy to knock before entering. He would just barge right in!

"I've brought you some supper, miss," Petersham said as he entered. "Cap'n said as how you weren't feeling too well at midday, but it's almost seven o'clock now, and you need something solid in you. This seasickness will leave you weak as a kitten if you don't take care."

"I am no longer seasick, Petersham," Cathy replied acidly, not moving from the chair. Petersham eyed her covertly as he set the meal on the table, his glance touching on her white face and tousled hair before taking in the final evidence of her quilt-clad body. It was plain what had happened. Master Jon, no longer hampered by the storm, had spent the morning enjoying what he would consider the spoils of battle. Well, men had their needs, as he, Petersham, knew full well, but it was hard on Miss Cathy. She was very young, and he'd stake his life that she had been an innocent.

"Be you all right, miss?" Petersham questioned huskily.

"Certainly I am all right, Petersham," Cathy snapped, suddenly afraid that he would somehow guess her shame. She would simply die if anyone knew! But Petersham didn't say anything else. He arranged the meal in silence, and left without venturing another word.

Sighing, Cathy uncurled herself, pulled the chair up to the table, and began to eat. She was surprised to find that she actually felt hungry, despite the trauma she had suffered.

She was just forking the last of the corned beef into her mouth when another tap sounded at the door. Her eyes flickered toward the oaken portal apprehensively. Who was it this time?

"Yes?" she called warily. Petersham poked his head around the door, and she relaxed.

"I thought you might enjoy a hot bath, miss. We've had an old tub down in the hold for months that nobody has had a use for. If you'd like, I'd be pleased to bring it up for you."

Cathy thought quickly. A bath sounded wonderful, and her abused body screamed for her to accept. But if this was a gesture from the captain, designed to ease what passed for his conscience, she would jump overboard before she would agree. She would take no favors from him!

"Whose idea was this?" she asked sharply.

"Why, mine, miss. Whose else could it have been?"

This was so true that Cathy was surprised into a wry smile. Did she really think that Captain Jonathan Hale would spend his valuable time worrying about her comfort, especially now that he had taken what he wanted from her? Not likely! To him, she was just an inanimate body without thoughts or feelings.

"Thank you, Petersham, I would like a bath." she answered.

Petersham beamed at her, then disappeared around the door. Cathy leaned back in her chair, suddenly faintly ashamed of her earlier behavior. After all, what had been done to her could hardly be blamed on Petersham. He at least had shown her nothing but kindness since she was taken prisoner.

Cathy was prepared for the brief knock this time. When the door opened in response to her summons, Petersham entered, closely followed by a husky sailor lugging a large hipbath, and another bearing one of her own small trunks.

"My clothes!" Cathy exclaimed joyfully.

"Cap'n gave permission to bring up some of your things, miss," Petersham said, smiling at her. "I took the liberty of selecting the trunk with your night attire. Was that right?"

The mere mention of the "Cap'n" was enough to make Cathy see red, especially in connection with him giving permission for something to do with herself, but bit by painful bit she was growing wiser. There was no point in cutting off her nose to spite her face. If she instructed Petersham to take that

71

trunk back to the gloating devil with the message that he could wear the dratted clothes himself, she would gain nothing but a fleeting instant of satisfaction. Better to make the best of things now, and bide her time. As Martha had often said, all things come to he who waits. And Cathy was prepared to wait forever, if need be, for her revenge.

"It was very thoughtful of you, Petersham," she murmured, her face a cool mask hiding her thoughts. Then, as the sailors brought in steaming buckets of water and proceeded to fill the tub, she added gruffly, "Petersham, about this evening, when you brought my supper. . . . I—I wasn't myself. I'm sorry if I was rude." It was the first time in her life that Cathy had ever apologized to anyone for anything, and she felt absurdly shy. But Petersham's beaming smile was her reward.

"That's all right, miss. Everyone has a bad day now and again."

That was the understatement of the year, Cathy thought, but said nothing. When the sailors had the tub filled to Petersham's satisfaction, the three men left her alone in the cabin.

The first thing that Cathy did was to take one of the wooden chairs and wedge it firmly against the door. Although it wouldn't keep Jon out for long if he was determined to get in, at least she would have enough warning so that she wouldn't be caught naked in the bath!

That done, she went across to her small trunk and opened it lovingly. Just the sight of something from

72

home was enough to make her eyes water. What she wouldn't give to hear Martha scolding, or her papa bellowing as he did when everything didn't go his way! Firmly she wiped a wayward tear from her cheek. Crying made everything seem so much worse.

Carefully, she lifted out the little tray of scented soaps and perfumes that fitted neatly over her clothes. She sprinkled attar of roses liberally in the bath water, sniffing appreciatively at the cloud of scented steam that rose to her nostrils. Picking up a bar of rose-scented soap and a small washcloth, she stepped into the tub. The feel of the hot water closing about her body as she sank down into it was pure bliss. She rested her head against the rolled back of the tub, not moving, luxuriating in the knowledge that she would soon be thoroughly clean again from head to toe. After a moment's enjoyment she began to scrub vigorously at her arms and legs and body, almost rubbing away the skin in her zeal to be rid of Jon's touch. Finally she splashed her face until her cheeks were pink and glowing. The only thing left to do was her hair, and taking a deep breath, she plunged her head beneath the water. Her hands worked their way through the long strands, wetting them thoroughly, and soaping them.

Cathy was rinsing her hair, her head under water again, when the doorknob rattled. The sound was closely followed by an impatient curse, then a shrill scraping as a strong shoulder set against the door pushed the detaining chair steadily over the planked floor. Jon squeezed through the opening he had made, looked about the cabin warily, then broke into a broad grin. All he could see of the little she-cat was a hank of dripping dark-gold hair and a pair of creamy shoulders. He crossed quietly to the side of the tub. Her face when she surfaced should really be something to behold!

At that moment Cathy came up for air, and Jon chuckled audibly at the absurd picture she presented. Her wet hair trailed limply over her face and shoulders to float around her in the water like trailing strands of seaweed. At the sound of his chuckle she stiffened, her hands coming up to push the hair out of her eyes. When she could see again, she glared at Jon as he towered over her, her face contorting with fury.

While she searched for her tongue, Jon amused himself by studying her soft curves through the water. Very nice, he thought appreciatively, admiring the impudent thrust of her breasts and the tender turn of her hips. Very nice. A slow grin was stealing across his mouth when, with an inarticulate cry of pure rage, Cathy hurled the bar of scented soap straight at his head. It struck him hard as a rock in the corner of his left eye. Jon staggered back, his hand clapping disbelievingly over the injured place. His temper, never placid, began to simmer in its turn. If the little vixen wanted to play rough, he would see to it that she got more than she'd bargained for!

"Get out!" Cathy shrieked, finding her voice at

last. While he was still off balance she tried to leap from the tub, grabbing frantically for the quilt to wrap herself in. Jon caught her in mid-leap, his hands clamping around the slippery skin of her waist. Twist and turn though she might, Cathy was unable to free herself as he thrust her forcibly back down into the water.

"Why should I? It is, after all, my cabin," Jon drawled, his hands on her shoulders holding her firmly in place. Only the steely look in his eyes warned her that she was on dangerous ground. But Cathy was too furious to heed any warning.

"I'm taking a bath!" she screamed, her fists clenching as his eyes moved over her body with insolent appraisal.

"I can see that you are." His voice was approving, and his eyes echoed the sentiment. The little flicker at the backs of them should have given her pause, but Cathy stormed on regardless.

"I hate you! Get out of here!"

When he continued to stand there like some great immovable object, Cathy began to kick and beat the water with her fists like a child in a tantrum. Jon's mouth clenched as the soapy water sloshed over his dry clothes. He moved around behind her so swiftly that Cathy had no chance to prepare for what happened next.

"You were rinsing your hair when I so rudely interrupted, I believe," he said silkily. "Let me help you."

Cathy felt a large hand pressing down on the top of her head, and just had time to take a deep breath before her head was forced under the water. She squirmed and twisted, clawing frantically for the surface, but Jon held her under until she thought her lungs would burst. Finally he relented, removing his hand while she came up for great gulping breaths of air.

"You swine!" Cathy gasped when she could speak. "Isn't rape enough for you? Or do you drown all your victims afterwards?"

"Not all of them, no," he told her, sitting down on the edge of the tub and playing idly with the wet strands of her hair. Cathy jerked the locks away from him angrily, tossing him a fearsome glare. He smiled mockingly back at her. "Just cheeky little brats who need to be shown who's master."

"Master!" Cathy screeched, recovering at this jab to her pride. "You're not my master and never will be, you insufferable animal!"

"Now, that's where you're wrong, my sweet," Jon's eyes narrowed until they were nothing more than glittering slits in his dark face. "I've been your master since the moment you first set foot on this ship. If you haven't realized it yet, then I've been too damned soft with you. Something which I intend to remedy right now."

His hand was on the top of her head again. Cathy didn't even have time to draw breath before he was forcing her back beneath the surface of the water. She slipped and slid on the bottom of the tub like an eel, finally managing to free herself. He grabbed for her again as she sucked air into her starved lungs.

Cathy caught one of his reaching hands in both of hers, burying her teeth in it until they touched bone.

"Bitch!" he yelled, snatching his hand away. This was the chance Cathy had been waiting for. She jumped up, flinging the soapy washcloth in his face. During the instant he took to free himself from its entangling folds she grabbed the quilt and sprinted for the door. The knob turned easily under her hand, but the blasted thing wouldn't open! She pulled at it frantically. It had to open, it had to!

"It's locked," Jon growled menacingly from across the room, and Cathy whirled to find him advancing toward her, his face tight with anger. He had wrapped the washcloth around his hand where she had bitten it, but blood was already beginning to seep through. Cathy felt a momentary triumph. Whatever the outcome of this night's work, at least he wouldn't escape totally unscathed!

"So the big, brave pirate had to lock the door, did he?" she jeered recklessly, edging toward the corner where she had strategically placed the chamber pot. "What's the matter, Captain? Were you afraid a mere female might get the better of you?"

Jon moved slowly toward her, his eyes promising a painful retribution. Cathy was too incensed to notice, or care if she had. At least she was getting a little of her own back on him! She made it over to the corner and bent to retrieve the chamber pot, straightening and hurling it at him so quickly that Jon didn't even have time to duck. It hit him squarely on the shoulder, making him stagger backwards. Cathy cursed her poor aim even as she grabbed furiously for another weapon, this time a book of plays. If he'd had a blow like that to the head, he would no longer be any threat to her!

"That's torn it, you little hell-cat!" Jon roared, making a lunge for her. The book bounced harmlessly off his muscular chest. Before she could launch another missile his arms closed around her, squeezing like a boa constrictor until she could hardly breath. Cathy kicked and clawed at him, but only managed to bruise her bare feet on his hard legs. Her nails had more success, scraping down the side of his face before he jerked his head back, out of reach. She fought frantically as he half-dragged, half-carried her across the room, screeching hysterical curses at him. He seemed unimpressed by her vocabulary. Cathy screamed in earnest as he jerked the quilt from her, leaving her totally naked in his grasp. Teeth bared and nails flaring she reached for him but was left holding air as he twisted her effortlessly around. Before she knew quite what was happening he was sitting in one of the wooden chairs with her up-ended and furiously squirming across his lap, her long wet hair trailing the floor and her bare bottom wriggling ingloriously.

"I think it's time you learned a few manners, my lady," Jon snarled, and took a hard swat at her heaving backside. Cathy gasped as his hand found its target with all the force of a bullwhip, then screamed as he spanked her again and again. In a short time she was reduced to hiccupping sobs.

"Let me go, you filthy swine," she managed with creditable defiance, but his hand thudding down hard on her buttocks refused her even that small measure of pride.

"From now on, you're going to do exactly as I tell you, right?" he questioned grimly, his hand hovering over her tender flesh.

Cathy said nothing. The hand stung against her bottom in a resounding slap.

"Right?" he asked again.

"Right!" Cathy screamed furiously, mentally condemning him to all the tortures of hell. He'd be sorry for all the indignities he was forcing upon her! She had her pride, and she would see him dead at her feet if it was the last thing she ever did!

"Who's your master?" he went on.

Cathy hesitated. She couldn't, simply could not, give him that satisfaction. Jon whacked her again, harder than before, and Cathy shrieked with pain and humiliation.

"I'm waiting," he said ominously.

"Oh, you are, you bastard!" Cathy sobbingly hurled the admission at him and braced herself, sure he would beat her even more for her phrasing. But to her surprise he let her go, shoving her off his lap contemptuously as he stood up.

"See that you remember it," he growled, and went to retrieve the chamber pot from where it had landed beside the door. When he picked it up he saw that it had broken cleanly in half. He regarded it grimly, then turned to survey the havoc in the cabin.

Water stood in a lake around the half-empty tub, and the bar of soap lay forlornly beneath the table. The quilt was wet and lay in a soggy heap of color near the bunk. Cathy huddled on the floor where he had pushed her, her knees drawn up in front of her and her arms wrapped around herself to shield her body from his gaze. Her eyes blazed with hatred as she glared up at him. Jon smiled menacingly at the feral picture she presented. By God, it was time the vixen was tamed!

"Get up!" he snarled. Cathy looked at him mutinously.

"I won't!" she hurled back.

"I said, get up!" Jon thundered, his voice cracking like a whip. Cathy glowered at him, prepared to defy him further, but what she saw in his face dissuaded her. He looked ready to strangle her if she disobeyed him.

"I can't. I—I don't have any clothes on," she muttered sullenly, not quite daring to openly contradict him.

"If you don't do as I tell you, right now, I'll make you very, very sorry. And that's a promise." His voice was deceptively soft, but Cathy could see a muscle twitching angrily at the corner of his mouth. As she looked at him he took a step toward her. Cathy scrambled hastily to her feet. Arrogant bully! She knew and he knew that she had no choice but to submit to him now. But later, she promised herself, later he would pay in blood for every humiliation he was making her suffer!

As she rose quiveringly to her feet he looked her over slowly, his bold eyes stripping her of the last remnants of her self-respect. Her cheeks flushed crimson as she tried to shield her body from his perusal using her hip-length hair. The damp strands were woefully inadequate as covering. This was just another form of rape, Cathy thought angrily, as his eyes searched out and lingered over her body. Innate pride kept her chin up, her mouth firmly set. She refused to give him the satisfaction of seeing her cower.

Jon took his time, letting his eyes caress her lovely quivering breasts, long ivory thighs and the alluring triangle of reddish hair between them. Almost reluctantly he acknowledged the hot stirring in his loins. The little witch was really beautiful, he had to admit. He would have to watch it or she'd be getting under his skin. She could already make him madder than any female he had ever encountered, and that was a bad sign.

Wasn't there some saying about a man having to be careful what he wished for because he just might get it? Well, he had wished for the taming of the little shrew the first time he'd set eyes on her. Now he had it, and it wasn't working out quite as he had expected. She was too soft, too lovely, too totally feminine despite her quick temper. Already an unfamiliar twinge of remorse was beginning to gnaw at him as he saw the bruises darkening on her white flesh. With a muttered curse he swung away from her, striding to the door and flinging it wide.

"Petersham!" he bellowed. Then, over his

shoulder to Cathy, he added in a quieter tone, "Cover yourself."

Cathy snatched the damp quilt from the floor, wrapping it thankfully around herself until she could retrieve her wrapper from the bowels of the trunk. Jon watched her broodingly as she crossed the room to rummage through her belongings. His eyes never left her as she dropped the quilt, her back to him, to shrug into the flimsy blue garment. If she had been looking Cathy would have seen him wince at the livid marks which marred the soft flesh of her buttocks and the backs of her thighs.

By the time Petersham came hurrying to the door, Cathy was respectably covered and standing by the bunk. Her bottom was too sore to permit her to sit. Petersham glanced at her briefly, his eyes widening as he noted the tearstains on her cheeks. Hurriedly he transferred his attention back to the captain.

"Sir?"

"Bring more hot water. I feel the need of a bath myself."

"Yes, sir!"

Petersham moved off with alacrity to do as he was bidden, knowing better than to interfere with Master Jon in any way when he looked like that. The captain had a temper to rival the devil's when he was roused. Petersham only hoped that Miss Cathy hadn't had the poor judgement to set it alight. But from the looks of things she had, and there was nothing anyone could do to save her from the consequences of her actions.

Cathy silently rubbed her wet hair with a towel as Petersham brought more water to fill the tub. Jon was equally withdrawn. Petersham, glancing from the captain's set face to Miss Cathy's subdued form, knew when it behooved him to keep his tongue between his teeth. He busied himself with wiping up the puddle of water that had spread to cover half the floor. When Jon finally dismissed him with a nod, he departed with a feeling of heartfelt relief.

Still Jon said nothing. Cathy almost wished that he would rant and rave and shout at her. The silence was more unnerving than anything he could have done. As he was probably well aware, she told herself resentfully as she watched him undress from the corner of her eye.

Naked, he was an awesome sight. His muscles rippled under their sleek covering of skin like a jungle cat's. Hair covered his chest in a thick black pelt, tapering down his flat belly in a narrowing trail to thicken again at his burgeoning maleness. The flickering candlelight cast shadows over his face, making it look sinister, almost evil. He looked almost unnaturally tall and strong and masculine. Cathy shivered, then flushed as he glanced casually in her direction, his eyes meeting hers in a brief, mocking salute. Mortified that she had been caught looking at him, she turned hastily away.

"Wash my back."

The stern tone brought her out of her reverie to find Jon ensconsed in the tub, looking slightly ridiculous as the water lapped around his waist. If Cathy hadn't been feeling so tired, so sore, and so thoroughly humiliated she would have smiled at the sight of his big body folded into the dainty porcelain tub. As it was, she could barely hold back her tears.

"I said, wash my back."

The command was a growl this time. Cathy stared at him disbelievingly. He couldn't be serious! He couldn't actually expect her to. . . .

"Damn it. . . . !" Jon roared. Cathy jumped hastily to her feet.

"Yes, master," she said bitterly, crossing the cabin to where he waited. Jon silently handed her the bar of soap and she moved around behind him, biting her lip. What she wouldn't give for a knife now, she thought venomously, staring down at that broad back. The muscles of his neck tensed suddenly, as if he expected to be attacked, and Cathy's lips twitched. The man must be a mindreader, as well as everything else. But he needn't worry, he was in no immediate danger. She would have been more tempted if her stinging backside hadn't reminded her of the consequences of a similarly violent act.

"What are you waiting for?" Jon snarled over his shoulder. Cathy pushed back the trailing sleeves of her wrapper and bent to the task. His shoulders quivered slightly as she began to work the soap into their hard contours, but other than that he was still as she hurriedly scrubbed at his back. His skin was as smooth as silk under her fingertips, and gleaming brightly. She badly wanted to rake her sharp fingernails in long furrows down his back to repay him for his use of her, but common sense restrained her. To do so would only invite more trouble. Gritting her teeth, Cathy finished the job with workman-like efficiency, sighing with relief as she straightened away.

"Will there be anything else, master?" Cathy could not resist a jeering emphasis on the last word. She jumped a foot straight up in the air when Jon's hand shot out to catch her by the wrist.

"You can damn well wash the rest of me, since you're so anxious." The angry muscle was twitching again at the side of his mouth. He pulled her around until she was standing where he could see her. Cathy resisted, horrified at the impasse into which her rash tongue had led her. He couldn't really expect her to wash him all over! It would be the final, humiliating straw!

"I won't!" Cathy muttered, then started as the hand tightened like a vice around her wrist.

"You'll do just exactly as I tell you, my girl. Get on with it."

He stretched back to give her access to his chest, releasing her wrist. Cathy made a quick move as though she would dodge away. He looked at her warningly.

"If you put me to the trouble of getting out of this tub and fetching you, you'll regret it." His voice was expressionless, which made it all the more convincing. She had no choice but to do as he said, and they both knew it. Better to go ahead and get it over with.

Cathy bent reluctantly over the tub, wetting the soap and then running it in slow strokes over Jon's chest. His body hair curled into loose little circles under her ministrations, its coarseness rasping against her sensitive fingertips. Cathy felt a sudden, almost irresistible temptation to drop the soap and let her hands run over the dark furring. Shocked at herself, she did just the opposite, letting the bar of soap wash him while she touched him as little as possible. Jon was aware of her ploy, she knew, but he said nothing, closing his eyes and relaxing while she did her job. She finished his chest hurriedly, splashed water on it to rinse the soap away, and stood up. He opened one eye to stare at her consideringly.

"Finish what you started."

Cathy glanced involuntarily down at his long body, clearly visible through the water. He was already swollen with desire! She couldn't do it! She simply could not!

"I—I can't!" she murmured despairingly just as his eyes began to narrow with anger.

"You can't?" he repeated slowly, questioningly, as though weighing her statement.

"Don't make me," she whispered, voice humble, despising herself for her weakness but unable to help it.

Jon stared up at her for a long moment. Her lips were trembling and those beautiful eyes swam with tears. He was suddenly reminded of the time he'd jumped his best filly over a fence she had tried at first to refuse; the animal had caught her hoof on the

86

top bar, fallen, and broken a foreleg. Her eyes had held the same expression of stricken entreaty that Cathy's held now.

"Get to bed," he said brusquely, surprising even himself, and straightened to finish the job with a wry grimace.

Cathy did as he ordered, huddling under the bedding on the wall-side of the bunk. She was too miserable even to think of reaching for the candlestick which still reposed beneath the mattress. What was the use? He would only take it from her and punish her for the attempt. Tears slid down her cheeks and dampened the pillow. Always before she had been surrounded by people who loved and cared for her. To this man she was nothing more than an object to be used like a—like a chamber pot! Cathy stifled a sob. Why had this had to happen to her? What had she ever done to merit such a fate?

She stiffened when Jon blew out the candle, huddling as close to the wall as she could get. He crawled into bed beside her, and she shrank from the feel of his hard nakedness as he settled down into the mattress. His hand reached for her, and she gave a little moan of distress. Surely he couldn't mean to force her to go through that filthy act again? Could men do it more than once a day? She didn't know. She had never had anything to do with the darker side of a man before.

His hand caught her around the waist, pulling her against his hard body. Cathy tried to free herself, but her efforts were futile. He drew her effortlessly against his side. She struggled weakly as his hands moved over her, seeking, caressing.

"I—we—you can't!" she finally protested in a wailing whisper. "Not twice in one day!"

She could just make out his hard mouth as it curved in a smile.

"Even more than that, little innocent, if I have anything to say about it," he said in her ear, putting his lips against the soft skin of her neck and slowly stroking it with his tongue. Cathy shivered. She knew now what he was leading up to, and she didn't think she could bear it again so soon. But she had no choice. She was his prisoner, and he could rape her until she died if he wanted to. There was no one to stop him.

Fresh tears rolled down her cheeks at the thought, and she pulled away a little. He caught her around her thighs to bring her back to him. As his hand closed around the tender flesh Cathy whimpered painfully.

"Damn!" Jon muttered, pushing her away. The next instant he was on his feet beside the bunk, lighting the candle.

Cathy stared up at him wide-eyed as he turned back to her. Was he angry at her for her resistance? Surely he didn't expect her just to melt in his arms!

"Turn over," he ordered harshly.

Cathy's mouth went suddenly dry. He was going to beat her again. Oh, God, please no! Her skin was swollen from his earlier blows, and this time would be even worse.

"I—I—please don't hit me," she whispered brokenly, making no move to obey him. Jon caught his breath sharply as he saw the tears coursing down her cheeks.

"I won't hurt you," he promised tightly, rolling her over despite her slight effort at resistance. Cathy shuddered as she felt him lift the skirt of her wrapper, but lay submissively still as he examined her. He was too strong to fight, far stronger than she was, and she was too tired! She would just have to endure whatever he meted out to her. It couldn't be worse than what he had done to her already!

Jon stared down at the soft curves he had so sickeningly bruised and despised himself. No matter what she had done to provoke him, she had not deserved this! The ivory flesh of her bottom and upper thighs was hot and red, punctuated with rapidly darkening yellow marks. It must hurt like the very devil! He turned abruptly away to rummage in a sea chest, then stood up seconds later with a first-aid kit in his hands. He felt like the biggest rogue unhung, as he sat down beside her on the bed. She neither moved nor whimpered as he began to smooth a healing lotion into her burning flesh.

His long fingers stroked the cream into her skin. Cathy tried not to flinch from the intimacy of his touch. His hands on her were worse than the pain, she thought dully. That *she,* willful, pampered, accustomed to every care and luxury, should be brought so low was unbelievable. Yet it was happening.

"Is that better?" he asked softly after a few minutes. Cathy wanted to scream at him, but it was too much effort. She nodded listlessly.

"You bruise easily," he continued in a faintly accusing tone, as though the marks on her were somehow her fault. Cathy made no reply. After a moment he said brusquely, "I suppose you think that if you sulk long enough, I'll apologize."

Apologize! Cathy quelled an insane desire to giggle. He actually thought that three little words would make it all right for her again. Still, she thought, it would be something. The first step on the road to humbling that proud black head!

"Don't worry. I know better than to expect anything like that from you," she managed bitterly, then shivered as she heard the sharp sound of his jaw as it snapped shut.

Jon saw her shudder and cursed himself. He hadn't meant to hurt her, God knew! But she'd been enough to try the patience of a saint, much less someone as hot tempered as himself. Anyway, how was he to know she'd bruise so easily? He blew out the candle slowly and got back into bed, lying on his back and making no attempt to touch her.

"All right, I'm sorry," he said stiffly after long moments.

The remark out of the blue surprised Cathy. She hadn't really expected him to apologize. Was there any way she could turn his remorse to her advantage? Perhaps if she pretended to forgive him. . . .

"W-what?" she asked cautiously.

90

"Damn it, I said I'm sorry." The words were ground out through gritted teeth. Cathy almost smiled. It was obvious that the admission was difficult for him. If she could actually wring an apology from him, it might be just a matter of time until she had him right where she wanted him: groveling at *her* feet. Not that that would satisfy her. Nothing would, until she saw him dead!

"You asked for everything you got, you know," he said as if he had to justify his actions.

"I asked for it?" Cathy gasped, forgetting her plan to be sweetly forgiving. "How can you say that? I certainly never asked you to rape me!"

"It wasn't rape, and you know it as well as I do," Jon said roughly, raising himself on one elbow and leaning over to peer at her face.

"Not rape!"

"You wanted it, too. Where I come from, if the lady's willing, there's no question of rape."

"Willing! I was certainly not willing! You forced me! I had no choice!"

"I admit I would have forced you if I'd had to. As it happened, I didn't. From the first time I kissed you, back on the 'Anna Greer,' I knew you were mine for the taking. You're a very passionate woman, sweet, or at least you will be when you learn a little more of what it's all about!"

"You beast!" Cathy shrieked, sitting bolt upright in the bed as his words flicked a raw spot. "I hated everything you did to me! I hate you to touch me! I hate you, period! You raped me, you filthy cad, and now you're trying to soothe your conscience by saying that I wanted it!"

"Didn't you?" he murmured provocatively.

"No!" Cathy was outraged.

"Shall I prove otherwise?" he asked, voice soft as one hard arm snaked around her waist to pull her back into the bed.

"But you—you can't! You apologized! How can you want to do the same thing again when you're sorry for the first time?"

"You misunderstood me, sweet. I apologized for spanking you, richly though you deserved it. I never regretted taking what you were dying to give me."

"You let me go, you lying swine!" Cathy railed. "Can't you get it through your conceited head that I despise you? I said let me go!" Her voice grew shrill as he dragged her against him.

"Don't be frightened, sweet. I told you that the next time would be better. This won't hurt you at all, if you'll just relax and let me. . . ." His voice trailed off as he buried his mouth in the soft, rose scented valley between her breasts.

"I'll never let you do anything!" Cathy got out in a strangled whisper, pulling fiercely at his black hair. "Anything you want from me, you'll have to take! You'll have to rape me again and again and again, and still I won't give in! I hate you, I tell you, and I'll die before I submit to you!"

"I doubt it, my girl. Not unless you plan to do it mighty fast."

These words were murmured against the curve of

her breast as Jon reached up to secure her hands. Cathy wriggled and squirmed as he leisurely suckled at first one taut peak and then the other. Strange yearnings shivered through her body at the touch of his hard mouth, but Cathy fought the tentative urge to surrender. This time, she knew what he was leading up to. She had experienced the knifelike pain that had felt as if it would split her in two. Oh, God, she couldn't take it again! She couldn't. . . .

He was lying on his side facing her, careful not to turn her onto her sore back, holding her clamped tightly to his muscular body. With one hand he stripped her wrapper from her. When she was as naked as he, his arm snaked out, catching her leg and hoisting it high around his waist. Cathy struggled frantically, horrified at this fresh indignity, but to no avail. Cathy wanted to scream, to cry, to plead with him to spare her this new torture, but his mouth was on hers, stifling her cries, suffocating her. She felt his hardness probe between her legs, and tensed for the pain she was sure must follow. To her surprise, she felt none, only a hot, sweet fullness as he slid inside her. She gasped at the strange sensation, but not from pain. It felt good. . . .

"I told you the next time would be better," he murmured smugly into her ear. Cathy longed for the familiar surging rage to flood her veins. Instead she felt a melting weakness as he moved gently inside her. She moaned at the unexpected pleasure, her arms coming up to twine around his neck of their own volition.

"Ahhh, Cathy," she vaguely heard him groan through the mists she was lost in, but she was too caught up in her own response to spare a thought for his.

His thrusts were carrying her away on a spinning cloud, and she was too weak to fight them. All she wanted was to get closer, closer, closer to that hard, warm body. She began to move with him, her untrained body writhing seductively against his. He moved faster and harder, groaning, and Cathy clasped him to her as though she would never let him go. Then with one final deep thrust it was over. Cathy was brought resentfully back to reality to find him sprawled beside her, one hand cupping her breast and his breathing ragged in her ear. She moved her leg experimentally over his. That couldn't be all! She had felt on the verge of something—something momentous! What had happened?

"Jon?" she murmured tentatively.

"So I'm Jon, now, am I? I thought you hated and despised me?" She could just make out the mocking curve of his mouth. "Ah, well, just goes to show how fickle is woman."

"Oh, you. . . ." Cathy gasped, flouncing away and turning her back to him. He had succeeded in shaming her again. But just you wait, she thought, steaming. Just you wait, my fierce pirate captain. You'll get your comeuppance, and before long.

Just as she finished the thought, Jon's arms came around her, pulling her back against him so that she was cradled by his warm body. Her head ended up nestled cozily on his arm.

"Go to sleep, vixen," he whispered, dropping a light kiss on her tumbled hair. She thought she saw the bright gleam of his teeth as he added softly, "While you have the chance."

Four

Jon awoke the next morning feeling more alive than he had in months. He stretched, yawning, and the movement brought him up against the soft body huddled in a little ball on the far side of the bunk. Even in sleep, he thought wryly, she stayed as far away from him as she could get. But he'd change all that, he promised himself. The day would come when she'd want his body as badly as he wanted hers. And he wanted hers pretty damned badly, he had to admit. Even now, knowing that the sea and his ship were waiting for him, he had to exercise extreme control not to roll her over onto her pretty little backside and pump out his lust between her legs. Jon grinned. He must be getting old. He'd always heard that as men approached middle-age they got yearnings for girls young enough to be their daughters. But if what he felt was typical of middle age, then let it come. So far, it was fantastic!

His hand moved beneath the bedding, but Jon drew it back before it reached its goal. Enough of that! He had a ship to sail. The men would be thinking he'd gone soft, lazing in bed until the sun was high up. It was the first time he'd slept past

95

dawn since he had first put to sea as a boy of sixteen. At the thought he frowned a little. Women had been the downfall of many a man. He'd have to watch out, so that the fascination the little she-cat's body held for him didn't get out of hand. Not that it was likely, he assured himself. He had bedded many women, most of them lovely and all of them far more experienced in pleasing a man than the child beside him. If he was gentler with her than the others, well, it was because she was younger and more tender. The unprecedented guilt he had felt after bruising her delectable flesh was only natural. After all, it might interfere with his enjoyment, which was what the game was all about! Just let him get to Cadiz, where a certain merry widow waited, and he'd get the little shrew out of his system once and for all. Like too much whiskey, the cure for intense sexual attraction was hair of the dog. And any dog would do.

A knock sounded discreetly at the cabin door. Jon bounded out of the bunk. The last thing he wanted was to be caught day-dreaming on his back like some lovesick child. He stepped hurriedly into his breeches, doing up the buttons and shrugging into his shirt before calling brusquely, "What is it?"

The door opened a couple of inches and Harry poked his head through. His eyes widened at the sight of Jon, frowning and tousle-haired and obviously just out of bed. At Harry's bemused expression, Jon's scowl deepened.

"Well?" he barked.

"Sorry, Cap'n," Harry said hastily, barely repressing a grin. "The crew was getting worried about you. Some of them heard all the ruckus in here last night, and . . . uh . . . well, they thought she might have killed you. When you didn't come on deck this morning, sir."

"Very funny," Jon said sourly. "You can tell whoever's interested that I'm still breathing. And if you don't wipe that damned silly smirk off your face, you soon may not be."

"Yes, sir, Captain, sir!" Harry was grinning openly as he started to withdraw. Then he paused. "Oh, uh, by the way, Cap'n, that's one hell of a shiner!"

"Get out!" roared Jon. Harry beat a hasty retreat.

"Is something wrong?" Cathy, awakened by Jon's infuriated bellow, struggled to sit upright. Jon turned frowningly in her direction. With her long golden hair cascading in bright waves around her nakedness and her sapphire eyes wide as saucers, she was breathtakingly beautiful. Just looking at the soft mounds of her breasts, almost completely exposed above the quilt, made his temperature shoot up. God, he wanted her! His muscles ached with it. Jon knew suddenly that he'd better make arrangements to get rid of her mighty fast. If he didn't, he might find himself in real trouble.

"No. Go back to sleep." He answered her question shortly, angry that she should have the power to disturb him. Last night she had even brought him to the point of telling her, like some lovesick swain, that he was sorry for having beaten her—when she'd

97

begged for every lick and more besides! Maybe the jade really was the witch he'd called her. It bore thinking about. Such things were not unknown, after all, and he was beginning to believe he had all the symptoms of a man pursued by a devil.

"What are you staring at?" he asked belligerently, seeing that her blue eyes had widened even more as she looked at him.

"Your—your face," she whispered, the corners of her mouth twitching in a quivering smile.

"What the hell is so funny about my face?" Jon turned to search for the small mirror he used to shave with. Come to think of it, Harry had said something about a shiner. He probed his left eye experimentally. It did feel a trifle sore. But he had had black eyes before and they'd never amounted to much. His skin was so tough from the sun and sea air that it took a powerful blow to bruise it.

Jon found the mirror and peered at his reflection. What he saw appalled him. He looked like the lone loser in a twenty-man barroom brawl! His eye was ringed with deepening shades of purple streaked with the faintest tinges of a sickly yellow-green. Three long scratches adorned his check. And now that he thought about it, his hand throbbed where the little bitch had bitten it. Even his shoulder felt sore! He cast a dark look at Cathy, who was trying to hold back her mirth with scant success.

"So you think it's funny, do you, miss?" he growled, advancing on her menacingly. Cathy shrieked and tried to leap from the bed, but hard arms came down

98

on either side of her, holding her in place.

"No. Oh, no," she quavered, then broke into help-less gurgles of laughter. "I'm sorry!" she got out be-tween spasms. "I—I truly can't help it!"

"You won't laugh long if I take you up on deck with me and display your wounds to the world," Jon threatened gruffly, knowing even as he said it that he wouldn't be able to stand the sight of other men drooling over her sweet nakedness.

"You wouldn't!" Cathy gasped, her hand flying automatically to protect her still tender posterior.

"I might," he warned.

"I won't—I won't laugh any more," she promised, only to collapse in a gale of giggles as she took an-other look at his battered face.

"Jade," he said without heat, and turned away from her to sit on the edge of the bunk while he pulled on his high boots.

"Jon," she ventured when her amusement had abated somewhat. "I didn't mean to hurt you—at least, I did—but—but I'm sorry now. Really."

"Are you?" He turned to look at her intently. Cathy felt her heart give a queer little lurch at the expression in his eyes.

"Y-yes." Not even Cathy herself was certain whether or not she meant what she said. It could have been just a ploy to get him to lower his defenses, or it could have been sincere. He had her emotions in such a turmoil that she just didn't know.

"Prove it."

"H—how?"

"Kiss it better." The gray eyes were mocking, but a tiny flame burned steadily at their backs.

"I—I—all right." The thought of being kissed by him after the intimacies they had shared the night before was oddly pleasurable. Cathy held her face up submissively, her eyes closed and her rosy lips puckered in the proper position for a kiss. Jon laughed shortly.

"I meant for you to give the kiss, trollop, not the other way around."

"Oh." Cathy rocked back on her heels, thinking furiously. She was surprised to find that she actually liked the idea of placing her mouth against his injuries, of soothing his hurts with her lips. The game was getting dangerous. She was no longer sure whether she wanted to win or lose, or even what winning or losing was. But anything that would make him soften toward her must work to her advantage, she reasoned. Therefore, giving him a willing kiss would fit right in with her plans.

She knelt beside him where he still sat on the edge of the bunk, keeping the quilt tucked carefully about her. His eyes darkened as she slid silky white arms around his neck. Cathy was surprised to find that her own heart beat faster. It wouldn't do to forget her purpose, she warned herself, moving close. This was all part of her revenge. . . .

Her mouth went first to his eye, drawing out the soreness with a series of butterfly kisses, then trailed over the long scratches that her nails had raked across his cheek. His skin felt hard and firm against her mouth, tasting of salt from the sea and smelling of man. Cathy was beginning to like the smell. . . .

Jon's arms came around her abruptly, his hand tangling in her long hair to pull her mouth down to his. His lips feasted hungrily on hers and then were still, letting her take the initiative. Her lips parted against his and still he didn't move, keeping his emotions on a tight rein as he let her learn by herself what she needed to know about kissing. Her small tongue flicked his shyly and was hurriedly withdrawn. Jon's physical reaction was so intense that he felt real pain. More than anything he wanted to push her back against the pillows and love the breath out of her. But he didn't want to scare her. . . . He was astonished to realize that rape no longer seemed as satisfying as it once had. He wanted her full, willing cooperation.

"Miss?" Petersham's voice on the other side of the door broke them abruptly apart. Damn, Jon thought frustratedly, then acknowledged with a grimace that it was really just as well. The wench was beginning to get under his skin. He needed to get out in the fresh air where he could get the way she made him feel in some kind of perspective. He heaved himself off the bunk, casting a quick glance over his shoulder at her as he strode to the door. Her lips were tucked into a damned irritating little Mona Lisa smile. She looked smugly self-satisfied, and Jon began to wonder if perhaps he was being taken for a ride. . . .

"I should throw you overboard," he said slowly, a thread of seriousness lacing the words. "Drowning's one way to kill a witch."

"It wouldn't do you any good. Witches float." She wrinkled her nose at him impishly. Jon didn't even smile.

"Master Jon! Uh, Captain! I didn't realize you were still in your cabin. Are you ill?" Petersham, exclaimed, flustered, as Jon flung open the door. His eyes widened at the sight of his captain's bruised face, but he quickly swallowed the exclamation that leapt to his tongue. Some things were better ignored.

"No, I'm not ill," Jon answered shortly, scowling at Petersham. The old fool's thoughts were painfully obvious. "I had some—uh—business to attend to this morning that could best be handled indoors."

"I understand, sir." Petersham permitted himself a small smile. Jon stifled a curse and brushed by the valet irritably, disappearing out the door.

"I've brought your breakfast, miss." Petersham entered the cabin hesitantly. After seeing Master Jon's wounds he hated to look at Miss Cathy. The master was a strong man, and with his temper he wouldn't have taken kindly to being so attacked. At the very least he expected the girl to be similarly marked. His mind reeled when she smiled at him saucily.

"Good morning, Petersham. I'm starving. What have you brought me to eat?"

Petersham set the meal before her, still in something of a daze. To his knowledge, the captain had never before had any qualms about bestowing a

102

hearty buffet upon a female if he felt it was deserved. And if one had scarred him up the way Miss Cathy had, well, knowing Master Jon he would have expected him at the very least to give as good as he got. He was soft where this girl was concerned. Petersham puzzled over it, but rejected the only solution that occurred to him as ridiculous.

"Petersham." Cathy called out, as he turned to leave her to eat her breakfast in privacy. "I'd like my other trunks, please. I'm being allowed up for air at last." She smiled sunnily as she spoke.

"Certainly, miss," Petersham replied, his thoughts in a turmoil. "I'll have them brought to you. Uh . . . with the Captain's permission, of course."

"Of course," Cathy agreed, her voice sugary. If all went well, the captain would soon be agreeing to anything she wished. How she'd love that! And how she'd make him grovel!

The same two sailors who had carried in her bath the night before brought her trunks. They were carefully respectful, but, as she thanked them, Cathy was taken aback by the knowing grins they turned on her. What was so funny, she wondered confusedly, looking down at herself to make sure that she was adequately covered. She was. Cathy shook her head, dismissing the matter. Men were strange creatures at best.

She spent the next hour sorting through her clothes. Her underwear was neatly folded and tucked away in the wardrobe. Some of Jon's shirts had to be removed to make room, but as Cathy stuffed them into a sea chest she shrugged. He wouldn't object, she was sure. He was not overly picky about his clothes. A few of her dresses that were not too badly wrinkled were also hung in the wardrobe. The rest were thrown across the foot of the bed until they could be pressed—if the "Margarita" carried anything so civilized as an iron. . . . All Jon apparently asked of his garments was that they be clean, and sometimes he was not even too concerned about that.

A white, muslin day dress sprigged with tiny, mint-green leaves was the least crushed of the lot, and Cathy decided that it would suit her purpose nicely. It was wrapped about the waist with a green silk sash that tied in the back in an enormous bow, and had little green slippers and a small flat hat to match. The hat added just the right touch, she thought, turning this way and that as she admired her reflection in the long mirror that hung inside the wardrobe door. Its light green color set off her golden hair and made her eyes look even more blue. The simple style of the dress called attention to her tiny waist and the rounded curves above and below it. Jon could not fail to be bowled over, she decided. And bowling him over was a necessary part of her plan.

He had taken her twice more during the night. And if she was honest, she would have to admit that he was right: it got better as one went along. Still, the knowledge that he could use her body whether she liked it or not rankled. Her pride demanded that he be brought to his knees, and making him fall in love with her was the best way she knew how to do it.

It was past noon when Cathy ventured out on deck, and the sun was floating almost directly overhead. Its brightness made her close her eyes momentarily, and then she lifted her face to the heat, enjoying its fierceness against her skin. She opened her eyes to a cerulean sky with small, white clouds scuttling across its surface like sheep. A sharp sea breeze cooled the air. The "Margarita" rocked up and down gently like a baby's cradle, rigging snapping in the wind, timbers creaking. Cathy felt suddenly marvelous. It was good to be out in the hustle and bustle of life again!

"Lady Catherine."

Cathy turned to find the young man who had refused to help her when she was first brought on board behind her. Harry, she'd heard Jon call him. Her good mood cooled somewhat. His presence was a nagging reminder that she was, after all, still a prisoner on this ship, subject to the captain's orders and good will. At the thought she tossed her head, blue eyes flashing. Not for long, she vowed.

"Ma'am, Captain's compliments and all that, and would you please join him on the quarterdeck. He says the air up there is healthier for a young lady."

Cathy looked down her nose at him. He hadn't been nearly so concerned about her well-being the last time he had spoken to her. In fact, he had delivered her straight into the jaws of the proverbial lion! But she had since learned that the lion, though fierce, was not greatly to be feared. And the lion's protection allowed her to ignore the baying of lesser beasts, such as the man before her.

She turned studiedly away as if suddenly afflicted with acute deafness. Her eyes wandered with determined casualness around the deck. The men had all stopped their various tasks and were staring at her as a pack of dogs would stare at a particularly juicy bone. Cathy shivered under the regard of so many lascivious eyes. There was little doubt about what was in their minds! If Jon had not afforded her his protection, she guessed that they would have passed her around like candy. Compared to what might have been, her fate suddenly seemed almost bearable.

"My lady," Harry began with desperation, only to be cut off by an angry bellow from the quarterdeck.

"Harry! Quit your lallygagging and get her up here. And the rest of you men get back to work! You'll have plenty of time to do your wenching when we make port!"

"Aye, Cap'n, we will, but the question is will we be able to find a piece so lively! Bedding a she-tiger beats the hell out of lying with a tame cat—ain't that right, boys?"

Hoots and guffaws followed this sally. Even Jon laughed, Cathy noted irritably as she turned her hot face up to where he stood braced on the quarterdeck. Vile, obscene animals, all of them! Their crudity was enough to make her sick! Obviously the crew had correctly guessed the cause of the marks on Jon's face, and had been making lewd jokes about it for some time. Well, they could think what they liked! She was not about to feel ashamed before a rag-tail bunch of pirates!

Jon frowned suddenly as he took in the full glory of her low-cut, thin-as-air dress, and Cathy scowled right back at him. How dare he let his men make her the object of their lewd jests! She stared at him haughtily as she ascended the wooden steps. He looked hard and fierce as he watched her approach, legs straddled to keep him upright against the intermittent roll of the ship, hands clenched over the rail. The breeze had blown his dark hair into raffish disorder. Sunlight glinted along the blue-black stubble which shadowed his cheeks. He wore a white shirt, torn in places, open to the waist to expose his sweat-dampened chest to the breeze. Pistols and a long knife were thrust into a sash which bound his trim waist, and his powerful legs were encased in snug black breeches. Cathy privately thanked God that he had not looked so fearsome when he had taken her from the "Anna Greer." She would have been frightened witless!

"You look like a pirate," she accused as she joined him on the quarterdeck.

"I am," he answered shortly. "A fact which you would do well to remember, sweet, lest I be forced to remind you."

Cathy was taken aback at the curt warning. After his gentleness with her that morning and his impassioned lovemaking of the night before, she had been confident that she would soon have him eating out of her hand. Suddenly she was not quite so sure. He had experienced many women; was her woefully ignorant body strong enough to give her the upper hand in their relationship? She didn't know. But it was the only trump card she held, and she had no choice but to play it.

Looking up at him coquettishly, she was piqued to find his attention fixed not on her, but on some far distant spot on the horizon.

"Looking for my rescuers?" she needled.

He glanced at her briefly, expressionlessly, then looked away.

"Your rescuers, as you call them, lost us in the storm. There's been no sign of them for some days. And as the 'Margarita' is now sailing a totally different course than she was when they last set eyes on us, I have no expectation of ridding myself of you in such a satisfactory way."

"If you were so anxious to be rid of me, why didn't you put me adrift in one of those little boats that first night? I'm sure the Royal Navy would have been delighted to pick me up."

"Ahh, but I had a use for you that first night." The wicked glance he sent her way left Cathy in no doubt as to his meaning. Cheeks flushing, she glanced quickly around to see if anyone besides herself was within hearing distance. Only Harry and an older, heavy-set sailor were near, and they were both stolidly concentrating on the tasks they had to hand. But something in their expression made Cathy certain that they listened to what she and Jon had to say with great interest.

"I notice that you express no concern over the fate of your fellow captives."

Jon's words brought her eyes swinging back around to him.

"I—why, of course I'm concerned," she said mendaciously. To tell the truth, she had been far too concerned over her own safety to worry unduly about three relative strangers. But Jon didn't have to know that. "I merely assumed that, since you stand to make a great deal of money from their ransoms, your own self-interest would assure that they were kept safe. Was I wrong?"

"Not wrong, my cat," he murmured. "Just a little too sharp-tongued. A fault which a bout with another cat would soon remedy."

Cathy was disconcerted by his inexplicable change of manner toward her. What ailed him? They hadn't quarreled. Was he angry with her for some unknown reason? Well, she would endure twenty cat-o'-nine-tails before she would beg for quarter from him! He could do his worst!

"Do what you deem necessary, Captain," she said coldly. "I was always told that pirates should be feared as a cruel, bloodthirsty lot!"

"And were you never told that pride goeth before a fall, my lady?" His voice was hard. "A single stroke with the cat on your bare back would have you crawling on your knees to me for mercy."

"But then you'd cheat yourself of your pleasure, wouldn't you, Captain?" Cathy smiled triumphantly,

109

knowing that she had him there. He would not whip her for the simple reason that he would then no longer be able to bed her. The rogue's own selfishness and lust were her protection.

"Would I?" He smiled slowly down into her eyes. "Your being whipped would not hamper my love-making particularly. True, you might find it painful, but pirates are notoriously unconcerned with the comfort of their prisoners."

"You . . ." Cathy began hotly, only to stop short as Harry came to join them at the rail. Jon glanced at him impatiently. Harry looked uncomfortable.

"Begging your pardon, Cap'n, but it's time for the prisoners to be brought up for exercise. Shall I see to it?"

"Aye," Jon answered brusquely, then swung away so that his broad back was facing Cathy.

She stood, biting her lip, as her companions in misfortune were brought up from the hold. She only glanced their way as they came stumbling up the stairs by the forecastle, her mind more concerned with Jon's strange behavior than their plight. Then she looked again. All three of them were blinking against the bright sunlight, their faces pale and thin, their clothes dirty and crumpled. They looked as if they hadn't had a square meal or a wash since being brought on board the "Margarita" almost a week before. Cathy's mouth formed a little "oh" of shocked amazement. If she had thought about her fellow captives at all, she had assumed that they were being fed and housed much the same as she was, the only difference being that they were not forced to share anyone's bed. She now saw her mistake. Except for one detail, her fate had plainly been far better than theirs! She felt a sharp stab of indignation at Jon that he should treat them so inhumanely.

Head high, back stiffened angrily, she gathered her skirts in her hand and began to regally descend from the quarterdeck. Jon called after her peremptorily, but she ignored him with a defiant toss of her head. After all, what could he do to her that he hadn't already done? His remark about a bout with the cat crossed her mind, but she shrugged it aside. He would find that she was not so easily cowed!

"Your Grace?" Cathy had crossed the planked deck quickly and was at the Duchess's side. The old woman turned her head at Cathy's words and then, as she saw who it was that had addressed her, a slight smile broke through the strain that etched her face.

"Lady Catherine! It's good to see you looking so well. I had begun to fear for your safety, when you did not join us."

"She was obviously offered a warmer berth," the merchant's wife, not so fat as she had once been, put in snidely, looking Cathy up and down as if the girl had just crawled out from under a rock. "I see they gave you at least a change of clothes, my lady. But then, the Duchess and I didn't share our favors with them."

"You will kindly be silent, Mistress Grady," the

111

Duchess said, speaking with the authority to which her high rank had accustomed her. "If Lady Catherine has fared better than ourselves, then I am sure it is through no fault of hers. If not . . . well, I'm sure that was through no fault of hers either."

Chastened, Miss Grady turned sullenly away. The Duchess looked keenly at Cathy.

"Have you been ill-treated?" she asked in a low voice.

Cathy could feel color rushing to her cheeks, but she answered as calmly as she could. "No, your Grace. Not—not really."

As a general rule Cathy scorned lies and liars, but she knew, with a sinking feeling in the pit of her stomach, that her whole future depended upon not allowing anyone to guess what she had actually suffered. The stigma of rape was all pervading. Once it had attached itself to her, her hopes for a brilliant marriage, or indeed any marriage at all, would be gone forever. In Victoria's England, an unchaste, unmarried female was automatically labeled a whore; the circumstances under which that female had become unchaste made not a particle of difference.

"I see." The old woman's eyes scanned Cathy's face thoroughly, but there was nothing in her expression to indicate disbelief. Cathy heaved an inward sigh of relief. "Where have they put you, child?"

"I—I—the captain has been kind enough to let me have the use of his cabin." Which was certainly true. She did have the use of Jon's cabin. It was no business of anyone's what price he exacted from her for the privilege.

"That was gentlemanly of him. I must confess that I'm surprised. Most likely you remind him of a young sister, or even a daughter. Even cutthroats have their soft spots, I suppose."

"Yes. Yes, I'm sure that's it." Cathy was feeling more and more uncomfortable. She felt that her shame must be branded into the soft flesh of her forehead. Quickly she changed the subject. "Tell me, your Grace, how goes it with you and—um—Mister and Mistress Grady?"

The Duchess looked ruefully down at the stained dress that hung on her now bony frame. "Things have not been too well with us, as you can see. But at least we are alive, and I suppose we must thank God for it. These pirates usually think nothing of murdering innocent people out of hand. They are a brutal, lawless bunch."

"Indeed, ma'am, you are right. We are both brutal and lawless."

Cathy jumped as Jon's hands bit hard into the thinly covered flesh of her shoulders. She should have guessed that he would come after her. His arrogant pride would not allow him to let her get by with ignoring his commands in front of his crew. The question was, would he give her away? She threw an unconsciously pleading look over her shoulder at him, trying very casually to shrug free of his touch. To her surprise, he let her go.

"I'm glad you realize it, young man. If you keep to your present way of life, you will surely hang." The

Duchess's voice was scornful. Jon's mouth tightened, and Cathy suddenly feared for the old woman. He was in no mood to take impertinence lightly.

"Undoubtedly, ma'am." Cathy relaxed as Jon replied with only a slight impatience. "But my men and I infinitely prefer hanging to starving."

The Duchess stared at Jon icily. She was an old woman, her life almost over. She did not fear death, but neither did she intend to invite it prematurely. This man was a pirate, and by definition murder was his trade. She modified the harshness of her tone.

"Lady Catherine tells me that her accommodations have been somewhat better than ours. For that I am grateful. She is still very young, and it would be an abomination if she were to be misused." Her words conveyed an unmistakeable warning to Jon. Cathy swallowed convulsively. Surely he would not expose her! After all, he would gain nothing from her disgrace.

"As you say, she is very young," Jon replied slowly, his face expressionless. "I thought it best to put her where she would be out of harm's way. As for the lack in your accommodations, for that I am truly sorry. But you must realize that the 'Margarita' is not a luxury vessel."

"That's quite obvious, young man. When may we expect to be released?"

"Arrangements will be made, as soon as possible, after the 'Margarita' makes port. Possibly some ten days from now."

"I assure you, Captain, that you cannot move too quickly for any of us."

"I am sure I cannot. And now, ma'am, my men have other duties which call them. If you are ready, they will escort you below."

"Ah, certainly. It never does to pull a tiger's tail, does it?" the Duchess said grimly, and, without waiting for a reply, turned to go below.

A sailor who had been loosely guarding the prisoners caught the old woman's arm none too gently. Another shooed the Gradys before him like a pair of squawking geese. Cathy, watching the Duchess's gaunt face as it set into an expression of tired endurance, felt an almost physical pang of pity. She had to do what she could to help. Her conscience would never let her rest, otherwise.

"Wait!" she cried impulsively. Then, to Jon, "You cannot continue to treat them in such a barbarous fashion! It's cruel, inhuman! If they are to be treated so unkindly, then I insist on suffering with them!"

Jon looked her over from the top of her head to the tips of her toes. Cathy felt chilled by that hard look, but she proudly stood her ground. It was possible that he would take her at her word, and order her to be taken below. If so, then she would have exchanged good food and a soft bed for the return of her honor, slightly tarnished. If not, if he refused to deny himself the comforts of her body for the sake of teaching her a lesson, then she could likewise refuse to submit to him unless the other prisoners were decently fed and housed. Of course, he could

115

always resort to brute force. But she was beginning to suspect that he might find that highly unsatisfactory. Or so she hoped.

"What did you say?" His voice was softly threatening, meant for her ears alone. Cathy's eyes flashed defiantly.

"I demand that you treat the other prisoners decently. It's brutal of you to abuse them in such a way! If they are to be starved and kept locked up, then so shall I be!"

"My sweet, if you insist on being starved and locked up, then I have no objection. But it will be done on my orders, not yours."

His voice was still low. Cathy hoped that the others had not heard the casual endearment with which he had preceded his words. Common sense told her to back off while she could still do it gracefully. Pride refused to let her.

"We should all be treated the same way," she argued recklessly. "If I am to be well-fed and housed then they should be, too."

Jon shook his head at her. "You don't learn very quickly, do you, little cat? I am captain of this ship, and I give the orders. Don't think that just because you share my bed that you can tell me what to do!"

Cathy gasped, looking quickly over her shoulder, praying that his crude words had not been overheard. Her hopes were in vain. Mister and Mistress Grady were eyeing her with shocked avidity while the Duchess's eyes were sorrowing. Cathy turned fiery red. Though she had brought this publicity of her disgrace upon herself, she refused to admit it. She felt that she hated Jon almost more for betraying her shame than for causing it. She would never forgive him, never!

"I hate you!" she whispered fiercely as he motioned the grinning sailors to take the other three prisoners below. He caught Cathy roughly by the arm, dragging her after him as he strode toward his cabin.

"Save your tantrums until we are alone, if you please," he said crisply. "Otherwise I'll be obliged to quell them in an equally public way!"

"You didn't have to say what you did! Isn't it bad enough what you've done to me, without telling the world? Are you so vain about your conquests, Captain, that you must make certain that everyone knows of them?"

"I said shut up!" The barely restrained savagery of his tone got through to her. She wisely did as she was told, but her chin jutted mutinously as he half-shoved her before him into the cabin.

"You did that deliberately," Cathy charged in a shaking voice as he kicked the door shut after them.

"I didn't have to." Jon's reply was calm as he leaned back against the door, arms crossed over his chest. He showed no trace of the anger he had exhibited just seconds ago. "They knew anyway. Do you think they're fools?"

"They didn't know for sure until you came right out and told them," Cathy hissed. "Do you have any conception of what you've done? You're ruined my whole life, that's what. No one will want to marry me now! No gentleman would want the—the leavings of a pirate!"

"But you're not leavings—yet." Jon grinned suddenly, eyes dancing wickedly. "And who knows, you might get lucky: I might decide to keep you for a pet. You purr very satisfactorily at times, my cat."

Cathy caught her breath furiously. "You filthy swine, do you think that my father won't come looking for me? He will—and he'll find me. Your only hope is to let me go as soon as we reach land. My father is a powerful man. He'll hang you twenty times over for what you've done to me!"

She was so angry that she barely knew what she was saying. Jon's grin turned derisive.

"He has to catch me first, little cat, and that's hard to do. Men have been trying for years, yet here I still stand. What makes you think that your almighty father will succeed where so many others have failed?"

"He just will, that's all," was all Cathy could think of to reply. She spat the words through gritted teeth to make up for their inaneness.

"He might not even try, if you were to send him word you had decided to stay with me of your own free will." It was said in an offhand manner, but Jon's eyes were suddenly intent on Cathy's flushed face. She was too angry to notice.

"Stay with you?" She laughed scornfully. "You can't be serious! Do you think that I'd give up my whole future, my family and friends, to stay with a man who thinks nothing of raping an innocent

118

young girl, a man who murders and steals, who would starve a helpless old woman? You must think highly of your abilities in bed, Captain. Speaking for myself, I disagree."

"You're a conceited little cat, aren't you, sweet?" Jon drawled, his eyes glittering strangely. "What makes you think I'd have you? I was just mentioning a possibility. Once we reach port, there will be plenty of women eager to warm my bed. Women much better at pleasuring a man than you, I'm glad to say. You'll become redundant."

Cathy glared at him, too incensed at this cavalier dismissal of her importance to be able to frame any kind of a reply. "And," Jon continued coldly, "as for the rest of your remarks, I'll take them point by point. First, I thought we'd already agreed that no rape occurred. Second, I steal to survive. If you'd ever gone hungry you'd be more sympathetic. Third, if I don't kill my opponents, they'll kill me. And I prefer to live, thank you. And finally, as to starving those pudding-bags, let me inform you that the 'Margarita's' rations are carefully calculated before each voyage so that there's enough to get us where we're going and back—no more. We have no room for stores. When we took the 'Anna Greer,' our food supplies were already low. We had followed her for some days longer than I had originally planned, you see. If your three friends were allowed to gorge themselves, then I or my men would have to go without sufficient food to make up the difference. And the prisoners are not needed to sail this ship. They get enough to keep body and soul together, and we'll reach port before they suffer any real ill-effects. You should be grateful that I was sufficiently taken with your soft curves to want to keep them that way."

"I despise and detest you," Cathy said slowly after a long moment. "You have the hardest heart of anyone I've ever met. If you even have a heart, which I'm beginning to doubt."

"I have one, never fear." His long lashes dropped to mask his eyes. "But I also have sense enough to realize that if I don't take care of me and mine, no one else gives a damn. Something you'll doubtless realize as you grow older, my child."

"I'm not a child any more, thanks to you," Cathy replied bitterly. "You've seen to it that I've grown up fast."

"And I've enjoyed every minute of your education." The mocking light was back in his eyes.

Cathy abruptly turned her back, too sick at heart to argue further. She crossed to the window to stare pointedly out.

"Would you please leave? I'd like to be alone for a while." Her voice was icy.

"Then alone you shall be, my lady. For a while. Just don't get too fond of solitude. Remember, it's only temporary."

Cathy clamped her lips together and refused to dignify his needling with a reply. After a moment she heard the door open, and then click shut behind him. Through the window, the sunlight was making sparkling, ever-changing patterns on gently breaking waves. Cathy stared at them blindly. She felt shattered, drained of all emotion. For the first time she acknowledged to herself how completely she was at the pirate captain's mercy. Then she smiled, her expression grim. Only a fool would expect mercy from a merciless man.

Five

Eleven days later the "Margarita" sailed into the Spanish port of Cadiz. The weather had turned hot and sunny again, after almost a week of intermittent squalls. Since their quarrel, Cathy had spoken to Jon only when she absolutely had to, and he was equally terse with her. The only use he now had for her was to take her body roughly, quickly, at least once, and sometimes even two or three times a day. Cathy found it increasingly easy to lie as unmoving as a stone statue beneath him while he did his worst to her. It had become a point of pride with her to feel nothing—and make sure that Jon knew it.

His temper had deteriorated steadily as her resistance increased. Even Harry tiptoed around him as one would around a live and extremely volatile bomb. Petersham took care to stay away from the cabin when Jon was there, telling Cathy frankly that he had no wish to be present when the inevitable explosion occurred. Cathy resolutely refused to be intimidated. Her tactics, though admittedly dangerous, were working.

Her attitude was as irritating to him as a small

stinging fly was to a large horse. He was being exasperated to the point where he found it impossible to conceal the fact that she was getting under his skin. Only the night before, as he began what Cathy was coming to think of as his ritual assault, he was goaded into revealing just how much her total lack of response irked him. She was lying flat on her back on the bunk where he had thrown her, as limp and unresisting as a rag doll while he systematically stripped her. Finally, with a muttered curse, he stopped with one large hand hooked around the waistband of her pantalets to glare at her. Cathy clenched her eyes tightly shut, refusing to respond to him by so much as a look.

"That's right, bitch," he sneered savagely. "Just close your eyes and think of England. Do you think I give a damn how you feel?"

With that he lowered himself on her stiff body and proceeded to take it brutally. Cathy made neither sound nor movement to help or hinder. She lay like a corpse, inwardly triumphant. He might walk off with an occasional battle, but she was winning the war.

His hands and mouth were deliberately ungentle, inflicting bruises that were still sore the following day. When he had finished, he rolled cursing onto his side. After a few moments he had risen from the bunk and dressed, stomping out of the cabin without a word. She hadn't seen him since. Cathy smiled, remembering. She was making him suffer, and the thought brightened her day.

The unaccustomed sight of land out of the small window beckoned Cathy irresistably. She decided to end her self-imposed exile. After all, she was the only one to suffer from her confinement. As Jon had repeatedly said, she could stay in his cabin until doomsday as far as he was concerned. All he cared about was having her body available whenever he cared to avail himself of it. Unspeakable animal, she thought bitterly, and then dismissed him from her mind. She was determined to enjoy the day.

Cathy dressed hastily, suddenly so tired of the four walls of the captain's cabin that she could have screamed. A simple, peach-colored linen dress seemed the best choice considering the heat, not to mention the way it blended with her creamy skin, giving the illusion at first sight that she was naked. A large straw hat tied beneath her chin to protect her complexion from the sun completed her toilette, and she was ready. She opened the cabin door and stepped out on deck.

Her arrival caused not the slightest ripple in the smooth running of the ship. Indeed, no one even so much as glanced her way. The men were busy taking in the sails so that the "Margarita" could safely drop anchor. Bawdy songs and jovial curses floated down to Cathy's ears from the rigging, where the men clung like chattering monkeys.

Jon was not on the quarterdeck. Cathy looked around for him on the theory that it was always safest to know the location of the enemy. He didn't appear to be anywhere on the ship, in fact.

Her eyes were beginning another disbelieving swing when she heard his deep voice high above her. She looked up, searchingly. When at last she spotted him her heart stood still for a frightened instant before resuming its beat double-fast. He was in the rigging with his men, high up near the tip of the main mast, climbing even higher as Cathy watched to release the rope that held the topsail to the spar. At last he succeeded, after several precarious tries, and the canvas came fluttering down like a huge white moth. Jon yelled triumphantly, then began to back down the pole after the sail, legs wrapped tightly around the smooth wood as his hands moved one beneath the other. He was grinning, and Cathy could have cheerfully slapped the ridiculous smirk from his face. It was dangerous to go up that high! He should have left it to the men! She was too disturbed to wonder why the thought of his falling from such a height should so upset her. She just knew that it did.

"Michaelson, you and Finch check that canvas for tears," he bellowed, as the sail floated down to the deck.

"Hell, Cap'n, we ain't tailors!" a man called back amiably.

"You are if I say you are!" Jon retorted, still grinning. "Now get to it!"

The men complied with much good-natured grumbling. Cathy wondered that they dared, considering the mood Jon had been in lately. Even he seemed cheerful, though. Lately he had been about as lighthearted as a graveyard. Then the words to one of the songs began to make sense. Jon had said that when the "Margarita" made port there would be plenty of women willing to warm his bed, and apparently the crew was of a similar mind. Cathy shut her mind to the obscene lyrics, her eyes beginning to narrow. If Captain Hale chose to sleep with whores, she could only be grateful to them for relieving her of the onerous duty! She shrank back against the wall beneath the quarterdeck, suddenly anxious not to be seen. The arrogant beast might take her presence on the deck as a sign that she was weakening toward him!

"Ahoy, Cap'n!" Harry came to stand beneath the mast, neck craned back to look at Jon as he still worked high aloft.

"What is it?"

"About the prisoners, Cap'n. You want me to see about their ransoms while I'm ashore ordering supplies?"

"Hell, yes! The sooner we're rid of the stinking pests the better!"

Cathy was shocked at the pain this callous dismissal caused her. She stood biting her lip, unnoticed by all, and told herself sternly that she was elated. Soon she would be free to resume her life where it had been so rudely interrupted, to go to parties and balls, to meet handsome young men. She would return to Portugal, she planned. No one there would know what had happened to her, and

125

she could be assured of her good name. Eventually she might marry. . . . Then the "Margarita" and all that had happened aboard the ship would seem no more real than a bad dream.

"Harry!" Jon yelled after a moment's silence. The second officer had already turned and was making his way toward the rail; far below a small boat waited to take him to shore. He turned back at Jon's summons.

"Aye, Cap'n?"

"Uh—just arrange ransoms for the old lady and the couple. I've a mind to keep the girl for a while." This was said in an offhand tone, but Jon had to repeat it at a bellow before Harry could hear him properly.

"You sure about this, Cap'n?" Harry asked worriedly, when the words were made clear to him.

"Damn it, don't argue every time I give you an order. Just do it."

"But, Cap'n. . . ."

"Look, consider her part of my share. Does that make it easier for your puritan soul to accept?" Jon sounded thoroughly exasperated. Harry cleared his throat nervously, remembering the Captain's temper of late.

"Yes, sir," Harry said smartly, but he was shaking his head as he walked away.

For just an instant Cathy was conscious of a quick stab of delight. Jon meant to keep her with him. . . . ! Then she took herself firmly in hand. Yes, he meant to keep her—until he tired of her. Then she would be cast aside like a pair of worn out breeches while he found another to take her place. She wouldn't even have exclusivity while she was with him! Not if she had read his plans for the night correctly. Was that what she, daughter of an Earl, wanted out of life? To be the transient receptacle of a pirate's lust? Not a chance! She would throw herself overboard before she would submit to being so degraded! Her pride hotly rebelled against the picture she had conjured up. She wouldn't take it, she wouldn't! She would escape . . . !

Cathy looked toward where the breakers pounded the curving shoreline, some seven hundred yards away. She had always been a strong swimmer—an unusual accomplishment for a girl. But she had insisted on learning, and, as always, had gotten her own way. For once her willfulness would stand her in good stead. She was certain that she could swim the distance to shore. True, she had never swum so far, but then she had never had so much reason. She was positive that she could do it. Just the thought of thwarting Captain Jonathan Hale would give her the necessary strength.

Eyes glittering triumphantly, Cathy slipped back into the cabin. Jon mustn't know she had overheard what he'd said to Harry. He must think that she still believed that she would be released while they were in port. He would go blithely ashore tonight, not knowing that she could swim. . . . Cathy smiled. He would soon learn that she was not so easily tamed!

It was about an hour after dark when Jon returned

to the cabin. Cathy, demurely dressed in her blue wrapper over a matching nightgown, was already curled up with a book on his bunk. She favored him with a haughty glance as he entered, but said nothing. Neither did he. Cathy kept her eyes trained zealously on the book while she inwardly rejoiced. He was going ashore! Instead of stripping off and attacking her as he usually did as soon as he came in, he was carefully setting out his shaving gear. She watched, gloating, as he cleared the thick stubble from his face. Moments later, wiping the excess soap away with a small towel, he pulled on breeches of a good, gray broadcloth that would not have shamed a Court dandy. Then he shrugged into a white linen shirt, clean and whole for a change, which sported a small ruffle down the front and at the wrists. That done, he peered into the wardrobe mirror, carefully tying a white, silk cravat around his neck. Finally, he donned a black velvet frock coat. He looked almost extremely handsome. If she had met him, dressed like this, at a party or a ball, she would certainly have exerted her charms to attract him. But, as Martha had frequently told her, handsome is as handsome does. By that reckoning, though, Jon should look like the toad prince!

"Going somewhere?" Cathy asked at last, her voice as cold as ice. To display no curiosity at all might invite suspicion.

"I'm honored!" Jon sneered, turning to stare at her with exaggerated awe. "Her ladyship deigns to speak at last! Well, for your information, my lady,

I'm going to visit an old friend. A female friend," he emphasized. "I've a fancy for a livelier tart in my bed tonight than you've become of late. You should be thankful. Your rest tonight will be as undisturbed as a virgin's."

"I *am* thankful," Cathy assured him, firmly suppressing what felt almost like a prick of jealously. "I only wish you'd decide to replace me altogether. If you're worried about wounding my sensibilities, don't. I believe that they would survive the blow."

Cathy was justifiably proud of the careless tone of her speech. If he'd had any inkling of what she had planned, that should help gull him.

"I'm giving it serious thought," Jon answered coldly. Cathy had to fight back an urge to scream "liar!" at him. She knew better! The perfidious, dog was planning to have her as a main course while he took any other woman he happened to fancy on the side! Well, not for long, she vowed, and almost smiled. Luckily, though, she caught herself in time.

Jon turned back to the mirror to smooth his unruly hair with his gold-backed brush. It looked ridiculously dainty in his big hand. Cathy watched him, triumph glowing in her eyes. The arrogant thing hadn't even considered that she might try to escape him. Would he ever be in for a shock? Hastily she lowered her eyes, afraid he might be able to read her rising excitement in them.

She maintained a stony silence while he finished his toilette, refusing even to look up or answer when he bade her a mocking good-night.

Cathy had to force herself to remain where she was as he shut the door behind him. She had to give him time to get clear of the ship. . . . This might be the only chance she would have. She'd better make the most of it.

Finally the splash of oars told her that he was on his way. Cathy jumped up and raced to the window. He was going, all right. She could see the light bobbing on the water as he rowed himself to shore.

She dropped the curtain and raced across to Jon's sea chests. Slow down, she told herself, as she almost tripped over the leg of a chair. There's plenty of time. If he had told her the truth about his destination, he'd likely be gone all night. Yet her fingers flew as they searched his sea chest for suitable swimming gear.

Moments later she stood up with her prize. Breeches and a shirt would have to do. They would certainly be better for swimming than her own long dress. Its material would quickly have become water-logged, dragging her down with its weight. And besides, Jon's clothes would serve her better once she had reached the shore. She would pretend to be a boy until she was sure she was in good hands. One thing that this voyage had taught her firsthand was a young lady on her own faced danger at every turn.

She dressed hastily, thanking God for the bagginess of the clothes. They allowed not the smallest hint of her shape to show through. Except for her hair, she could easily pass for some ragtail lad. She would have to do something about her hair. Weekly she braided it into two long plaits, then secured them across the top of her head. With one of Jon's caps pulled low over her forehead, she'd do, she thought, surveying herself critically in the mirror. Anyway, it would be dark, and she would take good care to stay out of the light as much as possible.

Taking her plainest shoes from the wardrobe, she tied the laces together so that they could be hung around her neck. She couldn't swim in shoes, but on the other hand she couldn't walk through the town barefoot. The sight of her dainty feet would be a dead giveaway.

Finally, Cathy stripped the two sheets from the bed, tying them together lengthwise and pulling on the knot with all her might to test its strength. Jon had undoubtedly left some of his crew on guard, so she would have to leave by the window, and lower herself by the sheets to avoid the noise of diving. With a lot of care and a little luck, she shouldn't be missed until Jon returned the next morning. By then she would be safely in the hands of the authorities. When she told her story they would arrest him, and he would hang. . . . Well, maybe she wouldn't tell the whole story until the "Margarita" had sailed away. She wouldn't want any man's death on her conscience. Thoughtfully, Cathy blew out the candle.

Getting out of the window proved to be easier said than done. Cathy was a small girl, but the window was smaller yet. She heaved and panted and struggled and finally, just as she was beginning to think she was stuck forever, popped clear, like the last olive from a bottle. Luckily she had decided to go feet first, and had maintained a grip on the rope. If she hadn't, she would have tumbled headfirst into the water with a splash loud enough to alert every ship in the harbor. As it was, except for a few very unladylike words, Cathy managed to lower herself down the "Margarita's" side in comparative silence. She gasped a little as her bare toes first encountered the waves. The water was colder than she had expected. Well, no one had ever promised her that escape would be fun, she told herself, gritting her teeth as she lowered her body into the chilly depths. After all, a little cold water never killed anyone. Yet, her traitor brain added. Cathy quickly shushed the thought.

The swim to shore should warm her at any rate, she mused, paddling for a moment to get her bearings. It would be dreadful if she were to accidentally swim out to sea! The water was dark, because the moon had not yet risen. Fortunately, the shore was even darker, an inky black line punctuated with tiny pin-pricks of light. Taking a deep breath, Cathy pushed off toward them, using the "Margarita's" hull for leverage. She swam steadily, arm over arm as she had been taught. Her only problem was the hat. It floated away the first time her head touched the water, and every time she crammed it back on her head it did the same thing again. Finally she took it off, fighting an urge to throw the pesky thing in as far away from her as she could. Once ashore, she would need it. She gripped it between her teeth and held it like a dog with a bone. It tasted vile—like someone had soaked it in a bottle of rum. Which they probably had, knowing Jon's proclivities!

Cathy had been swimming for what seemed like hours and the shore looked as far away as ever. She glanced back at the "Margarita" to make certain she was still headed in the right direction. Yes, the ship was still directly behind her. Cathy was just congratulating herself on her navigation when her mind was struck by what she had seen. She almost sank herself in her haste to look at the "Margarita" again. Sure enough, down the side of the ship like a telltale white serpent snaked her sheet-rope! Damn and blast, Cathy swore under her breath, borrowing one of Jon's favorite oaths without even realizing it. If she could see the rope so clearly from her position more than halfway across the bay, it must be just a little less visible from the town. She should have pulled it down! Too late now, she thought grimly, striking out for shore with renewed vigor. Now she was certain to be missed the first time one of the crew looked toward the ship.

Well, there was nothing for it but to swim as hard as she could and pray that the men would be so taken up with their revelries that they wouldn't spare a glance for the ship. Cathy pushed herself relentlessly, swimming until her arms felt like they would drop from their sockets. Her breath rasped in her throat and her teeth chattered with cold, but still she kept going. Just as she was beginning to despair of ever making it, her feet smacked hard into something solid. With an inward whoop of triumph, Cathy realized that she had succeeded. She stopped swimming and stood up. The muddy bottom felt like the finest carpet beneath her feet. Grinning happily, and wrapping her shivering arms around her equally cold body, she waded towards the shore.

The smell hit her even before she reached dry land. Sweet and rotten, it was a compound of equal parts of rotting fish, garbage, and human waste. Cathy gagged. She had never smelled anything like it in her life.

As she squelched onto the sand beneath the rickety wooden dock, it became obvious that her navigation had steered her into an extremely disreputable section of town. Cathy hastily pulled on her shoes and clamped Jon's cap down on her head. All her instincts warned her not to linger.

She set off toward what she perceived to be the center of town at a brisk walk. Sinister looking men and women prowled the streets alongside her. Cathy closed her mind as well as she could to her surroundings, thankful that the people she passed were too intent on their own questionable business to spare her more than a casual glance. Clearly, it behooved her to find the authorities as quickly as she could. To wander aimlessly through this hell-hole of a town was to risk having her throat slit.

The alley she had been walking down turned off into a wider street, lighted at either end with flaming torches. Drunken men laughed uproariously as they staggered from one rowdy establishment to another, their arms more often than not tight about the waist of a blowzy woman. Cathy started to go back the way she had come, then stopped. If she was ever to be safe, she needed directions. Surely, dressed as she was, there was no harm in asking.

As far as Cathy could tell, all of the open establishments seemed to be saloons of one sort or another. One adobe building, a trifle quieter than the others, had a hanging sign out front proclaiming it to be the "Red Dog." In English, Cathy's Spanish was practically nonexistent, so it seemed the logical choice. Yet some latent instinct for self-preservation caused her to hesitate.

She had to do something. She couldn't just wander through the streets all night hoping a constable would happen by. In the first place, it was dangerous. In the second, Jon would be looking for her as soon as he had discovered that she was missing. She had to be somewhere safe before then. Anyway, what harm could she come to dressed as a young boy, even in a saloon? She looked down at herself. Not the smallest hint of her sex showed. All she had to do was remember to lower her voice, and no one would suspect that she was a female. For some reason, Cathy was certain that in this section of town, at this time of night, female was not a good thing to be.

Taking a deep breath, Cathy pulled Jon's still damp cap low over her forehead and marched boldly through the swinging door. Faint heart never got anything done! Still, her movements became considerably more cautious once she was actually inside. Men sat drinking at round tables, rough, dirty men who looked far more like pirates than the "Margarita's" crew. They were certainly not gentlemen, with their raucous voices and filthy language. And the women who waited on them, bringing them ale and whiskey and sometimes lingering for a pinch or cuddle, were certainly not ladies! Whores would be more like it, Cathy thought contemptuously, barely controlling a blush as one would-be Lothario tugged at a gaily dressed woman's bodice, causing her ample bosom to spring free. The woman giggled, pressing the jiggling mounds wantonly against the perpetrator's face while the other men urged her on with obscene cries.

"Animals!" thought Cathy with a shudder, as she sidled around to the bar. It appeared that all men were dirty, disgusting beasts—it seemed to be inbred. She was beginning to think that, even when she got home again, she would never marry. She had a sneaking suspicion that even the most gentlemanly-seeming of men might share at least some part of that built-in brutishness.

Cathy stood at the bar, pulling her hat down over her eyes again and being very careful to attract no undue attention. She wanted time to get her bearings before asking anyone for anything. The barkeep seemed the most likely choice. He was a huge, meaty fellow with grizzled red hair and a white butcher's apron that was liberally adorned with stains. Although he looked no less of a ruffian than

136

any other man in the room, he had one advantage—he was cold, stone sober.

"Sir?" How did one address a barkeep? Oh, Lord, she should have thought of that. Somehow she couldn't imagine any of the louts around her using such a courtesy title. Still, she didn't have to worry. Her "sir" had produced no response.

"Hey, you!" she tried in a louder, gruffer voice. This time she got results. The burly barkeep turned slowly around as if he couldn't believe his ears.

"You talkin' to me, boy?" he bellowed in a belligerent tone. Cathy blinked at him, dismayed, before hastily recovering herself.

"I am." She tried to inject a note of boyish confidence into her voice as the man swaggered down the bar toward her. As he got nearer, she swallowed. Somehow she hadn't expected anything quite so overpowering. At close quarters he looked exactly like a huge, hairless red ape.

The barkeep seemed to be making an inspection of his own. His eyes lingered consideringly on the soft white skin and wide blue eyes beneath the too-big cap.

"Why, we got us a pretty boy here!" he called to the room in general. The men stopped drinking to stare at Cathy. She paled under the regard of so many hostile eyes.

"Haul him up so's we can see him!" one of the men at the opposite end of the bar shouted.

"Hey, Mac, I didn't know you was interested in boys!" His drinking companion jabbed the first speaker in the ribs with his elbow, grinning hugely. "Whatsa matter, has Bella turned you offa women?"

A red-haired, very generously endowed woman, who was plainly the maligned Bella, turned around to give the second man a playful tweak on the cheek.

"I'll turn you on to women, honey. All you have to do is say the word!" she giggled.

During the course of these events, Cathy perceived that she had made a grave mistake in coming into this particular saloon. The best thing she could do was leave again just as quietly as she had entered. She moved unobtrusively toward the door, hoping to pass through it unnoticed while everyone's attention was centered on Mac and his companions. Unfortunately, the bartender saw her sidling away and stopped her with a meaty hand on her shoulder just as she thought she was going to make it.

"Not so fast, boy," the man growled. "You never did state your business!"

Cathy looked up at him a trifle wildly. "I—uh—I just wondered if there was a place around here where I could get a bed for the night!"

She felt proud of her inventive abilities. Obviously, the mention of her true purpose would find no favor with these thugs. They all looked to be on the shady side of the law themselves.

"You need a bed for the night?" the giant asked ruminatively. "Well, I misdoubt that Bella there would be willing to share hers. She's always had a hankerin' for baby-faced lads!"

This remark brought more hoots and catcalls.

A black-haired woman, a local resident from her appearance, flounced over to stare at Cathy speculatively.

"Nah, he's too little!" she pronounced after a critical inspection. "Throw him back!"

The men exploded with hilarity. Cathy, ears burning at the lewd jests, tried to wriggle out from under the barkeep's hand while the pouting Maria held center stage. It was no use. The man's hand stuck to her shoulder like glue!

"Here, boy, there's no reason to hurry off now. Just you sit up here where you can watch the fun!"

So saying, the man grabbed Jon's shirt by the collar and hoisted Cathy up until she was sitting on the bar. To her utter horror she heard the material give with a loud ripping noise. Oh, no! But maybe it wasn't too bad. Maybe nothing showed. . . .

"Sorry about the shirt, boy," the barkeep said, looking down at her. His eyes widened fractionally. "By damn, would you look at that!"

His booming voice attracted the attention of everyone in the room. Cathy followed the barrage of eyes down her front. Dear God, she thought weakly, she was undone. Her whole left breast was exposed in all its pink and white glory! Quickly she jerked the material back up to cover herself, but one harried glance around told her that it was too late to do any good. Every man in the room was staring at her avidly.

"Goddamn!" a hoarse voice yelled from the back of the room. "It's a wench!"

"It's a wench! It's a wench!" The inebriated gang at the bar took up the chorus.

"Show us that tit again, Big Jim!" another man urged. The chorus echoed, "Show us that tit! Show us that tit!"

The barkeep, apparently Big Jim by name, caught Cathy around the waist with one huge arm. With his free hand he snatched the hat from her head. Her braids, loosened by the long swim to shore, tumbled down. The meaty fingers ran through her damp hair, separating the strands so that they fell over her shoulders and curled around her waist. Cathy, more frightened than she had ever been in her life, tried frantically to free herself. But an iron-thewed arm held her mercilessly, its fingers digging painfully into her waist.

"Man, show us that tit!" a man in the far corner called urgently. Big Jim caught Cathy's hands, pulling them down to imprison them at her sides. The torn shirt, with nothing to hold it in place, fluttered down like a dying bird. Cathy felt her whole body flush as every male eye in the saloon turned lustfully upon her exposed breast. Oh, God, what would happen to her now? Would they all rape her? Suddenly Cathy wished with all her heart that she was back safely on the "Margarita." Safely? Yes! Although Jon made disgusting demands on her body, he had never actually harmed her. Certainly his use of her was preferable to gang rape!

"Eh, Jim, pass her down here! I haven't set eyes on such a bellisima in years!"

140

"Nah, hand her over to me! It wouldn't take me more than a brace of seconds to toss her on her pretty little ass and give her me all!"

The badinage continued, growing gradually hotter. There seemed no doubt in anyone's mind as to Cathy's eventual fate. The only question was, who got first go?

"I seen her first!"

"Like hell you did! I seen her first!"

"You goddamn liar! I did! Green, you remember me tellin' you to look at that kid?"

Cathy began to feel sick. This couldn't be happening! Those animals would tear her apart! She had to do something to save herself. Fighting a man the size of Big Jim was likely to earn her a broken jaw. He didn't look like he'd have any qualms about hitting a woman. On the other hand, maybe she could bribe him. . . .

"Big Jim," she whispered to the man whose huge arms held her as much a prisoner as a helpless babe. "How would you like to make some money? My father's a rich man. He'd pay you well—let me go."

"I hate women," Big Jim remarked dispassionately. "And I especially hate lyin' women. Last woman who lied to me, know what happened to her? I broke her neck with these two hands."

He flexed the fingers that held Cathy's arms penned to her waist and Cathy trembled at the feel of his huge chest pressed against her back. He had the strength to do it, without a doubt. But she couldn't give up. . . .

"I'm not lying, Big Jim," she whispered urgently. "My father. . . ."

"Even if you're not lyin', wench, your father ain't here, is he?" Cathy had to forlornly shake her head. Big Jim looked sad. "I didn't think so. Then we got nothin' to talk about, do we?"

"Big Jim. . . ." Cathy began desperately, only to be silenced by his impatient snort.

"What you so scared about, anyway? These fellows ain't gonna hurt you none. They just want a little fun for tonight, and tomorrow they'll let you go about your business as nice as you please. O' course, you might be a little sore, but that don't matter to the likes of you."

Cathy wanted to scream, to cry, to laugh hysterically. Apparently he thought she was of the same type as the women who worked for him! Oh, God, this was out of the frying pan and into the fire—with a vengeance! But she wouldn't make it easy for them, she vowed. She would fight. . . .

The two men who were arguing the loudest about which of them had seen her first suddenly jumped to their feet, knives flashing. Before they could fall on each other, Big Jim's meaty fist crashed down hard on the bar beside Cathy, making her start nervously.

"Hold!" he bellowed. "There's to be no bloodlettin' in here! I say every man who wants the wench should roll for her!"

"Aye! Aye! We'll roll for her!" The suggestion was enthusiastically embraced by all. Cathy was fright-

142

ened as well as bewildered. Roll for her? What in the name of heaven—or should she say hell—was that? She was enlightened seconds later.

"Who's got some dice? All right, high roller gets first turn, second roller next, and so on. That agreeable?" The men boisterously indicated their approval. "In case of a tie, the winners roll again. Right?"

"Right!"

The men gathered around a large round table in the center of the room. One of them produced a pair of dice from his pocket. Another looked back over his shoulder at Cathy, his eyes glistening appreciatively.

"Bring the prize!" he roared suddenly. Cathy blanched.

"Yeah, put her in the middle of the table so's we can see what we're gaming for!"

Two men crossed the room eagerly to grab Cathy away from Big Jim. He let her go without a murmur. Cathy kicked and clawed in a frenzy of fear as she was carried bodily across toward where the rest of the men had gathered in a tight little circle about the table. The man who was holding her under her armpits took advantage of his position to squeeze her bare breast painfully. Oh, God, this couldn't be happening! She bit savagely at his arm. He cursed, almost dropping her. The man holding her feet chortled at his companion's pain. Cathy tried to kick him, but he was holding her about her ankles and she couldn't get free. When they set her on her

143

feet at last, the man she had bitten drew back his arm and deliberately slapped her across the face. The blow was so hard that Cathy reeled backwards. Another man caught her, grinning, and ran his hands over her body intimately. Cathy kicked him in the shin. He howled, grabbing the injured place. Before he could retaliate, Cathy was grabbed from behind and swung off her feet

"Tie the bitch up!" the bitten man growled. His companions needed no urging. Before Cathy quite knew what was happening, she was hoisted to the center of the table, and her hands were tied tightly behind her back. She tried to kick at her tormentors only to have her ankles bound too. For good measure they even passed a rope around her waist securing it to a meat-hook high overhead. Cathy was completely immobilized, and unable to help herself in any way. The only thing she *could* do was express her terror and rage with her tongue.

"You filthy pigs, you'll answer for this!" she screamed, her voice shaking. "If you don't let me go . . . !"

Her words were choked off abruptly, as a grimy rag was thrust into her mouth. Cathy gagged and spat, but she couldn't rid herself of it. God, she was suffocating! But that would be preferable to the fate these animals had planned for her. Through a haze of shame and horror she felt her shirt being ripped completely off.

Cathy's knees threatened to give way as she stared down at the leering circle of men. She couldn't faint! Then she would be completely at their mercy. Grimly, she forced herself to breathe deeply through her nose. After a moment she felt her strength returning. The man she had bitten reached both hands up to pinch hurtfully at her bare nipples. Cathy cringed in pain and fear.

"Hey, Billy, that ain't fair! You gotta wait your turn like the rest of us," one of the men protested. The man called Billy dropped his hands reluctantly. Cathy tried her best to shield her body from their devouring gazes, but it was impossible. She was forced to stand, gagged and bound, in the center of that table, surrounded by drooling men whose eyes feasted on her bare breasts. Summoning the last reserves of her will, Cathy stiffened her spine, standing straight and glaring at them ferociously.

"Hell, what're we waitin' for? Let's get on with it!" Billy said impatiently. A man grabbed the dice, shook them with intense concentration, and released them to roll across the table. They came to rest at Cathy's feet. With a tremendous effort she jerked both her feet against the dice, sending them flying to the floor.

"God, it was a ten!" the man who had cast the dice mourned, while Billy jumped up on the table beside Cathy. He made her wait as he very slowly drew his arm back. The blow, when it landed, snapped her head back on her neck. She straightened slowly, tears starting in her eyes. Her jaw throbbed with a strange, burning numbness. She was afraid it was broken.

"Try that again, bitch, and I'll take my knife to you," he growled. "You won't be so purty with a slit nose!"

Cathy had enough sense to realize that he meant it. He was a man who enjoyed inflicting pain on others, especially women. It made him feel good.

The game began again at Cathy's feet. This time she ignored it, staring with intense concentration at the smoky lantern that hung from the ceiling.

"Oh, God, please help me," she prayed desperately. A tear coursed helplessly down her cheek. Her jaw ached badly, she was mortally ashamed by her nakedness, and, looking at the repulsive men below her, she was conscious of a shaft of mortal fear. Was there to be no escape from these animals? She would welcome the devil himself if he would set her free!

"Is this an open game, gentlemen?"

Cathy's head swung around disbelievingly at the velvet drawl. Jon! Thank you, God, she thought fervently, not caring about the incongruity of seeing Jon as her deliverer. Her eyes met his with joyous relief, but he looked back at her warningly before ignoring her and walking over to the crowd of men. Cathy suddenly realized that her rescue was very far from being a sure thing. Jon was alone, armed with only one visible pistol, while there were at least a dozen, all armed to the teeth. Still, just the fact of his presence made her feel very much better, she believed that no harm would come to her while he was there to prevent it.

146

The men turned, as a body, to stare at Jon as he approached them.

"Who the bloody hell are you?" Billy demanded suspiciously, his bushy brows coming together in a menacing frown.

"Name's Jon Hale. I'm captain of the 'Margarita,' anchored yonder in the bay. Big Jim knows me, don't you, Jim?" Jon's tone was easy, but his eyes never left Billy's.

"Yup," the barkeep agreed, his brow furrowing. "We don't see you in here much any more, Captain. What brings you tonight?"

"I was on my way to visit a certain lady when I heard all the commotion. My curiosity was piqued. Now that I've seen the cause—she's certainly worth the noise. Does she belong to any of you gentlemen in particular?"

Cathy glared at Jon with unfeigned viciousness as his eyes ran over her insolently, lingering with languid appreciation on rosy peaks that quivered at him as she drew an outraged breath. His glance just touched on her swollen jaw before moving away, but the sudden glitter in his eyes reassured her. She had known him long enough to know that it boded ill for someone!

"The wench's what we're gaming for!" a voice explained jovially.

"Ah, I see. Well, then, may I join you?" His voice was very calm. As Cathy knew from experience, that deceptive quietness was a mask for fierce rage.

"I dunno." Billy sounded dubious. "You weren't

here when she came in. I don't see how as it would
be fair to let you take a turn."

The others nodded with solemn agreement.

"Suppose I buy one of your turns, then?" Jon proposed. "Say, two hundred dollars to the man who
sells me his place. Two hundred dollars will buy a
cathouse full of whores!"

"Three hundred and you can have my turn!" a
man who hadn't spoken before said.

"Two hundred and fifty."

"Done!"

Money exchanged hands and the game resumed.
The first three throwers rolled a three, a five, and a
two, respectively. From their curses it was plain that
they knew themselves to be out of the running.
Throw after throw was made. Billy rolled an eleven,
which stood as the throw to beat. Finally it was Jon's
turn. Cathy held her breath. What would they do if
he didn't win? The possibilities were unthinkable.

Jon picked up the dice, shook them, and let them
go almost casually. They landed near Cathy's feet.
She had to strain to see them. It looked like . . . a five
on one, and a six on the other. An eleven!

"We roll again," Billy growled.

He cast the dice and came up with a nine. Jon
threw. The onlookers muttered appreciatively. This
was more sport than they'd hoped. Another nine!

"Cast again!" Billy snarled.

"This could go on all night," Jon answered
lightly. "And I for one prefer to get on with more
pleasurable matters. Why not let the lady choose

her partner?"

"Aye! Let the wench choose!" Those who had lost their chance were eager to prolong the fun. There was nothing Billy could do but agree.

Cathy flinched violently as one of the men clambered onto the table beside her and plucked out the filthy gag. She was running her tongue around her dry mouth when his hand slid familiarly over her buttocks, fondling her intimately and giving her a lusty pinch. She gave a little choked cry and Jon whirled, his eyes blazing murder.

"Well, wench, which lusty stag will ya have? Both are hot for ya, I vow." Big Jim's voice brought Jon back to his senses.

Cathy looked first to Jon, her eyes touching on the lean, handsome face, set hard now with tightly reined anger, and then sliding over his broad shoulders and powerful chest, unfamiliar in their formal dress. As her gaze met his she had to bite back a wry smile. How certain he was of her! His confidence showed in his eyes. Well, he had reason. Much as she would have enjoyed discomforting him by choosing the other, she dared not. This was no time for childish games of vengeance. Jon was risking his neck to save her, and she was suddenly conscious of a weak desire to be held tightly in those strong arms. Devil that he was, he spelled safety to her now. He was her only security in a very insecure world.

She barely glanced at Billy. He held his arms up to her as though to lift her down, and she shuddered away. The light from the lantern fell on his outstretched hand, the bite mark she had made a livid circle around the thumb. Jon's eyes went swiftly from the wound to Cathy's injured jaw, and flushes of angry color stood out on his cheekbones.

"Choose, wench!"

Cathy swallowed. "I choose him," she said clearly, nodding at Jon. The men roared their approval, clapping Jon on the back and making lewd jokes at Billy's expense. Jon responded in kind to the quips, some of his remarks putting Cathy to the blush. But his hands were gentle as his knife cut through her bonds. At the tenderness of his touch Cathy felt an overwhelming surge of warmth for him. He could have been killed as a result of her willfulness. She knew that had he lost, he would have fought to the death to protect her. The knowledge brought a lump to her throat. When her legs and arms were free, she held out her arms to him wordlessly. He reached up to lift her down, catching her around the waist and swinging her as lightly as a thistledown to the floor. With a quick movement he shed his coat, wrapping it around her shoulders to cover her breasts. His arm stayed loosely around her waist as he ushered her toward the door.

"Hold, there, Captain!" Billy cried, watching the two with obvious hostility. "Where do you think you're going?"

"My friend, if you don't know without me telling you, I pity the women of this town. They're in for some mighty poor sport," Jon answered lazily, turning to face the man as he spoke. The onlookers

150

guffawed. Billy flushed a mottled purple.

"You can't take the wench away, Captain," Big Jim told Jon in an aside from behind the bar.

"Nah, she stays!" another of the men cried.

"How is this?" Jon's voice was deceptively cool. He pushed Cathy casually behind him, and she felt her heart quake. "I won her in fair play, didn't I?"

"That's true enough," someone chortled. "But you didn't wait to hear the rules of the game! You didn't win her outright! You just sort of rented her for a while. Then she goes to Billy, then to Joe, then to Harper, and so on. We was just playin' for first turn on her, ya see!"

Cathy could see the muscles of Jon's back tighten beneath his thin shirt. She looked at him anxiously. From her place behind him she could just make out the granite set of his jaw as he looked over the assembled men. Two of them had sidled over to block the exit. Cathy's hand went to curl instinctively about Jon's hard forearm. He didn't respond, but the others in the room saw and were amused.

"The wench is sure hot for you, Captain. Why don't you take her right here? We'd all like to watch!"

"That's a right good idea, Captain," Billy said. "Then we can be sure that you don't take off with a property that rightly belongs to all of us. If it's privacy you want, I'm sure Big Jim will be glad to move out from behind his bar."

Big Jim nodded his agreement. The men began to finger their knives, grinning at Jon openly. He looked them over for a long moment, and beneath her hand Cathy could feel his muscles tensing like a tiger's for the spring. But then he shrugged and said easily, "With a wench like this, I could bed her in the mud and think myself between the softest sheets."

The men snickered. Jon swung around, pulling Cathy into his arms. His back was turned to the room and his broad shoulders protected her from the sight of the men. He bent down to nuzzle her neck lustily, then whispered in her ear, "When I give the word, run as hard as you can. There's a constabulary about half a mile to the west. Tell them who you are and what's happened. They'll send you safely back to your father."

Cathy's eyes widened endlessly. Why should he actually be helping her to get away from him—unless he thought he would no longer be around to enjoy her?

"What about you?" she whispered tremulously.

"Worried about me, little cat?" The corners of his lips lifted in the ghost of a mocking grin. "Don't be. I've managed to take care of myself quite well for years. Now, enough talk. Just do as I say. Understand?"

Cathy's eyes met his wonderingly, and what she saw in the gray depths melted the hard little core of defiance that had knotted her belly ever since he had first taken her.

"Yes, Jon," she whispered.

"That's my girl," he murmured in her ear, then his hands were molding her to him as his mouth found hers in a passionate kiss, much to the delight

152

of the guffawing onlookers.

Cathy's mouth returned the sweet pressure, opening to him endlessly with no thought of denial. Her arms clung tightly around his neck. She felt bereft when he suddenly let her go.

"Now!" he hissed, whirling to take a punch at the men who guarded the door. Caught by surprise, one crashed to the ground, leaving just enough room for Cathy to slip past and out into the street. Her last frightened glimpse of Jon showed him reeling beneath the blow of a ham-like fist as the rest of the men closed on him angrily.

Cathy flew down the street followed by the outraged bellowing of the men in the saloon as they realized that she had escaped. The sharp pop of a pistol cracked like a whip behind her. She ran as she had never run before in her life, lungs aching as she labored for air. But she didn't head west for the constabulary. She ran for the "Margarita," and help.

Six

"He is lucky to still be alive," Dr. Sandoz grunted, stepping back from the bunk. His eyes ran over Jon's unconscious body, pale and corpse-like in the flickering candlelight of the ship's cabin. "If he were not so strong a man, the loss of this much blood would already have killed him. As it is, he is very weak, and his temperature is high. We may still lose him."

Cathy bit down hard on her trembling lower lip. Jon mustn't die, he mustn't! Especially not as a result of rescuing her from the consequences of her own wilfullness! She would never forgive herself. Oh, God, why had she ever been so foolish as to try to escape to a strange city where she had no friends? She had known he would come after her, and had secretly relished the thought. She had wanted to teach him a lesson. . . . And she had killed him instead! If only she could have brought Harry and the men back faster, before Jon was stabbed—and stabbed—and stabbed. . . .

"Young woman, are you listening to me?" Dr. Sandoz's voice broke impatiently, into her thoughts. "I am a busy man, with many patients left waiting. I do not have time to waste while you day-dream."

Cathy flushed, and started to reply sharply. She was still not accustomed to being spoken to so harshly. But she remembered how totally dependent Jon was on this man's skill, and held her tongue. If the doctor could save him, then she would let the doctor speak to her any way he wished.

"I'm sorry, doctor. What were you saying?" Cathy's tone was meek.

"He is going to need constant care for the next several days—maybe even weeks. His recovery depends on two things: his reaction to the high fever that is setting in, and whether or not his wounds become infected. The dressings must be changed every four hours, from now until I tell you otherwise, and the wounds themselves must be sprinkled with a powder I'll leave with you. And he must also take one of these pills each day," the doctor said, holding up a small, glass vial. "Not to follow these instructions would be the same thing as shooting him here and now. Can I rely on you to be his nurse?"

His stern, dark eyes fixed on Cathy. She nodded fervently.

"Yes, doctor. Of course."

"You can rely on the crew, too, Dr. Sandoz," Harry broke in coldly from the foot of the bunk. "We'll take it in shifts to nurse him. This—lady—has already done enough!"

"I'm going to nurse him!" Cathy glared at Harry, who scowled back at her. "And I'll make a far better job of it than you and your filthy sailors would, you insufferable little prig! If you had only listened to what I was telling you, instead of trying to drag me back aboard the 'Margarita' when I kept saying that Jon needed help, you might have been able to get there in time to keep him from being hurt!"

"Cap'n set us all to looking for you," Harry retorted, stung. "How was I to know you were telling the truth? I thought you were trying to trick me into letting you go! Besides, if you hadn't crawled out the damned window leaving a trail that a blind man could see, you'd be long gone by now and we'd all be happier! And the captain. . . ."

"That is enough!" Dr. Sandoz broke in, his eyes flashing from one to the other. "The rights and wrongs of the situation do not concern me! If you are going to quarrel like children, I will leave now, and not return. And Captain Hale will almost certainly die."

155

Cathy and Harry exchanged sullen looks, and apologized to the doctor.

"Very well," he said at last. "Young woman, I am making Captain Hale's care your responsibility. I have found that females, through their gentler natures, tend to make better nurses than men. You," he said, looking at Harry, "can see to it that she is relieved from time to time. I take it that you are in charge of this ship during the captain's disability?"

Harry nodded wordlessly.

"*Bien!*" Dr. Sandoz smiled at them both. "Now, young woman. . . ." He proceeded to give Cathy detailed instructions on Jon's care.

"I'll be watching you," Harry said fiercely to Cathy after Dr. Sandoz had gone, leaving behind the promised pills and powder. "And I'm warning you now, that if Jon dies and there is even the remotest possibility that you did or did not do something to cause it, I'll hang you from the highest yardarm. Lady or no lady. Understand?"

"Oh, go to the devil!" Cathy replied rudely, and was about to enlarge on this theme when a muffled groan from the cause of their quarrel brought her attention back around to him.

"Jon?" Cathy asked anxiously, leaning over the bunk and placing one hand on his dark forehead to see if it felt feverish. It did.

"Captain?" Harry said at the same time.

Jon moaned and tossed, his long body thrashing from side to side beneath the piled quilts.

"She's gone!" he began to mutter. "By damn,

156

she's gone! In Cadiz, of all places. Den of cutthroats. . . . Like a lamb wandering in a wolf-pack. . . . Won't stand a chance! Cathy! Cathy!"

"Hush, Jon, I'm here, and perfectly safe as you can see," Cathy murmured soothingly, trying to calm him. Her words were unable to penetrate the haze of fever, but Jon seemed to take comfort from the soft touch of her hand as she gently stroked it over his hot brow.

"See what you've done?" Harry spoke in a low tone that was vicious none the less. "I knew you'd be trouble from the moment Jon brought you aboard. I warned him, but he wouldn't listen. He was crazy over you, and now you've damned near killed him! Witch!"

"I have had just about enough of your insolence and abuse," Cathy said through her teeth, her temper surfacing through the pall of guilt that weighed her down. She refused to let herself dwell on the one warming part of Harry's speech—that Jon was crazy about her. Her heart melted at the thought. Was it true?

"Don't come the fine lady over me!" Harry snapped. "I've seen you with him, remember, and I know that inside you're no better than those women out there walking the streets! You're dying for what he can give you—it's obvious whenever you look at him. And then you have the gall to pretend that you hate it! God, deliver me from women!"

"Get out of here!" Cathy's voice was icy cold and laced with contempt. "I won't have you in here

157

spewing such filth! If you truly cared about Jon, which you don't, you'd see that our quarreling will only hurt him!"

"If I truly cared . . . ?" Harry choked disbelievingly. "And I suppose you do? Pray enlighten me if I'm wrong, but I seem to remember that you hated him just over a week ago! Rather a quick change, wasn't it?"

"I was angry," Cathy confessed, her wrath abating somewhat. "Of course I don't hate him. He—he saved my life tonight. I'll take good care of him, Harry, I promise. Only it would make it much easier on me if you wouldn't watch every move I make like you think I'm going to poison him!"

Harry's own anger and guilt subsided as he read the sincerity in Cathy's eyes. He stared at her indecisively for a moment, then nodded.

"All right, I trust you. But if something happens to him. . . ."

"It won't, if I can help it," Cathy said with quiet assurance. "Now, would you please leave? Dr. Sandoz said that Jon needs to be kept as quiet as possible, and we can't be sure that our voices aren't getting through to him."

Harry wavered, then moved toward the door. He paused with his hand on the knob.

"I'll send Petersham down to help you when he comes back aboard. And—uh—Lady Catherine. . . ."

"Call me Cathy," she said wearily. "Jon does."

"Cathy." Harry hesitated for a moment, then took the plunge. "I'm—I'm sorry for anything I may have

158

said to offend you. I'm only concerned for Jon's well-being. We've been friends a long time."

"I understand." Cathy smiled at him, then gestured toward the door. Harry took the hint. She thought he looked somewhat relieved to escape.

"I'll send Petersham when I can," he repeated, and then departed.

Cathy turned back to check on Jon. He was still unconscious and was muttering unintelligibly. His dark face was pale beneath its tan as his head tossed back and forth against the soft white pillow. His lips and eyelids had a bluish tinge, Cathy noted worriedly, due, she supposed, to the loss of so much blood. When she had arrived with Harry and the hastily assembled rescue force back at the "Red Dog," Jon had been lying unconscious in a congealing crimson pool. At his side had been the bodies of three men he had managed to kill before being brought down like a proud wolf. The slobbering beasts had left him for dead, and gone back to their drinking. Not that many of them would drink again, though, Cathy thought with satisfaction. For the few who had escaped the bloody vengeance of the "Margarita's" crew would be in no shape to enter a saloon again for a long time to come. As Jon's body was borne away, Cathy tripped over a familiar form sprawled lifelessly near the saloon's door. It was Billy, the man who had slapped her. He'd been shot through the head. . . .

"Cathy?" Jon called, his voice fretful. Cathy bent over him tenderly, catching his big hand in hers. It

159

was fiery hot.

"I'm here, Jon," she said with quiet insistence, but her words didn't get through to him. He continued to call and mutter and thrash about for the next several hours. Cathy could only sit beside him, holding his hand. Once he asked hoarsely for water and she gave it to him, pouring some from the pitcher by the bed into a glass, holding it to his lips and letting just a few drops dribble into his mouth. He swallowed, then seemed to sleep. But the quiet lasted only a short while, for his fever began to rise rapidly soon after his brief rest. Cathy poured more water into the basin and then pulled the covers down to his feet, taking a cloth and sponging his naked body as naturally as she would have her own. His maleness held no terrors for her now. The cool bath seemed to bring him some relief, and he lay still. Cathy's eyes stroked the hard length of him, admiring the muscular limbs that even in illness were corded and strong-looking. He was a handsome man. . . .

Almost reluctantly she pulled the covers back up to his chin, tucking them firmly about him. She was surprised to see pink heralds of dawn streaking the sky through the window. Soon it would be time to change his dressings again. . . .

She was so tired. Taking a quilt from the wardrobe, she spread it out on the floor next to the bunk and sank down upon it, leaning her head back against the mattress wearily. If she could just rest her eyes. . . .

"Miss Cathy?" Petersham's voice roused her from a sound sleep. "Miss Cathy, it's moving toward noon. I've brought you something to eat."

Cathy jerked upright, immediately alert. Her eyes flew automatically to Jon, moving restlessly beneath the pile of covers.

"How is he?" she gasped. How could she have fallen asleep when he needed her . . . ?

"He's much the same," Petersham reported gravely. "I came in several hours ago, and I've been sitting with him. You're not to think he's taken some hurt because you've slept."

Cathy stood up, shaking the sleep from her eyes.

"I must see to his wounds. The doctor said every four hours. . . ."

"I've already done it once. Mr. Harry came in and told me what to do. He said to let you sleep—that you'd been through a bad time yourself."

"That was so kind of him," Cathy said, wondering at Harry's unprecedented concern for her.

"If you hurry, miss, you'll have time to eat and freshen up a bit before anything else needs to be done." When Cathy shook her head he added severely, "You won't be any good to Master Jon if you're half dead from not taking care of *yourself* properly."

Cathy thought about it for a moment. Not eating certainly would not help Jon, and it might actually hurt him. She needed to keep up her strength so that she could nurse him. Petersham had tended his master's wounds for the last time, she vowed. From now on she was going to do everything herself. She owed it to him. . . . And besides, she found that she

161

actually wanted to tend him.

Petersham urged her into a chair and Cathy felt her muscles, stiff from sleeping on the floor, scream as she sat. She ached all over. Her jaw throbbed as she moved it experimentally. Every inch of her felt like it was bruised. But she had brought her injuries on herself, she admitted silently. If she hadn't been so foolish, neither one of them would be in such bad shape now.

An appetizing breakfast was pushed before her by Petersham. There was fresh orange juice, toast with fruit conserve, and even ham and eggs. After the dried salt pork and hard biscuits that had been the "Margarita's" bill of fare at sea, the food looked and smelled marvelous. She fell to with a will and managed to eat every last bite. Finally she sat back, replete. Petersham beamed at her approvingly.

"That was delicious, Petersham. I feel much better."

"I thought you would, miss. There's warm water in the basin, if you'd like to wash. Master Jon's dressings aren't due to be changed for another half-hour."

"Thank you, Petersham. I'll call you when I need you."

"Very good, miss," he said gravely, and left the cabin.

Cathy laid a gentle hand on Jon's forehead before performing her morning ablutions. He stirred restlessly, muttering, but his eyes remained closed and he gave no sign that he was aware of her presence.

His forehead was burning hot against her palm. Cathy frowned as she turned away to dress. To her untrained eye he seemed even worse than he had the night before. She thought about sending for Dr. Sandoz again as she began to wash, but decided that she would wait until she had checked the condition of his wounds.

While one of the men had run to fetch a doctor the night before, Cathy had hastily shed Jon's torn and filthy clothes and pulled on a dress. At the time she had been far more concerned with modesty than fashion. Now she saw with a grimace that she had donned her pink morning dress inside out. She changed it quickly, brushed her hair into a simple chignon, and then gathered up the basin, fresh bandages, and the powder Dr. Sandoz had left.

She set her supplies down on the bedside table and pulled back the sheet. Jon's naked body was long and dark and hairy against the white linen. She sat down on the edge of the bunk and began to ease the bandages gently away from his wounds. There were six lacerations, varying in their severity, scattered randomly over his body. The one on his right thigh was the worst, she decided. Long and jagged, it looked like it had been made with a broken bottle. The swollen, angry looking tear ran from just inches beneath his manhood to his knee. Cathy felt tears start in her eyes as she looked at it. She could imagine the feel of the sharp glass gouging deep into Jon's flesh, ripping his leg apart. God, it must have hurt! And he had endured the pain for her. . . .

The wounds themselves were serious, but Dr. Sandoz had assured her that Jon would survive them. Infection and its accompanying high fever were the real danger. In his weakened state, Jon would be unable to fight gangrene if it should set in. Cathy shuddered, wiping the crusted blood away from the wounds. The only known cure for a gangrenous limb was amputation. And Jon, debilitated as he was from loss of blood, was equally unlikely to survive that. If he did, he would be maimed for life and she knew that Jon would prefer death.

He began to trash wildly as Cathy gently bathed his torn thigh. She called for Petersham to help her, afraid that his struggles might re-open the wounds and start them bleeding again. Petersham, when he came, stopped dead in the doorway at the sight of Cathy leaning anxiously over Jon's naked body, a single strand of her golden hair, which had worked itself loose from the pins, mixing with the black furring on his chest.

"I'll finish this, Miss Cathy. It's not a proper sight for a young lady like yourself," Petersham said when he had recovered his powers of speech. Cathy glanced around at him impatiently.

"Don't be ridiculous, Petersham. I have seen a man unclothed before, you know. This man," she emphasized. "Now, would you please hold him still while I put this powder on his wounds? I'm afraid it may hurt him, and if he jumps around he may do himself injury."

Slowly Petersham moved to do her bidding, his

reddened face stiff with embarrassed disapproval. Cathy sensed rather than saw his shock, but there was little she could do about it. Jon's well-being had to come before Petersham's notions of propriety.

Jon moaned piteously when the healing powder was poured over his wounds and it began to penetrate his torn flesh. After a moment, his moans turned to howls of pain. Cathy wanted to flee from the sight of his agony, but she could not. He needed her now as she had needed him the night before. So instead of hiding, she cradled his head in her arms and murmured soothing words to him while Petersham did his best to control Jon's flailing limbs. If Jon had not been so weak, it would have taken four men of Petersham's size to hold him. Cathy trembled fearfully at the loss of strength that allowed her bold pirate captain to be so easily subdued.

At last the pain lessened and Jon rested more quietly. Petersham stood away from the bunk, but it was a moment before Cathy gently lowered the dark head to the pillow. Jon stirred uneasily as her comforting presence was removed. Cathy's hand came up to stroke his brow and he was still.

"Will there be anything else, my lady?" Petersham was still being stiffly formal, a sign that he was gravely offended, as Cathy knew from her years with Martha. She sighed.

"Petersham, you must see that this is not the time to be concerned about conventionality," she tried to explain. "Captain Hale is very ill, and needs care. The rest of you have duties about the

165

ship, which leaves me to be his nurse. Would you have me shrink away because he is naked, and leave him untended?"

"I will be glad to take over the nursing, my lady. When Mr. Harry told me that you were to do it, I did not fully comprehend the—uh—delicacy of the task."

"Oh, for goodness sake, Petersham!" Cathy exclaimed, exasperated. She was too annoyed to pussyfoot around. "You must be aware that I—that he—well, that our relationship is scarcely that of brother and sister. In short, I know all about the Captain. The sight of his body is no novelty to me."

Cathy blushed at her own boldness. Three weeks ago she would never have believed that she could have spoken with such a total lack of modesty. But her words were the plain truth, and there was no sense in wrapping them up in fancy clothes. She looked up to see Petersham regarding her coldly.

"Be that as it may, my lady, such sights are not fit for one of your sex and tender years. Will that be all, my lady?"

Cathy sighed, and dismissed him. Petersham's unexpected prudery was a difficulty she did not feel equipped to deal with at the time.

For the next five days Cathy nursed Jon devotedly. She cleaned and tended his wounds, and called Dr. Sandoz anxiously when they showed signs of swelling. The gash on his thigh began to putrefy. Dr. Sandoz lanced it, draining off the yellow pus with its streaks of red blood into the basin which Cathy held for him. Jon's hands and feet were tied to the bunk frame for this operation, and his screams of pain were bloodcurdling. Tears rained down Cathy's cheeks, but she steadfastly kept to her place. She gathered up the gory bandages afterwards, and then when Dr. Sandoz untied Jon's limbs she gathered his sweat-soaked head to her breast, holding it tightly while she crooned over him. Her wordless murmurings seemed to soothe him and he dropped off into a troubled sleep, his head still cradled on her breast.

In addition, she fed him, spooning thin gruel into his mouth at regular intervals and holding his lips pressed tightly together until he swallowed. She gave him water, and applied hot compresses to his inflamed thigh. As his fever rose she bathed him almost hourly with cool water, but this no longer served to lower his body heat even slightly. His natural functions she tended to herself, knowing that Petersham would faint with disapproval if she were to ask his assistance. Her total dedication to his well-being surprised everyone, including herself. Cathy would never have imagined that she, who had never so much as picked up one of her own discarded dresses, could care so intimately and selflessly for another human being.

Despite her tender nursing his condition steadily deteriorated. Dr. Sandoz, when he came, looked grave and shook his head, which drove Cathy almost out of her mind with worry. Jon's continued high fever was the most serious threat he faced now. The doctor could only advise Cathy

167

to bathe him frequently, and see that he had plenty of liquids. Otherwise, the captain's recovery was in the hands of God.

Jon frequently became agitated beyond her ability to control him as his temperature soared, and Cathy was forced to summon either Petersham or Harry to help her with him. Both men gradually lost their stiffness with her and came to look upon her as one of themselves. Cathy pacified Petersham by assuring him that, as soon as Jon's condition permitted, he would be dressed in a proper nightshirt. But for the time being, even Petersham realized that Jon's illness was too severe to allow Cathy to spend time worrying about such a nonessential as modesty.

Cathy's complete devotion to their captain's well-being won her friends among the crew as well. They would speak to her respectfully when she went out on deck for a breath of fresh air, their manner completely devoid of the lewdness that had marked their earlier perusals of her. For this, Cathy was thankful.

On the sixth day, Cathy could see, and Dr. Sandoz confirmed, that Jon had reached a crisis. His temperature had to be brought down or he would die. The doctor advised frequent cool baths mixed with a large amount of prayer. Cathy snorted angrily as he left. Prayer was a good thing, as she had frequently found, but one of Martha's most-loved axioms was that the Lord helped those who helped themselves. With that in mind, Cathy sent for Harry and told him that he was to send the entire crew of the "Margarita" out to scour Cadiz for ice. When

Harry protested that there was no ice to be found in the humid Spanish city, Cathy refused to listen. If Jon was to live, she must have ice to lower his temperature. The Lord could work on providing the ice.

He did. Harry returned less than an hour later with a huge block of it. Cathy's pale face mirrored her relief.

"Thank God! He's getting worse! Here, help me with this." Cathy set Harry to chipping off small chunks of ice and floating them in a large basin full of water. When the water was icy cold, she had him soak a sheet in it and then wrapped it around Jon's fever racked body. He moaned, but Cathy repeated the operation relentlessly, replacing the sheets as soon as Jon's body heat warmed them. They worked for what seemed like hours, soaking, wrapping, then soaking again. Finally perspiration popped out in tiny beads on Jon's brow.

"It's broken!" Cathy whispered, scarcely able to believe that the small droplets were real. "Oh, Harry, the fever has broken!"

In an excess of joy she flung herself into Harry's arms. They closed around her automatically. It took her only an instant to recollect herself and pull blushingly away. She looked up at Harry, suddenly shy, and what she saw in his face stunned her. He was gazing at her with naked adoration, his eyes showing that he was in love.

"Let me go, Harry," Cathy ordered tremulously, greatly disturbed by this new complication.

"Lady Catherine—Cathy. . . ." he began. Cathy

knew that she had to cut him off before the situation got out of hand.

"You mustn't forget Jon, Harry," she said gently, glancing back at the bunk and trying to free her hands.

"Jon." Harry repeated blankly. Then, coming to himself, "Yes, the Captain."

"Yes, Jon, the Captain," she repeated with gentle mockery. Her eyes warned him to say no more. After a moment his hands fell away from her.

"I'm sorry. Please forgive me," Harry muttered, then turned on his heel and strode from the cabin. Cathy shook her head, moving back to hover over the bunk. Jon was still unconscious, but he seemed to be resting much easier. If not for the little scene with Harry, this would have been one of her happiest days since Jon became ill. Oh, why was everything always so complicated?

Love was a funny thing, Cathy mused later, as she wandered across to look out the window. It could grow in the most unlikely places. It was absurd and yet a little sad that Harry, who had so despised her, should now be helplessly in her thrall. Why was it that adoration in the eyes of one man was a matter of total indifference, while if another man were to look at her in such a way. . . . Cathy's breath caught as she pictured Jon's gray eyes soft with love. Then she grinned. Jon would never plead with a lady for her affections. He would demand them as his right, and, if they were withheld, he would fall into a towering rage!

"Cathy?" Jon called weakly as he had many times over the last few days. Her presence never really penetrated his clouded mind, but he seemed to find it comforting to have her sit beside him, holding his hand or bathing his fevered brow.

"Yes, Jon, I'm here," she answered, coming to stand beside the bunk and looking tenderly down into his dark face. What she saw this time surprised her. The gray eyes were open and seemed to be comprehending as they fixed on her.

"Jon!" she exclaimed joyfully. "Can you see me?"

"Of course I can see you." His voice was weak, but a thread of irritation at her seemingly ridiculous question laced the words.

"How do you feel?" Cathy sat down on the edge of the bunk beside him, her hand going automatically to stroke his forehead. It felt cool, she noted with relief.

"Like hell," he said bluntly. "What day is it?"

"Wednesday, the twenty-second of June, 1842. You've been unconscious for the past six days."

"What happened?" he asked, a frown wrinkling his brow as he tried to remember. Then, before she could attempt to explain, his eyes fastened themselves on hers, anger burning in their depths. "You little fool, don't you know you could have been killed, or worse? Beautiful blondes like yourself fetch a mint in the brothels around here. If that had happened, no one would ever have heard from you again, and they would have used you until you died of it! God, of all the cities in the world to run away

171

in, you pick Cadiz! And of all the places in Cadiz, you wind up at the 'Red Dog,' the hangout for every hunted man on this coast! I couldn't believe it when I saw that ridiculous sheet and followed your trail there! God, when I heard all those bastards laughing inside, I thought I was too late!"

He was growing increasingly agitated. Cathy caught his hand, trying to calm him before he caused himself an injury. The long fingers fastened around her wrist with surprising strength.

"You're not to try such a thing again, do you hear?" he asked fiercely. "I'll keep you safe if I have to lock you up! I'll . . . !"

"You don't have to, Jon," Cathy told him quietly, not even trying to free herself. "I won't run away from you again, I promise. I'll stay until you're ready to let me go. Now, you must be quiet. You've been very ill. Would you like some gruel, or a drink of water?"

Jon stared up at her, his eyes plumbing the depths of hers. What he saw there must have reassured him. He released his stranglehold on her wrist to sink back more comfortably against the pillows.

"Gruel!" he snorted. "If that's all you've been feeding me, no wonder I feel weak as a newborn babe! I want real food, and a bottle of red wine!"

"Not until Dr. Sandoz has seen you," Cathy denied firmly, a small smile tilting at the corners of her mouth. "For now, you can eat gruel and like it!"

Jon started to protest, caught her eye, and grinned himself.

"It seems that I'm at your mercy for a change, my cat. Well, do your worst. My turn will come again soon enough."

Cathy stuck her small tongue out at him playfully, then got off the bed and crossed to the door to yell for Petersham. She could feel Jon's eyes boring into her back as she moved. When the valet appeared at a dead run, she smiled at him.

"The Captain is awake at last, and hungry. Would you please bring the usual, Petersham?"

"Thank God!" Petersham exclaimed, and hurried away to do her bidding.

"The old goat was worried about me, huh?" Jon grimaced as Cathy came to perch on a corner of the bunk.

"Everyone was."

"Everyone? Even you?" The words were said casually, the long lashes dropping to veil the gray eyes.

"Even me," she answered honestly, smiling at him when he flicked a quick glance at her. "Especially me," she could have added, but she didn't.

"Then you know how I felt when I found you gone," he murmured, his lips twisting a little as he caught her hand and carried it to his mouth. The touch of his hard mouth against her palm jolted through both of them like an electric shock. Cathy pulled her hand away, laughing shakily.

"Enough of that! You mustn't get excited, you know. You've had a very high fever and. . . ."

"Just looking at you excites me," he said half under his breath, his fingers reaching again for her hand.

173

Cathy's heart quickened but she refused to give in to the warmth that flooded her. Instead she jumped to her feet and moved jerkily toward the door.

"Where on earth is Petersham?" she wondered aloud, then mentally scolded herself for the inane question that revealed all her sudden nervousness.

"Cathy. . . ." Jon began, only to stop abruptly as Petersham appeared in the open doorway, carefully bearing a bowl of steaming gruel. Behind him came Harry. Cathy took the bowl from Petersham and set it on the bedside table as the two men crossed to the bunk. Jon grinned up at them weakly.

"Sorry to disappoint you gentlemen, but I'm not dead yet."

"Thank God!" Petersham's voice was fervent.

"It's good to have you back with us, Cap'n," Harry reached for Jon's hand, pumping it vigorously until Cathy felt forced to intervene.

"Harry," she warned. "You'll start him bleeding again if you're not careful."

"Oh, sorry," Harry said, dropping Jon's hand as if it had suddenly burned him. Jon's eyes narrowed slightly at the familiarity between the two of them, but he said nothing.

"How do you feel, Master Jon?" Petersham asked.

"I'll live," Jon grunted.

"He's very weak," Cathy put in. "And he needs to eat this gruel and then rest. If you'll excuse us . . ."

"Of course." Both men took the hint, shook Jon's hand again, and left.

"Bossy little madam, aren't you?" the invalid

174

said when they were alone once more. He eyed her thoughtfully as she carefully stirred the bowl of gruel. While she was so occupied he tried to lever himself into a sitting position only to fall back with a groan.

"God, my leg!"

"You're not to move," Cathy told him severely, coming to sit beside him, the bowl of gruel within reach. "If you start bleeding again, you may very well not live."

"And just how am I supposed to eat?" he asked crossly, disgruntled at his own helplessness.

"The same way you've been eating up to now. Like this."

She wiggled over until she was sitting behind him, carefully lifting his head onto her lap. Then she tucked a pillow beneath it so that he was propped in a half-sitting position with her body supporting his weight. He grunted derisively, but allowed her to situate him as she wished.

"Now, if you'll hold the gruel," she said finally, placing the bowl in his lap. "You can eat."

Dipping the spoon into the steaming mush, she raised it to his mouth. Jon rolled his head around until his eyes found hers.

"Are you actually meaning to feed me like some just-weaned infant?" he asked disbelievingly.

Cathy looked down at him admonishingly. "Yes, I am. And I've been doing so every day since you've been ill. If you object, I'll have Petersham feed you. But you're not strong enough yet to do it yourself,

175

as you would quickly find if I let you try it."

Jon stared up at her, then broke into a reluctant smile.

"The next time I take a female captive, I'm going to pick a nice, gentle, timid one. Not a bossy little spitfire who takes the bit between her teeth the first chance she gets."

"Very funny," Cathy snapped, not liking his reference to other females *or* captives. "Open your mouth."

Jon slanted another quick glance up at her. "Yes, ma'am," he said meekly, and opened his mouth.

When the gruel was finished and the bowl set away, Cathy started to gently extricate herself. Jon caught her wrist, holding her in place while his mouth moved to nuzzle at the inside of her elbow.

"Don't leave me," he whispered huskily.

"I have to," Cathy's voice was weak as she battled the shivery sensations invoked by his warm lips. "You need to rest."

"Stay with me," he murmured, his mouth tracing down the soft underside of her arm. "You look like you need some rest, too. We can rest together."

"Jon," she warned in a shaky voice. "You're too weak for . . . for. . . ."

"I know." He looked up at her appealingly. "I just want you beside me. I sleep better that way. I have nothing else in mind, I promise. If I try anything, you have my permission to slap my face and get up."

"Well . . ." Cathy wavered.

"Please," he said softly.

"Oh, all right," Cathy capitulated with a sigh. "Just as long as you remember. If you start to . . . to. . . . Well, I'll get up."

"I won't," he promised, and watched as Cathy slid off the bed to lock the door.

He said nothing as she slowly came back to stand beside the bunk, a faint flush staining her cheeks. Knowing the cause of her sudden confusion, he grinned.

Cathy turned her back as she slowly unfastened her gown. She undressed down to her last petticoat, feeling absurdly shy. Now that Jon was awake and aware, she was regaining some of her former reserve with him. Don't be a fool, she scolded herself, feeling a blush creep over her cheeks as she turned back to face him. The blush deepened as his eyes rested hungrily on her scantily covered bosom. His mouth crooked teasingly as the warm gaze traveled gradually up to her face.

"Blushing, my cat?" he mocked gently. "There's no need. I have seen you in less, you know."

Cathy forced herself to meet his gray eyes, determined to downplay her ridiculous embarrassment if she possibly could.

"I know," she managed evenly. "But that was . . . was different."

The stutter in her last words dismayed her. That too-knowing grin was making her even more uncomfortable.

"Because then I took your clothes off and now you're doing it?" Jon guessed astutely. "Well, never mind, sweet. Consider it your duty to humor a sick man."

"Oh, hush," Cathy said, annoyed.

"I will," he promised, seeing that she was about to turn away. "Come to bed. Please."

Cathy glared at him, but then broke into a reluctant smile as she pretended to cower away.

"You really are impossible, you know. I've a good mind to have Petersham take care of you from now on."

"Petersham lacks your—er—skills. Come to bed."

Cathy frowned at him severely, then gave up. The dratted man was really beginning to get to her, she thought vexedly as she slid into the bunk on his uninjured side. She would have to watch that she didn't grow too fond of him. That would mean only heartbreak.

But despite her reservations she allowed him to draw her close against his side, her head snuggling cozily into his shoulder of its own accord.

"Go to sleep," he murmured, his arm tightening around her.

And to her surprise, she did.

Seven

"Why did you run away?" The question, asked in a carefully offhand manner, caught Cathy by surprise. She stared down at the playing cards she held for a long moment before replying.

"I should think that was obvious." When she

looked up at last, she found Jon's eyes fixed on her intently. He frowned, as if considering her answer, then shook his head.

"Not to me." His hand of cards lay forgotten on the quilt beside him. Cathy sighed. Plainly he was not to be distracted from the subject.

"You must have known that I'd try to escape if I could. Heavens, you act as if I'd done you some grievous wrong! You're not my father, brother, husband, or even friend, you know. You're the pirate who abducted me and forced me to . . . to. . . . Well, I was and am under no obligation to stay with you."

"Are you saying that you ran away because your pride obliged you to do so?" Jon frowned at her thoughtfully. Cathy sighed again, not feeling adequately prepared to cope with the conversation. But she resolved to do her best to make him understand her position, without giving away the ambiguity of her own emotions at the present time.

"Jon, I don't think you realize the enormity of what you've done to me. I was brought up to be a lady. A lady does not—uh—uh. . . ."

"Make love?" he interjected, smiling a little. Cathy tilted her chin at him haughtily.

". . . does not allow a man to take liberties with her person before marriage. You raped me brutally—not once, but many times. Of course I was going to run away from you the first chance I got!"

"So you're telling me that you ran away because you couldn't stand me making love to you?"

"Raping me!" Cathy corrected sharply.

"Call it what you will." Jon dismissed the nomenclature as unimportant. "Is that why you ran away?"

"Yes!" she answered, relieved to be done with the subject at last.

"You are lying to me, my cat," he chided. "You like the way I can make your body feel. You can't hide it from me. I know."

Cathy flushed bright crimson under his penetrating gaze. How had she ever gotten involved in such a conversation, she wondered desperately. More important, how was she ever going to get out of it without revealing to him more than she meant to?

"You're very conceited, Captain, if you think that," she managed, not quite meeting his eyes. She could not, for the life of her, control the betraying redness of her cheeks.

"So I'm back to being Captain, am I, when you've called me Jon very nicely for the past two weeks. Very well, if that particular subject displeases you, we will return to another." Jon's voice was sardonic. "Tell me, my cat, since the damage to your virtue had already been done, wouldn't it have been wiser to wait until I was ready to let you go? Why run away, and put yourself in such danger? Good God, you're not going to try to tell me that you weren't glad to see me when I walked into that hell-hole! Hosannas sang out of your eyes!"

"I was glad to see you, I admit." Cathy bit her lip. "But the circumstances were unusual."

"Agreed." Jon said nothing more for some time,

his brow furrowed as he mentally worried the subject like a dog with a bone.

"You went for help." The words sounded like an accusation. Cathy just managed not to squirm uncomfortably, staring down at the cards in her hand as if fascinated by them. This was the point she had been dreading ever since he began the conversation.

"Would you prefer that I hadn't?" she countered defensively.

"No, I confess I like living." Jon paused, intent on the small face that was carefully averted from him. "Cathy, look at me."

Unwillingly her eyes lifted to his. His regard was frankly speculative, while hers was wary.

"Why did you go for help? If you dislike my love-making so much, you had the perfect opportunity to be rid of it—and me—forever. I even told you where the constabulary was located! Why didn't you take advantage of it?"

Cathy met his probing eyes defiantly. If he was waiting to hear her confess to an undying love for him, he'd wait for a long time, she vowed. Anyway, it was nothing like that!

"I'm not like you, Captain. I couldn't just stand by while you were murdered!"

"Is that it?" His eyes were beginning to take on a mocking glint. "Or is it that you're—ah—growing fond of me?"

"Don't be more conceited than you can help!" Cathy snapped angrily. "You're twice my age, and not at all my type! I infinitely prefer gentlemen to rampaging pirates!" His words had flicked her in a vulnerable spot, and Cathy was determined to hide it. "Anyway," she continued, bouncing the ball back into his court. "Why did you come after me? After all, as you said, there were plenty of women in Cadiz who would have been happy to share your bed! So why not just let me go? Could it be that you're— ah—growing fond of me?"

Deliberately she aped his words, wanting to prick him as he had her. Jon's eyes glinted at her.

"I have a very simple answer to that, my sharp-clawed little cat, and one that you would do well to take heed of: What is mine, I keep."

"And am I yours?" she asked, her blue eyes sparkling up at him provocatively.

"For the moment, yes." Then it was Jon who seemed anxious to drop the subject. He picked up the cards he had let fall and attempted to teach Cathy the intricacies of the game of veinte-un. Cathy allowed the conversation to lapse, but kept it carefully in the back of her mind to ponder over at her leisure. Was it possible that her fierce pirate captain was beginning to fall just a little bit in love with her? The thought warmed and excited her in a way she hadn't thought possible. If Jon were to love her, she mused, she'd have him just where she wanted him—at her feet! And from time to time she might even relent and let him kiss her. But no more. Captain Hale still had much to learn about the correct way to woo a lady! She grinned at the thought of her lusty pirate captain being forced to content himself with the chaste pecks grudgingly permitted in polite society. He wouldn't like that at all! Well, perhaps after he had suffered sufficiently she might relent. . . .

"You look like a very smug little cat who's just finished off a big bowl of cream," Jon observed laconically, breaking her out of her reverie. "Care to tell me what you were thinking about?"

"Veinte-un, of course," Cathy replied pertly, wrinkling her nose at him. Her fantasy vision had restored her good humor. "What else?"

"What else indeed?" he asked enigmatically, and then turned his attention back to the cards. The subject was finally allowed to drop.

Once restored to consciousness, Jon was a difficult patient. He was mocking and irritable by turns, chafing at his inability to get out of bed or perform any but the simplest chores for himself. He flatly refused to let Cathy feed him again after that first time, but he had to let her cut up his meat for him before he could fork it into his mouth. This annoyed him considerably and he took it out on Cathy, throwing barbed remarks at her like darts as she helped him. Cathy managed to stifle her natural impulse to tell him to go to the Devil, knowing that his helplessness grated on him like a sore tooth. Even though it occasionally cost her an effort, she used sweet reason when she dealt with him, pointing out that if he wanted to be shaved and bathed, either herself or Petersham would have to do it for him. He submitted with bad grace to her ministrations, which he grudgingly preferred to Petersham's.

He was acting just like a spoiled child, as Cathy told him hotly when he sulkily refused to let her change the dressings on his wounds. His nostrils flared angrily at this description, and angry color seeped high into his cheekbones. He opened his mouth as if he would hurl abuse at her, but then with a wry grimace closed it again, and let her change his bandages and give him his pill. Later he kissed the inside of her elbow penitently. Cathy glared at him, sighed, and forgave him.

Under Dr. Sandoz's supervision, he had been just barely manageable, but once the "Margarita" was back again on the high seas he was at his autocratic worst. In deference to Petersham's sensibilities, Cathy had persuaded him to allow himself to be attired in the nightshirts he despised. He gave in to her grudgingly, then complained about how uncomfortable he was in the pesky things until Cathy longed to tell him to be naked and be damned. The only way she could handle him at all was to threaten to turn him over to Petersham's tender mercies. This he refused to hear of. He wanted Cathy at his side constantly, reading to him, playing cards or chess, talking, or even just sitting there. She was only able to get away for a scant fifteen minutes or so each day while he very reluctantly napped.

"You're looking pale, Cathy," Harry said to her with concern late one afternoon as she joined him on the quarterdeck. The "Margarita" had been at sea again for over a week. Today the ship was moving briskly through gently rolling waves, a sharp

184

sea breeze at her back. Cathy took a deep, invigorating breath of the salty air before replying.

"I must confess that I'm feeling a little pale." She laughed, her blue eyes twinkling up at Harry roguishly. "Jon's like a child. He demands constant attention."

"You're not much more than a child yourself," Harry answered sharply, his eyes cloudy with disapproval. "If I'd known from the first how young and sweet and—and everything you were, I would never have let Jon have you. He was a brute to take advantage of your innocence!"

Harry's unaccustomed frankness took Cathy aback. Of course, she had realized that he was aware of the unorthodox nature of her relationship with his captain, as indeed every man aboard ship must be. Her constant presence in Jon's cabin was enough to make it plain. The captain was a lusty man, and before he was wounded there was nothing in the world to stop him from taking her. Still, it was not a subject that was easily discussed. Cathy blushed a little, but her answer was wryly honest.

"You couldn't have kept him from—well, doing what he did. And as you see I've survived, and will continue to survive. One day, when I'm back home again, this will probably seem like a tremendous adventure."

Cathy smiled whimsically as she spoke, thinking that it was not likely that she would be going home again for a very long time. Jon showed no disposition to rid himself of her at any time in the near future.

"The other hostages were freed in Cadiz," Harry told her abruptly.

"I know." Cathy's smile widened. "I heard Jon tell you to see to it the day I ran away."

"So, that's why you did it! I wondered, you know. By then, it was too late to. . . . Well, it was just too late." Harry broke off, color suddenly staining his cheeks.

"Yes, it was too late," Cathy agreed gently, her eyes on the distant horizon.

"I could kill him for what he's done to you!" Harry burst out, losing his control in the face of her placidity. "He's one of my oldest friends, and I swear I could kill him!"

Several of the crew looked around, surprised at the unexpected loudness of Harry's voice, then grinned knowingly as they saw Cathy on the quarterdeck beside the young second officer. There was bound to be another explosion when Cap'n got wind of what was going on between those two. He wasn't a man to share his women!

Cathy saw the speculative looks that the men were casting their way, and felt suddenly annoyed at Harry. This infatuation he had for her was beginning to get out of hand! She prayed that Jon would remain in blissful ignorance of Harry's devotion. Like the crew, she had no illusions as to what Jon's reaction would be if he found out that Harry fancied himself in love with her. Jon was a violent, possessive man, and once returned to full strength could easily crush Harry like an insect beneath his

186

heel. And if Harry made the slightest claim to herself, Jon would be very likely to do so!

"It's really none of your business, Harry," Cathy rebuked quietly, hoping to dampen his ardour before Jon got wind of it.

Harry stared down at her disbelievingly.

"You're in love with him, aren't you?" he bit off viciously. "God, I can't believe it! I thought you were too pure, too fine. . . . But all he had to do was get you into his bed, and you fell in love with the swine! Tell me something, Lady Catherine," he emphasized her title deliberately, leering down at her, "would you have fallen in love with me if I'd bedded you first?"

Before she thought, Cathy's hand came out and slapped him hard across the face. Then, biting her lip as she listened to the hastily muffled guffaws from the crew, she could have kicked herself for giving vent to such a display. Now it was just a matter of time before Jon heard that something was going on between herself and Harry! In a closed community like the "Margarita," talk spread like wildfire!

"Excuse me," Cathy whispered, stricken, and hurried below to calm herself before Jon woke.

"Where have you been?" he demanded sharply as soon as she entered the cabin. Cathy fought the urge to press her cool hands against her hot cheeks, knowing that if Jon were to suspect something was amiss he wouldn't let her rest until she had told him everything.

"On deck," she answered equally sharply, then ignored him as she crossed to where her brush and comb set were kept on a shelf of the wardrobe. Still not looking at him, she took the pins out of her hair and shook it until it hung in a coppery cloud around her face. Picking up the brush, she attacked the shining mass vigorously, feeling the need for physical activity no matter how slight. Jon watched, captivated by the length and glorious brightness of her tresses, but gradually, as Cathy continued to ignore him, a frown puckered his brow.

"I'm thirsty," he said at last, his voice plaintive. He had found that if he wanted her attention, pleading some physical need was the best way of getting it.

"There's fresh water in the pitcher by the bed. Pour it yourself," she snapped. Jon did as she suggested, eyeing her with some puzzlement. A spreading warmth began to grow in his loins as he watched her. Her face, reflected in the wardrobe mirror, was as smooth and delicately tinted as a peach. His eyes moved lower, lingering on the swelling curves of her breasts, and then slid to caress her tiny waist and rounded hips. She was so lovely that just looking at her could set him aflame, he thought half-humorously, enjoying the rush of physical desire that sent blood flowing through his muscles. He decided that if he was strong enough to want her, he was strong enough to take her, and smiled broadly in anticipation of the pleasurable event.

"Come here," Jon said, leaning his head back against his pillows and feeling pleased with himself.

"I'm not your slave," she retorted, throwing him a sharp glance over her shoulder. Jon began to feel annoyed himself, able to find no reason for her shrewish mood.

"No, you're not," he conceded, nettled. The little witch was getting above herself, and needed to be reminded of her place. "You're my mistress, and I intend to take advantage of the fact. Come here."

"What-did-you-say?!" she cried, whirling on him, her eyes flashing fire and her arms akimbo. Jon instinctively lifted his good arm to protect his head from attack. Her reaction both amused and angered him. Little vixen, did she think to rule him now that he was confined to bed?

"I said you're my mistress and I want you," he repeated boldly, keeping a wary eye out for unexpected missiles.

"I am not your mistress!" Cathy spat through taut lips, and suddenly the humiliating events of the past several weeks seemed to all crowd in on her at once. Her soft lips began to quiver, tears shimmered in her eyes, and then overflowed in shining rivers down her cheeks. Jon stared, amazed that his words, meant half in jest, should cause such an outpouring of grief.

"I - am - not - your - mistress!" she repeated with shaky composure, then broke down completely, turning her back and covering her face with her hands as shuddering sobs racked her slender form.

"Cathy! Cathy, love!" Her tears wrenched at him. He hadn't meant to cause her pain, God knew.

"Cathy, listen to me. I was only teasing you. I take it back. I'm sorry!"

She continued to cry as if her heart would break. Jon swore succinctly and profanely, then tried to haul himself out of the bunk. He managed to get to his feet by using the headboard as a lever, but when he tried to take a step toward her his legs refused to support him. His knees buckled and he collapsed onto the floor, cracking his head on a corner of the table as he went down. The air in the cabin turned blue with his curses.

"You bloody stupid fool!" Cathy railed, running to kneel beside him. "Go on, kill yourself! Do you think I care?"

Tears still poured from her eyes like rain. Jon, wincing with pain, caught her by the wrist.

"Let me go, you ungrateful oaf!" she cried, trying to pull away from him. Jon was weak from loss of blood and his long confinement to bed, but even so he was stronger than Cathy. He held on to her grimly, not even able to raise his other arm to protect his head from her blows because of the half-healed knife wound in his shoulder. Finally she stopped struggling and crouched limply beside him, doing her best to gulp back the sobs that shook her.

"Cathy." Jon's leg ached from its rude contact with the floor and his head throbbed where he had cracked it on the table, but he scarcely noticed the pain. His attention was concentrated on the keening girl beside him.

"Cathy, love, I'm sorry. Please forgive me." His

voice was soft, coaxing, his fingers caressing her wrist even as they refused to release her.

"You're despicable," she got out between gulps. "Your mind is as filthy as a gutter. I wish I'd let them kill you! I wish I'd killed you myself!"

"I'm sorry," he murmured again contritely, lifting her resisting hand to his lips to kiss the slender fingers. "I didn't mean it the way it sounded." He pulled her fingers into his mouth one at a time to suck at them gently.

"Stop that!" she screamed, startling him, and at the same time gave a tremendous jerk on her hand. He was so surprised that his hold loosened, and in that instant she was free, leaping to her feet and running for the door.

"Cathy, come back here!" he called after her furiously, but his only answer was the taunting slam of the door as she flung it shut behind her.

"Cathy!" he roared, knowing it was useless even before her name left his mouth. You goddamn fool, he raged at himself, trying to maneuver into a sitting position. He felt a tearing in his leg and sank back, cursing loudly.

"Petersham!" The bellow shook the ship. He had to repeat it several times before Petersham at last appeared.

"Master Jon!" Petersham rushed to his side. "What in God's name happened? You're bleeding!"

"Never mind that now," Jon answered sharply. "Get me back into that damned bunk and go find Miss Cathy. Bring her back here if you have to drag her by the hair! And hurry up! There's no telling what the silly chit might take it into her head to do!"

Petersham did his best, but he was not up to handling Jon's weight. Jon swore at him, and at himself for being so helpless.

"All right, leave me!" he grunted after several futile efforts. "Go find Miss Cathy. Send Harry and another man in here."

"But, Master Jon, you're bleeding. . . ."

"Goddamn it, man, go find that girl! I tell you she's upset, and she's liable to do something stupid!"

"Yes, sir, Master Jon." The valet's eyes turned suddenly disapproving, as if wondering what Jon had done to cause Cathy such distress. Jon didn't blame him. For the first time in his life, he heartily disapproved of himself.

Harry and Finch, the gunner, strode through the door some few minutes after Petersham had left. Between them they managed to get Jon back into the bunk. The white nightshirt was stained with blood from the wound on his thigh, but neither Jon nor Harry was inclined to worry about it. As soon as Finch was no longer needed, Harry dismissed him and turned on Jon angrily.

"What did you do to her?" he rasped, his mouth white around the corners. Jon stared up at him, surprised. After a moment his eyes narrowed.

"I fail to see that it's any of your business," he said evenly.

"I'm damned well making it my business!" Harry choked, his face mottling with anger. "We've been friends for a long time, Jon, but, so help me God, if you've hurt that girl I'll kill you!"

"You're mighty concerned about my property, aren't you?" Jon drawled bitingly. "I'm grateful. But I think you ought to remember something— she *is* my property. I can do what I damned well please with her!"

"Over my dead body!" Harry flared.

"If you insist." Jon's eyes glittered with all the warmth of a cobra's. "Now, if you don't mind, get the hell out of here. This is still my ship!"

"Yes, sir!" Harry said bitterly, and, turning on his heels, stalked out.

It was half an hour later when Petersham finally tapped at the door. Jon had been cursing his own helplessness and stupidity for most of that time. Also, an ugly suspicion was forming at the back of his mind. What had been going on between Harry and the little jade while he was confined to bed and safely out of the way? Had they. . . . ?

Petersham's knock put a halt to these musings.

"Come in!" Jon snapped impatiently, glaring at Petersham as the valet stuck his head around the door. The man was obviously alone.

"I told you to bring her back here!" Jon roared angrily. Then a sudden fear darkened his eyes. "You did find her? She's all right?"

"Yes, Cap'n, I found her, and she's all right, except that she's still considerably upset. She was crying." Petersham's eyes met Jon's accusingly. Jon sighed.

"I know." He thought for an instant about telling Petersham precisely what had happened. From the chit's tears, anyone would be excused for thinking that he had done some vile and unspeakable thing to her. Then he dismissed the idea. After all, he was the captain of this ship! Damned if he would let some sniveling twit reduce him to the point where he was forced to explain his actions!

"So why didn't you bring her back with you?" he asked sharply instead.

"She refused to come. Begging your pardon, Captain, but she said to tell you to go to hell!" Petersham's eyes gleamed triumphantly as he repeated Cathy's message. It was plain to see where his sympathies lay!

Jon stared at Petersham for a long moment. He had known from the first that the chit would likely cause trouble, and here it was, the closest thing to a mutiny a crew could get without actually drawing weapons. Two of his oldest companions had turned on him, in her behalf, in one day! Jon's eyes snapped, and the glare he turned on Petersham was ferocious.

"I didn't lay a hand on the little she-cat, if you must know," Jon ground out, seeing that if he wanted to talk to Cathy he would have to enlist Petersham's support. "I said something to hurt her feelings. I want to apologize, and now she won't listen. So, would you please see if you can get her to come in here? I give you my word of honor that I won't hurt her."

This last was a lame attempt at humor to cover the angry embarrassment he felt at having to confide so much to Petersham. Things had reached a pretty pass when the captain of the ship had to plead with his crew to get them to follow orders! He scowled, but Petersham's face relaxed, and his tone was warmer when he answered.

"Very good, Master Jon. I'll—uh—I'll tell her that the wound on your leg has broken open, and I can't stop the bleeding. That should get her back in here." He started to turn away, then looked back. "And— uh—sorry, Cap'n, I should have known that you wouldn't hurt Miss Cathy."

Jon's brows snapped together, but Petersham was gone. What had he meant by that remark? Petersham knew from long experience that he, Jon, had no aversion to striking a woman if he felt it was deserved, so why should the valet have known that he wouldn't do such a thing to Cathy? Unless Petersham, suspected that he was getting soft where she was concerned. Damn the troublesome chit anyway! He should have listened to his instincts back there on the "Anna Greer" and let her be. Now she was threatening to turn his whole life upside-down!

"If you lay a finger on me, I'll hurt you," a truculent voice warned from just inside the door. "I'm going to see to your leg, and then I'm leaving. I'll stay somewhere else until the 'Margarita' reaches wherever she's going, and there's not a thing you can do to stop me. When we dock, I'm going home to my father. Petersham can take care of you if you still need help."

Jon's eyes widened in surprise at this cheeky speech from what was, after all, a prisoner. Little bitch, who did she think she was talking to? He'd cut her down to size so fast. . . . He glared at her, then reluctantly felt his anger fading. Her tear-stained little face looked so woebegone that he didn't have the heart.

"My leg's bleeding pretty badly," he groaned cunningly, knowing that he would have to get her close enough so that he could grab her again before she would listen to anything he had to say.

"Serves you right!" she answered, sniffling a little as she approached the bunk, as warily as a young doe. As she got closer she could see the bloodstains on the white nightshirt, and her guard dropped somewhat.

"Does it hurt?" she asked with the faintest hint of sympathy, gathering up linen and water before coming to perch on the edge of the bunk. Jon gauged the distance carefully, then sighed inwardly. The wily little cat was clever enough to stay just out of his reach.

"Like the devil," he lied, watching closely for his opportunity to grab her.

"Good!" she sniffed, remembering her anger. Jon eyed her frustratedly as she pushed his nightshirt up to expose the hard brown expanse of his bandaged thigh. He still wasn't quite sure of reaching her. He would only have one chance, he knew. If he missed she would fly from him like a frightened bird.

Cathy was looking worriedly at the bright crimson stains that were soaking through the linen wrappings. She began to unwind the cloth from about his leg. When at last the jagged wound was laid bare, she sucked in her breath sharply at the sight of the dark red ooze that had broken through the thin scabbing. Even Jon managed to wince without too much trouble. Thank God it looked much worse than it felt!

She maintained a stony silence as she washed the blood from his leg, her hands cool and steady against his torn flesh. Jon was devoutly thankful for the protective covering of the nightshirt over his lap. If she could see the effect she was having on him, he doubted that she would be sitting there quite so calmly!

Jon winced again in earnest as she sprinkled some of that devilish powder over the open sore. It burned like the fires of hell! He gave a crafty groan and was rewarded by the feel of her soft little hand patting his leg consolingly. God, it was too much! If his need of her was frustrated much longer he was afraid he might burst!

When the wound was finally dressed to her satisfaction, Cathy set the bowl of water and the powder aside, then began to gather up the bloodstained bandages. Her movements brought her within reach at last, and as swiftly as a tiger Jon pounced. His hand closed around her wrist and he jerked her across him so that she was lying half on him, half on the bunk. An ache throbbed through him at the

197

sudden movement, but he ignored it. What he had to say was more important than any pain. He turned so that he could look at her, and found her red-rimmed eyes glaring up at him angrily.

"It was a trick, wasn't it?" she asked quite calmly. "You bullied Petersham into making me think you were seriously hurt. He didn't even try to stop your leg from bleeding, did he?"

"I wanted to apologize," Jon murmured, painfully aware of how her nearness tightened his muscles.

"Do you think an apology can wipe out what you said?" she challenged, her eyes beginning to fill up with tears again. "Or its truth? You're right. I am your mistress, even though it happened against my will. Do you have any idea how filthy that makes me feel?"

"Oh, Cathy, I didn't mean it that way," he said remorsefully. "You're my lover, my woman. Mistress was an unfortunate choice of words."

"But it's true," she whispered in a tiny voice. Jon felt his heart contract at the shame in her face. It was shame that he had caused, not only by his words but by his actions. She looked so small and helpless lying there on her back, her tear-filled eyes defiant and her red-gold hair cascading wildly over his chest and the pillows. Her soft pink mouth was quivering uncontrollably. Jon suddenly knew that he had to stop that shaking before it tore him apart.

Cathy's eyes widened as he bent over her, but before she could resist in any way his mouth was on hers, hot and sweet and almost unbearably gentle.

198

She wanted to scream, to hit him, to bite down on his encroaching tongue as hard as she could, but she didn't. Deep inside she knew that she needed his kiss like flowers need rain. It was balm to her sore heart, and unguent to her pride. Her mouth fluttered like a trapped butterfly beneath his, and then she opened it to him helplessly. Her hands came up to caress his black head, her fingers stroking through the thick strands, tugging at them. He gave a muffled groan of satisfaction as she began to kiss him back.

When at last he lifted his head it was only to bury his lips in the warm curve of her neck. Cathy's hands, which should have been bruising him, instead stroked his bristly cheek.

"I'm crazy for you," Jon muttered at last, raising himself so that he could look down into her face. What he saw there made his muscles stiffen longingly. Her sapphire eyes, their radiance enhanced by the sparkling drops that filled them and clung to her lashes, glowed up at him lovingly. Her small mouth had the deep redness of the lushest rose. As she smiled at him tremulously, he caught his breath as at a physical blow.

"I didn't mean what I said, sweet. Please forgive me."

His voice was humble as Cathy had never heard it before, and the hard core of shamed anger inside her melted away, like butter under a hot sun. I love this man, she thought, amazed, and the thought so bemused her that she could only stare at him wonderingly. After a moment her hand came up to caress his unshaven jaw, delighting in the feel of its roughness against her palm.

"Forgive me?" he asked again, his voice low, and his eyes plaintive.

"Does it mean so much to you, to have me forgive you?" she asked softly, hopefully. Jon's eyes glinted down at her, and his mouth curved in a self-mocking smile.

"Well, you see, my cat," he confided in her ear. "I want you so badly that I ache with it. And I have this minute resolved never to make love to you without your full consent again. So I need your cooperation if I'm not to spend the rest of my life stooped like some poor hunchback."

Cathy laughed with a little catch in her voice at this audacious speech. It was just like him to make lewd suggestions while trying to win her forgiveness for his earlier lewd suggestions! His eyes gleamed with corresponding laughter as he lowered his head.

The soft peak of her breast was his target. His lips burned moistly through the fabric of her dress, but Cathy made no attempt to push him away. She gave an involuntary moan of pleasure as a spreading warmth began to pulse inside her. Her nipple hardened under his searing caress.

"Your body forgives me," he murmured. Cathy's hands fluttered to his shoulders, knowing they should be pushing him away but unable to gather sufficient strength.

"All right, I forgive you," she gasped desperately, hoping that her capitulation would cause him to stop before she disgraced herself completely.

"That's my girl." The words were said against her lips as his mouth moved up to claim hers. Cathy responded to his kiss hesitantly at first, and then with growing passion. Her arms twined around his neck and she moved against him instinctively, forgetting his injuries in her ever-increasing need of him.

"Ahh, Cathy," he groaned, his hand coming up beneath her dress to press intimately against her lace-covered buttocks, molding her tightly against him. Cathy writhed against his hardness, suddenly craving the feel of him inside her, like a starving man craves food. It had been so long—and now she loved him. Maybe she always had. Her hand came up rather shyly to caress his thigh, then drew back as her fingers encountered the linen bandage.

"Jon, Jon, wait!" She tried to draw away. "Darling, you can't! You might start to bleed again!"

"Do you think I give a damn?" he muttered fiercely, pressing hot kisses over her neck and the exposed part of her bosom. "What did you call me?"

Cathy could feel herself flushing, but there was no help for it.

"I—darling," she answered simply, and he drew back a little to look at her. His gray eyes, cloudy with passion, were intent on her pink-hued face.

"That's what I thought you said," he said with satisfaction, his hand leaving its distracting occupation to move to the hooks at the back of her dress.

"Jon, really, no!" Cathy was breathing hard, but she was perfectly serious. "You're not well enough yet."

His hand freed the last of the hooks, tugging her dress down over her shoulders. Cathy caught at it before he could move it past her swelling bosom. He looked at her.

"I am—if you'll help me. I want you so badly. Please." His gray eyes pleaded with her like a small boy's begging for a sweet.

Cathy sighed, letting him pull the dress from her. She wore just one petticoat beneath it for coolness sake, and she had left off her stays for the same reason. Jon didn't even give her time to take it off. His hand slid up the back of her thigh to tug down her pantalets, tearing the fine lace a little in his haste. As she obediently kicked free of them he pulled her on top of him, shoving the skirt of her petticoat up around her waist.

Cathy caught her breath at the feel of his fiery hardness burning against her soft belly. Instinctively she rubbed against him until they were both gasping.

"Cathy—love me. Cathy—love me," he moaned. Cathy stared down at him, willing to do whatever he wanted, by now knowing quite what that was. His eyes, glazed with passion, flickered open. Seeing her obvious confusion, they darkened even more.

"Ride me," he directed softly. Cathy felt bright scarlet embarrassment stain her cheeks as she caught his meaning at last. Jon showed her what to do and she did it, both of them barely breathing as he slid deep inside her. Her movements were untaught, and rather shy, but they were enough to send both of them spinning with an intensity that neither had ever dreamed was possible.

Eight

Cathy was more than a little appalled at what had happened to her. It seemed impossible that she could have actually fallen in love with a man who had abducted her and subsequently forced her to perform the most intimate acts with him. A man, moreover, who was a thief and a murderer and made no bones about it. A man without lineage or money, whose only possession in the wide world so far as she knew was a ship!

He didn't even treat her that well, she mused, eyes beginning to cloud moodily. Since her outburst of two days ago he had been gentle and almost tender with her, but Cathy knew him well enough by now to be sure that his mellow mood would not last. Sooner or later she would do something to put him in a temper, and he would flare at her with all his usual fury. Well, at least she was no longer afraid of him. He wouldn't hurt her physically, she knew, and verbally, she could return what she got!

He was handsome, Cathy allowed, as she tried to discover what it was about him that made her heart go pit-a-pat. He was so tall and strong and worldly that, beside him, she sometimes felt like the child he mockingly called her. Just thinking about the wicked glint in those gray eyes when he looked at her, about the mocking curve of his mouth and the slash in his cheek when he smiled, warmed her. The memory of his lovemaking was enough to stop her breath. She grimaced, pushing the hair out of her eyes with an impatient hand. For whatever reason, she might as well admit it. She was in love with the dratted man.

That settled, the question now was, what to do about it? The only satisfactory solution would be for him to fall equally in love with her. She sometimes thought that he was not far from it. Whenever she was near, his eyes followed her hungrily, and if she came within reach of his hands she could be sure of a lusty pat or pinch. She knew that he wanted her body with an insatiability that never failed to amaze her. And she could move him—yes, in bed she could move him to the heights. But even in his most passionate moments he had never hinted at love or affection, or, indeed, anything but an intense desire to possess her physically. Which reduced her to the honorable status of his whore, she thought savagely. With a decided toss of her head she resolved to change that mighty quick! She would make him fall in love with her if it killed her—or him.

Jon had progressed to the point where he could lever himself out of the bunk and hop to a chair near the window. He was anxious to be out on deck again, but Cathy was afraid for him to venture too much, too soon. She knew that the only reason he acceded to her wishes was because he didn't like to display the full extent of his disability to his men. As he had once told her, a pirate crew was much like a wolf pack: they respected strength above all. For a leader to exhibit weakness was to invite trouble. His crew had been with him for years and he was convinced of their loyalty, but one lesson Jon had learned in his life was that no person was entirely trustworthy. He set one of the men to fashioning him a crutch, and in the meantime stayed grudgingly out of the way. He would return to the quarterdeck when he could get there without being carried like a baby. There was no point in taking chances.

Cathy sighed. Harry's devotion had become obvious to all, and Petersham had even gone so far as to warn her, with a meaningful look, that the captain was a jealous man. Once Jon resumed command of the ship, he was bound to become aware of the situation. She had tried everything she could think of to discourage Harry's attentions, but nothing had worked. Hopefully, Jon would see the younger man's devotion as the natural interest of a male in the only female within miles, and let it go at that. Or better yet, maybe Jon's presence on the quarterdeck would quell Harry sufficiently so that Jon need never know anything about it.

It was a beautiful day, warm and sunny. If not for the gentle breeze it would have been almost hot. The "Margarita" was moving on a southerly course, and Cathy could only suppose that Jon had concurred with Harry's orders when they were set. Their stores of food and water were getting low again. But when she pestered Jon about where they were headed, he teasingly refused to answer. She would see, was all he would say. Cathy shook her head. Really, he was becoming more like a mischievous small boy every day.

She was smiling when she walked back into the cabin, her cheeks flushed by the sun and her hair blown into curling disorder. Her smile changed to a severe frown as she saw Jon, clad in a pair of black breeches that were far too tight around his heavily bandaged leg, sitting at the table and studying some charts. She crossed to stand behind him, her thighs pressing into his broad, well-muscled back and her hand coming to rest on his bare shoulder. He grunted a hello without looking around. Cathy grimaced. As an impassioned lover, he had some definite failings.

"You shouldn't be up," she told the back of his head sternly. His arm came out to hook her waist, and he pulled her around so that he could see her. He was smiling, the gray eyes twinkling roguishly. Cathy felt her heart melt with tenderness for him.

"You look like an angel," he said by way of a reply, his eyes warm on her reproving face. "But a very bossy angel. I think I've spoiled you. Don't you know that you're supposed to quake at my every frown? I'm a vicious, bloodthirsty pirate, remember?"

"And I'm not an angel, I'm your nurse," Cathy replied lightly. "If you don't do as I tell you, I'll be terribly clumsy when next I change your bandages."

Jon laughed, and pulled her around so that she was sitting on his good knee. His arm squeezed her waist while his hand wandered upward to trap tenderer game. Cathy pushed his hand away with a show of indignation, but was soon distracted by his warm mouth nibbling teasingly at the curve of her neck. His hand stealthily returned to caress its prize. She stiffened automatically, then relaxed. The feel of his hand on her breast tingled pleasurably down to her toes.

"Let me up," Cathy ordered without much conviction. "The door is wide open. Anyone could walk in."

"Who cares?" Jon murmured abstractedly, his attention centered on the tempting valley revealed by the gentle scoop of her bodice.

"I do!" Cathy flashed him an admonishing look. His lips traced lightly along her cheekbone and down her nose before coming to rest at the corner of her mouth.

"Do you really?" he asked against her quivering lips. Then his mouth took hers with leisurely expertise and Cathy had to admit that at this moment she didn't care about anything except the delicious way he was making her feel.

"What are you doing?" When he lifted his head at last, Cathy's heart was thudding unevenly. Cathy hoped that the question would serve to distract him.

"Admiring your beauty," he answered promptly, his hard arm moving up close beneath her breasts to hold her tightly and cause the neckline of her gown to gape away from her curving flesh. His eyes feasted pleasurably on the bounty thus exposed to his view.

"I meant with the charts." Cathy nipped his arm sharply with her fingers. With an aggrieved sigh his attention turned to the papers spread out on the table.

"Calculating how long it will take us to get where we're going. Harry tells me that we've run into some strong westerly currents which have pulled us slightly off course."

"And where *are* we going?" Cathy asked casually, hoping that he would answer without thinking. Instead he grinned down at her.

"Curiosity killed the cat, sweet," he teased.

"And satisfaction brought it back," she retorted smartly. Then, on a coaxing note, "Please tell me where we're going."

"Persuade me," he murmured in her ear. The wicked glint in his eye left her in no doubt as to the type of persuasion he had in mind.

"Certainly not," Cathy answered primly, but couldn't resist trailing a provocative finger down his hard arm. Jon rewarded her boldness with a playful bite on her ear.

"If you must know, my nosy cat, we're going to Las Palmas," he said, leaning back in the chair and shifting her so that he could hold her more comfortably against him. One brown finger played idly with a strand of golden hair. Cathy rested back against his hard chest contentedly.

"Las Palmas?" Cathy questioned, eyes dreamy. She was no longer particularly interested in his answer. The warm male smell of him was acting like a drug on her senses. Idly, she continued, "I've never heard of it. Is it a city?"

Jon smiled slightly, shaking his head as he pulled

one of the charts closer.

"No, my lovely ignoramus, Las Palmas is not a city. It's an island. We use it as sort of home base between voyages."

"Between thieving expeditions, you mean," Cathy corrected, a slight edge sharpening her voice.

"All right, between thieving expeditions, if you prefer," he agreed carelessly, his eyes narrowing a little as he looked down at her.

Cathy's eyes flicked away from his to return to the charts.

"Have you ever thought about giving it up?" she asked, deliberately offhand.

"What, my life of debauchery and sin?" he mocked. "No, why should I? I like what I do."

"How can you like murdering and stealing?" Cathy snapped, straightening away from him.

"It has its rewards," he replied, joggling her up and down on his knee, as an adult would a fractious infant. Cathy glared at him, and he grinned. "I earn a good living, I call no man master, I sail my own ship, and—uh—I have a very pretty bedmate."

His eyes ran over her with exaggerated lasciviousness before twinkling down into her own.

"I'm serious," Cathy insisted, frowning at him irritably. "You can't be a pirate forever. It's against the law. One day you'll make a mistake and you'll be caught. Then you'll hang."

"And does the thought bother you, my cat?" One silky black eyebrow twitched quizzically. "Not so very long ago, I could have sworn that if you had

had access to a pistol or a knife, my life would have been abruptly terminated."

"Oh, you're impossible!" Cathy stormed, struggling to get off his lap. His words made a mockery of the concern he must know she felt for him. Thank God he had no idea of the true state of her emotions where he was concerned! He would really have a field day if he knew that!

"I wouldn't want to see any man hang," Cathy added with what dignity she could muster, still squirming to be free.

"Not so fast, little cat," he murmured, restraining her easily despite his injuries. Cathy could have effected her release by kicking or hitting his wounded thigh, she knew, but she didn't. Her love for him was such that she wouldn't willingly hurt him. "Why is it that you always want to leave just as the conversation gets interesting?"

Reluctantly Cathy stopped struggling, aware that to insist on being set free might reveal more than he had any right to know. She rested back against him guilelessly, aware of the prickle of his wiry chest hair through her dress.

"Would it matter so much to you, if I was hanged?" he persisted.

Cathy lowered her lashes to screen her eyes, careful to let no hint of her emotions show in her face. He could read her expressions like a book, she knew. For a moment she was tempted to confess her love, but cool caution restrained her. It would be a powerful weapon in the hands of a man who was, after all, a rogue and a blackguard. Unless he was rendered similarly vulnerable, her confession would leave her wholly at his mercy. She decided to confound any suspicions he might harbor by skating as close to the truth as was possible without actually revealing it. He wasn't stupid, after all. He must already know that her care of him meant something.

"Of course I wouldn't like to see you hang," she answered coolly, her blue gaze untroubled and candid as it met his piercing gray one. "Against my better judgement, I've grown rather fond of you."

The flickering light in his eyes died at her words. They grew harder, unreadable. His teeth came down to nip punishingly at the creamy bare flesh of her shoulder.

"So you're 'rather fond' of me, are you?" he murmured silkily, his mouth resting on the pulse that pounded just beneath her ear. "Your heart's beating mighty fast for mere fondness."

"You're a conceited animal, aren't you?" Cathy asked, her voice chill as she tried to get her wayward pulses under control. "You're lucky to get fondness. I should hate you forever after the beastly way you've treated me."

"I've treated you like a queen, my cat, and you know it." His voice had hardened to match his eyes. "Have I starved you, hurt you in any way? Have you ever stopped to think how you would have fared, a prisoner in the hands of any other man? You should be grateful."

"Grateful?" Cathy flared disbelievingly, her eyes

snapping sapphire sparks at him. "You kidnapped me and kept me prisoner! You raped me and humiliated me! And you think I should be grateful?"

Her voice cracked indignantly on the last word. Jon looked down at her, bristling on his lap like a small ruffled hen, then smiled ruefully. For the past few days his she-cat had purred like a kitten for him, and he had grown to like it. Too much, as he now realized.

"Oh, Cathy," he murmured with half-amused resignation. He definitely was not in the mood for a quarrel. Indeed, he had something altogether different in mind. "I take it back. I was undoubtedly brutal to you, and I apologize."

"So you should," Cathy told him severely, trying again to get up off his lap. He restrained her with ludicrous ease. From the hardening of the muscles beneath her, she could tell that her movements had merely succeeded in exciting him.

"I seem to spend half my time telling you that I'm sorry for something or other," he lamented in her ear. "This has to stop. I'm afraid it will go to your head, and then I'll be spending the rest of my life apologizing for trifles."

"But I won't be around for the rest of your life, will I, Jon?" Cathy asked sweetly, taking advantage of the opening. "Sooner or later you'll have to let me go."

Jon's eyes gleamed briefly. He buried his face in her bright hair, breathing deeply of its soft fragrance, without replying.

"When are you going to let me go, Jon?" she

212

prodded softly.

"When I get good and ready." His answer was clipped. "You weren't so anxious to leave me in Cadiz, if you recall. You had the chance."

"The other prisoners were released in Cadiz," she reminded him. "But you were planning to keep me even before you were hurt. Why weren't you going to let me go with them?"

"Because, my beautiful shrew, I have this strange craving for the taste of your skin. I don't propose to let you go until I've had my fill of it." His eyes leered down at her, but the rest of his face was guarded. Cathy began to feel that she was making progress.

"Not my leg, sweet," he grinned. "But other parts of my anatomy ache sorely."

"The cure is in your own hands," she replied unsympathetically, catching his meaning. "Let me up."

"I prefer another solution," he growled, his hands moving suggestively over her. Cathy shook her head at him, not bothering to evade his caressing fingers. She wasn't in the mood for any more verbal sparring. Deliberately she curved a soft arm around the back of his neck, pulling his head down to plant a soft kiss on his sandpaper cheek. Let him think about that as well!

"Your bark is much worse than your bite, Captain, as I know very well. Now let me up. I have things to do."

The look in Jon's eyes warmed. That kiss was the first spontaneous gesture of affection she had ever given him, and it made his heart beat faster. He felt for all the world like some infatuated schoolboy. Somehow this soft, little female on his lap was succeeding in making him feel things he would have scoffed in the past. The experience wasn't to his liking at all, but there didn't seem to be much he could do about it. He had already tried to cast her out of his mind by every means he could think of, and failed.

Cathy twisted in his hold, her eyes widening at his arrested expression.

"Jon, is anything wrong?" she purred.

His eyes glinted down at her rather dazedly for a moment, as if he was having trouble getting his bearings. Then his gaze focused on her face, and he bent his head to return her kiss right on her sweet little mouth. This wench was not like the others, he was certain. She was as innocent of guile and feminine schemings as a newborn babe.

"Excuse me, Captain." Harry's voice was wintry as he spoke from just inside the cabin door. "I'd like to go over the charts with you." He slanted a burning look at Cathy, pink-faced and cozily ensconced on Jon's lap. "If you can spare the time."

Cathy frowned at Harry as Jon reluctantly released her, and pointedly ignored him as she turned away. Really, if he weren't careful, Jon would get wise to his pursuit of her—for pursuit was what it had become—and then the fat would be in the fire for sure! Her pirate captain had a fierce temper and a strong sense of possessiveness where she was concerned. His eyes were already suspicious as they looked at Harry.

The two men talked for some time, drawing lines on the charts and measuring the distance to various points. Their conversation was largely unintelligible so she soon stopped listening. She wandered over to one of the bookcases and selected one of the volumes, and then settled herself in the alcove beneath the window to read. The book was extremely dull, and eventually she put it aside, passing the time instead by looking out at the ever-changing sea. She was unaware that the afternoon sun had turned her loosened hair into a fiery aureole around her face, or that her averted profile had the sweet purity of a perfect cameo. Both men's eyes wandered from time to time to feast on the enchanting picture she made, Jon's openly and Harry's whenever he thought his captain wasn't aware of it. Their conversation became more and more desultory and finally ceased altogether. This cessation in the flow of talk attracted Cathy's attention, and she turned to find both men eyeing her hungrily. She smiled warmly at Jon, ignoring Harry, and got to her feet, stretching a little as she rose.

"Would you like me to leave?" Perhaps they had something to discuss that was not for her ears.

"Not at all," both men assured her at the same time. Jon turned a razor-sharp look on Harry.

Cathy saw that look and crossed quickly to Jon's side, placing a slender hand on his shoulder and smiling down at him.

"It's time you had a rest." Her voice was caressing,

partly for Harry's benefit and partly because she couldn't help herself. Jon was distracted, as she had meant him to be. His hand came up to cover hers, pressing it down into the hard muscles of his shoulder. Cathy felt a twinge of excitement run through her fingers. Harry watched them resentfully, and then abruptly stood up to go, his eyes hard.

"We can finish this another time, Captain," Harry said stiffly. Jon flashed him a glinting look as he stalked from the cabin.

To Cathy's uneasy surprise, Jon said nothing at all when they were once again alone. The silence was heavy as he hobbled across to the bunk and began to undress. A deep frown furrowed his brow and his mouth was tight as he tugged painfully out of his breeches. When he had levered himself into the bed Cathy could bear the ominous stillness no longer. She came to sit beside him, pulling a pillow out from under his head so that he was forced to lie flat, and tucking the quilts up around his chest. His eyes were fixed on her, broodingly, as she ministered to him. It was stupid, she knew, but she felt absurdly guilty under that dark gaze.

"Cathy." His hand caught her wrist as she would have turned away. "Has Harry been—pestering—you while I've been laid up?"

She knew he must have felt the nervous start of her pulse under his hand, but there was nothing she could do about it. Damn Harry anyway, for putting her in this position! She didn't want to lie, but on the other hand she didn't want to cause trouble between Jon and one of his oldest friends.

"No," she answered coolly, not quite meeting his eyes. "Why do you ask?"

"He watches you like a gull after fish. I don't like it. If he's been making a nuisance of himself, tell me. I'll put a stop to it mighty fast." With an effort, Cathy smiled at him, hoping to lighten his mood.

"If I were conceited, I'd think you were jealous, Captain," she teased. Jon's eyes held hers for a moment as if struck by what she had said. His voice was strangely husky when he replied.

"And if I were, would I have reason?" His eyes burned into hers like hot coals. Cathy couldn't suppress a tiny shiver of triumph. If he were jealous, and it seemed very much like he was, then he must be far down the road to being in love with her. Jon saw the brief flicker in her eyes, and frowned heavily, his hand tightening painfully around her wrist.

"I said, have I reason to be jealous?" His voice was stark.

Cathy grinned down at him, her eyes twinkling impishly.

"I should let you stew," she said reflectively. "I think it would do you good."

Jon's face darkened thunderously as he glared up at her. His grasp on her wrist tightened so much that she winced.

"Don't play games with me, my cat," he warned, eyes menacing her. "You might not like the consequences. I'll ask once more: have I reason to be jealous?"

Cathy would have been angry at his threat if the disquiet in his eyes hadn't made her so happy. She pursed her lips, looking down at the floor as though dreading his reaction to what she had to tell him, then bent quick as a flash to whisper in his ear, "No, but I think you are anyway."

She could see the red come up under his skin as he absorbed the full import of her statement. His eyes flashed to hers as she straightened, their expression both wary and faintly sheepish. Cathy waited expectantly, but he was not yet ready to admit to feeling any tender emotion where she was concerned.

"What I have, I keep," was all he said. Cathy didn't really mind. It might take a little time, but one day he would love her and admit it. She felt sure of it. In the meantime, she could wait.

The next day was hot and airless, with the kind of heavy sultriness that presages a storm. It took all Cathy's ingenuity to keep Jon amused. He was itching to be back in charge of his ship, fretting that Harry would not do a proper job of preparing for the bad weather that seemed to be ahead of them. Tactfully Cathy tried to discourage him, and when that didn't work she told him bluntly that he was not yet strong enough to even stand on the quarterdeck. His wounds were healing nicely, but he still tired easily, and his appetite had not yet returned. Cathy scolded him roundly for leaving almost his entire portion of salted pork untouched at midday. He scowled up at her sullenly, like a thwarted small boy, and Cathy had to smile. She was still smiling as she called to Petersham to take the remains of the meal away, and then came back to sit beside Jon who was propped up in the bunk.

"How do you feel?" she asked, her eyes running over him proprietorily. He had lost weight since being wounded, but not enough to mar the splendid lines of his body. His leanness only served to accentuate the strength of his corded muscles.

"Like some puling infant," he answered grumpily, his eyes resting on the swelling curves of her breasts. Cathy remained stoic under his rapidly warming perusal. Bedding him whenever he wished wasn't getting her anywhere, she reflected. Perhaps it was time to try a new tactic. Let him go without her for a while, and his affections might suddenly blossom.

Jon, undeterred by her indifference, stretched out a questing finger to follow the trail blazed by his eyes. Cathy slapped his hand away only to find herself dragged across his lap to lie half on him, half on the bunk. His mouth came down to twist across hers hungrily. Cathy returned the embrace for a moment before lightly biting her teeth down on his tongue. Jon yelped, jumping back, his hand going up to test the injured member.

"It's a pity you're not as hungry for food as you are for me," she said lightly. "You might regain your strength sooner."

"I'm strong enough to tame a vixen," he grunted, his hands reaching for her purposefully. Cathy did her best to elude him, but she was hampered by her own desires. Eventually she surrendered to greater force of arms, and returned his kisses warmly. But when his hand groped behind her back for the fastenings to her dress, Cathy set it away from her firmly.

"No," she said. His eyes opened to stare at her.

"Why not?"

"Because I don't want to," she told him haughtily, tilting her fine-boned little nose at him. "I'd—I'd rather talk."

"Talk!" Jon groaned, rolling over onto his back with a pained expression.

"Yes, talk." Cathy was determined not to surrender to him again, operating on the theory that abstinence makes the heart grow fonder.

"Go ahead," Jon sighed, crossing his hands behind his head. Cathy wriggled upward until she lay full upon his chest, her chin propped in her hands as she looked at him, her legs between his, so as not to jar his injured thigh. His eyes warmed appreciatively at the method of her conversation, but when he would have kissed her again Cathy held him off, flickering her small tongue out at him playfully.

"Have you ever been in love?" Cathy began when they were settled at last.

"Oh, God!" he mumbled, closing his eyes as if pained. "She wants to talk about it, and I want to do it!"

"Many times." He grinned devilishly, entering into the spirit of the conversation. "And each time lasted about half an hour."

"Very funny," Cathy said sourly. "I meant, really in love?"

"When I was sixteen I was totally infatuated with my stepmother," he answered lightly, his eyes on the ceiling.

"Really?" Cathy asked suspiciously.

"Yes, really," he replied. "She was twenty when my father married her, a beautiful black-haired wench with flashing dark eyes and all the right equipment. At the time I thought she was the loveliest thing in the whole world."

"What happened?" Cathy asked a trifle stiffly, not able to control a prick of jealousy. Yet how ridiculous it was to hate a woman she had never heard of before, and for something that had occurred almost twenty years before.

"I was so infatuated that I followed her everywhere. I was just a boy, remember, and I worshipped her like a goddess. She didn't even know I was alive, I don't think. I certainly never remember her looking, let alone smiling, at me. I put her up on a pedestal, and never even thought of touching her. Such a thing would have seemed like a sacrilege. Anyway, I followed her to the dressmaker one August afternoon. She went to the dressmaker about twice a week, and usually I just hung around outside until she came out. This time, for no reason in particular, I happened to wander around back and saw her leaving by a rear entrance. Quite naturally, I was intrigued, and followed her. She walked to a little house set well back from the street, and went inside.

I didn't know what to think. In my innocence, I supposed that she must be visiting another dressmaker, or perhaps a milliner, for some reason. After a while, curiosity got the better of my sense of propriety, and I went up to the house and peeped through the windows. My dear stepmother was as naked as the day she was born on the floor of the library, mewling like a bitch in heat, while a man I'd never seen before in my life rode between her thighs."

"Did you tell your father?" Cathy gasped, fascination overcoming shock.

"Certainly not. He wouldn't have believed me, anyway. He was in love with her, and thought she was the most perfect creature on earth."

"Then what did you do?"

"I packed my few clothes and left that night. I couldn't stick around after that. The thought of what I'd seen made me want to throw up. If I had stayed, I might have killed her." Jon's voice was still deliberately light, but Cathy was able to discern the harsh note of remembered disillusion that lay beneath it. She placed a consoling hand on his bristly cheek. He turned his mouth into the palm, then grimaced down at her.

"Save your sympathy, sweet. Although I didn't think so at the time, I know now that the slut did me a service. I was never that young or that naive again."

"And—and did you soon fall in love with someone else?" Cathy's voice was very sweet and a touch wistful. Jon's eyes glinted down at her.

"Not in the same way. My other loves were all of

222

the type you're too young to hear about." He was teasing her, and Cathy twinkled back at him, glad that the harshness had left his face.

"I'd ask you if you'd ever been in love," he twitted her, "except that you're just a baby. You haven't had time."

"I most certainly have!" Cathy protested indignantly. Then, seeing the sharp look he turned on her, she amended hastily, "Well, I've had lots of beaus."

"I can imagine," he answered dryly, his eyes moving over the winsome beauty of her face and form. "And did they bring you flowers and kiss your hand?"

"Of course," Cathy replied with dignity.

"That's all they did," Jon muttered under his breath.

"How do you know?" Cathy looked at him flirtatiously from beneath her long lashes, hoping to provoke him to another display of jealousy. She felt cheated when he merely grinned.

"My cat, it was obvious the first time I kissed you. You were totally untouched by man."

"That's your opinion," Cathy sniffed, nettled.

"That's a fact." Jon pinched the tip of her nose playfully. "I've bedded enough women to know when one has had experience. You hadn't. Not a bit."

The tips of Cathy's ears turned pink with embarrassment. She stared at him reproachfully.

"You make it sound like I'm just one in a very long line." Her voice was stiff despite her attempt to speak naturally.

Jon looked at her through narrowed eyes. She sounded hurt, and he hadn't meant to do that.

"Jealous?" he teased to distract her.

"Not at all," Cathy replied coldly. "I'd certainly never be jealous over you."

"Good. I hate a jealous woman," Jon told her cheerfully, and when her eyes snapped at him he grinned and rolled over with her.

"Enough talk," he grunted, pushing her down into the soft mattress. "I'm hungry. And not for food."

When Cathy left the cabin some two hours later, Jon was still sleeping peacefully. There went her plan to win his heart by denying him her body, she thought ruefully. He hadn't even had to force her. His sensuous caresses had set her body afire, and, after that, making love to her had been as easy as rowing downstream. Oh, well, she thought, shrugging. At least she had enjoyed losing.

The sun was sinking beneath the horizon, its bright orange globe only half visible above the rippling, gold-edged sea. Streamers of pink and lavender clouds curved around it like a pinwheel, making a sunset so breathtaking that Cathy stepped to the rail to get a better look. The deck was deserted except for the officer of the watch, and the silence was broken only by the creaking timbers and the popping of sails. Cathy stood leaning lightly on the rail, drinking in the utter peace of the hour before darkness, not thinking of anything in particular, not even Jon.

"I see he rides you well," a tight voice jeered behind her. Cathy sighed deeply, knowing who it was before she turned. Harry, of course! Really, she wished he would get over this ridiculous notion that he was in love with her. It was growing exceedingly tiresome.

"Good evening, Harry," she said coolly, ignoring his taunt.

"Good evening, Harry," he said, mimicking her well-bred tone angrily. "I'll wager that's not how you greet Jon."

"But you're not Jon," Cathy pointed out with a slight edge to her voice. She gathered up her skirts and started to sweep past him, but his hand on her arm stopped her. Cathy stared pointedly down at the restraining hand, silently demanding to be released.

"Let me go, Harry," she ordered grimly, hoping that she would not be obliged to call for assistance. After Jon's questions of the day before, it would not take very much to reawaken his suspicions. And if she should be forced to make any kind of commotion to get away from this bumbling ass, Jon would surely hear of it.

"Not yet." His voice was low, and he was looking at her with half-shamed desire. "I want to apologize for the way I've been acting lately. I—I can't seem to help myself. You're so beautiful and I love you so much. Just the thought of you in his arms is driving me crazy."

"I accept your apology, Harry," Cathy said, deeming it wiser to ignore the last part of his speech. She tugged gently at her arm. "I really have to go in now. It's getting quite dark."

"God, you won't even listen to me, will you?" Harry burst out savagely. "Well, maybe you'll listen to this!"

Before Cathy knew what he intended his arms came around her, dragging her protesting against him. Cathy tried to pull free, but he was too strong. He was not as big as Jon, or as muscular, but he was wiry and he was determined to kiss her. She went limp in his embrace, hoping that by her lack of response she could convince him that his pursuit was hopeless. Just wait, Cathy thought furiously, keeping her teeth tightly clenched against his probing tongue. When you let me go I'll slap the daylights out of you, you stupid fool!

Cathy's eyes were wide open and filled with disgust as Harry's lips and hands beseeched her. As she glanced over Harry's shoulder her eyes grew even wider. Not three feet away stood Jon, leaning heavily on a hand-whittled crutch. As Cathy watched, horrified, the blood rushed into his lean face and his eyes, darkly furious as they met hers, showed murderous anger.

Nine

Jon felt a deep, boiling rage build up until he thought its force would blow him apart. "The cheating little bitch!" he raged silently. He had begun to think that she was different, sweet, innocent—even that she was starting to care for him.

226

"Fool!" he castigated himself furiously. He should have known that all women were basically the same. Like some besotted addlepate he had allowed a lovely face and soft flesh to lead him around by the nose. It enraged him to realize that all the time the two-faced slut was murmuring breathless little endearments to him, she had been planning to meet another man on the sly. But no more, he promised himself grimly. He would take her apart with his bare hands. And as for Harry. . . . Jon smiled savagely. That he would really enjoy!

Cathy's horrified shovings at Harry's shoulders finally had some effect. He released her reluctantly and started to speak, staring passionately down at her white face. What he saw there made him swing around. Oh, God! Jon! He looked more furious than Harry had ever seen him, his dark face suffused with blood, a muscle twitching convulsively in his cheek. His gray eyes stared at Harry like icy harbingers of death. Harry felt the color drain from his own face and devoutly thanked God that the other man had not yet recovered his full strength.

The three of them stood frozen in place for a long moment, like some ghastly tableau from a play. Cathy finally recovered the use of her limbs and ran across to Jon, catching him by the arm and shaking it slightly.

"Darling, it's not what it seems," she told him urgently. The set stillness of his face and those awful, leaping eyes frightened her far more than any amount of ranting would have done. "Jon, you must believe me! I can explain. . . . !"

Jon stared down at Cathy, his eyes glowing like twin coals on the devil's hearth. When she called him darling in that insidious little voice, he felt like he'd been stabbed in the gut. His pain was so intense that he was almost sick with it.

"You lying little bitch!" he snarled softy.

The arm she was clinging to swept violently against her, sending her staggering, and she fell heavily on the hard boards of the deck. She cried out at the force of the impact. Automatically Harry started to go to her assistance, only to find Jon blocking his path.

"Don't touch her, you damn bastard," Jon said through his teeth. His voice was icy cold, his hands twitching in their eagerness to close around Harry's neck. Harry backed off. Normally he was no match for Jon, but in the captain's weakened state he just might stand a chance. Or he might not. Rage had been known to give even the weakest of creatures incredible strength, and Jon, even leaning on a crutch, looked capable of tearing him to pieces. But Cathy needed him. . . . And what Jon might do to her after he was finished with Harry himself did not bear thinking of.

Jon settled the matter. He began to advance on Harry slowly, menacingly, the cold purpose in his eyes enough to send Harry backing away from him. If ever death had looked out of a man's eyes, it was looking now out of Jon's.

With deadly purpose Jon withdrew the long knife

from the scabbard at his waist. His fingers stroked along the finely honed blade almost caressingly. Harry was backed against the rail and could go no further. He looked about him desperately for a weapon. There was nothing. He felt terror rise in his throat like bile.

Cathy saw what was happening and scrambled to her feet with an inarticulate cry of horror. She ran frantically across to Jon and caught hold of the arm holding the knife in a grip that refused to be shaken off.

"Jon, you can't!" she screamed at him recklessly. "Harry didn't do anything! You can't kill him! It was me! I tell you, it was me!"

Her lie was the only thing she could think of that might save Harry's life. A kiss wasn't worth killing a man! Give Jon time to get over his first wild rage and he would agree, she knew. But in the meanwhile he must be kept from doing something that he would regret forever.

Her words succeeded in attracting Jon's attention. He stared down at her, his burning gray eyes going first to the saucer-roundness of hers and then firing on her trembling lips. That soft mouth, only a little over an hour ago, had been driving him mad. . . . Now it was driving him mad in a different way. His eyes blazed at her, one hand moving up to grab her hair. Cathy gasped as her head was jerked back suddenly, and she thought for a second that her neck might snap. Jon held her cruelly, his big hand purposefully hurting her as it dug into her scalp. The fingers twined themselves painfully around the silky strands, twisting her head back so that it was forced to rest against his hard shoulder, her face turned up to his. Cathy didn't attempt to struggle. Despite his fury, she didn't really think that he would hurt her. But if she were to resist him now, he might be driven to ungovernable lengths.

The straight line of his mouth closed over hers, prying her lips apart, purposefully bruising her. He kissed her as if he wanted to hurt her, to insult her, to imprint his total possession of her in her mind. Cathy quivered under his assault, but instead of trying to pull away she returned the full sweetness of her mouth to him. A miniscule portion of the rage had died out of his eyes when he released her.

"This is mine!" he barked at Harry, who had watched the scene in frozen silence. Jon's bullet-like speech was so abrupt that Cathy started nervously in his arms. He whirled her around so that she stood with her back against his chest facing Harry. The arm holding the knife was tight about her waist, the sharp blade facing out. Harry took in its glittering menace, and paled.

"This is mine," Jon repeated savagely. "If you ever attempt to touch her again, I'll kill you on the spot. Understand?"

Harry stared at Jon, then nodded wordlessly. He felt like a condemned man who had just been granted a reprieve. Jon's eyes raked over him, still flickering with anger, and then turned his attention to the trembling girl whose soft body he held so brutally. Roughly he shoved her away from him, sending her reeling to the deck.

"Get back to the cabin, slut," he growled. When Cathy made no move to obey him he lifted a hand as if he would strike her. Cathy's eyes flashed angrily at him, but before she could speak Harry broke in.

"She lied," he said as if the words were being dragged from him. "She didn't do a thing. I kissed her, and wouldn't let her go even though she tried to make me. She's completely innocent, as you would know if you weren't so goddamned stupid. She's far too good for you; you treat her like a whore, and yet she calls you darling."

Jon's eyes turned to Harry. Cathy stood up, her mouth shaking. That last display of violence had both frightened and angered her. She couldn't believe that he would treat her so brutally, not now, not after. . . . Pressing a trembling hand to her mouth, she turned her back and walked with dignity back to the cabin. She could feel his hard gaze boring into her back as she went.

While Jon's attention was concentrated on Cathy's retreating form, Harry took the opportunity to slink away below. When Jon turned back toward the rail he found that he was alone. He stood staring out at the darkening sea for some minutes before finally limping after Cathy.

"Is it true?" he asked heavily, leaning back against the closed cabin door. Cathy stood in the far corner of the room, sapphire eyes enormous in her white face, arms hugging herself to stop her body from

231

shaking. The look she turned on Jon was stony.

"Is it true?" he repeated, voice grating. "Did he force you?"

"Believe what you like," Cathy said coldly. "It makes no difference to me."

Jon's gray eyes, like twin shards of glass, seemed to impale her shivering body. Cathy stared back at him, icily angry herself. If he thought of her as a slut, after the slavish devotion she had lavished on him, then he didn't deserve an explanation!

"I asked you a question." Jon's voice rumbled ominously, like a volcano before it erupts. "I advise you to answer."

Cathy shot him a withering look.

"I'm not afraid of you," she sniffed contemptuously.

"By God, you damned well should be," Jon snarled, coming away from the door in a lunge. Cathy bravely stood her ground, chin tilted defiantly, eyes flashing as he closed in on her. She could not stop from cowering instinctively as he reached for her with savage imprecation, but she made no sound. His big hands came around her neck, squeezing the soft flesh just enough so that she could feel his strength. His thumbs pushed her chin up until her face was tilted to his.

"I could break your neck in less than a second," Jon growled, tightening his hands slightly.

"Then why don't you?" Cathy dared recklessly, her growing anger swamping her fear.

"I will," Jon promised grimly, "if you don't answer

my questions. Was Harry telling the truth? Did he kiss you against your will?"

"You're jealous again, aren't you?" Cathy taunted, wanting to hurt him. "You're so jealous that you're crazy with it. Well, as I've told you before, you've got no hold on me. I can do as I please!"

Jon's eyes darkened furiously.

"Cathy," he warned very softly. "This is one time when I would advise you to keep a hold on that sharp little tongue. I mean to have an answer. Did he force you?"

"And what if I say he did?" she challenged. "Will you believe me? You were ready enough to think the worst of me out there." She nodded in the general direction of the deck.

"I'll believe you," Jon muttered after a long moment. "God knows why, but I'll believe you."

"All right then, he forced me. Are you satisfied?" Her voice taunted him.

Jon looked down at her mutinous little face, and felt the slender fragility of the white throat he held in his hands. He could kill her so easily. . . . His hands tightened until he saw the blood rush into her pale face, then loosened again. She had said that Harry had forced her. . . .

"Is that the truth?" he demanded, his eyes burning her. Cathy stared up at him angrily.

"I've said it was. I thought you said that you'd believe me."

"All right, all right. I believe you." Jon felt the killing pain that had been throbbing in his belly subside. His hands slowly released her throat, then dropped to his sides.

Cathy glared after him as he turned away, limping across to the bunk. His crutch lay where he had dropped it by the cabin door, and he stopped to pick it up and lean it against the wall by the bed. Then he sank down in a sitting position on the mattress, his back toward her, and his leg thrust out stiffly in front of him. Absentmindedly he began to knead his wounded thigh. Watching him, Cathy felt herself soften slightly. After all, she wanted him to fall in love with her, and jealousy was a healthy symptom of love. Or maybe not. Maybe he was equally possessive with everything to which he had staked a claim.

"Does your leg hurt very much?" she asked, almost unwillingly. The broad shoulders shrugged.

"I'll live," he grunted, slanting a look over his shoulder at her. Then, as if compelled, he added tightly, "Has he ever touched you before?"

Cathy's antagonism bristled anew.

"If what you want to know is, have I slept with him, why don't you just come right out and ask me?"

"Have you?" he growled, turning to look at her almost as if he hated her. Cathy thought she could detect traces of pain in the gray eyes that had nothing to do with his leg. He was hurting, she realized with a pang. His violence stemmed from acute suffering. Realizing this, and remembering what he had told her about his stepmother, she felt her anger drain away. Her skirts rustled as she crossed the room to kneel at his feet, catching his long brown hands in hers. He allowed her to hold his hands, but the look he bent on her was wary.

"Jon, I had never known another man," she began, her eyes searching his sceptical face. "And if you remember, I didn't surrender to you willingly. You had to force me, didn't you?"

It was a measure of his hurt that he didn't even argue the point, but merely nodded curtly.

"What makes you think that I would be any easier for anyone else?" she questioned seriously. "I'm not a slut to fall into bed with any man who wants me. I was brought up respecting a certain moral code. You took my innocence, but my principles haven't changed."

Her eyes were steady as they looked into his. Jon began to feel better. What she said was true. She was born and bred a lady, and she'd been a virgin when he took her. It was unlikely that she could have developed whore's tricks so soon. His hands tightened around hers, his hard mouth curving in a slightly rueful smile. Cathy smiled back at him, her eyes glowing up at him warmly. Despite his faults, or perhaps even because of them, her love for him remained unchanged.

"It seems I owe you an apology yet again," Jon sighed, carrying her hands to his mouth one at a time. "But you shouldn't have lied to me. Did I hurt you, sweet?"

"No," Cathy answered. "Not really. Just scared me half to death."

"Now that I don't believe," Jon murmured,

235

smoothing the hair he had mussed away from her brow. "You spat at me like a she-tiger on the hunt. You weren't scared a bit."

"I didn't think you would hurt me." Cathy lowered her eyes demurely. "Was I wrong?"

Jon grinned at her, a teasing light chasing away the last traces of suspicion from his eyes.

"You'll never know, my cat, will you? Now, enough of this nonsense. I want my supper!"

"Yes, sir, master. Right away, master," Cathy teased back, bowing before him like a Chinese coolie. Jon rewarded her with a slap on the rear, and she went to tell Petersham to bring in the evening meal.

The subject was dropped until they had finished eating. Petersham cleared the dishes, and when they were alone once more Jon coaxed her into playing a game of chess. Cathy laughingly told him that the only reason he liked to play with her was because she was so bad. It was while her hand was hovering undecidedly over two different pawns that he brought the topic up again.

"Has Harry ever bothered you before?" His voice was casual, and his attention on the chessboard.

"He's never kissed me before, if that's what you mean," Cathy answered, moving a pawn at random.

"But he's been bothering you in other ways?" Jon persisted, his eyes lifting to fix searchingly on her face.

Cathy bit her lip, not wanting to cause more trouble between the two men, but realizing that the time had come for truth.

"He thinks he's in love with me."

Jon's eyes darkened as they stared at her fixedly. Cathy held her breath, braced for another explosion.

"And you—do you think you're in love with him?" The question sounded almost idle, but Cathy knew better.

"Now what do you think?" she replied lightly, while inwardly she rejoiced. From the tone of that last question, it would not be long before he was in love with her—and would admit it. For the time being, though, she was careful to hide her jubilation. The last thing she wanted was for him to get the idea that she was trying to manipulate him. He didn't trust women anyway, and, if he thought that she was setting her cap for him, he would probably run in the opposite direction.

Jon's eyes flickered, and his attention turned back to the game. He checked her move easily before replying.

"I'll see to it that he doesn't bother you again," was all he said, but Cathy read a wealth of meaning into the promise.

Jon was as good as his word. He stuck to her side like a large, lame shadow until the "Margarita" sailed into the bay at Las Palmas. Harry was kept busy on the forecastle at the opposite end of the ship. Jon resumed command the morning after the contretemps, disregarding Cathy's worried protestations. By the time the threatened storm had blown itself out he was almost back to normal. He still limped slightly, but he was able to get about without the aid of the crutch. Once the weather had cleared enough for her to venture out on deck again, she was careful to remain on the quarterdeck under his eyes. If, for some reason, his duties took him elsewhere, he detailed Petersham to act as her bodyguard. Cathy was both amused and touched by these elaborate precautions for her safety. The captain took good care of his possessions, it seemed.

It was the first of August when the "Margarita" reached her home port at last. By that time Cathy was so sick of ships and the sea that she would have welcomed hell itself if it would only not rock up and down. And Las Palmas was genuinely beautiful. She was entranced with the small island, set like a tiny, perfect emerald in its nest of blue ocean. The coconut palms which had given it its name were everywhere, swaying with the breeze, and making gentle music. Gleaming white sand formed a perfect crescent beach up to a line of trees, and large, exotic birds made brilliant splashes of color as they fluttered about the thick foliage. The sultry perfume of lush tropical flowers floated on the air.

Jon's house was set on a small cliff overlooking the beach, about a quarter of a mile away from the cluster of thatched buildings that served as a town. Cathy loved it on sight. It was a long, low, rambling building, built of shell-studded brick that caught the sun and sparkled like thousands of tiny diamonds. Inside, the rooms were large and airy, whitewashed to maximize coolness, and equipped with a minimum of furnishings. Huge windows, looking out over the sea in front and the vividly colored garden at the rear, made the interior as light as the outdoors. There were two native servants, the housekeeper Juta and her husband Kimo. They were almost comically respectful of the new "mam," and assured both Cathy and Jon, in their pidgin English, that every care would be taken of her. Jon was carelessly offhand as he showed her through the house and surrounding grounds, but Cathy could tell that he was anxious for her to like it. So she smiled at him and told him that everything was simply beautiful. Jon grinned at her, swinging her up in his arms and bestowing a sound kiss on her sweet mouth. His exuberant tenderness made her feel like a cherished bride instead of his paramour, and Cathy relished the sensation.

About two hundred Europeans lived on the island, and Cathy was shocked to learn that they all earned their living in the same way: through piracy. A very few of the men had European wives or mistresses, but the rest contented themselves with casual couplings with native girls. Cathy wondered, with a sidelong glance at Jon, if this was his usual practice when he was in residence, but didn't say anything. Petersham had told her that she was the only woman he had ever had in his home, and with this she was content. After all, the man was thirty-four years old; he was certainly lusty, and she couldn't expect him to have lived like a monk. So she banished the faint stirring of jealousy with determination.

Cathy was amazed when Jon pointed out a white-haired, grandfatherly looking man to her and identified him as Red Jack, so called because of the blood of his victims that was said to stain his hands. When Cathy stared after the man with shocked horror and then turned wide, doubting eyes on Jon, he laughed out loud.

"You should see him at sea," Jon said, grinning.

Cathy *could* believe it, after seeing the change Las Palmas made in Jon himself. Once away from the "Margarita," the hard mantle of authority dropped like a cloak from his shoulders, and he seemed years younger—almost boyish. He laughed a lot, and bent over backwards to amuse and please her. She loved him even more in this new guise, and was beginning to be afraid that he would be able to read her secret in her eyes. Determined not to speak of her love until she thought he felt the same, she was in constant fear of giving herself away. Jon thrived on her affection and Petersham told Cathy, privately, that the captain seemed a changed man.

The pristine beach and sparkling sea invited exploration, and Cathy spent her first morning on Las Palmas stretched with Jon on the sand, and paddling in the bay. For swimming, Jon wore only a pair of shortened breeches which left his powerful torso and long, muscular legs bare. The long, jagged tear on his thigh showed brightly red in the brilliant sunlight, and the scars of his other wounds nestled like gleaming medals of valor on his chest. Cathy gave way to compulsion and pressed her mouth consolingly on these reminders of pain, making Jon catch his breath sharply. The rest of that day was spent in their big brass bed.

Cathy found, to her pleasure, that she was the better swimmer. Jon had been around the water for years, swimming in a rough and ready style that took him where he wanted to go, but Cathy's lessons had given her a polished form that he could not match. He was first piqued then proud of her ability, and quickly learned not to wager anything he didn't care to lose on the outcome of a race with her across the bay.

One hot afternoon, about a month after the "Margarita" docking, Jon was lying on his side on the sand, propped up on one elbow while he studied Cathy's sleeping face. She was about a foot away from him, stretched out flat on her back, eyes tightly closed. Her breath rattled in her throat in a little snore. Jon grinned, admiring the dark crescent of lashes that lay on her cheeks. Their lovemaking had been long and impassioned the night before, lasting until the morning sun was sending crimson feelers across the dark sky. Plainly, it had been too much for the wench. She had fallen asleep as soon as she had hit the sand.

Her creamy skin had taken on the golden bloom of a ripe beach, he saw, and her tumbling hair had been kissed into even more glorious brightness by the tropical sun. Her figure, clearly outlined beneath the knee-length, bleached muslin dress she wore for swimming, had matured in the months since he had known her; her lovely breasts had grown fuller, her waist and thighs longer and more lissome. She was more woman now, than girl. Jon felt his heart speed up as he looked at her. She was so exquisite that he sometimes didn't believe she was real.

Even more important than outward beauty, he reflected, was the warmth and sweetness of the girl. Her tenderness was like oil calming the stormy waters of his previous dealings with the so-called gentler sex. She was one in a million, he thought, a woman to be guarded against all comers. She was his, and he meant to keep her.

His thoughts turned broodingly to Harry, eyes darkening as he pictured the moment on the "Margarita's" deck when he had found Cathy in the other man's arms. God, he had felt murderous, and Cathy's taunts afterwards, though maddening at the time, had admittedly been right on target. He had been jealous—pure and simple. Even the memory of that scene was enough to make the green demon rear its ugly head.

Jon could never remember feeling jealous over any other woman he had bedded, and he could come up with only one explanation: jealousy was the by-product of love. He toyed with the idea that he might actually have fallen in love with the golden-haired little shrew, but then dismissed it as ridiculous. He had received his inoculations against such folly at the hands of experts long ago. Although she was undoubtedly comelier and more tender than most, there was nothing about her to cause him to abandon the hard-learned tenets of a life-time. Was there?

He sniffled, and patted around the thought like a bear wanting meat but scenting a trap. Was it possible that the fierce possessiveness he felt toward her had its roots in a softer emotion? Jon shied quickly away from the idea, but then sidled reluctantly back. If he was honest with himself, he would admit it: he was head over ears in love with a seventeen-year-old chit; her slightest smile could make his heart beat faster.

Jon turned to lie on his back, staring sightlessly up at the cerulean sky, and considered the facets of his unprecedented predicament. From the first moment he'd set eyes on the little jade, looking like a small, golden wildcat, bright hair cascading around her half-naked body and sapphire eyes snapping fire, he'd been in deep water. He had wanted her badly, and had taken what he wanted. And that, as the saying went, should have been that. But later, as she had defied him with a courage that had amazed him, his desire had deepened and become mixed with admiration. Here was no shrinking, timid wench, frightened out of her few wits by a fearsome pirate. Instead, he had found a woman of fire and passion who quickly learned to match him, kiss for kiss, and blow for blow.

Jon's mind wandered further, remembering other telltale signs. God, the worry she'd caused him that night in Cadiz when he realized that she had fled into town. He had almost gone out of his mind thinking of the dangers she was prey to in that degenerate city! And then, when he had walked into the "Red Dog" and seen her, eyes wide with fright and humiliation and her lovely breasts bared, rage had burst like a red bomb before his eyes. He had wanted to kill all of them immediately, but had restrained his temper until she was safe. He had promised himself, though, that the man who had dared to strike her would die—and he had kept his promise. His one bullet had found its way into the cur's brain.

He must have loved her even then, he thought, and not known it. The question was, did she love him? She was fond of him, he knew, and sometimes, when his lovemaking had excited her to the point of shivering ecstasy, she was more than fond of him. But he had pleased many women, and he knew how little their impassioned adoration really meant. His pride shrank from declaring outright that he loved her without some assurance of her feelings for him. If she didn't love him, confessing his passion would be tantamount to handing her a whip she could use to flail him with at will. Much better to charm *her* into loving *him,* he decided, supremely confident of his ability to do so. Eventually he might even marry her. . . .

Jon's new tenderness plunged at the thought. Marriage was for fools and lapdogs, he had always maintained. There was no woman on earth worth losing his freedom for! But how else could he keep

Cathy with him? He would have been perfectly content to keep her as his chit. His lips tightened as he thought of Cathy being shamed. What would marriage be, anyway, but his vow to protect and provide for her, and her vow to keep herself only for him? If she wanted it, he conceded, he would marry her. At least that way he could be assured that she would never leave him.

Jon frowned a little, thinking of Cathy as his wife. As contented as she seemed to be on Las Palmas, she was accustomed to a totally different mode of life. She was a titled lady, the daughter of an earl, and was entitled to a place in the highest circles of society. Every care and luxury had been hers until now. If fate had not intervened by pushing her into his arms, she could have married whom she chose. With her beauty and background, even royalty would have been within her reach.

But she's mine now, Jon thought defensively, and what is mine I keep. He was wealthy enough to support her stylishly, and, if it would make her happy, he would even give up his present way of life. England was closed to him—he had preyed on too many English ships—but he could take her back with him to South Carolina. Despite everything that had happened there, it was still his home. It was not quite what she was used to, but Jon felt that it might be enough. If she loved him. . . .

A handful of cool water splashed down on his sun-warmed midriff, jolting Jon abruptly out of his reverie. The subject of his musings stood giggling at his feet, her blue eyes alight with laughter and her golden hair curling wildly about her slender body. Her hands were cupped, and even as he stared at her she sprinkled more water on his chest.

"I'll teach you to throw water on me," he growled with mock anger, springing to his feet and grabbing for her. She eluded him easily, as light and quick on her feet as a young gazelle, her teasing laugh floating behind her as she sprinted for the safety of the sea.

"You'd better run, vixen," Jon called threateningly after her, and followed at a more sedate pace to frolic with her in the waves.

Jon was very quiet that evening, and Cathy found herself casting him anxious looks from time to time. Could he possibly be angry with her about something? His gray eyes, when they rested on her, were brooding, and his manner was distracted. He drank several glasses of wine with his meal, but left his food practically untouched. Was he sickening for something, Cathy worried. Or maybe his leg was hurting him and he didn't want to own up to it.

Finally she could contain herself no longer.

"Jon, do you feel well?" she asked anxiously.

He looked up, his eyes vague. It took him a minute to focus on her.

"What? Yes, of course I do. Why?"

"Does your leg hurt?" she persisted, his lack of attention puzzling her even more. Lately he had listened with great interest to her every word. What was wrong with him? Was it possible that he was beginning to tire of her?

"My leg feels fine. Why suddenly so worried about my health?" His eyes were lazy, his tone desultory. He still seemed to be about a million miles away.

"Then what's wrong with you?" she burst out. She had to know, even if the answer was unpleasant.

"There's nothing wrong with me, so far as I know. Should there be?" he asked with faint interest.

"You're so quiet. Are you angry with me about something?" Cathy hadn't meant to sound quite so abject, but she couldn't help herself. She couldn't bear it if he was even now thinking of a way to break it to her gently that he no longer wanted her.

Jon laughed, his gray eyes suddenly warm as they rested on her.

"I was only thinking, my love."

"About what?" Cathy asked suspiciously.

"You'll find out. One day." He was being deliberately mysterious, she thought crossly.

Jon grinned at her annoyance, standing up and moving away from the table.

"Juta, we've finished," he called to the housekeeper, then walked around to Cathy's chair and pulled it out for her with a gallant gesture. Cathy stared up at him, then looked suspiciously down the table at the half-empty decanter of wine. Could he be drunk? He certainly didn't look it, but then maybe he carried his drink exceptionally well. Some men did, she had heard.

She stood up at his urging, smiling at Juta as she came in to clear the table, and allowed Jon to lead her into the large sitting room. The long French windows were open to the night, their thin veiling of mosquito netting fluttering in the gentle breeze. The only illumination came from a pair of wall-bracketed candles.

"Come for a walk with me?" Jon asked, nodding toward the windows. Cathy acquiesced, still faintly puzzled as she followed him out into the lush garden. The moon was a large, pale disc floating high over the tops of the palms, and the garden was alive with a chorus of insects. Sweet perfume from the brilliantly colored hibiscus trees floated in the air. Cathy breathed the heady fragrance deeply into her lungs.

"It's beautiful here," she murmured, more to herself than him. Jon's arm came around her waist, pulling her loosely against his side, supporting her as they strolled away from the house.

"Beautiful," he agreed huskily, but his eyes were on her.

"You're very gallant tonight, Captain," she teased lightly. "Are you trying to soften me up for some bad news?"

"As a matter of fact, I do have something to tell you," Jon answered, his tone matching hers. "Whether it's bad or not I leave up to you."

He hesitated, and Cathy cast a quick glance up at him. Was he about to tell her what had been worrying him all evening?

"Well?" she prompted impatiently.

"I have to go away for a few days," he said finally.

Cathy felt faintly uneasy at something in his tone.

"Go away? To where?"

"There's another island near here—Tenerife. I had word this afternoon that a man there is willing to buy the 'Margarita's' cargo. I had meant to dispose of it in Cadiz, but circumstances intervened." He slanted a look down at her. Cathy walked slowly on, not noticing whether he was moving with her or not. Was he not planning to take her with him?

"May I come?" she asked in a small voice, not looking at him. Her feet came to the edge of the small cliff overlooking the beach and she stopped automatically, not even aware that she had done so.

Jon shook his head.

"Not this time, my cat. Tenerife's a rough place, and I'll be busy. I won't have time to look after you properly. I'd rather leave you here, where I know you'll be safe."

He came to stand behind her, his arms sliding possessively around her small waist, pulling her back against his chest. Cathy stared unseeingly at the reflected moonlight shimmering on the ocean below. The gentle roaring of the waves echoed in her ears.

"Will you miss me?" Jon asked huskily, his mouth nuzzling at the soft curve of her neck.

"You know I will," Cathy whispered, her pride deserting her. She turned in his arms to slide her own around his neck. Jon stared down at her small face, admiring the translucent gleam of her skin in the silvery light. With moonbeams catching in her hair and her lips softly parted, she was so lovely that she took his breath.

Cathy stood on tiptoe, reaching for his mouth with hers. At the same time Jon's head came down, and their lips met with an explosion of passion that set them both to shaking. Jon's big hands moved over her body, slowly at first and then with increasing urgency. Cathy moaned as his trembling fingers slid inside her bodice to cup her breasts. Before she quite knew how it had happened, she was standing naked in the moonlight, Jon's eyes dark with desire as they ran sensuously over her. Her fingers were unsteady as she helped him unbutton his shirt, and then with an animal-like groan he lowered her to lie in the tall grass by the cliff. The ground was cool and prickly against the bare skin of her back, but Cathy scarcely noticed as she held up her arms to Jon beseechingly. When he came to her at last, he was as naked as she. Their bodies coupled fiercely, with no thought of preliminaries, conscious only of a raging need so intense that they were both caught up in its flames.

Ten

Cathy was sick for the third morning in a row. She lay gasping over the porcelain chamber pot, racked by violent spasms of nausea. When her exhausted stomach was finally quiet, she made her way back to bed, trembling, and resting weakly against the cool linen sheets. What on earth was the matter with her? Had she contracted some strange tropical disease? If this morning was like the other two, she would soon feel all right again, able to go about her business as if nothing had happened. Besides her one bout with sea-sickness, she had never been ill a day in her life before. This intermittent vomiting was beginning to alarm her.

"I bring coffee, mam." Juta's cheerful brown face appeared around the door. Cathy smiled at her wanly. Useless to expect either Juta or Kimbo to knock. They treated Jon's house as their own, and herself and Jon were catered to as if they were honored guests. Cathy could not quite get used to them walking in unannounced, but Jon had told her with a shrug that there was nothing to be done about it. He had merely forbidden the servants to enter the little room Cathy used for dressing or the big bedroom that he and Cathy shared. Juta appeared to consider that Jon's absence negated that last prohibition.

"Mam, you all right?" Juta asked, concern in her velvety dark eyes. Cathy sat up to sip her coffee, still feeling a trifle shaky.

"I'm fine, Juta. I've just been a little nauseous lately. I don't think it's anything to worry about."

"Nothing to worry about," Juta agreed, turning to leave Cathy to drink her coffee in peace. "Baby's nothing to worry about. Cap'n will be pleased. Proves him plenty strong man."

Juta sailed majestically from the room while Cathy slowly put the delicate china cup back down on the tray, her hand unsteady. Baby! It couldn't be!

251

She thought back quickly, and blanched. So much had happened to her over the past three months that she had completely lost track of her monthly courses. The last one had been—let's see—about a week before she had sailed with the "Anna Greer." Her hand crept to her stomach, still firm and flat beneath the filmy nightdress, with a feeling of awe. Juta was right. According to all the signs, she was going to have a child.

Cathy's emotions dissolved rapidly into a wild mingling of happiness, worry, and fear. She would love Jon's baby as she loved Jon. Already her arms yearned to hold her child, to lavish care and affection on it. What would it be—a little boy with black hair and swarthy complexion—or a little girl with gray eyes? Cathy faltered. Would Jon be pleased? Would he learn to love her as the mother of his child, or would he turn from her, as she grew big and unwieldy, to seek out females with a more seductive shape? Perhaps he would even send her back to her father, once she was no longer able to please him? She suddenly knew that she didn't really care if she never saw her father or Martha again. Her life was with Jon now, and as long as he wanted her she would stay with him. And if she had her way, he would want her for the rest of his life.

A frown puckered her brow and her hand caressed her belly protectively. According to the tenets of society, her child would be a bastard—unless she did something about it. If there was any way she could manage it, her baby would have a right to his father's name, would be able to hold up his head with anyone as he grew to manhood—or woman-hood. In that moment she resolved to persuade Jon to marry her by any means available. Whether he loved her or not, he had a duty to their unborn child. She didn't think he would shrink from it.

She thought about Jon's background, and chewed her lip. Did she want a pirate for her baby's father—for her husband? A thieving, murdering brigand who would certainly hang if he were caught? Well, like it or not, he was the father of her child. And she loved him. She would marry him and take her chances on the rest.

Cathy got rather gingerly out of the big brass bed and began to dress. She would really have to see about getting a new wardrobe. Few of her clothes were suitable for the tropical heat. Then she thought about how her stomach would bulge in the coming months, and smiled. She would soon be needing a new wardrobe in any case.

Dressed, she wandered out of the house and down toward the smaller dwelling at the end of the garden where Petersham stayed. After the incident with Harry, it seemed that Jon was taking no more chances with her. He had ordered her not to go out of sight of the house without Petersham in atten-dance. The men on the island would keep their dis-tance as long as she was protected, but if some of the more unscrupulous characters were to come on her while she was alone, they might consider her fair game. Cathy obeyed Jon's instructions more from a desire for company than from fear for her own safety. The days were long and tedious without Jon, and Petersham was at least someone to talk to.

The valet was sitting on a chair outside the front entrance of the palm-thatched cottage, carving busily at a piece of wood. He smiled when he saw Cathy approaching, his faded eyes crinkling in appreciation of the lovely picture she made with her golden hair piled high on her head for coolness' sake and her simple white dress emphasizing her youthful sweetness. Master Jon was a lucky man, Petersham thought, had he but the sense to know it.

"You're late, miss," he grinned at her. "I thought you might have decided to sleep all day."

"Just most of it," Cathy twinkled in response, and waited while he carefully took the wood he was carving inside.

"Where to this morning, miss?" he asked, dusting his hands as he rejoined her in the garden. "Fancy another ride on one of them ponies?"

"Oh, no, I can't, thank you, Petersham," Cathy said hastily before she thought. She wanted to take no chances where her baby was concerned, but she didn't feel like explaining the facts of her condition to Petersham at the moment. Besides, she wanted Jon to be the first to know.

"You can't, eh?" Petersham said astutely, looking at her through narrowed eyes. Cathy, intent on one of the gorgeous parrots that were as plentiful here as sparrows in England, missed his words and tone. She surfaced to hear him say, "Well, how about the beach, then?"

She agreed smilingly to the beach. They crossed the garden and climbed down the cliff path onto the white sand. Cathy found a little outcropping of rock and sank down in its shade, resting her back against it comfortably while she watched the breaking of the waves. Petersham sat down beside her, his expression thoughtful. It wasn't like Miss Cathy to sit when she could be doing.

Cathy took off the leather sandals that Jon had fashioned for her out of one of his old jerkins and wriggled her toes in the warm sand. Petersham watched her, saying nothing. The merest germ of a suspicion was beginning to form in his mind.

"What was Jon like as a baby?" Cathy broke the silence to ask, her expression dreamy as she stared out to sea.

"About as mean-tempered and pig-headed as he is now, as I recollect," Petersham grinned. Cathy looked at him reproachfully.

"I'm serious," she insisted. Petersham chuckled.

"So am I, miss."

Cathy sent him an admonishing look and Petersham continued.

"Well, miss, he was a big baby as I remember, about ten pounds or so at birth. Mr. Hale was so excited about having a boy that we all thought he'd bust a gut. Passed out good Jamaica rum like it was water, even to the grooms—that's what I was, then, a groom. Then Miss Virginia—that was Master Jon's mother, a real fine lady, she was, too—up and died.

For a while there it looked like Mr. Hale might die too, of grief, or drink. But he didn't, though it might have been better for Master Jon if he had. After Miss Virginia's death Mr. Hale was a changed man. He was bitter, you see, and after a time we all saw that he blamed Master Jon for his mother's death. Mr. Hale got some women in to care for the boy, but none of them lasted long and Master Jon was sort of just passed around amongst the servants. His daddy wouldn't hardly even look at him. He was a real quiet, solemn little boy, miss."

"Poor little boy," Cathy said softly, picturing Jon unwanted and unloved. Then, to Petersham, "Go on, please."

"Well, Master Jon sort of had to grow up on his own, if you know what I mean. He was about ten when he started hangin' around the stables—no place else around there that he was welcome. Like most boys, he got into his fair share of trouble—just pranks mostly, nothing really bad. But Mr. Hale, he didn't see it like that. The only time he hardly noticed Master Jon was to wail the tar out of him for something he'd done wrong. Then one day Master Jon got big enough to fight back, and the whippings stopped. Things got a little better after that, because Mr. Hale found a pretty little girl he wanted to marry. Mr. Hale thought the sun rose and set with that woman, and Master Jon liked her too. Followed her around like a puppy-dog with its master, though she wouldn't hardly give him the time of day. Considered him a nuisance, I guess. Master Jon was sort of tall and gangly as a boy, nothing like as handsome as he is today." Petersham broke off to look at Cathy. "You want to be patient with Master Jon, miss. He didn't have nobody to love him growing up, and he's suffered because of it."

This last was said very earnestly. Cathy blinked away the moisture that was starting to form in her eyes. She would love Jon and her baby doubly hard to make up for everything Jon himself had missed as a child.

"And then he left?" Cathy asked softly. Petersham shot her a wary look.

"Master Jon told you about that?"

Cathy nodded wordlessly. Petersham shook his head.

"I didn't think he'd ever tell anyone about that. The only reason I know is because I found him throwing up his toenails afterwards, and when I threatened to get his daddy to bring a doctor to him he told me what had happened. I told him not to take it so hard, but I guess he did anyway. The next morning he was gone. Mr. Hale didn't much care for a couple of days, but after about a week the folks in town started asking after Master Jon. So Mr. Hale sent me out to see if I could find him and bring him back. Well, I found him all right—signed on board a brig called the 'Merciful' as a deckhand. Master Jon was set on going to sea, and said point-blank that he was never going back to Woodham again. Seeing as how I couldn't change his mind I went with him. I didn't blame him for not going back. The 'Merciful' wasn't much, but it was more than he'd had at home."

"Was Mr. Hale rich?"

"He had some money, but he was real stingy with it where Master Jon was concerned. Why, the stable-boys had better looking clothes than he did, and sometimes more to eat. Mr. Hale spent his money on cards and women. He even let the place go to ruin, last we heard."

"Has Jon ever been back?" Cathy asked slowly, her heart aching with pity. She had had so much as a child, love as well as material things, and Jon had had so little. She wished that he was here now, this second, so that she could make up for all that he had suffered.

"Never," Petersham said shortly. "And I doubt he'll ever go. He likes the life here. Suits him just right. Me, too."

Cathy was silent for a while, thinking over what Petersham had told her. It explained so much about Jon—his distrust of women, his toughness, his fierce possessiveness. Having had so little, he had become determined to take what he could, and keep it.

"And—and how did he become a pirate?" Cathy asked finally.

Petersham took up the tale again.

"Well, working on the 'Merciful,' Master Jon saved enough to go partners with this other fellow in a lugger. We sailed it up and down the coast of North America, taking as cargo anything we could get. Master Jon was captain on this one voyage, and

258

our cargo was guns. Somehow some pirates must've got word about what we was carrying, because they attacked. Naturally, not being trained in fighting and the lugger having only one gun, we lost. Anyone who refused to join up with 'em was killed on the spot. Master Jon's no fool, no more am I, so we signed where they told us and took up pirating. Master Jon had a real talent for it, and liked it, so we stayed on. No reason not to. It's a good life, and we have more now than we ever did."

Cathy digested the story for some time in silence, then turned to smile mistily at Petersham.

"Thank you for telling me," she said softly. Petersham nodded a wordless acknowledgment of her thanks, suddenly embarrassed by his own garrulity. They sat silently watching the waves. It was Petersham who spoke at last.

"You have something to tell Master Jon, Miss Cathy?"

The question out of the blue caught Cathy by surprise. She flashed Petersham a quick look, then felt burning color begin to creep up her neck and over her face.

"W—what do you mean?" she faltered unconsciously.

Petersham grinned. "You can't hide it from me, miss. I've seen too many female creatures when they're breeding. They get a look about them . . . like you have."

Cathy felt herself flush even more painfully. The idea of having Jon's baby was still new to her. Even though she was happy about it, she was conscious of a deep-seated shyness. A child was such an intimate thing to be having—and it was undisputable evidence of the use Jon had for her.

"I—I . . ." she stammered, then said more calmly, "You're right, of course, Petersham."

"I knew it," the man said with satisfaction. "Master Jon'll be as thrilled as a dog with two tails. It'll be the best thing in the world for him."

"Why do you say that?" Cathy asked with genuine curiosity. Her embarrassment was fading. After all, having a man's child was the most natural thing in the world—except that she wasn't married to the man in question. Like it or not, that did make a difference.

"He's always needed someone to love—and to love him. Now he'll have his child—and you."

"What makes you think he wants us, Petersham?" Cathy's voice was suddenly wistful.

"Miss Cathy, the way he feels about you is as plain as the nose on your face. Master Jon may not know it himself yet, but he needs you. You're good for him. He's been happier this last month or so than I've ever seen him. When he hears about the baby, he'll go over the moon. And he'll do the decent thing by you. You wait and see."

"I hope you're right, Petersham," Cathy sighed, dropping her reserve altogether.

"I am, miss. You can rest easy about that."

Cathy smiled at him, feeling like she had found a staunch ally. He smiled back. They lapsed into silence again, staring pensively out to sea. After a few minutes Cathy put her hand up to shade her eyes, squinting into the horizon.

"Petersham, is that a ship?" she asked excitedly. Petersham looked in the direction she indicated.

"I think so, miss."

"Is it the 'Margarita,' do you think?" Cathy was beginning to feel a little nervous at the idea of breaking her news to Jon.

"It might be, miss. There's a spy-glass up at the house. If you'll wait here I'll go get it. Then we'll know for sure."

"Oh, would you, Petersham? If it's Jon, I'd like to have a little warning. I—I have things to do."

"Get yourself all gussied up, eh, miss?" Petersham grinned. "Well, that's females, lord love 'em. You just sit here and I'll run up and take a look."

"Thank you, Petersham," Cathy said, blushing faintly at the valet's perception. She leaned contentedly back against the rock as he strode away across the sand. She was almost looking forward to telling Jon, with Petersham's words to buoy her. Still she couldn't help wondering how he would react. What would he say? More important, what would she say? How did you tell a man that you were going to have his baby? Especially when the man wasn't your husband, and might not be delighted at the news?

"Miss Cathy! Miss Cathy!" Petersham came huffing back toward her. "Miss Cathy!"

Something indefinable in Petersham's voice alarmed her. She got to her feet, shaking the sand

261

from her dress and slipping into her flimsy sandals.

"What is it, Petersham?" she asked sharply.

"It's not the 'Margarita,' Miss," he panted, coming up to her. "There are about eight ships out there, and they're headed this way fast. They were too far away for me to make out exactly what flag they were flying, but they mean business. They've got their big guns trained on the island!"

Cathy stared at him, aghast.

"What can we do?"

Petersham grabbed her arm, pulling her back along the beach with him.

"For a start, we can get off the beach. We're easy targets here, miss, if they start shooting."

Cathy half ran, half stumbled over the soft sand, then scrambled awkwardly up the cliff with Petersham keeping close behind her. With all her heart she longed for Jon—Jon would keep her, would keep all of them, safe. If the island was actually attacked, she might never see him again. He would come back to find her dead, or vanished—and he would never know about the baby. Suddenly that thought hurt most of all.

As if her prayers had conjured him up, he was anxiously striding through the front room when she and Petersham burst into the house. He was dripping wet, and furiously angry. Cathy uttered a glad little cry, and flew into his arms. They closed tightly around her, holding her against his hard body as if he would never let her go even while he bellowed curses at her.

"Jon! Oh, Jon!"

"Where the hell have you been?" he yelled into her hair, rocking her against him like a small child. "I've been going out of my mind! Didn't you see those ships out there?"

"Oh, yes, I did! I'm so glad you're here!"

"How did you get here, Cap'n? From what I could see, they've surrounded the whole damned island, begging your pardon, miss!"

"All except the southeast corner—they must think the reef makes it impassable. The 'Margarita's' hovering there, about a mile out. I swam through. The opening's not big enough for even one of the 'Margarita's' gigs, but I think a smaller boat could make it."

"Oh, Jon, are they going to attack us? Why?" She tilted her head back to stare up into his bronzed face. His teeth flashed suddenly in a savage grin.

"We're pirates, my love, or had you forgotten? We do get attacked from time to time. One of the less pleasant aspects of the business."

"Master Jon—will we fight?"

"Hell, yes, we'll fight—we have to. There's no way off this damned island now except through the reef, and not many can make it through there. There won't be time."

Jon looked down at Cathy, who was watching him anxiously, pressed a brief, hard kiss on her trembling mouth, and set her away from him. His voice turned crisp and authoritative.

"Petersham, I want you to take Miss Cathy to the

place where I came through and wait. If there's need, I'll either come myself or send someone to get you through the reef. The 'Margarita's' under orders not to move from that spot without you, so you don't have to worry."

"But, Jon, if you come now, too, we can all get away," Cathy protested, trembling. "You can't mean to fight so many ships. You'll be slaughtered if you try."

"Since when did you become a military expert, my love?" he forced a teasing note. "You just do as I tell you, and everything will be fine."

"Don't treat me like a dim-witted child, Jon Hale!" Cathy flared, glaring at him. "If you seriously expected everything to be fine, you wouldn't have the 'Margarita' waiting offshore to get me away. Not to mention taking the chance of swimming through a coral reef! Well, I'm not going, do you hear? I'm staying with you!"

"Don't be childish, Cathy," he chided in a bored tone. "The best thing you can do is stay out of the way. Good God, what kind of fight do you think I could put up, constantly worried about where you were and what was happening to you? Now, there's no time to argue. Go with Petersham, he'll look after you 'til I can."

"He's right, miss. You'd only get in the way," Petersham put in quietly. Cathy ignored him, her eyes searching Jon's lean face. Suddenly he smiled, his eyes warm on hers.

"Please?" he asked. Those silvery gray eyes and

that twisted grin were her undoing.

"All right," she said grudgingly, defeated. "But be careful, will you? For my sake?"

The words had a special meaning now, though he didn't know it. He had to be careful for their baby, too.

"For your sake," he answered, as if making a solemn oath, then gave her a little shove toward the bedroom. "Go get your warmest cloak, you may need it. It gets cold on the water at night."

Cathy did as she was told. As always, he was getting his own way. When had he ever not, with her? As she came back into the room, her cloak over her arm, she heard Jon say, ". . . see that she gets back to her father."

"Cap'n, there's something you ought to know . . ." Petersham began, only to break off as he saw Cathy standing in the arched doorway, eyes wide as the import of Jon's words sank in.

Jon turned slowly to face her, the set bleakness of his face, which he quickly tried to disguise, echoing the fear in her own heart. Tears started in her eyes and threatened to overflow as she ran to fling her arms around his neck, hugging him tightly.

"Jon, you must come with us," she whispered frantically into his ear. "I'm going to have your baby. You have to come!"

There was a moment of astounded silence. Jon's long body stiffened in her arms as if he'd been poleaxed. Petersham turned discreetly away.

"Oh, my God, no," Jon muttered at last in a

queer, strangled voice. "Are you sure?"

Cathy pushed away from him to look up into his face. He looked horrified.

"You're sorry, aren't you?" she cried tormentedly. "You didn't want anything as permanent as a child, did you? Well, you should have thought of that before you raped me!"

"Oh, Cathy, no, of course it's not that I don't want it! I . . ."

The unmistakable boom of a cannon cut him off.

"Christ, there's no time to talk about it now! Petersham, get her out of here!"

With a frustrated groan Jon's mouth covered hers in a hard, passionate kiss, his lips bruising hers with their intensity, and then he was pushing her away from him, giving her to Petersham as he turned to stride from the house. In seconds he was gone, and Petersham was urging her through the French windows and across the garden.

The distant booming of cannon could be heard as they made their way across the small island. Spirals of smoke began to float toward the sky with increasing frequency as the guns found their mark. An acrid, burning odor filled the air.

The stench of fire and destruction made a chilling contrast to the languid beauty of the countryside they were hurrying through. Parrots squawked in the palms and hummingbirds flitted from bush to bush, lunching on the lush tropical fruits and berries. The crimson of the bougainvillea blossoms blended with the pink and white hydrangeas to form

266

rolling banks of exotic color. After a twenty-0minute walk they reached the sea, sparkling like an endless silver carpet before them.

Petersham urged her down into the lee of a clump of small palms, and Cathy dropped to the soft ground. She huddled with her arms around her knees, her back resting against one of the trees. Petersham eyed her with some concern as she stared silently out to sea.

"He doesn't want the baby, Petersham," she said, finally. Petersham squatted down beside her, catching her small cold hand and chafing it briskly.

"Miss Cathy, Master Jon was upset. When all this fuss has passed, and he's back to normal, he'll change his tune, you'll see."

Cathy stared up at him blindly. "When all this fuss is over. . . . if Jon's even alive. Oh, God, life is such a mess!"

The thought that Jon might even now be dead or dying mixed with the horrible realization that their child was nothing more than an unwanted responsibility to him. Her lips trembled, and she bit down hard on her lower one, willing back tears. Her arms wrapped protectively about her midriff as she fought for control. Petersham could only sit beside her, aware of her pain but unable to do anything to alleviate it. From time to time he patted her drooping shoulder.

Cathy watched the breaking waves blankly, her mind in a turmoil. The one thought that consistently came through was that, more than anything, she was concerned for Jon's safety. If he came through this battle in one piece, she would ask nothing else of God!

Petersham's voice broke through her reverie, and Cathy looked up to find that he was leaning over her anxiously.

"Miss Cathy, someone's coming. We must move."

Cathy was suddenly fully alert. She got quickly to her feet, following Petersham in a crouching run until they were out of sight of the cliff. From their new position they couldn't see who was approaching, nor, however, could they be seen themselves. In the present situation, it was better to be safe than sorry.

"Cathy! Cathy!" A man's voice rang out from the overhang above them. Cathy and Petersham looked at each other, then scrambled out from their hiding place.

"Harry?" Cathy called disbelievingly. The man strode into view, and, sure enough, it was Harry. Cathy felt a cold little hand of fear clutch at her heart. Jon had said he would come himself if he could. Why hadn't he? Had something happened to him . . . or did he no longer want to be with her now that he knew about the baby?

Petersham drew closer to Cathy's side as Harry came toward them down the cliff. When at last he was near, the valet asked challengingly, "What are you doing here?"

Only then did Cathy remember the contretemps between Harry and Jon. Petersham was right to be wary, she thought. Jon wouldn't send Harry of all men to get them through . . . unless he no longer cared whether or not Harry wanted her.

Harry came right up to them, stopping directly in front of Cathy. She could see the marks of powder burns on his face and hands.

"Jon sent me," he said shortly to Petersham. Cathy felt the last little ray of hope die. If Jon had sent him, then it must mean that he himself no longer had any use for her now that he knew she was with child.

"Now that I find hard to believe." Petersham's hand closed over Cathy's arm protectively. Harry looked at him impatiently.

"Oh, for God's sake, Petersham, do you think I'm going to rape her now that she's pregnant? I know when I'm beaten, and Jon knew that I would feel that way when he told me."

"Jon—told you?" Cathy asked, slowly. If Harry knew, then Jon must have sent him. Besides herself and Petersham, Jon was the only other person she had told.

"Is he all right?" Cathy breathed.

"He was when last I saw him," Harry said, his eyes strangely hard. "He may not be now. You see, he was holed up with myself and three other men in one of those thatched cottages. The soldiers were getting ready to set it afire when I sneaked out. This uniform, you see."

Cathy stared blankly at the British navy uniform, singed and ripped in places, that Harry was wearing. He had worn it when she had first seen him on the "Anna Greer," she remembered. But what did that have to do . . . ?

"Soldiers?" Petersham was quicker on the uptake than Cathy. Harry smiled mirthlessly.

"Did I forget to tell you?" he said softy. "The ships were filled with soldiers—British soldiers. I assume they've come in your honor, Lady Catherine. After all, as you once told me, your father is a very rich man."

"Oh, my God, they'll hang him!" Cathy whispered, horrified. Already her mind was filled with visions of Jon being summarily executed. British soldiers were both quick and efficient, she knew.

"If he doesn't burn to death, I imagine that's what they have in mind," Harry agreed.

"I must go to him!" Cathy cried. Harry looked at her with the faintest glimmer of respect.

"I thought you'd feel that way," he said. "And I agree with you. You're the only chance he has. But going into that town could be dangerous. Those men are drunk with blood, and they're not liable to take time to ask your name before they string you up for a pirate lass!"

"I believe I can handle British soldiers, Harry," Cathy replied with unconscious hauteur. For almost the first time Petersham and Harry saw her assume the mantle of her rank, and were, in their different ways, impressed.

"Maybe you can, at that," Harry admitted.

"We can't waste time talking." Cathy was determinedly moving toward the cliff as she spoke. Harry and Petersham exchanged a quick glance, then fell in behind her. She looked back at them in surprise.

"What are you two doing? You can't come with me. They'll hang you!"

"And do you suppose either of us could ever face Jon again if we let you go alone?" Harry snorted derisively. "That's supposing we get there in time to keep them from hanging him!"

At this unnecessary reminder Cathy picked up the pace, almost running over the rough ground. A hand on her arm slowed her.

"Remember the baby, Miss Cathy," Petersham warned her, casting a concerned look at her flushed face.

"I'm not made of porcelain, Petersham!" Cathy snapped. "And if we don't hurry, it may be too late! Now come on!"

It was not far to the town, but to Cathy it seemed to take hours to cover the short distance. She rushed by the remains of Jon's house without giving it more than a glance. A cannon ball had apparently crashed through the roof, and the structure had caught fire. Nothing was left but a burned-out shell. But what did a house matter, she thought, compared to Jon? All she could think of was Jon hanging, his long body twisting and turning at the end of a rope, his handsome face blue and swollen. It didn't even occur to her that she had once longed to see him meet that exact fate. She loved him now, and she felt that if he died, so would she.

A pall of thick, black smoke hung over the cluster of once sturdy huts that marked the mouth of the harbor. Not one of them was left standing. Debris was everywhere, as though a giant hand had snatched up this side of the island, shaken it, and then flung it down again. Bodies of men, pirates and natives, lay where they had fallen. On one of the huge ships anchored in the bay Cathy could see more bodies dangling by their necks from spars. Oh, God, they had started the hangings! Was Jon even now choking at the end of a rope, his body twirled by the brisk wind in the movements of a macabre dance?

Harry and Petersham came up on either side of her to take her arms, both looking down at her worriedly. The complete absence of gunfire told its own story.

"The battle is over, Cathy," Harry said gently. "You'd do better to come away. You don't want to see Jon dead, do you? The shock might harm the baby. We'll look for him, and if there's need we'll fetch you."

"No!" Cathy exclaimed fiercely, snatching her arms free. "He's not dead, I know he's not!"

She ran toward the harbor, picking up her skirts and moving faster than she had ever moved before in her life. Harry and Petersham panted along behind her, muttering curses at her stubbornness. Both of them felt it was too late to save Jon, and in her heart Cathy was afraid that they might be right. He would have fought like a demon to keep from being captured, and if she were honest with herself she would have to admit that he was very likely one of those who had been killed in the battle before the hangings started. But if not, if there were even one chance, she was going to do her best. She didn't even know if she could stop the hanging if she got there in time, she reminded herself. A seasoned soldier might think twice before halting an execution on the say-so of a mere girl, no matter who she was. No matter, she had to try.

A troop of British soldiers stood on guard at the mouth of the harbor, obviously stationed to prevent any surviving pirates from escaping. As Cathy rushed toward them they drew their muskets, pointing them at her in a body.

"Halt!" cried the officer in charge, warningly, as he strode out in front of his men. Seeing Cathy's sex, he hesitated to give the order to fire.

"Don't shoot, you fools!" Cathy cried, not slowing until she was level with the officer. Her face was flushed and her breath was labored, but drawing herself up to her full height she still managed to look a lady. The officer stared at her, perplexed.

"I am Lady Catherine Aldley," Cathy spoke to the officer quickly but imperiously. "And I require to be taken out to the ship where they are hanging the pirates. At once, if you please!"

The officer looked her over suspiciously, then glanced behind her to run even more guarded eyes over Harry and Petersham, who had approached rather warily. Cathy knew that the only thing that was saving the two men from being seized out of hand was Harry's uniform. She turned to them quickly, holding out her hand.

"Thank you, gentlemen, very much for providing me with an escort," she said rapidly, catching first Harry's hand, then Petersham's. "I'm sure you must be anxious to get back to your duties. Don't let me detain you any longer."

The two men stared at her, then catching the warning in her eyes solemnly shook her hand and started to turn away. They had done all they could for both Cathy and Jon, and now knew that they must think of their own skins.

"Wait!" the young officer ordered suspiciously as the two men started back up the cliff. Harry and Petersham stopped, but before anything else was said Cathy whirled on the man.

"Lieutenant, I said that I require you to escort me to that ship immediately! I do not have time to waste while you bandy words with these men!"

The lieutenant stared down at her, undecided. He had no way of knowing if she was who she claimed to be, but he did remember hearing that a Lady Catherine something was either dead or captive at the hands of these pirates. If she were the lady in question, it behooved him to obey her commands. Apparently she had some powerful friends at Court.

"Immediately, Lieutenant!" Cathy's words cracked like a whip, and the officer visibly started.

"Yes, my lady!" he stammered, and turning back to his men ordered them to prepare a boat for her ladyship and look sharp about it! In the confusion,

Harry and Petersham were able to escape unnoticed.

When the boat was ready the lieutenant handed her into it reverently. Cathy almost gnashed her teeth at his pomposity. Even now Jon might be being hanged!

"Please hurry!" she exhorted the rowers, standing in the prow of the small boat while it skimmed through the white-capped waves toward the huge frigates. When they at last reached the ship where the hangings were taking place, Cathy directed them to pull up beneath the ladder snaking down the ship's side while she caught it. Once her hands and feet were firmly positioned on the ropes, she was up it like a monkey. Fear for Jon's safety made her impervious to fear for her own. As she reached the top, eager hands reached down to haul her the rest of the way aboard. She was set on her feet on the deck, barely conscious of the interest in the dozens of pairs of masculine eyes turned her way.

"And what might your business be on the 'Lady Chester,' miss?" a gruff voice demanded roughly.

"I demand to see the captain of this vessel at once!" Cathy said sharply, fear dogging her throat as she saw the limp bodies of men who had already been executed and were now stacked in neat rows against the "Lady Chester's" rail. A funeral service would be read over them after the last of the hangings, and then their bodies would be consigned forever to the sea. Cathy was just able to restrain herself from rushing over to the corpses and examining every face. After all, if Jon were among them she could not help him now, and if he wasn't speed was of the essence!

"Oh, you do, miss?" the voice sounded amused, and Cathy turned her most ferocious glare on its owner.

"Yes, my good man, I do! I am Lady Catherine Aldley, and these brigands have been holding me captive! I believe you will find that your captain knows very well who I am, and will be most sorry to learn that I was not immediately conducted to him!"

Under her freezing look the stocky, grizzled bosun's mate visibly wilted.

"Yes, ma'am!" he responded smartly. "If you'll come this way, ma'am!"

Head high, back ramrod straight, Cathy sailed after him through the crowd of sailors who had been detailed to watch the hangings. Halfway across the deck a cannon roared, so close that Cathy felt deafened by the noise.

"What was that in aid of?" she snapped, hurrying her pace so that she was beside her perspiring escort.

"It's a signal to the guards to bring out the next batch of prisoners for hanging. We can do five at a time, my lady!"

The pride in the man's voice sickened Cathy. She had come to know and like men like those being hanged, and had discovered that, despite their unsavory occupation, they were really no different from men anywhere. Suddenly she was devoutly thankful that the "Margarita's" crew were safely away. They had become her friends, and it would have pained her to watch them die.

She turned sharply at the sound of marching feet behind her to see a score of sailors bringing the condemned men to the makeshift gallows. The prisoners were blocked from her view by their uniformed guards, but some sixth sense froze her in place. An instant later she was thanking God that she had stopped. On a rickety platform, hastily erected beneath an overhanging spar, hands tied roughly behind them and blindfolds covering their eyes, stood the five parties who were soon to be hanged. Third from the left was Jon. And a black-hooded executioner was placing a noose around his brown neck.

Eleven

"Stop!" Cathy wanted to scream, but the words wouldn't come. She could only open and shut her mouth soundlessly, like a fish out of water, her throat closed up with pure terror. Her limbs seemed frozen to the deck, refusing to carry her across to where Jon stood with that horrible rope around his neck. Oh, God, this was worse than any nightmare! They were just moments away from hanging him, and she could neither speak nor move!

A hand caught at her arm, squeezing familiarly, and Cathy suddenly recovered the use of her limbs and whirled viciously on her assailant. The vituperations quivering on the tip of her tongue died a quick death as she stared up into the grim, tired, but suddenly vastly relieved face of her father.

"Cathy!" He made the words sound like a prayer. "Cathy, child, I thought you were dead. . . ."

"Papa!" Cathy cried on a note of thanksgiving. "Oh, papa, thank God! You have to stop them from hanging that man!" She pointed to Jon. The sailors about them turned at her desperate plea, their faces curious. Cathy didn't care. She was beyond feeling embarrassed, or thinking of the proprieties. Jon was the only matter worth considering.

When her father just stared at the blindfolded man, making no move to go to his rescue, Cathy shook his arm frantically.

"Papa, hurry! Oh, God, please hurry!"

"Is that the man who abducted you?" Sir Thomas asked viciously, his eyes never leaving the man on the gallows.

"Yes! Papa, stop them!"

"Let them hang him! Hanging's too good for the dog! I'd like to draw and quarter him! I want him to suffer as he's made you suffer! Bloody bastard!" Sir Thomas flashed a hateful look to where Jon stood, too far away to hear Cathy, pale and quiet as he nodded in answer to the earnest questions of a priest. As Cathy and her father watched, one horrified and the other gloating, the priest made a sign of the cross over him and moved on to the next man, where he started to repeat the ritual.

"Papa, you have to stop them! He's the father of my child!"

278

"What?" Sir Thomas cried, his voice cracking with pain and outrage.

"I'm going to have his baby! Oh, papa, I don't want my baby's father to hang! Please stop them! Hurry!"

Sir Thomas stared at Cathy for a full minute while she thought she would go mad. The priest granted absolution to the last of the five and stepped back. The drum roll that preceded all executions began.

"Papa, please!" Cathy begged urgently, clutching at her father's arm. It was too late now for her to appeal to the captain of the "Lady Chester." If her father would not relent, what was there left to do?

Sir Thomas's eyes moved from her pleading face to the man on the gallows and back again, his lips compressed in a straight line.

"Papa. . . . !"

"Halt!" His deep, authoritative voice rang out. "I want that man, third from the left, brought to me for questioning! Cut him down!"

The executioner hesitated with his hand just above the lever that would send the five men swinging into eternity, and looked to the officer in charge for confirmation of the brusque order. The officer identified Sir Thomas with a glance, then nodded curtly at the black-hooded man. With a shrug that clearly renounced all responsibility for what he was about to do, the executioner lifted the noose from Jon's neck. Cathy felt a lump rise in her throat as she saw the broad shoulders, which had been held rigidly erect in anticipation of the coming ordeal, slump a little. Two of the armed sailors dragged Jon down from the makeshift gallows and led him roughly away, still bound and blindfolded. Cathy turned to Sir Thomas anxiously.

"Where are they taking him?"

"To the brig, I imagine, until I send for him. He'll be quite safe." The bitter mockery in her father's voice made Cathy wince.

"Papa, I can explain . . ." she faltered uncertainly, wanting to ease the hurt anger in his eyes. He grimaced, catching her arm.

"I'm sure you can, daughter, but I think you had better do it in private. We seem to have attracted quite an audience as it is."

He glanced scathingly around at the grinning crowd of men who were listening unabashedly to their exchange. Cathy saw the lecherous looks being cast over her, and realized, sickeningly, that by her own words she had branded herself whore. An unmarried woman who was with child, no matter what the circumstances were, could be nothing else according to the morals of the time. She held her head high as she moved with her father to the stairway that led below, but could not control the crimson flood that rose to stain her cheeks. Behind her the execution went on. She flinched at a hoarse scream that resounded across the deck; it was followed by the sharp cracking sound of necks snapping. Cathy shuddered, her hand tightening convulsively on her father's arm, bile rising in her throat and threatening to choke her. Despite the irretrievable ruin of her reputation, she could not repine over what she had done. Better for her to be spat upon forever than for Jon to lose his life. But the shame wasn't hers alone to bear. There was her father. . . .

"Papa . . ." she began in a small voice.

"Hush," he bade her gently, pushing her before him down the stairwell. "You can tell me all about it when we're in my cabin."

Sir Thomas, as an extremely rich and influential man, had been given the best cabin on the ship. As he allowed Cathy to precede him inside she was taken aback a little at its luxury. Compared to Jon's neat but spartan accommodation on the "Margarita," this cabin was positively opulent, almost embarrassingly so. Her eyes flickered as she considered what Jon's reaction would be to such elaborate comfort. He would sneer, she knew, at the plush carpet and velvet drapes, the fine furniture and crystal ornaments, just as he had once sneered at her expensive clothes. Cathy looked at the ornate room with his eyes, and felt faintly uncomfortable.

"Now, child, I want you to tell me everything that happened," her father directed, his eyes grim as he directed her into a chair and took the one opposite her.

Cathy swallowed, blushed, and obeyed to the best of her ability, leaving out only the most intimate parts of her relationship with Jon. She emphasized that he had been kind to her, seeing that she was adequately fed and sheltered and protected from all harm. Describing how he had risked his life to save hers in Cadiz, her eyes glowed lovingly, although she was unaware of it. Sir Thomas, however, took full note of her expression, and his own eyes narrowed. She told about Jon's terrible wounding, and how she had nursed him, and her fathers eyes narrowed even more. Cathy became suddenly aware of his quietly rising anger, and broke off. He was silent for a long moment, staring blankly at the opposite wall. She fidgeted finally, and he looked at her.

"Are you sure—that you're with child, I mean?" Sir Thomas asked in a carefully neutral voice.

Cathy felt the hot, betraying color flood her cheeks again. In her present condition, she could be nothing but a liability to the father who had always been so proud of her. Sir Thomas Aldley's daughter with child by a pirate. . . . Cathy could almost hear the malicious talk. It would destroy her father as well as herself.

"Yes, Papa. I'm sure," she managed, not quite able to meet his eyes.

Sir Thomas saw her shame and his heart quickened with protective love for her. She was, after all, his daughter, and what had happened to her was not her fault. Fierce hatred rose in him for the man who had been vicious enough to visit such degradation on a seventeen-year-old virgin, a well brought up young lady. He thought of his own role in saving that man from a well-deserved death, and his eyes glittered. But he had just granted the pirate a temporary reprieve, he promised himself. For now, his daughter's happiness and good name had to be his first concern. But later. . . .

"My child, you have no reason to look so distressed," Sir Thomas said soothingly, catching her small hand in his and patting it. "Your condition came about through no fault of yours, I know. The child you carry was conceived through a brutal act for which you cannot be held accountable. We must now take steps to safeguard your reputation. It was unfortunate that you had to blurt out the news within hearing of every sailor on the ship, but I believe that we can remedy that mistake. Now, Cathy. . . ."

Cathy was feeling a resurgence of nausea. Plainly, in glossing over the intimate details of her association with Jon she had misled her father. For Jon's sake, he had to know the truth, no matter how much it might pain him.

"Papa," she ventured hesitantly, her eyes on their clasped hands. "Papa, it wasn't rape, you know."

"What did you say?" Sir Thomas exploded after a stunned instant.

"Jon—Jon didn't really have to force me, Papa," Cathy whispered, feeling more humiliated than she had before in her life. "I—I was willing."

"My God, do you know what you're saying?" Sir Thomas leaped to his feet in agitation, glaring angrily down at his daughter. Cathy looked up at him, going almost as white as her dress.

"Yes, Papa." Her voice was low, but her eyes met his steadily. Sir Thomas's florid face got even redder. Cathy bit her lower lip, but refused to drop her eyes.

"The bloody bastard!" Sir Thomas breathed finally. "I'm glad I stopped them from hanging him!

He's going to pay . . ."

The ugly light in her father's normally placid blue eyes alarmed Cathy. She stood up too, then swayed as a spasm of giddiness hit her. Sir Thomas reached out a hand to catch her, and Cathy clung to him, her eyes wide and frightened.

"Papa, I love him."

She looked like death, and Sir Thomas couldn't bring himself to berate her further. Even if the bastard hadn't actually forced her, he thought furiously, an experienced man would have little trouble seducing an innocent young girl. What he had done was no better than rape. Cathy must be made to see that. She couldn't be allowed to continue thinking that she was actually in love with such a man!

"Daughter, this man is considerably older than you, is he not?" he began gently. He realized that condemning her affection for the pirate out-of-hand would only serve to alienate her.

"He's thirty-four," Cathy replied faintly, sinking back down into her chair. Her father's sudden volte-face surprised her. She had expected him to rave for hours.

"I thought so." Sir Thomas sounded as if his gravest fears had been confirmed. "Have you reason to suppose that he loves you?"

"Well. . . ."

"Has he ever said so?" Sir Thomas pursued. A keen glance at Cathy's flushing face told him that he was on the right tack.

"N—no," she had to admit. Her eyes dropped to

study the rich red carpet, against which her sandal-shod feet looked totally out of place.

"I thought not," Sir Thomas sighed heavily and resumed his seat, once more taking Cathy's hand. "My child, a man of thirty-four, especially an un-principled brigand, will have known scores of women in the biblical sense. Any feelings you may have aroused in him were no novelty to him, believe me. But you, on the other hand, totally innocent, sheltered from men, you mistook your very natural physical awakening for love. It's normal for a young girl to imagine a deathless romance with the first man who makes her a woman. Haven't you noticed yourself that many young ladies who despise their husbands before marriage soon grow attached to them? Why do you suppose that is, daughter?"

Cathy thought. What her father said was true. She had known girls who had wept at the idea of marriage only to appear later to be perfectly resigned to their fates, and even fond of their husbands. But. . . .

"It's not like that, Papa," she said determinedly. "I really love Jon. He's handsome and strong, and he can be very gentle and sweet. . . ."

Her father gave a rueful bark of laughter.

"Of course he's been gentle and sweet with you, my poor child. Pleasure for a man is much en-hanced by a willing partner. I know. I myself have used that technique on a female to ensure her com-pliance with my wishes. And the sweet young things have all supposed me to be madly in love with them, while in actual fact it was no such thing. A man

285

doesn't dishonor a woman he loves, and a woman would be well advised to use the degree of respect a man accords her as a gauge of his true feelings."

Sir Thomas was satisfied with the effect of this speech. Cathy appeared to be struck, and if he could have somehow known her thoughts he would have been happier yet. It's true, she was thinking. Jon did prefer me when I was willing. Was his tenderness just a ruse to get me to accept his lovemaking? She could only judge by the depth of her emotions for him, but her father's words had opened even her own feelings to suspicion. Was what she felt for Jon really love, or was it the natural reaction of a young female to a handsome male? How could she be sure?

Seeing that he had given her food for thought, Sir Thomas wisely said no more on the subject. Instead, he turned his attention to an even weightier problem.

"Cathy," he said at last, startling her out of the maze she was lost in. "We must get you wed, child. As I see it, that's the only thing that will serve to restore your reputation."

Cathy looked up at him enquiringly, her blue eyes, so like his own, misty with thought. It was a moment before she answered.

"Wed, Papa?" she repeated stupidly.

"Yes, daughter. I have in mind a young lieutenant of good family who is presently stationed aboard the 'Lady Chester.' He's just three years older than you, a handsome, gentlemanly lad. Of course, it's nothing like the marriage you could have made, but under the circumstances any marriage at all is better than none. As it is, I am convinced that I can induce this young man to claim fathership of the child. His family is rather low on funds just at present, you see."

Cathy stared at him, the color slowly draining from her lips. Her hands clenched into tight fists in her lap.

"You propose to buy me a husband, Papa?" she asked tightly. Sir Thomas met her rapidly cooling gaze calmly.

"My dear, we have little choice. Not many men will take you without some inducement. Be realistic, daughter. Not only for your own sake, but for mine, and even for the child you carry. If any of us are to ever hold up our heads again, you must have a husband."

Cathy thought deeply. What her father said was true, and was indeed no more than she had told herself earlier. Did she want to bear a bastard child, to watch it suffer the stigma of illegitimacy? Did she herself want to face scorn and ridicule for the rest of her life, to be barred from polite society? No, she didn't. And marriage seemed to be the only way to prevent it.

"I agree with you, Papa," she said clearly. Sir Thomas regarded her with some surprise. He had expected an argument, not this level acceptance.

"Excellent!" His bluff features relaxed into a smile. "I'll make arrangements at once. The sooner you are wed, the sooner the talk will die."

"I have just one condition, Papa."

Sir Thomas looked at her fondly. "What is it, daughter?"

"I want my husband to be of my choosing."

Sir Thomas spluttered. "But, my dear, there is no time for you to meet eligible young men. We must act quickly if we are to act at all. If we wait, we will no longer be able to claim the child as premature when it comes."

"The man I have in mind will take no time to find, Papa."

Cathy's meaning crept up on Sir Thomas like a bush fighter on an unsuspecting enemy regular. His eyes narrowed at her.

"I presume that you're referring to the pirate?"

"His name is Jon, Papa. And yes, I'm referring to him."

"But, daughter, I have already explained to you that what this man feels for you is nothing like love. And you will soon come to realize that you don't love him, either. There's no reason for you to compound your mistake by marrying the fellow."

"There's a very good reason, Papa. I'm carrying his child." Cathy's blue eyes met her father's calmly.

Sir Thomas sighed. When he spoke, his voice had hardened.

"Cathy, you must understand that I will not permit you to marry this man. Why, he is a murderer, a criminal! You would be ashamed of him as soon as you came to your senses, and would reproach me for permitting such a thing to befall you! Good God, what do you propose to do with him after the ceremony? Take him back to London, and introduce him around the Court? We would be laughed out of England!"

Cathy's chin set in the mulish lines he knew and dreaded. Blast her stubbornness!

"Papa, if I don't marry Jon I won't marry anyone." The very coldness of her voice was horribly convincing. Still, Sir Thomas tried. He glowered at his daughter, his face suffusing with the angry color that used to alarm her into compliance.

"By damn, girl, you can't defy me! I am your father, and it is my responsibility to arrange your future. You will wed whom I name!"

"I am very sorry to disoblige you, Papa, but I will marry Jon, or I won't marry at all!"

Two sets of almost identical blue eyes warred with each other, both refusing to give ground.

"And what happens after the ceremony, if I were foolish enough to permit such a thing? You realize that your pirate is still under sentence of death, don't you? It is unlikely that he will escape the gallows forever. His kind rarely do."

"I know how much influence you have at Court, Papa. You could easily arrange a pardon, if you so desired."

While Cathy was talking, Sir Thomas's thoughts raced on ahead. Now that he considered it, perhaps there was something to be said for her scheme. He had never liked the idea of his daughter being forced to throw herself away on some young puppy with neither money nor influence to recommend him. If he could somehow restore her good name without saddling her with a husband, at least not on a permanent basis, then something still might be salvaged from this shambles. Say, if she were to become a widow. . . . Sir Thomas smiled inwardly. He had hit on the very solution. Cathy would be permitted to marry her pirate, and then steps would be taken to assure that the fellow was gotten out of the way. Not that he himself would ever stoop to murder, Sir Thomas thought cunningly. There would be no need. If the pirate were to be turned over to the Queen's justice, his end would be swift and sure—and perfectly legal. And Cathy would be free to choose another husband more in keeping with her own high rank. There were only two problems that he could foresee: the polite world must not know that Cathy's dead husband was a pirate, and Cathy herself must not be apprised of the man's fate until her infatuation for him had run its course. But there were ways to make sure of such things. . . .

"What did you say, daughter?" Sir Thomas smiled at Cathy genially. Cathy was taken aback by the constant shifts in her father's mood, but persevered with what she was saying.

"You could arrange a pardon for Jon, Papa."

Sir Thomas nodded slowly, his lips pursing as if he was thinking the matter over. "Yes, I suppose I could."

"I won't marry anyone else, Papa." Cathy's eyes challenged him. Sir Thomas sighed.

"And is that your last word, my dear?"

"Yes, Papa. That is my last word."

"I see that you leave me no choice." Sir Thomas relented grudgingly. "But mind you don't reproach me later! This is entirely your idea, and I refuse to take any responsibility for it!"

Cathy flew up out of her chair, throwing her arms around her father and hugging him tightly.

"Oh, thank you, Papa! Thank you!"

Sir Thomas patted her back consolingly.

"That's quite all right, my dear. You know I'm only concerned with your happiness."

"I know, Papa. I love you for it." The soft words, muttered into the front of his satin coat, cost Sir Thomas a momentary pang of conscience. But he stilled the pang, and continued to smooth her tumbled hair until she pushed away with a shaky laugh.

"I must look a mess."

"You do indeed, my dear. Have you no other clothes?" Sir Thomas eyed her crumpled white dress and untidy hair somewhat severely.

"I did—but they were in Jon's house. It got hit with a cannon ball and burned. I don't imagine there's anything left."

"Good God," her father said faintly. "If I had known for sure you were on that island, I would never have let them open fire. But Colonel Hugh— he's in charge of the soldiers that came with us—assured me that the pirates would have killed you long since, as there was no ransom demand. I thought you were dead, Cathy."

"Oh, Papa," Cathy said, tears filling her eyes at

the thought of her father's pain. "Jon didn't send a ransom demand because he wanted to keep me with him. I was never in any real danger," here she managed a glimmer of a smile, "at least, not until this morning."

"Yes, well," Sir Thomas turned away, clearing his throat. "I believe Martha packed some of your clothes in with my things in case you should need them. I'll have someone bring them in to you. I think that I had best make the arrangements for the marriage today, if that suits you. Under the circumstances, the sooner, the better."

"Anything you say, Papa." Cathy smiled at him lovingly, then impulsively ran across to press a kiss to his ruddy cheek. Sir Thomas hugged her to him lightly, then let her go. Cathy thought she saw moisture in his eyes as he turned to leave the cabin.

Left alone, Cathy wandered aimlessly around the room, too keyed up to sit still. She ran a hand over the curving backs of the elegant chairs, absentmindedly admiring their delicate beauty. After all, if one could afford it, there was nothing wrong with having the best, she thought defensively, imagining the sneer that her ideas would bring to Jon's handsome face. She picked up a delicate Sevres vase almost defiantly. Jon would simply have to grow accustomed to a different standard of living. Indeed, he would have little choice, if her plans worked out the way she hoped. It would be fun to teach him the modes and manners of society. She smiled, picturing her fierce pirate captain in the guise of an English gentleman. How he would scowl at first! But for her sake, and their child's, he would adjust. She knew he would, given time.

She was conscious of a faint, uncomfortable stirring of guilt about forcing him into what she was pretty sure would be an unwelcome marriage. He had been obviously displeased about the baby. It was unlikely that he would be any happier with the news that he was to become a husband as well as a father. But better wed than dead, as she would be sure to point out to him at the first opportunity afforded her. If not for herself, and the baby, he would have been hanged.

Her father had been certain that Jon didn't, couldn't, love her. Well, maybe not. Maybe she didn't even love him. But they had made a baby together, and, for the present, their own emotions were secondary. The coming child was what was important now.

A gentle tap sounded on the cabin door, and Cathy ran a self-conscious hand over her tumbling hair before bidding whoever was on the other side to come in.

"Mason!" she cried joyfully as the gentleman's gentleman, who had been with her father for years, entered.

"My lady," Mason beamed at her. "It's good to see you again, my lady, if I may say so. Sir Thomas has been like a man possessed since we had word that you were captured by pirates. He thought you dead, my lady, and the thought grieved him—

grieved us all."

"I know, Mason." Cathy smiled at the severely dressed little man. Mason was as much a part of her childhood as her father or Martha. He had always been reserved, as befitted the personal servant of a great man, but to Cathy he was as well-known as the drawing room in their Lisbon home.

"A sailor is bringing in Sir Thomas's trunk, my lady. If you require help in fixing your hair, or if your clothes need attention, please feel free to make use of my services. Sir Thomas tells me that you are getting married this afternoon. Allow me to offer you my best wishes for your happiness, my lady."

"Thank you, Mason." Cathy was touched by the prim speech. For Mason to offer his services as a lady's maid was tantamount to herself offering to scrub floors. "I may want you to fix my hair. I'm still not very handy at doing it myself."

"I should think not, my lady," sniffed Mason, plainly scandalized at the thought. He responded to another tap on the door, relieving the man in the hall of Sir Thomas's trunk without ever letting him catch a glimpse of Cathy. Cathy smiled. It felt a little strange to be so protected again. She realized that reverting to her rightful role as a high-born lady might require some adjustment. She had become accustomed to freedom on the pirate ship.

Cathy dismissed Mason with a smiling thank-you, and rummaged through her father's trunk herself. Martha had packed four dresses and a nightgown as well as the necessary underclothes, hairpins, and paraphernalia without which a lady could not claim to be properly attired. Her garments took up a goodly portion of Sir Thomas's trunk. Mason wouldn't like that, she thought, grinning. Mason had always been determined to keep her father dressed in the very height of fashion, and if he had consented to turn over some of his master's precious luggage space to her needs, then everyone must have been more concerned about her than she had imagined. It was a small sign of devotion, but it touched her as nothing else had done.

One of these dresses would be her wedding gown, she reflected as she shook out the garments. They were all lovely—all her clothes were, as Jon had once remarked—but she had always had visions of marrying in white satin, with a lace veil and a bouquet of orange blossom. She allowed herself a gentle moment of regret and then decided on a silk dress of a luscious peach, trimmed with yards of creamy Viennese lace. Martha had thoughtfully included the matching slippers, and her truly beautiful matched pearl necklace and earrings. With an elegant hairstyle she would do, she decided, and summoned Mason to iron her dress. While she was gone she bathed her face and hands in the basin of warm water, thinking with a momentary pang of the sweet scents that were most likely reduced to ashes in the ruins of Jon's house. Martha had pointedly not included any scent.

Cathy struggled into the three petticoats that were *de rigueur*, and laced her stays as well as she could herself. It was lucky that she was naturally slender, she reflected wryly. Somehow she couldn't quite picture Mason helping her lace.

When he returned with the dress, she had him wait outside the door while she donned it. Once respectably clad, she let him in to do her hair. He was surprisingly handy with a brush and hairpins, and Cathy teased him about his skill. He maintained a dignified silence as he swept her hair up into an elegant Grecian knot. Finally, he passed her a small hand mirror, and Cathy surveyed her reflection critically. Without conceit she decided that she looked as lovely as she ever had in her life. Under the gentle coaxing of the tropical sun her cheeks had taken on the same glowing color as the dress, while the rest of her complexion, down to the gentle swell of her breasts that was just visible above the filled neckline, was a lovely creamy white. The perfectly matched pearls were looped twice around her neck to rest with a cool heaviness in the hollow between her breasts. Pearl studs shone delicately pink-white against the lobes of her shell-like ears. Her months with the pirates had given her face a fine-boned purity of outline that had not been apparent before. She looked like a woman now, not a girl, and her cheeks flushed becomingly as she thought about her imminent marriage to the man who had made her so.

Mason went to inform Sir Thomas that she was ready. Cathy forced herself to sit quietly as she awaited her father's return. Suddenly she wished for a few moments alone with Jon before their wedding.

If he truly disliked the idea. . . . What could she do? She was committed to it now, and so was he. If he disliked the idea, then he would just have to dislike it. She was not going to draw back at this stage. If she were honest, she would admit that she didn't even want to.

Sir Thomas, when he rejoined her, assured her that all the arrangements had been made. Captain Winslow of the "Lady Chester" would perform the ceremony, and Mason and Sir Thomas himself would be the only witnesses. Besides Captain Winslow, no one outside of the family would know the details of her hasty wedding. And that was the way it should be, her father cautioned. If it became known that her new husband had once been a pirate, then the respectability that the marriage was supposed to achieve would be destroyed forever.

Cathy was caught by surprise when the door to the cabin swung open after only a perfunctory knock. Sir Thomas frowned at this breach of etiquette on the part of the two sailors detailed to guard the prisoner, but Cathy had eyes only for the man in the middle. His face was bruised and streaked with a combination of gunpowder, soot, and sweat. His clothes were torn and filthy, and his eyes glittered oddly as they moved almost contemptuously over Cathy's elegant form. She nervously moistened her lips with her tongue, and his expression changed to a savage sneer. It was only as he was thrust roughly forward by his two captors that she saw the heavy chains that swung between his wrists and ankles.

For the second time that day she could neither move nor speak. She could only watch with horrified compassion as he stumbled over the chain that stretched from ankle to ankle. He managed to right himself with an effort, and stood regarding her as her father dismissed the men.

"Well, well," Jon drawled, when neither Cathy nor her father spoke. "To think that I was worried about you. I should have remembered that cats always land on their feet."

"Why, you . . . !" Sir Thomas snarled, taking a hasty step forward. Jon swung around to face him, chains rattling, teeth bared like some savage animal. Cathy ran across to her father's side, clinging to his arm.

"No, Papa!" she said urgently, her eyes wide as they moved between the two men. Then, in what was almost a whisper, "I want to speak to him alone, Papa. Please."

"Impossible!" Sir Thomas growled, his eyes narrow with hatred as they fixed on the tall, muscular form of the animal who had abused his daughter. His mouth was dry with bloodlust. If it were not for Cathy's presence, he would have taken great pleasure in blowing the rogue straight to hell.

"Papa, please!" Cathy repeated, her eyes pleading with him. Sir Thomas looked down at her whitening face, his own softening.

"My dear, it is quite impossible," he said patiently. "He kidnapped you once before, and he looks quite capable of using you as a hostage again to win his freedom. I'm sorry, child, but there it is."

"Your father is right, Cathy," Jon said slowly, his eyes gleaming at her with an expression she found hard to define. "If you come too close I might wrap these chains around that sweet little neck and snap it with a single jerk. Better not risk it."

"Shut up, you!" Sir Thomas barked, the gun pointing unwaveringly at Jon's heart. "You can thank my daughter that you're still alive! If she hadn't told me of the child that you forced on her, I would have let you hang with great pleasure. As it is, you are going to do what you can to repair her good name!"

"Papa!" Cathy cried in despair as she saw Jon's face darken ominously. This was not how she planned to tell him! If they could only be alone, she could persuade him that marriage to her would not be the purgatory he was plainly expecting.

"I forced the child on her?" Jon repeated, his voice savagely mocking. "If that's what she told you, she lies."

Angry blood rushed into Sir Thomas's face. It was all he could do to restrain himself from pulling the trigger. His finger ached with the effort it cost him not to do so. Cathy flushed herself under the stinging taunt of Jon's words, but she clung steadfastly to her father's arm.

"I take it you want me to marry her," Jon said with a viciousness that tore at Cathy's heart.

"And why not?" she cried, stung. "It's your child,

you know it is, and you share the responsibility for it! The least you can do is make certain that it doesn't grow up a bastard!"

"You opportunistic little bitch," Jon snarled, and Cathy whitened under his raking glare.

"If you speak to my daughter in such a manner again, I'll shoot you down on the spot." Sir Thomas had regained his composure. His voice was icy cold.

Neither Jon nor Cathy replied. They glared at each other, anger and pain in both pairs of eyes, neither recognizing the other's hurt. Sir Thomas looked from one to the other and relaxed slightly. He was well satisfied with the way this interview was going. If the bastard kept on in this present frame, Cathy would be hating him before the ceremony was completed.

"And if I refuse?" Jon asked after a long moment.

"You'll hang," Sir Thomas responded positively. Cathy bit her lip. Jon's eyes swung to her.

"Do you agree with that?" he demanded curtly.

Cathy looked at him miserably. "Jon, I know you don't want to marry me, but I have to think of the baby. I'm sorry."

"You do agree." He swung around so that his broad back was turned to them, and swore savagely under his breath. Cathy longed to go to him, sliding her arms around that hard waist, but both Jon's own attitude and the presence of her father held her back. There would be time enough for making it up to him after the ceremony, she thought.

"It seems I have little choice," Jon said coolly at

last. The look he turned on Cathy made her flush. "I hope you're not expecting a proposal in form."

Cathy flinched from his cruel mockery. He really was a bastard, she thought furiously. Her father had been right. Jon definitely didn't love her!

Now that the minor matter of the pirate's consent had been settled, Sir Thomas dealt with the rest of the formalities with his usual efficiency. Less than twenty minutes later Cathy was standing at Jon's side in front of Captain Winslow, while that bewildered but game gentleman read the words that united them in holy matrimony. She was surprised at the cool sound of her own voice as it made the correct responses. Inside she was a quivery mass of pain. Jon sounded equally composed. Suddenly she found herself hating him. His callous disregard of her needs and the baby's was despicable!

When Captain Winslow got to the part about the ring, Sir Thomas hurriedly pulled the gold signet from his own finger. In the rush he had forgotten the need to procure a proper wedding band, but that could be attended to once they were safely in England. Jon took the ring from him without a word and slid it onto Cathy's finger, making as little contact with her as he possibly could in the process. Cathy could have wept at the feel of his warm hand holding hers so distastefully. Whenever she had imagined marrying Jon, it had certainly been nothing like this! His cold dislike of her almost made her sick.

She numbly signed the paper that Captain

Winslow held out to her, and Jon wrote his name below hers in a firm black scrawl. Then the captain was pronouncing them man and wife, and Cathy lifted her face to him hopefully. He stared down at her for a moment, his twisting in a jeering smile.

"I hope you don't expect me to give you a chaste bridal kiss after that farce," he drawled, and, before Cathy could think clearly, she slapped him hard across the face. The mark of her small hand was plainly visible against his dark cheek. He snarled, reaching for her, and his action mobilized the other three men who had been watching the little scene with stunned surprise.

Sir Thomas's pistol cracked down hard on Jon's head and Captain Winslow's caught him on the back of the neck. He went out like a light. Mason ran to the door and bellowed for the guards, who appeared on the double. They dragged Jon away between them while Cathy stood biting on her clenched fist to stop herself from crying out. She had provoked Jon's violence, she knew, and she bitterly regretted it. She hadn't meant him to be hurt.

"Papa, could you see that he's all right?" she asked after a moment, voice low. Her father looked at her sharply, then nodded, shepherding the other two men out of the cabin with him. Cathy was standing over by the window when he returned, tears rolling down her cheeks. Sir Thomas felt a renewed surge of hatred for the pirate.

"He wasn't hurt, was he, Papa?" she faltered. Sir Thomas crossed the room to her, putting his arm around her waist. Cathy clung to him miserably.

"Not at all, my dear," Sir Thomas said sorrowfully. Cathy looked up quickly at something in his voice.

"Papa. . . ."

"My child, I hope that what I'm going to say won't hurt you. You plainly don't love the pirate any more than he loves you, so I want you to look on this as a blessing."

"Papa. . . . !"

"He's escaped, Cathy. Abandoned you, and your child, and my promise of a pardon for him. Now, my dear, was I right?"

Twelve

London was nothing at all like Cathy had imagined it would be. Instead of stately mansions surrounded by acres of parkland, there were narrow townhouses separated from the streets by tiny yards and wrought iron fences. Carriages rattled over cobbled streets at all hours, while street vendors touted their wares from dawn to dusk. Garbage filled the gutters and no one seemed to pay the least heed to its stink. It was not at all unusual for the contents of a chamber pot to be emptied from a second story window onto the head of an unsuspecting pedestrian. The London of her dreams had been elegant and gay and extremely fashionable. The London of reality was merely dirty.

Immured in the opulence of her Aunt Elizabeth's house in Grosvenour Square, Cathy was at first restless, then bored, then totally disconsolate. Even though she had attained the dignity of matronhood, it was still considered improper for her to leave the house without a female attendant. Her readily apparent pregnancy precluded her participating in the parties and balls and musical soirees of the London Season. The only pastimes left to her were sedate walks, or carriage rides through the park with Martha in attendance, or a visit to the nearby shops.

Cathy's enjoyment of these diversions quickly palled. The thick chill of the coming winter made the park uncomfortable for one whose blood was used to warmer climes, and her thickening waistline kept her from taking any real interest in fashion. For several weeks she managed to amuse herself by selecting the baby's layette, but when that was complete, to the last tiny cap and satin coverlet, she could find nothing else to do. She moped about the house, smiling wanly in response to Sir Thomas's and Martha's attempts to cheer her. Resolutely, she refused to acknowledge that the inexplicable lowness of her spirits might have something to do with Jon's defection. As far as she was concerned, she told herself firmly, he was a chapter in her life that was now closed.

Elizabeth Augusta Anne Aldley Case, Lady Stanhope by marriage, and sister to Sir Thomas, had no patience with Cathy's megrims. In her considered opinion, the girl was very lucky to have escaped so lightly. If not for her willingness to cast the mantle of her sterling reputation over her niece, Cathy would have found herself a social outcast—despite the whitewash that Sir Thomas had tried to spread over the whole unsavory affair. For although the Duchess of Kent had refrained from discussing what had befallen Lady Aldley at the hands of the pirates, the Gradys had felt no such inhibitions. What they didn't know for a fact, they made up out of thin air. And the story they told was scandalous enough to ruin the reputation of even the most unimpeachably virtuous lady.

Lady Stanhope, sailing into the fray like a bosomy man o' war, dismissed the rumors as false lies. Her niece, said the lady with a look that dared her listeners to contradict her, was secretly married to an American in Lisbon before sailing for England. When the unfortunate bridegroom had fallen ill of a fever and died just days after the ceremony, a grieving Cathy had been packed off by her father to spend the summer with her aunt on the theory that a change of scenery might be what was needed to dispel the young widow's grief. When the "Anna Greer" was overrun by pirates, Cathy was already *enceinte*. The pirate captain, when made aware of her condition, had chivalrously offered the expectant mother the use of his cabin, and had behaved toward her thereafter with perfect propriety. Sir Thomas had recovered his daughter in Cadiz after the Duchess and those unspeakable chits were ransomed. And that, said my lady, was what really happened. Although polite society might titter behind its hands when Lady Stanhope was not present, no one quite had the nerve to openly dispute what she said.

Cathy, although not really ungrateful for these efforts on her behalf, was indifferent. Even after the baby was born, she did not anticipate feeling a burning urge to shine in society, or indeed to enter it at all. It would suit her far better to retire with her child to the country, she told her father. Sir Thomas was appalled. He foresaw all his careful machinations being made the casualties of an incomprehensible female whim. He appealed to Martha for aid in enumerating to Cathy the advantages accruing to a place in the polite world, and even a possible second marriage. When Cathy pointed out, with undeniable logic, that a second marriage was out of the question as she was not really a widow, Sir Thomas squirmed uncomfortably and told her not to bother her pretty little head about that. When the time came, he said, something could be arranged.

Besides Lady Stanhope, Cathy, Sir Thomas, and the servants, the present Lord Stanhope was also a resident of the house in Grosvenour Square. Plump, pompous, and pasty-faced, he was the widowed Lady Stanhope's only child and the apple of her eye. She thought Harold could do no wrong, and when Harold looked down his nose at his little cousin and pronounced her wild, Lady Stanhope could only agree. Cathy's degenerate tendencies had brought about her downfall, as Lady Stanhope told the girl repeatedly. Cathy, mindful of her father's career and the burden her adventure had already placed on it, held her tongue and submitted, with as good a grace as she could muster, to her aunt's homilies. But with Harold, she had no such scruples. She despised him, and did not care who knew it.

The first of December saw Cathy going into the sixth month of pregnancy. She felt as large and ungainly as an expectant sow, and her dissatisfaction with her appearance and general malaise caused her to be snappish and impatient with anyone who came near her. The tensions in the house grew to such an intensity that she was driven to spending much time in her bedroom. It was large and elegantly furnished, with a satin-draped four-poster, delicate chairs, a mirrored dressing table, and a plush gold oriental carpet. But the lack of fresh air and exercise made Cathy pale and listless. Her days were spent huddling apathetically in front of a roaring fire, a book forgotten on her lap as she gave herself up to wistful daydreams. "If only Jon had loved me" was their usual theme, and Cathy was too heartsore to banish them. But she finally managed to convince herself that her love of Jon, if indeed it had ever existed, was now dead. In its place was an implacable antagonism.

The coming child was becoming more real to her with every passing day. She could feel it moving inside her, its tiny kicks and rolls tickling like the flutterings of a trapped butterfly, and she thrilled to the knowledge that in less than three months she would be able to hold her child in her arms. Despite Jon's betrayal, she would love their child with every ounce of her being. The baby would be her whole life.

Martha was growing seriously concerned about Cathy's melancholia, and consulted with Sir Thomas endlessly on the subject. He too was becoming alarmed. Except for the bulge at her middle, the girl had lost weight, and she was uncharacteristically quiet. Sir Thomas began to wonder if he had done the right thing. The remedy was even now in his hands, he knew, but any change of plan must be worked out quickly. After the third of January, it would be too late. Cathy would in truth be a widow.

Newgate Prison was a horrible place, as Sir Thomas had found on the first of his numerous visits. To a prisoner without friends or money, and under sentence of death, it was hell itself. The guards had no scruples about dragging a condemned man out into the courtyard, tying him to a whipping post, and beating him until the blood ran. Sir Thomas learned that a carelessly tossed silver coin could assure such treatment on a weekly basis. He didn't have to waste his money bribing the guards to withhold food and drink. The standard prison fare was a piece of moldy bread, twice a day, accompanied by a scummy mug of water.

His craving for revenge was almost satisfied as he watched the weekly beatings, gloating as the once powerful-looking man was reduced to a wild-eyed skeleton. If Cathy could only see her pirate now, he thought, turning up his nose at the unwashed odor of the man's body and staying well back out of reach of hands that he knew itched to kill him, she would recoil with revulsion. There was nothing about the pirate now to awaken maidenly hearts, and the knowledge pleased Sir Thomas mightily. Still, he worried about what Cathy's reaction would be if by some unlikely mischance she were to discover that her pirate captain had been hanged at Tyburn instead of escaping as she supposed. Was it possible that after the passage of so much time she would be angry nonetheless?

No anger, however, could match that which Jon Hale felt for Sir Thomas. A homicidal gleam would come into the crazed gray eyes when they rested on their captor, and his parched lips would curve in a feral snarl. Although the man was chained hand and foot, and was under the constant guard of armed men, Sir Thomas was conscious of an occasional stirring of fear. The pirate only made the mistake of lunging for him once, when Sir Thomas had remarked deliberately on his plans for his daughter's future. The pirate emitted what could only be described as a howl and leaped like a wild beast for his throat, but Sir Thomas was able to jump back in time while the guards clubbed the man senseless. They then dragged the prisoner over to the whipping post, tied him to it, and beat him again as soon as they revived him. After that, the pirate feigned deafness when Sir Thomas mentioned how sorry Cathy was to hear of the treatment he was receiving. Feeling that his daughter's vengeance was being well and truly served, he began to tell the man before each beating that they had been ordered by Cathy, and not himself. And the malevolent glitter in the pirate's eyes or the twitching of a muscle in his cheek conveyed to Sir Thomas that his prisoner was indeed cognizant of what was being said to him.

Although Sir Thomas hated Jon Hale for having dishonored his daughter, he began, very reluctantly, to feel a glimmer of respect for the pirate's iron endurance. The man never uttered a sound, although the pain he suffered was excruciating, and the only time he showed any reaction was when Sir Thomas mentioned Cathy's name. Even then, the emotion in his gray eyes was so fleeting that Sir Thomas was unable to identify it.

Jon's hanging was scheduled for seven o'clock on the morning of January third. As Christmas came and went, Sir Thomas began to have serious misgivings about the wisdom of what he was doing. Was he indeed serving his daughter's best interests by having the pirate hanged? Or would she be better off with him for a husband? For instead of getting over her infatuations, as Sir Thomas had been certain she would, Cathy seemed no happier now than she had weeks ago. If anything, in fact, she was plunging more and more deeply into depression. If she genuinely loved the pirate, then Sir Thomas would reluctantly put her wishes before his own career. But he was still morally convinced that what Cathy felt was a mere girlish infatuation which time would remedy. It was just that it was taking rather more time to cure her than he had at first supposed. Anyway, it was too late now to restore the pirate to her, the man would very likely do her serious harm if he could get his hands on her, believing what he now did about her. Thus Sir Thomas decided that it was in the best interests of all concerned to let the execution take place. Even the pirate might welcome death as an alternative to his present sufferings.

New Year's Day, 1843, dawned clear and crisp and very cold. Snow lay thickly on the window sill just outside Cathy's bedroom. The antics of the child in her womb had awakened her earlier than had lately become her custom. For a long while she lay quietly in bed, one hand pressed to her belly, while she watched the sky turn from midnight blue to a leaden gray. From the looks of it, there would be more snow before the day was out, adding to the foot or so that was already on the ground. Cathy grimaced. The somberness of the day exactly matched her mood.

The fire in the hearth had burned down to a few glowing embers, and the room was chill. Cathy burrowed beneath the thick satin quilt, tucking it cozily around herself so that only the tip of her nose and her eyes were exposed to the raw air. She thought about getting out of bed to poke up the fire but then decided against it: it simply required too much effort. Martha would be bringing her morning chocolate in a few minutes, and the woman could do it then.

A knock sounded very formally at her bedroom door, and Cathy smiled ruefully. Martha usually acted far more like her mother than her servant, and when she made a point of remembering her place, it was a sign that she was gravely offended. Cathy sighed, because when Martha was offended she could be as difficult to placate as an outraged Brahma bull. Apparently the words she had flung at the older woman the night before still rankled. She hadn't meant to hurt Martha's feelings, God knew, but she was so cross now. Her personality had changed so much in these few short months that she scarcely recognized herself.

"Come in," she called, resigned to spending the better part of the morning soothing her nanny's ruffled feathers.

Martha entered with a dignity that would not have been out of place in Queen Victoria herself.

"I've brought your chocolate, my lady."

The stilted form of address told Cathy, more clearly than a diatribe would have, that Martha felt that she had been ill-used. Cathy sighed again, not feeling up to the task of placating anyone. It took a great deal of effort just to maneuver herself into a sitting position against the pillows.

"Please don't be angry with me," she coaxed as Martha arranged the tray of chocolate and warm croissants on her lap. "You and my father are the only friends I seem to have left. If you desert me, I'll have no one."

"There's no talk of anyone deserting you, Miss Cathy." The woman responded to the sadness of Cathy's tone just as she had been meant to do. "It's only natural that you should be a bit peevish now

312

and again, what with the baby and you not being in good health. When I see how you're changed, I could kill that pirate myself if I knew where to lay hands on him. What he's done to you is criminal!"

"Martha, please!" Cathy cried, biting her lip. Any mention of Jon was excruciatingly painful, and, as a rule, Martha and Sir Thomas were careful never to allude to him in any way. Although Cathy had done her best to banish his lean image from her thoughts, it was impossible to do so, with his child moving so strongly inside her. The man was beginning to haunt her night and day like some earth-bound ghost.

When she closed her eyes it was easy to picture feet braced wide apart, on the "Margarita's" quarterdeck while a warm wind ruffled through his thick black hair. By now he could be sailing any sea in the world, preying on weaker ships and making love to a procession of willing women. Cathy felt a long-denied rage begin to build inside her as she imagined him slanting his mouth across the eager lips of some sloe-eyed Polynesian beauty. Bastard, she thought vindictively, as she remembered how he had deserted her when he had found out about the child. He wasn't worth wasting a single tear on—not that she had any intention of crying over him. It was bad enough that he could abandon her, his wife, whether the wedding had been of his design or not. But that he could so coolly leave their coming child bore out every harsh word her father had ever said about him. Jon Hale was a heartless, merciless brigand who had taken advantage of her inexperience to make her think she loved him. His own actions condemned him in Cathy's mind.

"Sorry, Miss Cathy."

Martha's subdued tone brought Cathy back to the present. The woman was looking as if she wished she had bitten out her tongue before reminding Cathy of the author of all her problems. Cathy smiled at her nanny with sudden warm affection, because it grieved Martha to see her so unhappy.

"What dress shall I wear today?" The question was designed to shift Martha's mind to more mundane matters, and it succeeded admirably. Martha was visibly delighted to see her charge taking an interest in her appearance at last. Ever since the girl had been rescued from that heathenish pirate she had been dull and apathetic, totally unlike herself. Usually she allowed Martha to choose what she would wear for her, not even bothering to glance in the cheval glass in the corner of the room when she was ready for the day. Not that there was much to choose amongst her dresses, Martha had to admit. The ridiculous story of Cathy's widowhood sentenced the girl to wearing black, unrelieved by so much as a ribbon or an ornament. Indeed, the only jewelry that it was considered proper for her to wear was the plain gold wedding band that Sir Thomas had procured for her in London. Looking with disfavor on the dreary selection in the wardrobe, Martha didn't wonder at the lowness of her charge's spirits. Such gloomy dresses would be enough to depress any young lady.

"The silk is very pretty," Martha said, not betraying her true opinion of the garment by so much as a flicker of an eyelid. Cathy was undeceived.

"For a crow, maybe," she groaned, swinging her legs out of the bed and allowing Martha to help her with her toilette.

Special care had to be taken on this particular day to give the impression of sorrowing rectitude. It was the custom on New Year's Day for friends, relatives, and acquaintances to exchange calls. Lady Stanhope had decreed that, since Cathy could obviously not be allowed abroad in her present condition, she must remain in the drawing room to receive any visitors. Besides, Cathy could do much to aid herself by appearing sweetly innocent and brave in the face of her husband's untimely demise. To hide the girl away from callers would only give rise to more talk as Lady Stanhope had sharply informed both Cathy and Sir Thomas.

With Lady Stanhope's instructions in mind, Martha carefully arranged Cathy's long golden hair in a demure coronet on the top of her head. The girl's own paleness and ladylike demeanor should be convincing. If anyone were not convinced and dared to directly question Lady Catherine, Martha planned to ever-so-accidentally overturn a pot of hot tea in the impertinent one's lap. She had made up her mind to remain at her lady's side throughout the day, and no one, not even Lady Stanhope herself, was going to make her do otherwise!

"Martha, I look awful!" Cathy's voice was a

315

strange mixture of dismay and awe as she regarded her image in the long mirror. Her unaccustomed hairstyle made her appear unexpectedly meek, and the paleness of her face and hands seemed to speak of consumption. The severe black dress, high at the throat and sleeved to the wrist, hid every hint of her shape while emphasizing the bulge of her belly. Cathy could hardly believe that the girl who stared back at her, her blue eyes dulled by inactivity, could really be herself. I look ill, she thought with the faintest glimmer of alarm, and turned quickly away from the glass.

"You look like a proper widow," Martha reproved briskly, and caught up a light shawl as she prepared to follow her mistress downstairs. It would never do for the girl to catch a chill. As thin and peaky as she had become, even so slight an illness as that could be enough to carry her off.

The day passed with dragging slowness. Seated on an uncomfortable horsehair sofa that was all the rage, Cathy tried to school her itching limbs to proper stillness, while she neatly fielded the questions of the curious. Martha hovered at her side like some black-uniformed vulture, never straying from the room. The woman was unusually clumsy, and Cathy began to wonder if she might be sickening from something. Not once but four times had she overturned a pot of tea on a visitor's lap.

The last callers of the day departed at precisely four-fifteen. Cathy stood up with a sigh of relief, scratching her outraged legs vigorously. Her face still burned with anger at some of the prying questions that had been addressed to her. "And what was your dear husband's name?" one sharp-eyed old bat had asked her. When Cathy had answered with perfect truth, seeing no need to withhold such fundamental information, the woman had said "Ahhh!" as though she had just caught out her young hostess in some monumental lie. Her beady little eyes had gleamed, and she was just opening her mouth for another prying question when Martha knocked over the silver teapot once again. The Countess of Firth left immediately afterwards, as outraged as if the deed were deliberate. Cathy shook her head, smiling faintly. Knowing Martha, it might have been.

Cathy expressed a wish to take supper on a tray in her room, mendaciously saying that she felt tired after her ordeal. Truthfully, she felt better than she had in days. But she could not face the prospect of dinner, with her aunt and cousin quizzing her about who had called, what questions had been asked, and what she had replied. She was certain that, discreet as her answers had been, either one or the other of them would manage to find fault with her. If she had had only herself to consider, she would have told them to go to the devil long ago, but her father was almost pathetically eager for her to achieve a respectable place in society. For that, she acknowledged, she needed her aunt's help. Obnoxious as Lady Stanhope was, her reputation was unimpeachable.

Unfortunately, her retreat to her bedroom was ill-timed. Harold was in the entryway, being helped out of his coat by the obsequious Sims. Without the butler's assistance, it was doubtful if Lord Stanhope would have been able to free his stocky arms from the too-tight sleeves of his coat. He reminded Cathy of a sausage being skinned, and she did her best to stifle a giggle. She was unsuccessful. Harold heard the small, muffled sound, and turned toward her. When he saw who it was that had dared to laugh at him, his small eyes grew even smaller, almost disappearing in the puffy mound of pale flesh that was his face.

"Good evening, cousin," he said with dreadful affability, strolling toward her. Cathy inclined her head in haughty acknowledgment of his greeting, then turned away and walked with dignity in the direction of the curving staircase.

"Don't run away, cousin," Harold drawled, his affected voice grating on Cathy's ear. "You've become so quiet and mouselike of late, I declare, I find it hard to believe that you could be the same female who engaged in acts of such unspeakable depravity. But then, your—ah—condition is no doubt responsible for your meekness. Once you whelp your bastard, the innate weakness in your character will come out again, I feel sure."

Cathy whirled on him, clenching her fists. Temper sparked from her eyes, making her look more alive than she had in all the weeks she had lived in London. Harold eyed her with dawning interest. It might be amusing to have her in the house after she was free of the pirate's spawn. He began to toy with the idea of making her his mistress. It was a certainty that, with the reputation she had acquired, no gentleman would offer to take her to wife. Her flesh would begin to itch for a man sooner or later, he calculated. When the time came, he would be on hand.

"My child is not a bastard!" she spat furiously, every hair on her head seeming to crackle with temper. Harold smiled slightly. He was beginning to see how she had managed to attract the attention of a pirate. With a little spirit showing, she was quite something.

"I beg your pardon if I said something to offend you, cousin," he said in a bewildered fashion which Cathy knew was deliberately assumed. She seethed, longing to verbally assault him, but decided to restrain herself. If Harold discovered that he could wound her with his barbs, he would take fiendish delight in doing so.

Without another word Cathy turned her back on her cousin and walked gracefully up the stairs. Harry's high-pitched laughter followed her, making her grit her teeth. Place in society or not, she was moving out, she promised herself grimly. Not even for her dear papa would she endure Harold.

Cathy was still angry when Martha came in with her supper tray. The old woman took heart at the unaccustomed spark in her charge's eyes. Not since before the capture of the "Anna Greer" had she seen the girl display such animation. It was a healthy sign.

319

Martha prepared Cathy's bath and laid out her night things while Cathy ate her meal. She was quite hungry for a change, and it was no hardship to finish the entire portion of tender lamb. The baby gave a little kick as she put her fork aside, and Cathy smiled, touching the mound of her stomach.

Martha helped her to undress, tying up her long hair with ribbons. Cathy stepped into the bath, sinking down in the perfumed water with some surprise. She had not put any scent in the water herself, and Cathy eyed Martha questioningly.

"Roses is a good, decent scent," Martha said, defending herself stoutly in response to Cathy's unspoken question. Cathy smiled at her nanny affectionately.

"You knocked that tea over deliberately, didn't you, Martha?" she asked softly, her eyes teasing.

"Certainly not, Miss Cathy," the woman replied primly, pausing in the act of turning back the bedcovers. "I just must be getting a touch of arthritis. My hands are getting clumsy."

"Lying's a sin, Martha," Cathy mocked, but Martha was too pleased with the girl's liveliness to take offense.

When Cathy was finished she stepped from the tub and was enfolded in a warmed towel. Martha dried her thoroughly and then slid a pretty pink nightgown over Cathy's head; at night, in the privacy of her bedchamber, Cathy had her only chance to wear colors, and she took shameless advantage of it. Her nightgown was trimmed with yards of lace and ribbon; it was a frivolously feminine garment. With her hair brushed and braided into two long plaits for the night, Cathy felt almost attractive again.

Martha settled her in the large four-poster, pulling the covers well up around Cathy's chin. Cathy submitted patiently to the woman's ministrations. Despite all that had befallen her, Martha persisted in treating her like a child. But her devotion was total, and Cathy found the woman's care oddly comforting.

When Martha had gone, blowing out the bedside candle, the room was lighted only by the dim glow of the fire. It cast strange, leaping shadows across the room. Cathy watched them, fascinated, and fell asleep.

She had no idea what it was that woke her. The popping of a burning ember, perhaps, or the mournful bark of a dog. The room looked strange to her sleep-weighted eyes, and not quite real. The fire-shadows looked longer, and vaguely sinister. Cathy's eyes gradually widened as she stared at one in particular that seemed to be moving stealthily toward her. Finally she realized that it wasn't a shadow—it was a man! His tall frame was silhouetted by the light of the dying fire as he crept toward the bed. Cathy opened her mouth to scream, terrified, but only a tiny squeak emerged. Immediately the man was upon her, his big hand stilling further cries.

Instinctively Cathy fought, kicking and writhing in a hopeless bid for freedom. She bit down hard on the hand that covered her mouth. The man cursed, snatching his hand away, but before Cathy could draw breath for a shriek he thrust a rag between her dry lips.

Oh, God, what did he mean to do to her? First, he bound her hands in front of her with a strip of cloth torn from the sheet. Then, pulling back a little, he jerked the bedcovers down around her feet and hauled her upright. She stood swaying before him, trembling with fright. He struck a match, lighting the candle, and Cathy's eyes widened as he turned to face her. It was Jon! Her heart sang with thanksgiving. He had come for her, after all this time! But then she frowned, her forehead creasing in puzzlement. Why tie her up? He must know that she would be glad to see him! He was her husband, after all!

Cathy looked at him more closely, and she caught her breath in surprise. His handsome features were almost completely obscured by a full, black beard. His skin was yellow, as if he were ill, and he was thin to the point of emaciation. Cathy caught a faint whiff of his unwashed flesh, and her nose wrinkled in distaste. Jon saw her reaction, and smiled very slowly. The smile was a terrifying sight.

Jon looked as if he hated her—as if he might even kill her! Perhaps he had picked up a fever somewhere, and was delirious. That would explain his revolting appearance, as well.

Jon was making an inspection of his own. His eyes traveled slowly over her face, and a light began to glow in them. His gaze moved down over her throat, her breasts, and then froze on her belly. He stared at the bulging mound with the same horror he might have shown toward an abomination. His grip on her wrists tightened almost to the breaking point.

"My God!" he cried. A muscle in his jaw worked furiously. He seemed to be exercising control over some fearsome emotion. Cathy trembled a little as she sensed his force. Jon felt her quiver, and that terrifying smile returned to his lips.

"You're right to be afraid of me, wife." His use of that last word struck Cathy as being ominous in itself. Was it possible that he sought some type of vengeance on her for forcing him into an unwelcome marriage? Then why had he troubled to seek her out at all? On the "Margarita" he could have been as free as the air, and unobliged to recognize the bond that tied them together.

"I've been planning this meeting for months, wife. Ever since our last one, in fact," he said softly, his eyes trapping hers as he loomed over her. Cathy instinctively shrank away, and he laughed in a way that made her blood run cold. "You think you've defeated me, don't you? Well, partly right. Not even the thing that I have become would stoop to harming my own child. So I've decided to take you with me, and you'll stay with me until after the child's birth. Then, wife, we'll settle the score. You'll suffer. . . ."

The words trailed off menacingly. Cathy's eyes were frankly terrified. She was convinced that he had gone mad, and was raving like the poor lunatics in Bedlam.

"Where is your cloak?" he muttered, as he turned to look about the room. He spied the wardrobe, and dragged her in his wake as he strode toward it. She stumbled after him, afraid to resist, lest she should further inflame his maniacal rage.

He flung open the wardrobe door, and stopped short at the sight of her collection of mourning dresses. She heard him suck in his breath as at a mortal blow.

"Thus vanishes my last doubt," he muttered cryptically, jerking on her wrists with a violence that would have sent her stumbling to the floor if he had not held her upright. His eyes seared hers with hatred, and then he thrust his hand into the closet, tearing the dresses from their hangers in his search for her cloak. He found what he was seeking at last, and wrapped it roughly about her, lifting her clear off her feet and up into his arms. She could feel the bones of his chest and shoulders as he held her in a fierce grip that told her he enjoyed hurting her.

"Unfortunately for you, wife, your widowhood was a touch premature. A fact which I'm sure you bitterly regret."

Cathy squirmed in his arms, deathly frightened of being borne away by this dark, terrifying stranger. Dear God, he was not the man she knew and loved! He hated her, and he looked like the devil himself with all the fires of hell burning out of his eyes! This must be some strange, twisted nightmare. . . . Cathy prayed that she was having a nightmare, and writhed desperately in an effort to wake herself up.

"Lie still! Lie still, bitch, or by God I'll. . . ."

The threat trailed off as he crushed her to him. Cathy went limp, convinced by the violence of his tone that he was no apparition. Her heart was beating in frightened bursts, and she suddenly knew how a rabbit must feel in a snare when the hunter approaches. Was he going to kill her . . . ?

The bedroom door creaked open, sending a quivering circle of light spilling over the floor. Cathy could feel him freeze. She froze, too, in terror for the person coming into her room. He was mad, and violent. He was capable of murder. . . .

"Miss Cathy?" Martha said, venturing a step or two into the room, the candle she carried held high as she peered toward the bed. When she perceived a candle already burning by the bed, she faltered, and then looked around searchingly.

"Miss Cathy?" The voice was a quavery whisper. Cathy could feel Jon's heart beating in slamming thuds against her ear. He fumbled at his waist with one hand, and Cathy realized with a sickening sense of helplessness that he was carrying a pistol. She tried to scream, to warn Martha, but was able to force only a strangled, groan through the gag. It was enough. Martha swung toward them, her eyes widening as she dropped the candle with a crash, her mouth opening for a scream.

"Make a sound and I'll kill her."

Jon's voice sounded hoarse and menacing as he threatened Martha. The woman froze, the cry of alarm dying in her throat as she saw the pistol

325

pressed to Cathy's head.

"Come over here."

Martha stared at him with growing horror.

"You're . . . the pirate!" she gasped painfully. She went paper-white, as if she might faint.

"I said, come here!" Jon's voice, low though it was, cracked like a whip. Martha obeyed jerkily, like a puppet on a string. Cathy met her nanny's frightened eyes. Be calm, she willed silently. Do as he says. He's gone mad.

When Martha was within touching distance, Jon set Cathy on her feet, holding her with one arm around her waist so that she could not run away. The pistol was now pointed squarely at Martha. It didn't waver as he reached out to pull the sash of the woman's wrapper free. He deftly looped it into a hangman's noose with one hand and then slipped it over Martha's head to rest around her neck. He turned her around so that her back was to them, taking up the slack in the sash and tying it to his belt. Cathy could only stand by numbly, waiting to see what he would do next. So far, he hadn't actually harmed either of them. Perhaps if they were docile he would relax his guard long enough to give them a chance to escape. Martha had neither moved nor spoken since Jon had turned her around.

"When I give the word, we're going to walk very quietly out of the house. If one of you makes a false move, or a sound, I'll kill you both. Do you understand?"

Cathy nodded, hoping he could feel the movement of her head against his chest. She believed him. He was mad enough to do exactly as he had said. Martha's head bobbed in the same assenting gesture. Cathy looked around her wildly, searching for anything that might be used to delay or impede him until they could be rescued. There was nothing.

"Move!"

The command was like a bullet next to Cathy's ear. Martha took a tentative step forward, and Jon pushed Cathy after her. She stumbled over one of her crumpled dresses that he had pulled from the wardrobe and thrown to the floor. He swore furiously, kicking it out of the way, but the memory of it and the others lying like silent witnesses in front of the wardrobe comforted Cathy slightly. Her father would realize that they had been kidnapped when he saw such traces. She prayed he would be in time to rescue them. Jon was clearly not sane, and she and Martha were helpless in his hands. He could do with them what he willed.

Thirteen

Jon's cabin aboard the "Margarita" was unchanged. Martha and Cathy had been thrust roughly through the door, which was then slammed shut behind them. There was the sound of a key grating in the lock. The cabin was pitch dark, and icy cold, but Cathy at least was thoroughly familiar with it. Shivering slightly with cold, relieved to be rid of Jon's demonic presence, she crossed to the table and lit the candle that stood there. By its light, she could see that Martha was trembling, her arms hugging her plump body. Her bare feet were blue from having walked barefoot through the snow to the closed carriage that had been awaiting him further down the street. Cathy supposed she could attribute the fact that Jon had carried her to the child burgeoning inside her. His arms about her had felt heart-breakingly familiar—with one enormous difference: he had held her as if he hated her. Cathy was more than ever convinced that he had gone mad.

Martha's teeth chattered audibly, and with a little cry Cathy ran clumsily to embrace her nanny. The older woman's arms came around her to hug her tightly.

"Oh, Miss Cathy," she murmured brokenly. "Do you think he means to harm us?"

"I don't think so, Martha," Cathy denied, although she was far from sure herself. As she spoke she turned away to strip two quilts from the bed, wrapping one around Martha and one around herself.

"If he meant to hurt us, surely he would have done so already," Cathy argued, as much to convince herself as Martha. She knelt before the coal stove and stuffed a few sticks of kindling inside before striking a match and setting it ablaze. After a few moments the coals began to glow, and Cathy sank back on her heels, pleased with herself.

Martha's eyes were closed, and her head was flung back when Cathy turned around. The woman's face was pasty. Cathy was afraid that the experience they had just endured, had been even more frightening for Martha than for herself. For Martha was totally unfamiliar with Jon. Perhaps it had brought on some sort of attack. She got laboriously to her feet, weighted down by the seven-month fetus inside her, and walked to Martha's side.

"Why don't you lie down, Martha?" she asked gently. "The bed's quite comfortable. I can guarantee it."

Cathy smiled as she spoke, hoping to lighten the fear that clogged the very air. Martha opened her eyes and stared at the bed as one would at a poisonous snake.

"Is that where . . . did he bring you here after . . . my poor lovely, you must have been frightened to death. I never realized. . . ." Martha's words trailed off, and she regarded Cathy with loving pity. Cathy smiled at her.

"Yes, that is where . . ." she echoed teasingly, hoping to buck Martha up a little by a deliberately light touch. "But at the time I must admit that I was as much curious as frightened. I wondered what it was like, you see. Besides, Jon was . . . was . . . different then."

She bit her lower lip as she spoke, her eyes clouding over. Martha reached out to clasp her hand.

"Has he gone mad, Miss Cathy?" the woman whispered. Cathy shut her eyes. This was what she feared herself, yet to admit as much to Martha would only terrify the woman further. She returned the pressure of the hand, but then tugged at it briskly.

"Come on," she said, avoiding a direct answer. "Let's both get into bed. I, for one, am frozen, and we won't do ourselves any good by sitting here worrying."

Martha obediently got to her feet and followed Cathy across to the bunk. Cathy urged her between the sheets, then spread the two quilts back over the bed and got beneath them herself. They huddled together, their body heat gradually warming them, and at last Martha drifted off to sleep. Cathy smiled wryly at the woman's slight snores. Martha had always been able to sleep through anything. Something to do with a hardy Scots ancestry, she supposed, although Martha herself would doubtless attribute it to a clear conscience.

Try as she would, Cathy could no longer avoid thinking about Jon. He had not said a word to her since that tersely voiced "move!"—not even when he had roughly removed her bonds during the long ride to the coast. Obviously, he had come to repay her for some wrong she had supposedly done him. His whole attitude made that clear. But what could it be? Surely he was not enraged over the manner of their marriage! No, he was too violently angry to be nursing a grievance about something so unimportant to him. Then what had she done? She tried frantically to remember any injury she had caused him, but could think of nothing. Which left her first terrifying conclusion intact. He was, quite simply, mad. It was the only explanation.

Cathy shivered, pulling the quilts more securely around her. The thought of being helpless in the hands of a madman was unnerving in the extreme. What had befallen him to turn his brain in such a way? Would he, perhaps, recover his senses? Or maybe her father would manage to rescue them before anything too horrible could happen. She hoped so. She prayed so. The memory of Jon's gray eyes gleaming like the fires of hell made her sweat with fear.

The chance of rescue was becoming more remote every second, she realized. Above her she could hear the flapping of the "Margarita's" sails as they were run up the masts. The sudden plunging of the ship beneath her said that they were beginning to move toward the sea. Once away from the coast, they could head anywhere. It might be weeks, months even, before a rescue party could overtake them. Dear Lord! Her eyes widened with horror. This time there could be no rescue! The man who had stolen her away was her husband in the eyes of the law, and she was absolutely subject to his wishes. He owned her, like a slave, and any man who attempted to come between them would be legally in the wrong. The thought so stunned Cathy that she could only stare blankly into space. Her heart pounded as she realized that Jon had her well and truly trapped. And the hysterically funny part about the whole thing was that the web was of her own making!

Cathy drifted off despite her fear, and, the next thing she knew, she was being jerked awake to the sound of the key turning in the lock. Her eyes widened fearfully as the door opened and Jon strode into the room. Instinctively she pulled the covers high around her neck. His eyes ran over her derisively, jeering at the action, and then he turned back to whoever had followed him to the door.

"I want a bath," he said abruptly to the unseen person. The reply was unintelligible, although plainly affirmative. Jon swung back to face Cathy.

"Get her the hell out of here," he growled, brusquely nodding at Martha who was coming groggily awake. "Now!"

"W—why?" Cathy stammered, clutching instinctively at the older woman. Martha sat up, her gray hair in a wild frizz around her head, her arm going protectively about her charge.

"Don't worry, lovey. No one's sending me away from you!"

It was an unmistakable challenge. Martha, up in arms like a lioness protecting her one cub, glared at Jon ferociously. He scowled back, his thick black brows rushing together ominously over his nose. The rest of his expression was hidden by that fierce-looking beard. Cathy trembled, and Martha's arm tightened around her shoulders.

"I said get out." Jon's voice was even, but it had an underlying tinge of menace. "Unless you want to watch me bathe. It's your choice."

He shrugged indifferently, turning back to open the door for Petersham who struggled in with the porcelain bath that Cathy had used in happier times. Cathy's spirits picked up a little at the sight of her old friend. She was not to be entirely at Jon's mercy, it seemed!

"Oh, Petersham!" she exclaimed. "How are you?"

The joy in her voice made Jon's eyes narrow. Petersham glanced at her, his expression stony.

"Very good, ma'am," he answered, his voice like ice. Cathy fell back against the pillows. Good God, Petersham hated her too! What was it that she had done? Would no one tell her? Or did they suppose she already knew?

Jon's lips curved in the ghost of a satisfied smile. Cathy stared at him. The murderous light was gone from his eyes, and except for that revolting beard and his filthy clothes, he looked almost normal. Was he insane? Or was there something going on that she simply didn't understand?

Jon started to unbutton his shirt as Petersham filled the tub. His eyes never left Martha. Color rushed into the woman's cheeks as she realized that he would have no inhibitions about doing just exactly as he had threatened. Cathy saw her consternation, and pushed her gently toward the foot of the bunk.

"It's all right, Martha," she said softly. "You can go. He won't do me any harm."

Jon did not contradict her statement, and continued undressing lazily. Martha scrambled from

333

the bunk as he freed his shirt from the waistband of his pants. Then she turned back to Cathy.

"Shut your eyes, lovey," the woman said fiercely. "It isn't right, your seeing him like that."

Jon's lips lifted in a humorless smile. He shrugged free of the shirt, throwing it casually to the floor.

"He is my husband, Martha," Cathy said quietly. Martha's mouth widened in a soundless "Oh!" and she clapped her hand to it as Jon began to unbutton his breeches. He gave every indication that he was prepared to strip to the skin regardless of who was watching.

"It's all right, Martha," Cathy repeated rather wearily, and, with one last horrified glance at Jon, Martha scuttled from the cabin. Petersham, finished with his task, followed Martha without another glance at Cathy. Cathy stared after him, perplexed, and then her eyes swung back to Jon. He was stepping rather stiffly from his breeches.

The thick black hair that covered his body was dull now and matted. Cathy caught her breath at the sight of bones showing through the swarthy flesh. Before he had been a lean, finely-honed animal with smooth, powerful muscles. Now he looked like the survivor of a famine. The only thing about him that was unchanged was his manhood, standing tautly away from the surrounding black bush. Its burgeoning stiffness looked obscene amidst all that wasted flesh. Cathy averted her eyes hastily.

"A little late for maidenly modesty, isn't it, wife?"

Jon commented sardonically. The way he said the last word made it an unspeakable insult. Cathy flinched from the hatred that still licked like flames through his voice.

"Don't call me that!" she protested sharply, automatically. Jon leaped toward her, snarling, and Cathy cowered back against the pillows. His hands closed over her shoulders, tightening cruelly on the fragile bones. Cathy gasped with pain and fear. Jon's lips parted in a feral smile and he dragged her up so that her face was level with his.

"Do you know how close you came to being strangled, last night?" he asked almost conversationally, his face not more than three inches from hers. The crazed glitter had returned to his eyes. Cathy shook her head fearfully. Anything to placate him.

"Very close. In fact, if not for my child, you wouldn't be alive today. So don't try telling me what to do. I might decide that the child isn't worth enduring your bitchy ways."

His hands dropped away from her as if she had suddenly become distasteful to him. Cathy slumped back down in the bed, her eyes following his every move, her breath coming fast and shallow. He turned his back to move stiffly toward the steaming bath, and Cathy gave a little shocked cry of horror.

"Your back!" she breathed. "What happened to it?"

Jon swung around, the glow in his eyes so bright that Cathy felt scorched by its intensity.

"Don't pretend with me, slut," he growled. "I find

I'm extremely short of patience where you're concerned. It wouldn't take much to persuade me to show you just how excruciating a whipping can be."

Cathy stared at him. He looked mad, and yet spoke with the confidence that his attitude was justified. Petersham, too, had treated her with scathing contempt. Conjecture crystallized into fact: they were both blaming her for something of which she had no knowledge.

"Jon, I realize you're angry with me," she said softly, her eyes never leaving the blazing gray ones. She was going to add, "Won't you tell me why?" when he interrupted with an enraged bellow.

"Angry? Angry? You bitch, I could cheerfully cut you up for bait with a dull knife, and I may do it yet if you don't keep your goddamned mouth shut!"

His fists were clenched as if he were having great trouble restraining himself from hitting her. Cathy recoiled from the taut menace in his face. When she remained silent he gradually relaxed, and, turning away, crossed to the tub. He stepped into it, sliding down into the steaming water gingerly. A grimace of pain crossed his features as the hot water touched his raw back. From the bed Cathy could still see the suppurating sores. It looked like he'd been beaten not once, but many times. Where had he been, she wondered feverishly. What had happened to him?

"Jon, won't you tell me what happened?" she ventured after some minutes. His head snapped around, and he fixed his burning eyes on her. The bristly black beard made him look like a fearsome stranger.

"You have a very soft voice," he drawled in reply. "Soft and twining. It almost persuaded me that you were like that too. But you taught me better, didn't you, wife? You taught me that beneath that distracting exterior beats a heart of pure flint, and a selfish, grasping mind. Do you think you can play the same trick on me twice? I warn you now, don't try. Killing you would give me more pleasure than anything in my life, and if you tempt me I may not be able to deny myself even until the child is born."

Cathy gaped at him, feeling sick with shock. There was no mistaking the venom in his tone. Hatred stared implacably from his eyes. She started to protest her total bewilderment, then though better of it. Plainly he was determined to despise her. Besides, there was no way she could properly defend herself until she knew of what she stood accused. But if she couldn't tell her innocence in words, she could express it in deed. Swinging her legs over the side of the bunk, she struggled laboriously to her feet. Her swollen belly surged against the clinging pink nightdress and her plaits swung rhythmically against her breast as she moved toward him. Jon watched her warily, his eyes veiled. His gaze moved first to her delicately etched features then traveled as if drawn by a magnet to her surging middle.

"God!" he muttered, closing his eyes as if he could no longer bear the sight of her. Cathy flushed, thinking that he must find her pregnancy repulsive, but she refused to be deterred. She walked forward steadily until her thighs just touched the cool porcelain rim of the tub. Jon's mouth set grimly, but he still refused to open his eyes. Cathy stared doggedly down at his overlong black hair.

Jon opened his eyes at last, glaring ominously up at her.

"What do you think you're doing, bitch?" he grated.

Cathy's eyes sparkled at the expletive, but she bit her tongue and said nothing as she bent to scoop the soap and cloth from the water. Her fingers just brushed his chest, and his hands flew up to capture hers, tightening cruelly around her wrists.

"I asked you what you think you're doing?" he snarled, his eyes snapping at her like a wild beasts.

"Your hair needs washing," Cathy said coolly, masking her apprehension beneath a surface calm. She was gambling all on the notion that he wouldn't hurt her, at least not as long as she carried his child. If she were wrong, the consequences could be disastrous. But if she were right—well, her touch had been the key that freed his softer emotions once. Perhaps it would be again.

"Are you proposing to wash it for me?" he asked, his voice very soft as he jeered at her. "You really think you can touch me with those little white hands and erase everything you've done, don't you? Well, wife, it won't work, so you may as well not bother. I've found out about you the hard way, and I'm not likely to forget."

"I don't want you to forget, Jon," she said in a calm voice, freeing her hands from his grasp. She wet the rag and squeezed it over his black head. The water trickled down to his scalp, and he didn't move away. Cathy repeated the maneuver, then bent and scooped more water in her cupped hands, wetting his hair thoroughly. When he still didn't protest, she soaped the thick strands, letting her fingers run deeply through them. His hair and scalp were thick with grime; Cathy should have felt repulsed but she didn't. Her fingers massaged his scalp, softly working out the dirt. Jon tensed at first under her ministration, than at last began to relax.

"Hell, why not?" she heard him mutter, more to himself than her. "I've got your measure now, bitch, and you won't find me so easily taken in a second time."

Wisely, Cathy continued as if he hadn't spoken. After a while she took up the bucket of hot water that Petersham had left and tipped its contents in a steady stream over Jon's head. The grimy soap rinsed away, and Jon swivelled around to look at her. Whatever words he had planned to utter froze on his lips as his eyes narrowed ferociously on the large wooden bucket that was still half full of water and which she still held in her hands.

"Put that down!" he roared, his teeth snapping together furiously.

Cathy was so startled that she lost her grip on the bucket. It fell with a crash to the floor, cascading

339

water all over her nightdress. She was wet to the waist. Her eyes were huge as she stared at him incomprehendingly, one hand clasping her throat. Jon surged to his feet, cursing fiendishly, stepping from the tub and snatching up the towel to rub himself dry. All the while he rained oaths on her while she cowered dumbly away from him. What had she done to make him so angry this time? She couldn't understand it, and her blue eyes mutely pleaded with him to explain. Jon met those eyes, his own growing savage.

"So you think to seduce me again, bitch?" he ground out. "You think to make me solicitous of your condition, is that it? Are you perhaps hoping to be spared the punishment that awaits you after the child is born? I'll see you in hell first! Thinking of it, planning it—it was the only thing that kept me alive, and you're not going to weasel your way out of it. Your insidious little ways are wasted on me!"

While Cathy still struggled to make sense of his words, he threw on clean clothes and stormed out. The door banged behind him, and she was left staring blankly at the wall. The horrifying truth crashed over her head like a tidal wave. No matter how violent his rejection of her, or how fierce his hatred, her love for him remained unchanged.

Jon didn't return to the cabin at all that day. Martha came in, and bullied her into bed, and Petersham stiffly carried in their midday meal. But Jon didn't come. Cathy brushed aside Martha's care of her impatiently, and felt like screaming when Petersham turned a deaf ear to her questions. If she were going to be able to understand what motivated Jon's savage resentment, she must know what had happened to him, and why he blamed her. Besides Jon himself, who would undoubtedly meet her questions with furious invective, Petersham was the only one she could turn to.

Darkness fell at last, and the ship gradually quieted. Cathy waited with nervous expectation for Jon to retire to bed. It must have been around midnight when she at last faced the truth: he wasn't coming. He must really despise her if he couldn't even bear to stay in the same cabin with her, she thought forlornly. Tears trickled down her cheeks as she disconsolately blew out the bedside candle and settled down in the bunk. She felt lost and alone beneath the covers. Sobs tore from her throat, and, mindful of Martha's contentedly snoring form tucked up in a pallet at the side of the bunk, she muffled the sounds in her pillow. Come tomorrow, she comforted herself, she would get some answers to her questions. If not from Jon, or Petersham, then from the crew. Someone would tell her, she felt sure.

The weather defeated her. She rose the next morning to find that it was snowing, not in drifting fat flakes but in a driving curtain of white. From the window she could see icicles forming on the wooden overhang. The sea was gray and choppy, and if it had been possible to see the sky Cathy knew it would look the same. Common sense, and a lack

341

of warm clothes, kept both her and Martha glued to the small area around the coal stove. Any questions she had would have to be saved for whoever entered the cabin first.

Petersham arrived after a while bearing the midday meal. Cathy answered his curt knock, and instead of taking the tray from his hands she caught his arm and pulled him inside the cabin. Then she shut the door, leaning against it so that he would have to push her out of the way to get back outside. Knowing Petersham, she realized that his innate respect for a woman in a delicate condition would stop him from resorting to actual physical force. Unless he, as well as Jon, had suffered a severe sea change.

Petersham set the tray down on the table, and then, with great dignity approached the door. Cathy crossed her arms over her chest, leaning against it, smiling at him determinedly. With the thick quilt around her shoulders and her hair hanging in braids down her back, she looked like an Indian squaw. Petersham paused some two feet away, uncertain of what to do.

"If you'll excuse me, ma'am," he said stiffly, not quite meeting her eyes. His face was rigid with disapproval.

"I want to know what happened to Jon, Petersham," Cathy said softly. "And I'm not moving until you tell me."

"You'll have to ask the Captain that, ma'am." Petersham's tone was very formal, his eyes as they met hers hard with dislike. "It's not my place to discuss his personal business."

Cathy tried a different tack. "Petersham, I am his wife. I have a right to know what's wrong with him."

"There's nothing wrong with the Captain, so far as I know, Mistress Hale." The emphasis on the title was scathing. Cathy's temper, exacerbated by first Jon's and now Petersham's unreasonable antagonism, went up in flames. Her blue eyes snapped, and her mouth contorted furiously. She came away from the door, advancing on Petersham. The man backed before her, not knowing what else to do. Martha sprang up and ran to Cathy's side, clutching at her arm.

"Miss Cathy, you must remember the baby!" the woman cautioned, her voice shrill with alarm. Cathy saw the flicker in Petersham's eyes as they went from her face to her belly, and suddenly knew the way to get him to tell her what she wanted to know.

"Oh, Martha!" she gasped, clasping her middle and bending almost double. Martha's face went white, and Petersham mirrored her concern. Cathy moaned, and Martha turned furiously on the valet.

"Now see what you've done, you spawn of Satan!" she raged. "Upsetting Miss Cathy, and her so far gone with child! You'll have that baby stillborn with your cruel ways, and serve your fiend of a Captain exactly right!"

"I didn't mean . . . ," Petersham gasped, bending over Cathy. Cathy looked up at him, still moaning.

"Petersham, what happened to Jon?" she asked,

her voice hoarse with pretended pain. Petersham's face stiffened, but as she gave vent to another rending groan he capitulated, albeit unwillingly.

"You know the answer to that very well, Miss Cathy," he said severely, and Cathy stifled a triumphant smile at the familiar form of address that had slipped out. "But if it amuses you to have me tell you what you already know, I will. Master Jon was imprisoned under sentence of hanging. The execution would have been carried out this morning if Mr. Harry hadn't got word about what was going on. We rescued him, which I'm sure you're very sorry for. Any woman who would have her husband beaten and starved deserves whatever happens to her later, as we've all agreed. You'll get no help from us, Mistress Hale."

The freezing dislike was back in Petersham's voice. Cathy straightened quickly, forgetting her supposed pain in the shock of Petersham's revelations.

"I . . . had him beaten and starved?" she repeated disbelievingly, staring at Petersham as if she thought he too had gone mad. "In prison? I didn't even know he was in prison! He escaped the day the soldiers took Las Palmas! How was I to know he'd been captured again later? I tell you I didn't know, Petersham. I didn't know! You must believe me!"

"It's not me you'll have to convince, Mistress Hale." Again that hateful inflection was present in the last words. "It's Master Jon. But if I may give you a piece of advice, don't try that tale on him. He's too canny a bird to be taken in by such an obvious lie."

"But it's not a lie!" Cathy wailed, starting to go after Petersham as he walked with immense dignity to the door. Martha held her back, unaware that Cathy's physical distress had merely been assumed. By the time Cathy shook free of Martha's restraining hands, Petersham was gone.

"Martha, what am I going to do?" Cathy cried, turning wounded eyes on her nanny, who ducked sympathetically over her distress. The woman's plump arms came around the girl's shoulders, and Cathy allowed herself to be led over to the bed and tucked in beneath the quilts. Cathy thought furiously as Martha brought her meal across and set the tray on her lap. Somehow she had to convince Jon that she was completely innocent. But how was she to do that if he wouldn't even come near her? The answer was painfully obvious: she would have to go to him.

The storm the "Margarita" was caught in howled for the rest of the day. The ship was tossed around like a toy in the hands of a capricious giant, and Martha became violently seasick. Cathy, whose stomach had become accustomed to the ocean's vagaries on her previous voyage, made her nanny as comfortable as she could, but there was really no treatment for seasickness save time or the cooperation of the sea. At last she persuaded Martha to lie down in the bunk, where the woman curled up in a fetal position. Eventually her groans quieted and she fell asleep.

Cathy, huddled in a chair in front of the stove, pursed her lips thoughtfully as Martha's light snores drifted to her ears. This was the chance she had been waiting for. As long as Martha was awake, there wasn't any way she could leave the cabin. Martha would tie her to the bunk before she would permit her to venture out in such a storm. As far as Cathy was concerned, however, her need to talk with Jon was paramount. She dismissed the storm with little more than a shrug.

Her decision made, Cathy got to her feet and slid stealthily toward the door, casting an uneasy glance back over her shoulder at Martha. The woman slept on, oblivious.

She pulled a quilt high over her head so that it would give her some protection from the wind, and then attempted to venture outside. The force of the wind almost jerked the door from her hand, but she held on to it desperately, knowing that a crash would be sure to waken Martha. The muscles in her arms ached as she struggled to close it quietly be-hind her. Finally it was done, and she leaned back against it with a sigh to catch her breath.

The boards of the deck were icy wet beneath her bare feet. Cathy curled her toes against the cold, her eyes widening as she looked about her. What she saw was a study in gray and white. The sky and the sea were both the color of lead, the former seeming so low that it would almost crush the ship, and the latter straining upward to defy the heavens with menacing, white-tipped waves. Fine, grainy particles of snow and ice mixed with the freezing salt spray to sting against her face and hands like a thousand tiny bees. The wind howled as if outraged that such a puny thing as the "Margarita" should dare to challenge it. Cathy thought for an instant about abandoning her mission and going back inside where it was warm and dry and safe, but then squared her shoulders resolutely, squinting up at the quarterdeck. It was so close, and she would hold on to the rail every step of the way. If she wanted to talk to Jon, the storm was something she had to face.

Clutching the quilt about her with one hand and leaning into the force of the wind, Cathy struggled up the stairs. They were slippery with ice, and her frozen feet were so numb that she had trouble moving. Twice she fell to her knees on the shallow flight of steps, and twice she righted herself and went on while the ship heaved like a malevolent spirit beneath her. Splinters drove into her hand as it pulled her upwards, but Cathy was unconscious of the pain. Only one thought was in her mind: she had to tell Jon that she had had nothing to do with his imprisonment or subsequent torture. Only then could she hope for his love.

Finally she made it to the quarterdeck. She held on to the thin wooden rail, looking about herself disbelievingly. The quarterdeck was deserted. The wheel was lashed with rawhide thongs to hold the ship on course. Cathy turned to peer over the rest of the ship. The decks were completely bare of life. There was not a man in sight. Her heart began to pound erratically as a terrible thought occurred to her. Had everyone been washed overboard? Were she and Martha the only people left alive on the ship? Dear God, what had happened? What . . . ?

"Jon!" she screamed in a paroxysm of fear. "Jon! Jon!"

"Shit!" The enraged response whirled down on the wind. Cathy looked up, still frightened, unable to see a worldly source of speech, but at the same time registering dimly that a heavenly being would scarcely resort to such language. Her eyes widened and her mouth went dry as she saw men clinging like blurred gray shadows to the rigging as they hacked desperately away at the ropes that held the canvas at full sail. One man had left the work and was lowering himself toward the deck at a furious pace. His face and the clear outline of his body were obscured by the driving snow, but Cathy knew with an inexplicable certainly that it was Jon.

There was a dull roaring in her ears as he reached the deck. She could just make out the leaping fear in his eyes as he came toward the quarterdeck at a dead run. She shook her head to clear it of the buzz, holding tightly to the rail with one hand and feeling a smile quiver at the way he was forced to zig-zag across the deck in time to the pitching of the ship. The roar seemed louder as he reached the base of the steps, and Cathy glanced reflexively over her shoulder.

What she saw stopped her heart. Rushing toward her like hell itself was a huge wave, dark and terrifying as death. Cathy threw her hand up over her face in an absurd effort to ward it off, knowing that she could never reach safety in time.

Suddenly she was thrown to the deck and a heavy body crashed down on top of her. Hard arms came around her, holding her tightly against the railing.

"Hold your breath!" The words were screamed in her ear.

Automatically Cathy did as she was told. No sooner had she closed her mouth than tons of icy water came hurtling down on top of her, threatening to crush her, trying to pull her away from the strong arms that held her penned to the deck. She could feel the force of the water dragging at her, doing its best to suck her into the depths. Alone, she would have been no match for its force; with Jon, she stood a chance.

It was over in a matter of seconds. The "Margarita" bucked wildly, then righted itself, shaking off the deluge like a shaggy dog. Cathy felt herself being hauled to her feet, then the arms that had kept her safe shook her until her teeth were rattling in her head.

"You goddamned stupid little fool!" Jon raged, too angry to realize that the wind was carrying away his bellows or that Cathy could barely hear him above the sounds of the storm. "You damn near got yourself killed!"

"I had to talk to you. . . ." Cathy tried to explain, cringing in his rough embrace. With a feeling of frustration she realized that he could no more hear her than she could him. Still, she had to try.

"You have to listen to me!" she screeched, shaking his arm. He glared down at her murderously, his hands moving from her shoulders to meet around the base of her throat.

"Shut up or I'll throttle you here and now!" he yelled, his hands tightening around her slender neck. Cathy jerked free, her eyes widening as a stabbing pain tore through her belly. She screamed, its force bending her double.

"What the hell . . . !"

Cathy dropped to her knees on the quarterdeck, her arms clutching her middle protectively. Another pain tore through her. Oh, God, she was losing the baby! Jon bent over her, then divining what was wrong he scooped her up in his arms, cradling her against him as he battled his way to the stairs. The swirling wind carried away the curses that were falling in a steady stream from his mouth. Cathy stared up at his lean face, her eyes glazing over as pain ripped through her belly with increasing intensity. She moaned, trying to hold her baby safely inside her with both hands pressed frantically to the convulsing mound. Jon's eyes met hers, and she saw in them leaping flames of panic. Why, he's frightened, too, she thought with vague surprise. Then all thoughts vanished under another sweeping onslaught of pain. She screamed, then merciful blackness descended like a curtain. Jon swore profanely as she went limp in his arms, leaping down the stairs two at a time to carry her unconscious form to the shelter of his cabin.

Fourteen

The only thing that kept Cathy from losing her baby there and then was Martha's skilled nursing. Routed from the bunk by Jon's frantic bellow and ignoring her seasickness, Martha pressed cold cloths between Cathy's legs and packed them tightly around the heaving mound of her belly, hoping to stop the hemorrhaging before it was too late. Jon hovered helplessly until Martha turned on him like a ruffled hen, driving him from the cabin. Such things, she sniffed, were not suitable viewing for gentlemen. Her disparaging glance at Jon seemed to doubt whether in fact he belonged in such a category, but still she insisted that he leave. Knowing that there was nothing he could do to aid Cathy and their child, other than seeing to it that the "Margarita" was not sunk by the force of the storm, he complied with a meekness that did much for him in Martha's eyes. As a compromise, he sent Petersham along to help the woman in any way she needed it. Once the immediate danger was past, Martha gloried in using Petersham as an errand boy. She was in her element presiding over a sickroom.

Cathy did not return to full consciousness until two days later. By then the storm had passed, and the baby was once again a firm resident of her womb. She was weak from the ordeal she had passed through, though, and Martha insisted that

351

she remain in bed until after the baby was safely born. Jon added his command to Martha's, and Cathy was too frightened by what had almost occurred to disobey either of them. Jon's gruffly expressed words pleased her more than she had thought was possible with their implicit message of concern for her. He was wary, and distrustful, but she didn't think he hated her any longer. Rather shyly she mentioned the matter to Martha, who nodded at her comfortably.

"Captain Hale was sick with worry about you," she confirmed with brisk cheerfulness. "He's one who takes his woman's child-bearing hard. That fool of a valet tells me that his mother died in child-bed, so I guess it's not to be wondered at. You know, Miss Cathy, I think I may have been mistaken about the man. He's not nearly so fearsome as I thought. He might make you a proper husband after all."

Cathy had to smile at what was, from Martha, an accolade. If only *Jon* thought he might make her a proper husband, she would be content. Her love for him was devouring her, and it was all she could do to keep herself from telling him outright. Instinctive caution kept her silent, however, as she did not want to drive him further away from her. Time was her ally, she thought—time and the child she carried. After it was born he would surely let down his guard with her, realizing that the baby's birth bound her to him irrevocably.

Jon still slept out of the cabin, and Cathy reluctantly conceded that it was probably just as well. But he paid her a visit nearly every afternoon. Although his manner was stiff and rather formal, she delighted in his presence, and smiled at him warmly whenever he appeared.

One day about two weeks later Martha tactfully absented herself during Jon's visit. Cathy took the opportunity to catch his hand, drawing him down to sit on the edge of the bunk beside her. He allowed her to hold his hand, but his eyes as they ran over her were wary. Cathy could see the tension forming in the lines beside his mouth.

As simply and convincingly as she could, she told him that she had had no part in what had happened to him in prison. She hadn't even known he was captured again, she told him earnestly, not understanding why his face was beginning to poker up. Before she was finished he got to his feet abruptly, pulling his hand away from her grasp and glowering down at her.

"Jon!" she cried as he started to turn away. The pain of his disbelief cut through her like a knife. He glanced back at her, hesitating, the muscle working in his jaw the only indication he gave of feeling anything at all.

"It doesn't matter," he told her briefly, seeing her obvious agitation. "It's in the past, and we'll forget it. You're my wife, regardless of how it came about or what happened afterwards. We won't discuss the subject again."

With this curt pronouncement, he strode from the room. Cathy called after him frantically, determined that they would discuss it until everything was quite clear, but he neither answered nor turned back. She collapsed back against the pillows with a dispirited sigh. Beneath his polite exterior Jon still distrusted her as much as ever. It might take years, or even longer, to persuade him differently. Tears began to trickle down Cathy's cheeks, overflowing one at a time until her whole face was wet. When Martha came back into the cabin, Cathy was crying unrestrainedly. Martha threw up her arms in horror, then bullied her charge into drying her eyes and drinking a nice, bracing cup of tea. After that Cathy was told to go to sleep, and, rather to her own surprise, she did. From then on Martha was careful to remain in the cabin whenever Jon was present. And to Cathy's intense annoyance, Jon seemed almost relieved at the other woman's presence. Because of sheer lack of opportunity, Cathy grudgingly put the subject on hold. Once the baby was born. . . . The words beat like a Greek chorus in her mind. Once the baby was born, she vowed determinedly, he would not find it so easy to avoid the discussion she had in mind. She would badger him relentlessly until, from sheer exhaustion, he was forced to believe her. Her cheeks dimpled in a secret, droll smile. As she knew from experience, there were ways to make him listen, and believe. She wouldn't scruple to use them . . . once the baby was born.

Cathy was thankful to discover that Petersham at least was not so pig-headed. Gradually, by infinitesimal degrees, her relationship with the little man returned to where it had been before the soldiers came to Las Palmas. He mothered her almost as much as Martha, scolding her for not eating, or for allowing herself to feel depressed. The baby's welfare should be her main concern, he told her sternly, and he set himself to cheering her up.

Martha regarded this strange camaraderie with uncertainty. In her world, it was worse than improper for a man to enter the bedroom of a lady who was not his wife, much less to sit and talk with her for hours. But if the Captain saw no harm in it then she could find no grounds to object herself. The little man was harmless, she knew very well, and he did serve to bolster Miss Cathy's spirits. Grudgingly she concluded that his constant popping in and out must be endured for the sake of her charge. But that didn't mean she had to like the man, and she most emphatically didn't.

Cathy was aware of Martha's growing jealousy of Petersham, but she found the valet's snippets of information too intriguing to permit her to discourage his almost constant presence. From him she learned that they were bound for South Carolina because of a sudden inexplicable whim on the captain's part. Word had come while Master Jon was still in prison that old Mr. Hale had died, leaving Woodham and the rest of his personal possessions to his son. When Petersham had informed Jon of this, the captain's face had been a study for a few minutes before he curtly ordered that the "Margarita" be set on an easterly course. It was time, Petersham quoted Jon, that they returned home.

Harry came in to see her only once, and then reluctantly. Cathy supposed that he feared Jon's wrath. He need not have worried, Cathy thought dispiritedly. Far from showing signs of jealousy, Jon was coolly indifferent when she informed him of Harry's visit.

Petersham found some good quality wool in the hold, and Martha used it to clothe herself decently. Cathy, confined to bed as she was, was perfectly content to wear Jon's nightshirts again. If the sight of her small body enveloped in the too-big white folds brought back memories, Jon didn't show it by so much as the flicker of an eyelash. Cathy was forced to conclude that the only interest he now had in her was as the mother of his child. But if his emotions had warmed toward her once, they could again. And she meant to see to it that they did.

The "Margarita" sighted Nova Scotia some three weeks after setting sail. From then on they were never far from land as Jon sailed down the coast of North America toward his goal. The ocean during the winter months was unpredictable, and for the sake of everyone on board he elected to make the voyage longer but safer. Cathy, ruthlessly confined to bed, was not even permitted up at the first sight of land. Although Jon volunteered to carry her up on deck if she were set on looking, Martha firmly prohibited the notion. And, despite Cathy's sulks, Martha got her way.

The weather warmed gradually as the "Margarita" sailed southward. The child was due on the third of March according to Cathy's and Martha's calculations. Jon told them that they should drop anchor in Charleston sometime during the third week in February. His estimate was dead on target, as always.

Cathy insisted on going up on deck as the "Margarita" sailed into the bay at Charleston. She wanted to see her new home, she declared, and she would if she had to crawl. Jon overruled Martha's objections for once, wrapping Cathy securely in a quilt and then hoisting her up into his arms. Despite the added weight of the child he held her easily. Cathy twined her arms around his neck, secretly relishing the feel of his strong muscles against her skin. Soon, she thought, she would be in a position where she could use her female charms to convince him of her innocence. Until then, she would have to be satisfied with being held distastefully.

A small, anticipatory smile curved her lips as Jon bore her out into the sunshine. He saw the feline contentment in her face, and his eyes narrowed warily at her. Cathy, buoyed by her plans for the future, rewarded his suspicions with a blithe smile. His sure stride faltered, and he stared down at her with the dazzled expression of a man who has looked too long at the sun.

Cathy returned his look with candid interest. During their seven weeks at sea he had regained the weight he had lost, and he was now as big and powerful as ever. His arms about her were corded with muscles, and Cathy gloried in their sure strength. His face had regained its healthy bronze color, and the beard had been shaved to reveal the lean firmness of his jaw. His ruggedly hewn features were still compellingly handsome. Cathy felt a pleasant little tingle start at the base of her spine and shiver up her back as she stared at the hard mouth. She wanted to touch it with her own. . . . Her thought must have shown in her face, because she felt his breathing pick up as she looked at him. He wanted her too, she realized with a mingling of triumph and desire. The kindling fire in his eyes spoke not of anger, or distrust, but of naked passion.

"Excuse me, Captain, is something wrong?" Martha's worried voice behind them brought them both back to reality with a thump. Cathy saw a faint red color steal up to stain Jon's cheekbones. Her own face felt uncomfortably warm. Jon hitched her up as if he had merely stopped to make sure of his grip, speaking over his shoulder to Martha with wry humor.

"Your mistress has picked up a considerable amount of weight since I last had occasion to carry her," he grunted. "But I'll do my best not to drop her. After all the trouble she's caused us, it would be a pity to lose her now."

He glanced significantly over the side of the ship into the sparkling blue waters of the bay as he spoke. Cathy squealed playfully, knowing that nothing short of a hurricane would make him drop her, while Martha frowned at his nonsense disapprovingly. Cathy felt giddy with happiness as he bore her up to the quarterdeck, rejoicing in his gruff teasing. He was more like the Jon of Las Palmas today than at any other time since he had stolen her away again.

With her head pressed back against Jon's shoulder, she didn't notice the sudden tightening of his mouth or the grimness that came into his eyes as she nestled into him like a small, trusting kitten. He didn't speak, but then she didn't feel like talking either. Relaxing against the hard muscles of his chest, she looked with interest toward the city which was to be her home.

Charleston was a thriving seaport, a bustling southern town dependent for its sustenance on the ocean's proximity. Ships from all over the world were at anchor in the harbor, come to trade spice or rum or textiles for Charleston's most profitable export: cotton.

Cathy took a deep breath of the sweet air, enjoying the feel of the sun which shone warmly down even at the end of February. Jon had been born in this town, had spent his boyhood here. Despite the bitterness of his memories, Charleston was his home. Cathy was determined to make it her home, too.

She protested when Jon began to carry her back down to his cabin again. She could have watched the activity in the harbor all day. But when he insisted, she gave in with good grace. As he said, Charleston would be around for a long time. It wouldn't disappear if she went in for a rest.

Jon went ashore while Cathy napped. He was still gone when she awoke. To her surprise, Martha had accompanied him, leaving Petersham with Cathy. It was after dark before they returned to the ship.

Martha bustled in first, her arms loaded with packages. Jon followed, similarly burdened. Cathy sat up in the bunk, her eyes widening with astonishment. Her eyes flew to Jon's face. His eyes met hers steadily, then a slow smile curved his mouth.

"I couldn't take my wife ashore dressed in a quilt," he explained simply, dropping the bundles on the bed. Cathy looked from the packages to her husband and back, speechless. Jon continued: "And I like the idea of a naked baby even less. I think you'll find everything you both will need in there."

A nod indicated the packages. Cathy's fingers flew to open them while Martha beamed at her. There were three dresses, all sized to fit a very pregnant lady, in lovely yellow and palest green and peach. Petticoats and underwear designed specifically for an expectant mother were in another box. Cathy held up a pair of drawers with an elasticized middle panel made to expand as her belly did, her eyes quizzical as they turned on Jon.

"You didn't pick these out," she accused, half laughing at the idea. Jon grinned.

"I must admit that I didn't," he said. "Nor did I select the ungodly amount of infant paraphernalia without which I have been assured no child can be adequately cared for. Martha did. You must thank her."

"Captain Hale told me to get what I thought you both needed," Martha said, defending him stoutly. "And he paid the bills. Which is more than a lot of gentlemen would have done."

"I am unmanned," Jon murmured satirically in response to Martha's unexpected championship. Cathy smiled at him, and at her nanny. She caught at Martha's arm, pulling the woman down so that she could plant an affectionate kiss on her cheek, then turned to hold out her arms unselfconsciously to Jon. Red washed up under the swarthy skin of his face, and he looked undecided for a moment before Martha's expectant look forced him to bend rather stiffly toward her. Cathy's arms closed tenderly about his neck, and she brushed a soft kiss against his firm mouth. Under her touch his lips parted, hardening, and his hands moved convulsively as though he would crush her to him, belly and all. The sound of Martha discreetly clearing her throat in the background brought him to his senses. He pulled away, his breathing perceptibly harder. Cathy smiled at him tremulously. His eyes lingered on her face for a long, disturbing moment before swinging away.

"If you ladies will excuse me . . ." he said rather jerkily, turning on his heels. Cathy stared at him, her eyes warm, admiring the powerful swing of his tall body as he left the cabin. Martha had to speak to her twice before she managed to tear herself away from a rapt contemplation of the closed cabin door. The older woman's eyes were knowing as she watched her mistress lovingly unwrap the tiny infant apparel, but she refrained from mentioning what she had seen. It was plain as the nose on Miss Cathy's face that she was head over heels in love with the captain. As for him, well, men were better at hiding their feelings. Still, Martha smiled contentedly as she helped Cathy pack away the baby's things.

By the time Cathy was dressed in the yellow gown, her hair fixed in a demure style as befitted a young matron, and her and the baby's new things were safely packed in the sea chests, it was midmorning. Jon had been striding about the deck for an hour, impatiently sticking his head in the door from time to time to demand testily what in blazes was taking so long. Cathy smiled at him, but Martha was less forbearing. She shooed him away firmly, saying that a lady's toilette was an intricate business and that a real gentleman knew this and adjusted his schedule accordingly. Jon clenched his jaw, but knew better than to retort. A seasoned warrior, he had been in enough battles to recognize defeat. He retired with reluctant grace, leaving Martha in command of the field.

At last Cathy was ready. Jon was summoned to carry her to a waiting boat, and two sailors were told to take care of the luggage. Their jaws sagged when they saw the towering mound of trunks and packages, but they nodded valiantly in response to Jon's terse instructions as to how they were to convey them to the house. Jon picked up Cathy, one arm supporting her shoulders and the other beneath her knees. She held on to his neck carefully, smiling at him as her head rested against his shoulder. The scent of her freshly washed hair drifted to his nostrils, and he half closed his eyes. Only Martha's impatient hustling movements behind him kept him from stopping to press his lips to the fragrance's source.

When Cathy saw exactly how she was expected to get from the "Margarita's" deck to the small boat bobbing far beneath on the surface of the water, she balked. There was no way that she was going to sit in the sling Jon had devised and be lowered over the side. If she fell, she would fall all the way to China. If nothing else could be arranged, she would much prefer to take her chances with the ladder. Martha agreed with Cathy wholeheartedly. She misliked the look of the contraption herself.

Jon coaxed, cajoled, and ordered. Cathy refused to budge. Finally he lost his patience and dumped her bodily into the sling, still handling her as gently as he could in deference to her condition. Cathy, seeing there was no help for it, allowed him to tie her in, then closed her eyes and clung hard to the attached ropes as she was suspended over the side. A pulley lowered her carefully, and a sailor caught her at the other end, but Cathy was white by the time the operation was completed. She had always had an irrational fear of heights.

Once Cathy was safely aboard the punt, the operation proceeded speedily. Martha was lowered in the same fashion, screaming as she was suspended over the blue waters of the bay. Less care was taken to catch her than Cathy, and by the time Martha was safely installed on the wooden seat her skirt was thoroughly splashed. She muttered direly as Jon climbed down the ladder and jumped lightly aboard. Luckily the water was as smooth as satin. The journey to shore was completed without a hitch.

Jon had hired an open carriage and given it instructions to await them at the dock. He proposed to take Cathy to Woodham while Martha followed in a second carriage with the baggage. The ride should take no more than an hour, and then they would be safely home. Nobody would have to move again unless he or she wanted to.

This partly mollified Martha. She agreed, with an air of injured dignity, to wait for the luggage and to watch over its safe bestowal. Jon, inwardly blessing his father for not having endowed him with a nanny, swung up into the carriage beside Cathy and nodded to the driver to move off.

Cathy leaned her head back against the upholstered seat, drinking in the sights and sounds around her. As they moved over the cobbled streets, they passed avenue upon avenue of small shops, with wooden signs hanging out front advertising everything from a millinery to a tooth-drawer. After the child was born, Cathy anticipated, she would spend many a pleasurable afternoon in making the acquaintance of the local boutiques. Jon caught her hand as they drove out toward the residential section, and Cathy turned to look at him, surprised. Lately he had not been given to gestures of affection.

"I bought you something else, yesterday," he said, continuing to hold her left hand while he drew a small box from the pocket of his coat. As Cathy stared at him he drew the wedding ring from her finger. He held it briefly in his clenched fist, then opened his hand to let it fall carelessly over the side of the carriage. Cathy gasped as the small golden circle was left behind in the road, then turned on Jon indignantly. He thrust the box at her.

"Open it," he ordered brusquely, and Cathy took the box from him. When she hesitated to open it he flipped up the lid with his thumb. Cathy blinked bemusedly at the glitter of jewels inside. There were two rings; a diamond solitaire flanked by two smaller sapphires, and a plain gold wedding band. She looked from the rings to his face, her eyes questioning.

"My wife wears my rings," he explained sardonically, and when Cathy continued to stare at him he frowned at her impatiently.

"Put them on."

She made no move to obey, so he caught up her left hand and slid the rings onto her unresisting fingers. The gesture took her by surprise, and she felt an absurd knot of tears rise in her throat as the long brown fingers slipped the rings onto her slender white ones. It was almost as if they were getting married again, without the twisted emotions that had made a mockery of the real ceremony, and Cathy's unguarded eyes as she raised them to Jon's reflected her feelings.

"Jon, I . . ." she started to say, but something in his face made her think better of the confession she had been about to make. Instead, she decided to use this chance to protest her total innocence again. "I really didn't know that you were in prison. I certainly never would have had you beaten, or starved. Please believe me."

Jon's eyes narrowed coldly on her face.

"As I think I told you before, the subject is closed. There's no need for you to make ridiculous attempts to appease me. I have accepted the fact that we are married, for better or worse, so you have no need to fear that I'll exact some sort of vengeance on you for your actions. You're perfectly safe."

The sneering tone of the last words stabbed Cathy to the quick. She took a deep breath, trying to hold back the tears that started to her eyes. I must not cry, I must not, she told herself fiercely, willing back the tears that seemed to flow on the slightest provocation in these last weeks of her pregnancy.

"Christ, you'll try anything, won't you?" Jon muttered fiercely, looking away from the suspicious glitter in her eyes.

"Of course I will," Cathy retorted angrily, his contempt stiffening her spine. She tilted her chin at him haughtily. "Being married is a dull business. I have to do something to liven it up!"

"You bitch!" Jon swore under his breath.

Cathy's mouth tilted in a satisfied smile. Two could be nasty, she thought vindictively. If he thought that she were willing to play doormat, he could bloody well think again! She made up her mind to give back what she got.

The remainder of the ride passed in almost total silence. Only the steady clop clop of the horse's hoofs on the dirt road sounded in the air. Finally, Jon roused himself from the black study he was lost in to indicate a certain lane to the driver.

"We're here," he said laconically to Cathy.

Cathy sat up, willing to ignore what had passed between them in her eagerness to see her new home. The lane curled between two rows of tall oak trees. Sloping green fields fell away on either side. In the distance Cathy could just make out the misty outline of a two-story brick house. As they drew closer she caught her breath. It was beautiful, a stately mansion with soaring white columns guarding the entrance. A veranda ran the length of the house, and a leaded-glass fan light curved over the oak front door. Shallow steps led up to the veranda. Magnolia trees with their wavy white blossoms flanked the steps on either side.

The carriage halted on the circular drive just in front of the house. Jon made a move as though he would jump down, but was arrested in the act as a woman came out to the edge of the porch to stand staring down at him. Jon stared back, his face curiously hard, and got out of the buggy with calm deliberation.

"Good morning, Isobelle," Jon said, his voice expressionless. Cathy's eyes went from her husband's broad back to the fashionably dressed woman on the porch. The woman was very pretty in a black-haired, flashing-eyed kind of way, and her figure in the low-cut silk gown was voluptuous. But tiny lines marred the skin of her face, and her red mouth had a petulant droop. She was quite old, Cathy saw, even older than Jon. The merest glimmer of a suspicion as to who she might be began to lurk in Cathy's brain.

"Jon," the woman nodded in reply to his greeting. Her bold eyes ran over his tall form in a way Cathy didn't care for. They had widened appreciatively as they came back to linger on his face, and Cathy bit her lip. "You've changed, my dear."

"So have you, Isobelle," Jon answered, his voice tight. Remembering Cathy's presence at last, he turned to lift her from the carriage, holding her very carefully in his arms. Cathy flashed him a poisonous look. He smiled slightly at the anger smoldering in her eyes.

"And who have we here?" Isobelle's eyes narrowed as they ran over Cathy's round shape. Cathy regarded the woman haughtily. Her possessive attitude toward Jon was irritating in the extreme.

"This is my wife," Jon said coolly, carrying Cathy with easy strength as he began to mount the stairs. When he was on the second one from the top he paused. "Cathy, this is Isobelle. My stepmother."

Cathy's suspicions were confirmed. This, then,

was the woman Jon had adored as a teen-ager, the one who had so cruelly disillusioned him by her betrayal of his father. Much against her will she murmured something polite, which the woman didn't even bother to answer.

"Cradle-snatching, Jon?" Isobelle asked provocatively. "Or a case of needs must?"

Jon's mouth tightened at the woman's cattiness, and Cathy felt a blush heat her own cheeks. Like it or not, that last remark was too close for comfort. But she'd be boiled in oil before she would let Jon's stepmother guess her discomfiture. She summoned a polite smile, and kept it firmly glued to her lips as Jon continued up the stairs and across the porch. Isobelle followed them into the hall.

"When a man sees something as lovely as Cathy, he takes whatever steps are necessary to stake his claim to it immediately. Or has it been so long that you've forgotten, Isobelle?"

Jon's reply was negligent, but that it stung the woman was evident from her suddenly heightened color. She started to retort, but bit back the words as Petersham came hurrying into the hall from the back of the house.

"Ah, Petersham," Jon said evenly, "I wondered if you had somehow gotten lost. I see my—uh—instructions were not carried out."

"I'm sorry, Cap'n, but she insisted on staying. Said she wanted to meet the bride." Petersham's eyes were apologetic as they met Cathy's. She smiled at him.

"Of course I wanted to meet your wife, Jon," Isobelle trilled with assumed gaiety. "After all, I suppose she'll be my step-daughter-in-law. I shall have to introduce her to my friends. When Petersham showed up this morning with some ridiculous story about you wanting the house for your family, I knew I had to see this for myself. It's so hard to picture you as a family man."

"Well, now that you've seen that I am, indeed, a family man, perhaps you'll excuse me. My wife hasn't been well, and she needs to rest. Petersham, have you prepared a room?"

"The master suite, Cap'n."

Jon started to turn toward the stairs, but Isobelle caught at his arm. Cathy glared at the woman icily, but Isobelle ignored her, smiling archly up into Jon's face. Cathy was conscious of a sudden, shocking urge to rake her nails over that artfully painted face.

"I'm taking a house in town, Jon. You must call on me after you get your wife settled. We can discuss old . . . times."

"I may do that, Isobelle. I suppose you have taken the house slaves?"

"They were mine." Isobelle shrugged, her hand with its scarlet nails stroking his sleeve. Cathy gritted her teeth at the intimacy of the action. "Your father gave them to me just before he died. You're lucky to get the house. After all, you never came home."

"No, I never did, did I?" Jon answered coldly, then turned away. Cathy's arms tightened around his neck as he started up the stairs with her. Petersham was right behind them.

"You are welcome to make use of the carriage outside to take you into town," Jon said over his shoulder to Isobelle.

"You're too kind, Jon dear," the woman purred in reply. "Don't forget to come and see me. I know how . . . lonely . . . a man can get when his wife is in an interesting situation."

Cathy gasped audibly at this blatant invitation. Jon's jaw tightened, and he slanted a look down at the indignant girl in his arms as Isobelle left.

"You're not to go to see her," Cathy told him in a blunt undertone, not wanting Petersham to hear but unable to keep back the words.

"Are you giving me orders, wife?" Jon's eyes were suddenly glacial as they looked down at her. Cathy nodded, her blue eyes still burning with resentment over Isobelle's boldness.

"Don't," Jon said softly, his tone edged with cruelty. "Remember that you're very much on sufferance. You have no right to question my actions, now or at any other time."

Cathy stared at him, the pain his words caused stabbing at her chest like a knife. Her chin lifted defiantly.

"I wouldn't dream of questioning your actions, husband." Cathy stressed the last word in mocking imitation of the tone Jon used when he uttered "wife." "But on the other hand, you must not question mine. Remember, what's sauce for the goose is

371

sauce for the gander."

"I wouldn't stake my life on it," Jon answered grimly. "You just might lose."

Petersham came around him and opened the door into the master suite, thus averting a quarrel. Cathy glared at her husband resentfully as he placed her carefully in the middle of the big four-poster. His eyes gleamed with a stony implacability down into hers as he straightened up from the bed.

"I trust you'll be comfortable here." Jon's voice was distant, and Cathy knew that the words were said more for Petersham's benefit than hers.

"Certainly," she replied with equal coolness, determined not to be outdone at the game of polite disinterest. A spark flared in Jon's eyes at her tone, and that warning muscle began to twitch in his cheek. Before he could respond with the rage that seemed dangerously near the boiling point, however, Petersham spoke from his place by the window.

"Cap'n, that Martha woman is here with the rest of the things. Do you want me to see to them?"

"I'll do it. I have to go back into town anyway, and I'll bring them in on my way. You stay with Miss Cathy until Martha gets up here, and then you can go see what's left of the stables. If I remember my father correctly, there won't be much."

"We aiming to stay here for a while, Cap'n?" Petersham asked quietly.

"For a while," Jon said shortly, and strode from the room without another glance at Cathy. She bit her lip so hard, in her effort not to call after him, that it bled. He had to go back into town, he'd said—to see that woman, no doubt! He was a lusty man, and she knew for a fact that he hadn't had a woman in months. If he went to that woman she would never forgive him, she fumed. But then, a little voice inside her head mocked, she would probably never know. Who was there to tell her?

Suspicions ate at Cathy like cancer during the next ten days. Jon was hardly ever home, and when he was he was curt and preoccupied. Cathy could not be certain that he was seeing Isobelle, or any other woman for that matter, but it was more than likely, as she silently acknowledged. There was nothing to stop him, after all. Although she was his wife, he was not bound to her by the usual ties of love or even guilt. He would do just as he damned well pleased, she thought dismally, and if she didn't like it she would just have to learn to lump it!

The only thing that kept her from being totally convinced of his infidelity was the steady influx of slaves into the estate. There was a possibility that he was legitimately busy, spending his time seeing to the seed and fertilizer and human labor force needed if Woodham were once again to become a successful cotton plantation. That this was Jon's plan she learned from Petersham. The captain had decided to take up planting, which the little valet found hard to understand, and when Master Jon did something he went all out. Why, he, Petersham, wouldn't be surprised if they had a bumper cotton crop by next summer!

Cathy was patently uninterested in cotton. She was cross, and tired, and if she were honest she would admit that she was missing Jon. She longed for the baby's birth the way a jailed convict longs for freedom. Once her body was her own again, she vowed, she would have no scruples about using it to get what she wanted: the love of her husband.

Martha was appointed housekeeper for the time being, and she was growing more and more harassed. Unused to dealing with slaves, she was deeply suspicious of them, and refused to let any of them near Miss Cathy. She was sure they were all plotting rebellion, and would slit the girl's throat if given the chance. The constant upheaval caused by this attitude did nothing for Cathy's serenity. When she was on her feet again, domestic organization would be another problem she would have to deal with.

The weather remained warm and sunny through the first day of March. Then a gentle shower broke the monotony, its soft pattering noise against the closed windows lulling Cathy into drowsiness. She had felt strangely lethargic all day, and the burden she carried seemed even heavier than usual. Which was normal, she supposed, as the child was due any day now.

Jon had looked in on her that morning, inquiring with a cool politeness about her health. He had been dressed for town, and Cathy had eyed his handsome form with smoldering resentment. He was responsible for her discomfort, and he wasn't suffering one bit! She scowled at him, refusing to speak, and he had looked her over with bland disinterest before according her a mocking bow and proceeding on his way.

As she ate her dinner, propped up against a mound of pillows in the enormous bed, Cathy stared moodily at her engagement ring, the brilliant stones reflecting the light of the candle near the bed. Jon was a swine, she thought bitterly. Even now he might be with another woman, kissing her, making love to her. Cathy's whole body burned with jealousy. If Jon had been present she would have taken great pleasure in slapping that bronzed face.

Savagely she speared a piece of chicken with her fork, pretending it was Jon. As she bit into it with grim satisfaction her eyes widened. A rush of water spread over her legs, wetting the covers and mattress. What on earth? She stared down at her lower body with amazement. She had wet herself! Then the truth dawned. It was her time. The baby was coming!

She looked around for the bell that was supposed to stand on the bedside table. It wasn't there. Between Martha and the confused house slaves, nothing was in its place. But she had to have help. She tried calling out, but her voice echoed thinly and she knew it wouldn't be audible beyond the confines of the room. Gritting her teeth, she swung her feet to the floor and eased out of bed. She no longer had to worry about doing something that would force the arrival of the baby. It was on its way of its own accord!

Her legs were shaky from the weeks she had spent in bed, but she managed to drag herself across to the door by holding on to the furniture. The first pain hit her as she was stepping into the hall. She bent double, gasping, but it was gone almost as soon as she felt it. That wasn't so bad, she thought, heartened. Maybe childbirth wouldn't be the ordeal she had feared.

Her room was three doors away from the stairs. She made it to the top, hanging on to the banister as she looked down. She didn't dare attempt it. A fall might kill both herself and the child.

"Martha!" she called. Her voice was pitiably weak. She tried again. "Martha!"

The door to one of the rooms off the hall opened and Cathy could see the cozy glow of a lamp illuminating a filled bookcase. The study, she surmised, and opened her mouth to call out again just as Jon stepped into the hall with another man.

"Thanks very much for stopping by, Bailey," Jon said, shaking the man's hand.

"It was a pleasure, Captain Hale," the man replied.

Cathy tried to draw back into the shadows of the upper hallway, not wanting to call attention to her predicament with a strange man present, but another pain struck and a tiny moan escaped her.

Jon glanced almost casually up the stairs, his face freezing with disbelief as he saw Cathy doubled over at the top.

"My God!" he breathed, and came up the stairs two at a time. Cathy felt his strong arms go around her with almost womanly gentleness. She tilted her head back, trying to smile at him. The effort was contorted by another pain.

"It's . . . I'm having the baby!" she gasped, when the spasm had receded.

Jon nodded, his face white beneath its tan.

"I'm going to lift you," he said, his voice very calm. "You don't even have to put your arms around my neck. Just relax. You'll be all right." He lifted her with infinite care, then bore her swiftly back along the hall to her bedroom. Gently he lowered her to the bed, then strode back to the open bedroom door. His bellow for Martha shook the house to its rafters.

Fifteen

Cathy was in labor for almost twenty-four hours. As the night wore on Martha saw that the delivery would be difficult, and sent word down to Jon asking him to summon a physician. (It was the custom for babies to be delivered by female members of the expectant mother's household.) The message was unnecessary. Jon, white and shaken by the sounds that emanated from behind the closed bedroom door, had already done so.

The low moans were bad enough, but Cathy's occasional piercing screams were well-nigh unbearable. Jon broke out in a cold sweat, and had

377

to be physically restrained by Petersham and one of the new housemen from rushing upstairs and bursting into the room where his wife was enduring such agony.

Old Dr. Sanderson arrived more than three hours after being sent for. He responded to Jon's growling demand to know what the hell had kept him by pouring Jon a stiff whiskey and telling him brusquely to stay out of the way. As he mounted the stairs to the upper floor shaking his shaggy white head, the doctor was heard to mutter that he would rather deliver twenty expectant females than deal with one prospective father. The women were usually far more stoical.

To Jon's intense annoyance and Petersham's consternation, the whiskey helped only marginally. Jon downed great quantities of the stuff, but his mind was so desperately attuned to what was happening upstairs that oblivion eluded him. When Cathy's screams rose to such a pitch that he was sure she must be dying, all he could do was stride about the hall outside her bedroom, cursing and praying in the same breath. The thought of her suffering tore at his vital organs like red-hot pincers, making a mockery of the cold contempt he had convinced himself he felt for her. Bloody fool, he castigated himself, as emotions he had thought long dead struggled for resurrection. Would you love her now, after all she's done to you? No, his mind screamed in reply. Any love he might once have felt for her had been foully murdered by her treachery.

Another piteous moan from inside the bed-chamber made Jon flinch. Petersham silently passed him another shot glass of whiskey, and Jon bolted it down. It didn't help. With a great flash of insight it burst on him that his lust was solely responsible for Cathy's pain. Shuddering with self-loathing, he remembered how he had callously ignored her pleas that first time on the "Margarita," his own hungry passion driving him ruthlessly on until he had possessed her completely. And he had not been content with merely stealing her virginity. Oh, no! He had taken her time and again until the end result was the agony she was even now suffering. Listening to her anguished cries, he vowed never to touch her again as long as she lived. If she lived. He was hideously afraid that he might already have killed her.

All through the next day Jon refused to move from the vicinity of the bedroom, rejecting food with an impatient shake of the head. Petersham shook his head over him, thinking that Master Jon was drinking enough whiskey to fell a horse and hardly showing it. The valet did his best to coax Jon to lie down on the sofa in his study for a brief rest, or to step outside for a breath of fresh air, but Jon curtly dismissed all such suggestions. He continued to prowl the hall just outside the bedroom, swallowing shots of whiskey like water and morosely pouring himself more. Every time Cathy made the slightest sound he winced, and when she screamed he went as white as death. Martha, bustling from the room occasionally to fetch hot water or towels for Dr. Sanderson, was shocked at the state he was in and did her best to cheer him up. Really, the poor man seemed to be suffering almost as much as Miss Cathy!

Toward dusk Cathy's screams grew to a shattering crescendo. Jon froze outside in the hallway, his eyes fixed fearfully on the closed bedroom door. Finally he could bear it no longer. With a frenzied rush he burst through the door only to stand transfixed just inside the threshold, one hand still on the knob. Dr. Sanderson was holding a tiny, blood-covered infant by the heels, and, even as Jon watched, administered a sharp slap to the miniscule buttocks. Jon's mouth gaped open as the child let out a wailing cry, and then Dr. Sanderson was laughing and passing the baby to Martha, who was smiling with big glistening tears rolling down her plump cheeks. Jon felt his knees sag with relief. At last the ordeal was over!

"Cathy?" he questioned hoarsely. Both Martha and Dr. Sanderson turned shocked faces toward him, not having heard him enter. For a moment two sternly reproving sets of features regarded him, and then Dr. Sanderson's old face quivered into a smile.

"Relax, Captain," Dr. Sanderson said dryly. "From the looks of you, Mistress Hale is in better shape than you are."

"You've got a son, Master Jon," Martha put in joyfully, proffering the infant, wrapped in a blanket, for him to view. Jon glanced at it abstractedly, vaguely registering a red, wrinkled face and a thatch of black hair. It looks like a red Indian, he thought even as his gaze was leaving the sleeping bundle to fix hungrily on the girl in the bed.

"Wait until we get her cleaned up, Master Jon," Martha urged softly, seeing where his eyes rested.

"I want to see her now," Jon said stubbornly. At a resigned nod from Dr. Sanderson Martha discreetly withdrew a few paces.

"Cathy?" Jon's voice was husky as he came to stand beside the bed, staring down with pained eyes at her small, pale face. Her bright hair was wet with sweat and wildly mussed, trailing in great snarled strands across the plump white pillows. Her lips and cheeks were practically bloodless. Jon was afraid for one shattering instant that she had died while everyone in the room had been taken up with the baby. Then her eyes fluttered open, and she smiled weakly as she saw who was looking down at her.

"Jon," she murmured, her eyes great pools of tiredness. "I did it, Jon."

Her way of putting it brought a slight, rueful smile to his lips. Dr. Sanderson was right. She did seem to be in better shape than he was, mentally at least. Giddy with relief, he took her hand, carrying it to his lips and pressing his mouth passionately against the softness of it.

"Thank you for a son, my love," he murmured hoarsely, the endearment slipping past him before he could catch it.

Cathy smiled up at him tenderly, her sapphire eyes glowing. It was the first time he had called her that since the soldiers had come to Las Palmas. She badly wanted to hear more. He looked terrible, his eyes bloodshot and his jaw unshaven, his hair standing up wildly all over his head as if he had been running his fingers through it. He had been worried about her, she saw with satisfaction. Desperately worried, from the look of him. She took a deep breath, wanting to answer him, to encourage him to say other soft words. The unmistakable smell of stale whiskey hit her nostrils as she inhaled.

"You stink," she mumbled, surprised, and then her eyelids fluttered down and she was asleep.

Jon's mouth curved in a foolish grin at that, and he pressed another ardent kiss to her hand before tucking it reverently beneath the covers. He turned from the bed, still grinning, and walked on unsteady legs to the hall. No sooner had he reached it than his knees gave out and he collapsed with a crash. By the time Dr. Sanderson reached him, he was snoring loudly. The doctor shook his head, and called for Petersham to come and help him get the captain to his bedroom. The whiskey had finally, belatedly, had its effect.

Jon slept like a stone through the rest of that night and well into the next day. He finally surfaced, when the reedy cry of an infant pierced through his fogged brain. Frowning bemusedly, he shook his head to clear it, reaching for the water jug to rinse the stale taste from his mouth. What was a baby doing at Woodham? Then he remembered. The cry must be coming from his son! Why was no one seeing to the child? Groaning, he hoisted himself to his feet, running a hand over his wildly tousled hair as he walked very carefully out of the room and into the hall. The cry seemed to come from Cathy's bedroom and he approached it with grim determination. Jjust as he made it to the door, it opened before him. Martha's startled face blinked at him, then moved over his crumpled form. She grinned, then quickly assumed a serious expression as Jon frowned at her.

"Good morning, or should I say, good afternoon, Captain," the woman said demurely, squeezing around him as he stood swaying, blocking the doorway with his big body. "If you'll excuse me, Captain. . . ." Martha's words trailed off as she disappeared down the hall.

Leaning back against the door jam to recover his strength, Jon realized that the cries had stopped. Looking around the room, his slightly unfocused gaze came to light on the small figure that was regarding him with some amusement from the depths of the big four-poster. Cathy! Jon's eyes went over her appreciatively, feasting on the lovely picture she made. Her golden hair had been neatly brushed and swirled into a top-knot, high on the crown of her head, from which little curling tendrils escaped enticingly. Her eyes were as clear and blue and serene as a pool of water on a summer's day. Her cheeks were flushed rosily, and her lips were turned up in the smallest of shy smiles. As his gaze lowered, he found the reason for her shyness. Cradled against her bare breast was the tiny form of his son, the small head turned away as the infant suckled greedily. Cathy blushed even more rosily as she realized where Jon's eyes rested, but the look she turned on him was warmly welcoming.

"How do you feel?" Cathy asked solicitously after a moment's silence, her smile broadening as her eyes ran over his unshaven face, pale beneath its sunbronze. He looked as if he, and not she, had just passed through some death-defying ordeal.

Her question took a moment to penetrate the whiskey haze that still clung to him. When it did, he permitted himself a small groan.

"Like somebody tried to split open my skull with an axe," he admitted, the slash in his cheek deepening humorously. "But more to the point, how do you feel?"

"Oh, I'm fine," she assured him, her mouth curving in a tender smile as she glanced down at the infant at her breast. "Won't you come over here and meet your son?"

Jon stared from her to the baby and back again. His wife. His son. The fierce possessiveness that accompanied the thought rocked him back on his heels.

"I—I need to clean up," he stammered, thinking desperately that what he really needed was a breathing space. "I must reek of whiskey."

"You do," Cathy answered frankly, her eyes warm as they twinkled over him. "But never mind. Neither Cray nor I mind in the slightest."

"Cray?" Jon questioned absently as he moved almost against his will toward the bed. The tenderness in her huge eyes drew him like a magnet. During all those terrible weeks in prison, even under the lash of the whip that she had ordered, he had dreamed of her looking at him like this. . . . Despising himself as a weak fool, he nevertheless came to stand beside the bed. Cathy looked so small and helpless as she smiled up at him, almost as small and helpless as the infant in her arms. He wanted to stand between her and the world, and cursed himself for letting the lingering effects of the whiskey cloud his judgement.

"I thought we would name him Jonathan Creighton Hale, junior—Cray, to keep things from getting confusing around here as he grows older. Is that all right with you?"

Her eyes were caressing as they traveled over his lean face. Jon felt like he was being drawn helplessly into two deceptively limpid whirlpools. He didn't have the strength at this moment to resist her blandishments. When she reached out and caught his long-fingered hand in her smaller one, tugging on it gently, he obediently sat on the edge of the bed beside her. Cathy and the child were so close he could feel the heat of their bodies, could hear the small sucking sounds that Cray made as he nursed. His eyes met Cathy's and he smiled at her against his will. She smiled back at him tenderly, and then his eyes traveled down to rest on the child at her breast. My son, he thought with amazement, and reached out a finger to wonderingly touch the tiny, perfect hand that kneaded Cathy's breast. It closed over his finger with surprising strength. Jon stared at his son for a moment, then his eyes rose to meet Cathy's.

She laughed with a little catch in her voice at his astonished expression.

"Is Cray all right with you?" she repeated patiently, her eyes tender on his handsome face. Jon, dazzled by what he could have sworn was the genuine affection in her eyes, had to force himself with a strong effort of will concentrate on what she was saying.

"Yes, of course," he muttered, tearing his eyes away from hers before he drowned in them. He would have risen to his feet, but Cray still clutched his forefinger.

Jon stared at his son rather helplessly, not knowing how to free himself without hurting the child.

"He's strong," Jon said finally, unable to think of anything else to say. He was uncomfortably aware of her soft breast swelling warmly beneath the hand the baby held.

"Like his father."

Cathy's soft voice was deliberately seducing him, he thought desperately, urging him to abandon his distrust and fall once again victim to her spell. Her breast burned against his hand. His breathing quickened, and he had to grit his teeth against the impulse.

"Jon . . ." Cathy began, and the blue depths of her eyes, as he lifted his own to meet them, were his undoing. He leaned forward, his eyes never leaving hers, until his mouth was just scant fractions of an inch away from her soft lips. Some remaining instinct of self-preservation made him hesitate, but she defeated him. Her lovely, rose-colored lips moved up to press against his, warm and unbearably sweet, drawing from him a ragged groan. His mouth slanted over hers with starved passion, his free hand coming up to cup the back of her neck so that she couldn't move away. He kissed her hungrily, urgently, his tongue hotly exploring the willing hollow of her mouth. Long denied need flamed with searing heat in his loins. He wanted her with a greedy passion that threatened to consume him. No other woman would do, and he acknowledged the fact with a sick feeling at the pit of his stomach.

Cathy's hand came up to curve around the back of his neck, and she responded to his kisses with an ardor that matched his. Her fingers sensuously stroked his tense neck muscles, then curled wantonly into the cluster of black curls at the back of his collar. Jon realized with a fierce tightening of all his muscles that she wanted him as badly as he wanted her. The trembling of her slight body made that plain.

Drawing a deep, ragged breath, he started to push her back down into the bed, his desire for her so hard and furious that he was oblivious to everything but his need for satisfaction. An indignant squall halted him on the brink of a total, unconditional surrender. Shaking his head to clear it, he glanced down at his son, who was regarding him balefully. Apparently, the child did not take kindly to having his dinner interrupted. Thanking

387

God fervently for Cray's timely reminder, Jon determinedly drew back. Without his son's intervention, Jon knew that the witch would have had him once again hopelessly in her thrall.

Cathy could only watch distressfully as Jon's mouth hardened and his gray eyes iced over. She loved him so much, and had thought that he was beginning to soften toward her. But his eyes as they met hers were stony with hatred, his mouth cruel. Her own eyes filled with hurt tears as he stood up abruptly, almost jerking his hand free of Cray's grip.

"You must really think me a fool," he said softly, his eyes glittering maliciously down at her. "I may make a mistake once, but I'll be damned if I do it twice. Beneath that sweet face you're as hardhearted and calculating as the worst of the waterfront whores. I'd sooner bed with a snake than you!"

Cathy gaped at him dumbly, tears overflowing her eyes to spill helplessly down her cheeks. With a savage curse Jon swung on his heel, striding furiously toward the door. Cathy collapsed with hurt sobs as he slammed out of the room. Cray's frightened cries joined hers.

In the days and weeks following Cray's birth, Cathy scarcely saw Jon. He was working harder than ever before at making Woodham a paying operation. In his mother's time, free workmen had been hired to cultivate the fields, but when his father had married Isobelle she had insisted that money would be saved by buying and using slaves. Marcus Hale had given in to her demands as always. Jon himself had always despised the institution of slavery, but the economy of the south was now built around it. A large percentage of his money had been sunk into the planation, and if it did not turn a profit with this year's cotton crop he would be hard put to support his family. Of course, he could always return to the sea. But he considered this a last resort. For Cray's sake, and Cathy's too, if he was honest, he wanted to provide a secure, stable home.

In a rough compromise with his conscience, he refused to hire an overseer and directed the field workers himself. He worked from sunup to sundown, driving himself as hard as he drove the men. When he had finished for the day he was usually too tired to do more than eat his supper in silence and fall into his lonely bed. Sometimes he slept immediately, but more often he was haunted by images of Cathy. The remembered silken texture of her bright hair, the softness of her flesh, the feel of her warm body trembling with passion in his arms, dogged the hours between dusk and dawn. Many times he was tempted to go to her room, to ease his lust by taking what was after all his by right. But he was afraid that she would coax him into surrendering more than just his physical self. She would never be content until he was grovelling at her feet, he mused savagely. And he was damned if he would give her that satisfaction!

Other women were available and he was chagrined to admit that he didn't want them. On his occasional trips to town he was the recipient of certain unmistakable signals from some very lovely ladies, but he could not rouse himself to more than a mild interest in their charms. It was ironic to reflect that the one woman capable of exciting him to the point of frenzy was his legal wife, the mother of his son, and yet he was afraid to take her. If she was bent on revenge, she was exacting more than she knew! And fiercely he vowed to keep it that way.

A combination of fatigue, worry, and plain sexual frustration made his temper hair-trigger quick. Everyone from Petersham to the lowliest field worker felt the bite of his tongue at one time or another. Cathy was generally spared from these verbal attacks, but the glint in Jon's eyes when he looked at her told her that she was the real target. She returned his flaying looks limpidly, and redoubled her efforts to attract him. As water eventually wears away rock, she felt that she was making slow but steady progress. One night soon he would abandon the struggle and come to her, and she would be ready. And from his bed it was a very small step to his heart.

Jon was at first cynically amused and then infuriated by her transparent attempts to seduction. Soon after Cray's birth he had commissioned a fashionable Charleston seamstress to replenish her almost nonexistent wardrobe, and now he realized that he had made a tactical error. In the gossamer thin, low-cut, sleeveless gowns, that were best suited to South Carolina's climate, she was as tempting to him as Eve must once have been to Adam. Just the sight of her slender, curvaceous figure as she flitted about the house or gardens was enough to send him up in flames. The soft smiles and provocative looks she lavished on him were pure torture. He lusted after her with a fierceness that left him time for thoughts of little else. Night after night he was reduced to taking moonlight swims in nearby Miller's Creek in an effort to cool his ardor. It barely helped at all.

As the weeks passed and he realized that she had had sufficient time to recover completely from Cray's birth, his control was strained almost to the bursting point. There was no physical reason why she shouldn't assume the intimate duties of a wife. Grimly Jon clung to his sanity. The bitch had stolen his heart once, and then callously trampled it. He'd see her in hell before he would give her the chance again!

Word spread through Charleston's plantation community that another generation of Hales had taken up residence at Woodham. Hardly an afternoon passed without a carriage rolling up the drive to disgorge two or three fashionably dressed ladies come to make the acquaintance of their new neighbors. Cathy, well-dressed and demure, served tea and macaroons and fielded probing questions diplomatically. When the ladies discovered that she actually possessed a title (Cathy suspected Martha of divulging this information) they fell over themselves in an attempt to make the new arrivals welcome. Mistress Gordon, the neighborhood matriarch, set the final seal of approval on them by revealing that she had been close friends with Jon's mother, Virginia. After that, Cray was cooed over, Cathy pronounced "the sweetest thing," and Jon described by the dazzled ladies as too romantic for words. Jon was cynical about this approbation, but directed Cathy to accept a few of the invitations that were showered upon them. If they were to make Woodham their home, it would not do to live like recluses.

Cathy selected a ball given by a young couple named Ingrams for their social debut. Jon was unenthusiastic, but grudgingly consented to accompany her. Inwardly, he felt that it might do him good to be in the company of other beautiful women besides his wife. It was incredible that he, who had bedded scores of women over the years, had been reduced to wanting only one. Perhaps he needed to take a closer look at what else was available.

Cathy, for her part, looked forward to the ball the way a cat anticipates its Sunday bowl of cream. She would dress to kill, and flirt judiciously with all the handsome men present. Jealousy would bring Jon around if nothing else would, she thought smugly. She knew he wanted her, it was plain in his eyes, but he was too damned stubborn to give in. A slight smile tilted at the corners of her mouth. When he had begged sufficiently for her favors, she would very sweetly submit. In the flaming of his passion, she hoped to touch his heart.

Cathy's mouth went dry when she thought of Jon's lovemaking. It had been so long since he had possessed her—almost nine months. If she were honest, she would have to admit that she wanted him too. The lustful glances that had touched on her half-exposed bosom when he thought she wasn't looking, the imperfectly concealed tremor in his limbs when she oh-so-accidentally brushed her body against his, excited her more than she had dreamed was possible. She had always thought that only men were subject to physical needs, but she was painfully learning her mistake. It would have been very easy just to go to his room one night and offer herself to him, but she wanted more than just sexual gratification. She wanted his love, and if he had to be driven to the point of madness before he could recognize or admit it, then that was what she had to do.

The night of the ball Cathy made an elaborate toilette. Her ballgown was the most beautiful she had ever possessed, ordered especially for the occasion. It was cloth-of-gold, a whispering tale of enchantment as it shimmered in the candlelight. The tissue-thin bodice was suspended from two fragile straps that caressed her shoulders before widening to cross over her breasts in wide swaths of material. The material crossed again in back, then came around to hug her slender waist before billowing out into an enormous bell of a skirt. Her neck, shoulders, arms, and the gleaming upper slopes of her bosom were left deliciously bare. Perfectly plain yet daring in design, the dress was dependent for its effect on the wearer's own beauty. On Cathy, it was superb.

Martha styled her golden hair very simply, gathering it in a sapphire clasp at the crown of her head then coaxing it to stream down her back in cascading ringlets. Sapphire-and-gold earbobs swung coquettishly from her ears, and a delicate matching necklace which had belonged to Jon's mother was clasped about her neck. Tiny gold-heeled slippers and long golden gloves completed the outfit. With her wide, sapphire eyes and perfectly etched features, Cathy looked like a princess from a fairy tale.

"Lovey, you look a real picture," Martha said with satisfaction when Cathy was finally dressed. "Master Jon's eyes'll pop."

Cathy smiled ruefully at her nanny. Not much escaped Martha's keen eyes. But she was too excited, too filled with anticipation to reprove her nanny as she supposed she should do. Instead, she pressed an impulsive kiss on the plump cheek nearest her as she caught up her spangled stole.

"That's the idea, Martha," she twinkled roguishly, and then vanished out the door with a swish of her full skirt.

Jon was testily pacing the downstairs hall as Cathy descended toward him, and she had an opportunity to study him unobserved. Dressed in charcoal gray velvet with a silver waistcoat, he was incredibly handsome. Her eyes ran over his lean, powerfully muscled frame with possessive pride. He was every inch the arrogant male, and just looking at him made her heart beat faster. His hair was neatly brushed for once, and gleamed blue-black in the light of the candles. His dark face was smoothly shaven, emphasizing the hawkish cast of his features. Silky black eyebrows met over his eyes in an impatient frown. Cathy smiled. He looked like he wasn't in a very good mood, and, if her plan succeeded, he would be in a worse one before the night was out.

He glanced at his pocket watch, then up the stairs, stopping dead as he saw her seemingly float down toward him. His eyes flickered over her, touching on her shining hair, her face, the nearly naked globes of her bosom, her tiny waist. His mouth tightened angrily, and he swung away from her, but not before she saw the raw hunger that blazed for an unguarded moment in his eyes.

"Shall we go?" he asked with commendable coolness as she came up beside him, her head not quite reaching his shoulder. She laid her hand lightly on his reluctantly proffered arm, glancing up at him in time to surprise his eyes feasting greedily on the rounded flesh left bare by her gown. A dark flush spread over his cheekbones as she caught him out, but he said nothing more. Cathy was likewise silent as he escorted her out of the door and handed her up into the waiting carriage.

The ball was a tremendous success from almost every viewpoint but Cathy's. Dozens of candles lit the long ballroom, and an orchestra on a raised dais at the far end of the room played haunting melodies. Ladies, in floating gowns ranging in color from the demure pastels that were *de rigueur* for debutantes to the more daring scarlets and emeralds favored by dashing young matrons, twirled about the highly polished floor in the arms of soberly clad gentlemen. After greeting their host and hostess, Jon swung Cathy into the laughing throng for a stiffly silent dance. He held her at the correct arm's length, and vouchsafed not a single word to her. Nettled, Cathy hardly waited until the music stopped before pulling away from him to smile at a young man nearby. The boy, dazzled by her beauty and not deterred in the least by Jon's monitory scowl, immediately asked her to dance. Cathy agreed with a little curtsey, and twirled away without a backward glance.

After that, she was beseiged with invitations to dance from nearly every gentleman present. The young, unmarried ones were the most vociferous, and Cathy encouraged them with sparkling gaiety helped by the glasses of champagne punch that were constantly being pressed into her hand. From the corner of her eyes she caught occasional glimpses of Jon dancing with this or that lovely lady. He seemed to have no interest in the blushing girls, preferring the older, more experienced women. Cathy felt real physical pain as she saw him smile with devastating charm down into the face of a lady who, all too plainly, knew what men-women games were all about. Slut, thought Cathy furiously, turning away to redouble her own efforts at flirtation.

When supper was announced, Cathy allowed her partner of the moment, a handsome young man of twenty-five named Paul Harrison, to escort her. It was the custom for married ladies to dine in their husband's company, but her last glimpse of Jon had found his dark head bent intimately over the auburn one of that sluttish female. Cathy had no inclination to wait for him after that. So she laughed and flirted with Paul as if she didn't have a care in the world. No one would have guessed that her head hurt, or that her meal might have been sawdust for all the enjoyment she took from it. Finally, across the room she spied Jon—and his partner. It was the same woman, and she was looking at Jon with an avidity that positively sickened Cathy. Furiously she swallowed another glass of champagne punch, bestowing a dazzling smile on the bemused Paul as she begged sweetly to be taken back into the ballroom.

Paul danced with her twice more after that, each time growing just a little bolder. His hands caressed her waist discreetly, and Cathy, instead of pulling away, smiled up at him with deliberate enticement. This night was not going at all as she had planned, but she had no intention of letting anyone guess her sick dismay. If Jon had no care for her—why, then, she would have no care for Jon! When Paul swung her in the direction of the veranda, she made no demur.

The cool night air brought her to her senses. As Paul whirled her down the veranda she pulled back from him, and was just opening her mouth to tell him to take her back inside when she saw a long black shadow loom up over his shoulder. Jon's hand descended on Paul's shoulder with rather more force than was proper, and his voice had a steely ring to it.

"Excuse me, Harrison, but I'd like to finish this dance with my wife." The words were perfectly even, but Paul dropped Cathy like a hot coal. To his credit, he had forgotten until this moment that his *enamorada* had a husband. Now, confronted with Jon's formidable strength, he sketched a quick bow before retreating with more haste than dignity.

Cathy faced Jon boldly, tilting her chin at him as if daring him to make something of what she had done. Inwardly, she was not nearly so sure of herself. He had been furious enough to kill her that time with Harry—and this time she had deliberately invited another man's attentions. Besides, she was now his wife. But at the moment she didn't much care what he did. If he could bask under that predatory woman's advances, then surely she was entitled to a little harmless enjoyment!

To her astonishment, his voice when he spoke held none of the furious anger she had expected. Instead, he was icily controlled.

"I suggest that we go back inside and finish this dance. Your behavior tonight has already caused quite enough talk. I don't think we'll provide the gossips with a brawl to further their entertainment."

He reached out and grasped her upper arm with long strong fingers that bit deep into her skin. Cathy peered at him through the darkness, trying to read his expression. It was impossible. The shadows were too dense to permit her to see anything more than a tall, dark silhouette.

"What about your behavior?" Cathy hissed, trying to pull her arm free of his grasp. She was damned if she would let him intimidate her! If her actions had been reprehensible, his had been worse!

"Jealous, my wife?" Cathy could see the brief gleam of his teeth as they showed in a mirthless smile. "You have no reason to be. I turned the lovely Annabella down—in favor of you. You see, tonight I've decided to give you what you've been wanting."

He was drawing her inexorably toward the ballroom as he spoke. As the light fell on his face, Cathy caught her breath sharply. On the surface was the urbane mask of a gentleman; only someone who knew him as well as she did could detect the savagery in his eyes.

"Smile, wife," he said almost pleasantly, swinging her through the wide doors and into the movement of the dance. "We wouldn't want the good people to think we were fighting, would we?"

Cathy glanced about her, saw the interested eyes on them, and smiled. Inside she was a trembling mass of nerves. She had never before seen him in such a quiet, terrible rage. But still, she thought, tossing her head and dimpling at him for the benefit of the onlookers, what can he do to me? He wasn't a wife beater. If he proposed to share her bed, then that would fit in with her plans very nicely. Why then did she feel so frightened?

When the music ended, her husband led her through the throng, his arm about her waist in a gesture of casual affection. Only Cathy could feel the iron hard muscles that kept her clamped to his side. Mechanically she smiled and called gay answers to the men who still pleaded for dances. To the disapproving looks bestowed on her by chaperones she responded with suitable penitence. Privately she rebelled. Damn the old cats, she thought, and continued to smile.

When Jon went to fetch her wrap Cathy almost ran off and hid. The thought of being alone with her husband in a closed carriage for the half an hour or so it would take them to get to Woodham was unnerving. She had a feeling that he had some punishment in store for her—but what? As she considered the possibilities he returned with her wrap, and the chance for escape was lost.

Jon held her arm lovingly as they bade smiling goodnights to the Ingrams. Cathy was frighteningly aware of the strength in the hand that held her. The polite smile dropped from his face like a mask as they left the house. She was right—he did intend some punishment for her. The angry glitter in his eyes made that plain. Cathy felt her heart quake as he lifted her silently into the carriage, folding the steps himself before giving the coachman the order to drive.

The interior of the carriage was lit by a single stationary lantern. By its light Cathy watched the grim face of her husband as he took the seat opposite to hers. He met her eyes, and slowly smiled. The mirthless grimace gave him the look of a malevolent satyr.

"Come here, wife," he said very softly. When Cathy only stared at him, her eyes huge and wary, the smile left his face to be replaced by a snarling frown.

"I said come here!"

The command cracked like a whip. Cathy moistened her lips nervously with the tip of her tongue. Jon's gaze centered on her mouth, his expression savage.

"W—why?" she stammered, shrinking back against the velvet upholstery.

"I'm going to give you what you've been wanting from me for weeks now. You're surely not going to try to deny it?"

"I—I—if you mean to make love to me, I have no objection. You are my husband, after all, and I realize that you have certain rights." The words were meant to sound coolly reasonable. Instead they were pitiable. But she was inexplicably frightened of him. He knew it. She could see the brief flare of satisfaction in his eyes.

"Yes, I do. And I mean to exercise them. Now." His hand reached almost casually across the space between them and closed over hers, jerking her toward him, Cathy half-fell across his lap. He pulled her around until she was sitting on his knees, his hand around her throat. He stared down into her pale face, his own twisting angrily.

"Jon, please . . ." Cathy whispered humbly as his face loomed closer to hers. "Wait. . . ."

"Do you deny you've been trying to get me into

bed for the past month!" The words were growled against her ear. "Or that your little act with that unfortunate youth tonight wasn't designed to make me jealous? Well?"

"It wasn't like that . . ." Cathy protested feebly, responding despite her fear to the hardening of the muscles beneath her soft buttocks.

"Wasn't it?"

His eyes glared down into hers, and then his mouth silenced all further talk.

Sixteen

Jon was lost. He had known it from the moment he had watched. Cathy disappear onto the veranda with that swaggering pup. Jealousy, fierce and primitive, had ripped at his insides. He had wanted to kill, even though he knew full well that her whole performance had been designed for just that purpose. Well, she had succeeded in her aim: against his will he had come after her, and had only just stopped himself from making a furious scene. The thought of the triumph that would gleam in her eyes was all that held him back. For months she had been trying to wrest his heart from him. Tonight, he acknowledged with a furious anger, she had done just that. He loved the little bitch still, God help him. And God help him if she should ever find it out.

His mouth as it twisted over hers was deliberately brutal, his tongue raping her mouth with no thought of her pleasure or even comfort. The feel of her soft

402

little mouth opening under his, her arms twining around his neck, her small tongue caressing his lips and teeth lit the fuse of both his starved passion and his mounting rage. She was actually responding to a kiss that was intended to insult her! She thought she had won at last, he realized infuriatedly. The evening was ending just as she had planned—with him making love to her. Well, he would take her because he could no longer help himself. But my lady wouldn't have everything her own way. Jon smiled savagely, his hand coming up to clench over the top of her extravagant ballgown before jerking downward with all his might.

The flimsy material gave with a satisfying rip. Cathy gasped against his mouth, placing both hands against his chest and trying to push away. Jon let her draw back a little, wanting her to see his face—he knew it would be frightening with its furious mixture of hatred, passion, and rage. The sleepy satisfaction vanished from her eyes as she stared at him. Jon knew he must look mad, as indeed he was. She had finally succeeded in driving him insane.

He held his stare as he plunged his hand, with brutish strength, down the front of her chemise. His fingers closed over her breast, pinching cruelly at the soft peak. She cried out with shocked protest, trying to squirm free. His arm tight around her waist kept her clamped firmly on his knees.

"What's the matter, wife?" he jeered cruelly, jerking her chemise down over her shoulders so that her rounded breasts popped free. The neckline of the chemise trapped her arms at her waist, and she had no way of holding him off as he bent his head to suckle at her breast. His mouth clamped ferociously over the tender nipple, ravaging her, hurting her.

"Jon, don't," Cathy moaned, helpless in his arms. The violence of his mood drove all thoughts of lovemaking from her head.

"Isn't this what you wanted?"

He was angry—furiously and savagely angry. Cathy was more than a little afraid of him. He plainly meant to punish her for her behavior earlier in the evening. Just the feel of his mouth sucking viciously where little Cray still nursed did that. She felt her milk begin to flow, and flushed painfully. His use of her was humiliating.

Jon tasted the warm, sweet liquid as it gushed into his mouth, his face contorting fiendishly. His outraged desire rose with an infernal heat, and even as he knew that he had to have her, now, this minute, he felt a curious sneaking shame that he could so abuse the mother of his child. But the bitch deserved it, had asked for it in fact, and nothing could stop him from giving it to her. His fingers dug into her waist and he bore her back against the padded seat. Her eyes were wide and frightened as they stared up into his.

"Jon, please," she begged weakly. Her hands were still imprisoned by her chemise, and his weight on her made struggling impossible. Besides, he was her husband. He had the legal right to take her, when and where he pleased.

"Please what? Isn't this what you wanted?" he demanded viciously, his face just inches away from hers. In the flickering light of the lantern, he looked inhuman, diabolical. Cathy shivered beneath him. His mouth twisted as he felt her fear.

"No—not like this . . . !" she cried, shutting her eyes against the sadistic mask that his face had become.

"Like what then?"

"I—I wanted you to love me!" Cathy muttered in despair. His eyes blazed with demoniacal rage at her soft words.

"Far be it from me to disappoint a lady," he sneered, rising to his knees between her spread legs. He was kneeling on the golden skirt of her ballgown, leering down at the quivering, rose-tipped mounds of her bared breasts. His weight on the material of her dress held her legs immobile. Her arms ached from where the chemise cut into their softness.

Jon's hand went to the buttons of his breeches, and he began to unfasten them one at a time, his movements almost leisurely. Cathy's eyes widened with shocked horror. He couldn't mean to take her in the carriage! But apparently he did. His swollen desire jutted out at her obscenely amidst the dark finery of his evening clothes. Cathy couldn't take her eyes from it. Jon laughed, the sound ugly, and reached down to whip her skirts up around her waist. Her lace-trimmed linen pantalets still stood between him and his goal, and he ripped at them until they hung in ragged tatters from her waist. Husband or no, Cathy began to struggle, kicking at him frantically and trying to roll from the seat. Jon subdued her easily, seeming to enjoy her futile fight. His teeth gleamed at her wolfishly as he dragged her back in place. His hands closed hurtfully over her buttocks.

He held her like that, her bottom lifted toward where he knelt between her flailing legs, his eyes gloating on her squirming, shamed nakedness. Cathy's breath caught in her throat at the deliberate crudity of his look, her head thrashing helplessly from side to side against the velvet-cushioned seat.

"Jon, please don't!" she pleaded desperately, knowing that if he took her like this, in anger and hatred, something would be destroyed between them forever. When she imagined him making love to her, she had pictured the laughing, tender Jon of Las Palmas, not this hard, brutal stranger who seemed bent on hurting and humiliating her.

"Why the hell not?" His voice was vicious, his hands painfully kneading the soft flesh of her buttocks. "You're my wife, by your own unsavory little act. I own you. I must admit, keeping a wife is more expensive than paying an occasional whore, but I plan to get my money's worth. Starting right now."

With this speech he pulled her toward him, spearing her with his passion, his action brutal. Her cry of pain gave him almost fiendish pleasure. He wanted to hurt her, meant to hurt her. He took her like an animal, kneeling above her, plunging savagely in and out. Her pained whimpers drove him on like red-hot whips. His eyes glazed over with passion, his breath rasping harshly in his throat. Cathy's eyes were squeezed shut, tears trickling past her closed lids. She had accused him of rape before. By God, now she knew what the word meant!

A ragged groan was dragged from deep inside him as his seed spewed hotly forth. For some minutes afterwards he stayed imbedded in her soft warmth, then his eyes opened and he stared expressionlessly down into her tear-wet face. Sneering, he looked her half-naked body up and down, then freed himself and stood up, turning his back as he adjusted his clothing. Cathy lay where he had dropped her, making no attempt to cover herself. Shock and despair had combined to make her totally apathetic to anything else he might take it into his head to do. Jon turned around, his lip curling angrily as he saw that she hadn't moved.

"Hoping for more?" he mocked in an unpleasant growl. The carriage swayed over a pothole in the road, and he had to brace himself with one hand against the wall. "I'd be happy to accommodate you, but we're nearly home. Unless you want the coachman to take my place, I suggest you cover yourself."

Stiff Cathy didn't move. With a furious curse Jon reached down, grabbing her by the arm and jerking her into a sitting position. She cringed away from him, her blue eyes swimming with tears. Jon's face tightened ominously.

"I said cover yourself!" he grated. Cathy made feeble attempts to obey. Her hands were shaking so badly that she was barely able to tidy herself. Jon watched, mouth compressed in a grim line, as she managed to slide the straps of her chemise back up over her shoulders, hiding her full breasts from his view. She smoothed her skirt down over her legs, but there was nothing she could do about her torn bodice. It gaped open, revealing her flesh through the thin silk of her chemise.

Jon swore under his breath as the carriage came to a rocking halt. Cathy clutched the front of her dress together with both hands, twisting around so that her back was toward the door. Quickly Jon doffed his coat, draping it around her shoulders before leaning over to blow out the lantern. No sooner had the interior of the carriage plunged into darkness than the door was swung open. The poker-faced coachman stood waiting for them to descend.

Jumping easily to the ground, Jon turned to hold up his arms for Cathy. She submitted woodenly to being lifted down, but when Jon's hands would have left her waist she swayed, feeling suddenly dizzy. Her knees no longer seemed to have the strength to hold her upright. Jon stifled a curse as he felt rather than saw her weakness, and tightened his hands on her waist. Unable to help herself, Cathy closed her eyes, leaning heavily back against him. She was sure she was going to faint.

With an indrawn breath, Jon slid one arm around

her shoulders and the other beneath her knees, picking her up as if she was a small child. Her head lolled weakly on his shoulder, looking ghostly in the faint moonlight. The coachman stood gaping at the pair of them, and Jon scowled at him.

"Put the carriage away, and see to the horses," he ordered tersely, then moved with long, angry strides up the front steps and into the house.

The hall was deserted, the servants long since in bed. A pair of candles had been left burning on a table at the foot of the stairs for use by the master and mistress of the house when they returned home in the small hours of the morning. His hands full, Jon was unable to take advantage of their light to ease his way up the stairs. Cursing under his breath, he bent to blow them out, mounting the stairs in a thick darkness that was relieved only marginally by the silvery moonlight streaming through the fan-shaped window above the door. Agile and keen-eyed from his years at sea, he managed to negotiate the curving steps without too much difficulty. Cathy lay limply in his arms as he strode along the upstairs hall, not even bothering to put her own around his neck. She felt foully, churningly sick.

Jon paused outside the door to her bedroom, his grip shifting slightly as he struggled to turn the knob. Cathy felt herself slipping and instinctively clutched at his shoulders just as the door swung open.

The warm glow of a many-branched candelabra lit the room that was designed to be shared by Woodham's owner and his wife. The huge four-poster, its covers turned down invitingly, loomed large in the center of the floor. A small fire burned in the grate, and in front of it, curled up in a chair, Martha slumbered peacefully.

"You can put me down now," Cathy whispered stiffly, not looking at him, mindful of Martha's sleeping form. "I feel quite recovered."

"You look recovered," he retorted in a stinging undertone, his gray eyes blazing with anger and something else as he looked down into her pale face. "Your face is as white as death. What the hell's wrong with you, anyway? Did I hurt you?"

This last question was ground out with an effort. Cathy could tell from the anxious look in his eyes that he was afraid his assault might have damaged tissues not yet fully recovered from Cray's birth.

"Yes, you hurt me!" Her response was no less fierce for being whispered. "I thought that was the whole idea!"

"Miss Cathy, is that you?" Martha sat up, blinking sleepily as she looked around the room.

"Yes, Martha, it's me." Cathy was glad of Martha's presence. The sooner Jon left, the happier she would be. To him, she whispered fiercely, "Put me down."

"As I've told you before, I don't take orders from you," Jon growled in her ear, but the arm beneath her knees relaxed its grip, allowing her feet to slide to the floor. His other arm stayed firmly about her waist, and Cathy was secretly glad of its support. Her head swam alarmingly, and if he had released

410

her she was afraid she might have fallen.

"You're late, lovey, and I was. . . ." Martha began reprovingly, just making out Cathy's shape in the shadows beyond the firelight. The woman broke off, her eyes widening perceptibly as she saw Jon standing behind her charge, one arm clasping her possessively about the waist. Martha's sharp eyes traveled from Jon's arm to Cathy's tumbled hair, then touched on her huge, slightly unfocused eyes and bee-stung mouth. Clearly, Miss Cathy would have no need of her services tonight! From the looks of the two of them, all they wanted was to be alone.

"Well, it's plain to see that you won't be needing me tonight, lovey, so I'll get along to my own bed. Don't worry about Master Cray. If he wakes, I'll tend him. Do that young gentleman good to get a taste of a sugar-tit, for a change!"

She smiled at them beatifically as she spoke, her gray hair in its two neat plaits swaying in time to her stately walk toward the door.

"Martha . . ." Cathy gasped out convulsively, frightened anew at the idea of being left alone with her husband. Jon's arm tightened like a vise around her waist, his fingers digging painfully into her flesh as Martha looked inquiringly back over her shoulder.

"Yes, Miss Cathy?"

"Let her go. Do you want her to see you like this?" Jon hissed in Cathy's ear as Martha spoke. Cathy thought of her torn dress, of the unmistakable signs

411

of Jon's possession that still soiled her body, and swallowed.

"Have a good night, Martha," she forced out from between dry lips.

Martha smiled at her whimsically.

"You too, lovey," she twinkled, and left the room, pulling the door closed very gently behind her.

Jon didn't release her immediately. Cathy's every nerve was aware of the strong body behind her, of his heart beating rhythmically beneath her ear, of his breath stirring her hair. She stiffened, trying to pull away. His grip didn't slacken.

"You can let me go now. We're quite alone. There's no need to continue with your touching display of concern." Sarcasm edged the words.

"Can you stand?" Jon's voice was harsh as he ignored her taunt.

"Certainly," Cathy replied with icy dignity. The hard arm around her waist slowly removed itself. Without its iron support her knees quivered, but she forced herself to remain upright. All she wanted now was to get rid of him as quickly as possible.

"Good-night," she said pointedly, taking a few steps toward the bed and then turning to face him. Very casually she leaned against a bedpost, conscious of his eyes on her. He made no move to leave.

"I'd like you to go now, if you don't mind. I'm tired." Despite herself a little quiver racked her voice. She glared at him glacially, hoping he hadn't heard it.

"Get undressed," he said, almost casually,

strolling forward into the light. He thrust his hands deep into the pockets of his gray breeches, rocking back and forth on his heels, his eyes hooded as they met hers. Cathy gaped at him disbelievingly, then shut her jaw with a decided snap.

"You've had your fun for the night," she bit off, her knuckles showing white where she still clutched his coat to her. She tried stiffening away from the bedpost only to sink back against it. Without its support, she would have fallen.

"I'm not looking for fun, as you call it," he answered evenly, his eyes never leaving her pinched face. "I want to be sure you're all right. Now, can you undress yourself or do you want me to help you?"

Cathy stared at him furiously. He looked so tall and invincible standing there, so cool and collected, as if the events of the night had affected him not at all. As they probably hadn't. She was the one who had been hurt and humiliated, she reminded herself. He probably only felt relieved!

"It's a little late for you to worry about me, isn't it?" she spat venomously. "After all, if I'm unwell, you're the cause!"

"Get undressed, Cathy," he repeated brusquely, strolling over to the fire and seating himself in the chair Martha had vacated. Cathy glared at him, then snatched his coat from her shoulders in a sudden spurt of rage and threw it at him.

He caught it easily. Cathy clenched her fists impotently, then sagged back against the bedpost. That little display of temper had completely snapped her strength. She felt light-headed, but she would rather die than have him undress her after the unforgivable way he had treated her!

Thank goodness he was no longer watching her! He had extracted a thin brown cigar from his coat pocket and was leaning toward the fire to light it on a burning ember. Smoking was a habit he had acquired since returning to Woodham, and Cathy was not sure that she liked it. It made him seem more than ever like a stranger.

Taking a deep breath, Cathy reached around to fumble with the hooks that fastened her dress in the back. Jon was sprawled in the chair, his long legs thrust out in front of him, staring abstractedly at the dancing flames as he puffed at his cigar. The smoke wafted above him, its smell oddly strong. As it floated toward Cathy, surrounding her, suffocating her, she felt her stomach give an ominous heave. She clapped a hand to her mouth, but it was too late. She was violently sick where she stood.

When the spasm was over, Cathy became aware of Jon's presence beside her. He reached down and caught her by her upper arms, lifting her gently from where she had collapsed to her knees. He was smiling faintly as he looked down into her woebegone face, and if Cathy had had the strength she would have clawed that superior smirk from his mouth.

"It was your damned cigar!" she choked defensively as he sat her on the edge of the bed, wiping her face carefully with a dampened towel.

"I don't think so," he answered, kneeling to remove her small shoes. Cathy felt too weak to sit upright. She flopped back against the mattress, her feet still dangling over the edge. Jon continued, "How much did you have to drink?"

"I'm not drunk!" Cathy protested indignantly. How dare he imply such a thing! "All I had to drink was punch."

"Champagne punch," Jon corrected calmly. "I saw you swilling it, but it never occurred to me. . . ."

"Oh, shut up!" Cathy snapped, giving vent to her outraged feelings. "Nobody gets drunk on punch!"

"You managed very nicely, my dear." The laughter in his voice infuriated Cathy. After all he had done to her tonight, he had the gall to laugh at her! With a tremendous effort she forced herself into a sitting position again, her hand swinging in a wide arc that smacked satisfyingly against his hard cheek.

Cathy stared at him defiantly as he raised a disbelieving hand to his face. He was still kneeling at her feet, his startled eyes almost on a level with hers.

"You deserved that!" she told him decidedly, then sank back down against the mattress.

"Deserved or not, you'd be well-advised not to repeat it," he drawled after a moment's silence. "Next time, you might be repaid in kind."

"Bully!" Cathy murmured resentfully, closing her eyes tightly as the ceiling whirled around above her. She opened them again to find Jon towering over her. As she blinked at him his face came closer, swimming into focus.

"Go away!" she hissed, and was rewarded with a reluctant smile.

"In a few minutes," he promised gravely, his hands gentle on her shoulders as he turned her over onto her stomach. Cathy could feel him deftly unfastening the hooks at the back of her gown. He tugged it down over her body, tossing it aside, then began to struggle with the lacing of her stays. The strings had apparently worked themselves into a knot. Cathy heard his muttered "Damn!" as he tried to undo it. Succeeding at last, he deftly loosened her stays, pulling them from beneath her.

"I feel sick," she moaned suddenly as her stomach twitched again warningly.

"I know you do." His voice was soothing, his hands caressing as they lingered briefly against her thighs before sliding her stockings and garters down her legs. "When you're undressed, I'll bring you something that will make you feel better."

"Like strychnine?" The question was pure bravado, and Jon ignored its provocation. He turned her over onto her back, and Cathy was too weak to even want to resist him. She lay limply on the bed, her eyes closed as he peeled her petticoats away. She was left in her nearly transparent chemise and her ruined pantalets. Jon pulled the chemise over her head with a swift movement, then untied the ribbon waistband of her pantalets with deliberate care and slid them down her legs. His hands felt warm against the nape of her neck as he removed first her necklace, then her earbobs, and finally the ornament in her hair. Cathy was drifting off into a troubled sleep when she felt a cool wetness slide across her belly and down over her soft thighs.

"What are you doing?" she gasped, her eyes popping open. Jon continued to sponge her body with a damp cloth, washing her with an intimacy that made her blush furiously.

"You need a bath," he said, glancing up at her briefly, his look almost tender. He drew the cloth one final time between her legs then threw it aside. She was left lying naked on the bed, her feet dangling ridiculously over the side as he turned away and strode across the room to the armoire.

"Where are you going?" she asked before she could catch herself, feeling strangely bereft. Jon slanted a wry look at her over his shoulder, his hands busy pawing through the stacks of her undergarments.

"I presume you want to sleep in a nightdress?"

"Oh," Cathy murmured, then nodded. Her earlier anger with him was fading, along with her memory of its cause. The crazy spinning of her head was banishing all before it.

"You hurt me," she accused, vaguely remembering a hard, thrusting pain with him as its author.

Jon found what he was looking for and turned back toward the bed, a wisp of silk dangling from one hand.

"You hurt me back," he reminded her, one hand moving to lightly touch the cheek she had slapped. "That makes us even."

This seemed reasonable to Cathy, who was getting dizzier by the minute. She submitted docilely as he pulled her to her feet, leaning heavily against the hard wall of his chest while he dropped the nightgown over her head. The musky man-smell of him was oddly pleasant. Cathy burrowed her face against the cool silk of his shirt as he twitched the sleeping garment into place.

"Into bed with you, temptress," she heard him mutter, his voice husky. His arms slid around her and he was lifting her, then depositing her all too quickly on the soft mattress, this time up near the headboard in a proper sleeping position. Her blue eyes blinked at him reproachfully as he pulled the covers neatly under her chin.

"My head hurts," she said as if it was somehow his fault. He smiled down at her, his face suddenly charming.

"I'll fix it," he promised, running a teasing finger down her small, straight nose. "I'll have to get you drunk more often, minx. You're irresistible."

Before Cathy could do more than frown at him sleepily he was gone, only to return a few moments later with a brandy snifter full of some noxious looking concoction.

"Drink this." He sat down on the edge of the bed, holding it out to her.

Cathy struggled up on her elbows. Even that slight movement made her head spin.

"What is it?" she asked suspiciously.

"Hair of the dog, my love, with a slight addition. Drink it."

His arm came around her back, holding her upright, and he thrust the glass against her lips. Cathy had perforce to swallow. It was vile, and she gagged. But when her stomach had subsided and she was lying once more against her pillows she had to admit that she did feel better. She seemed to be floating, her body weightless, her mind soaring free. The mattress creaked and then sprang upwards as Jon rose lithely to his feet.

"Don't leave me," Cathy murmured, her eyes barely opening as she clutched at his hand. "Please."

"I won't."

"Martha would be so disappointed. . . ." The words trailed off, and her long eyelashes fluttered down against her pale cheeks. Jon grimaced. Despite his firmest resolutions, the chit could twist him around her finger with ludicrous ease. He wandered over to the fireplace and stood staring blindly down into the flames, musing wryly on the follies of love-smitten men.

The pop of an exploding ember woke Cathy some two hours later. The room was dark and peopled with mysterious shadows. Cathy blinked groggily, pushing herself up on one elbow to peer around the room. The faint odor of cigar smoke lingered in the air, reminding her irresistibly of her husband. The events of the night were not very clear in her mind, but she could vaguely recall him undressing her gently, his dark voice calling her his love. His love. A smile curled her mouth.

The bright orange glow of a cigar tip caught her attention. She stared at it, just barely able to make out the long, lean shadow that sprawled behind it in the chair before the fire.

"Jon?" she breathed, knowing it could be no one else. The cigar was flipped into the fire, and the dark figure got to its feet and crossed toward the bed. Cathy sank back down, pleased. It was, indeed, Jon.

"How do you feel?" he asked softly, his face in shadow as he leaned over her.

"Lonely." Cathy sighed the word, feeling no need to hide her love for him any longer, now that he had admitted his. His love. His love. The words echoed like a benediction in her brain.

"What do you mean?" Jon asked after a long moment, his voice strangely guarded. Cathy wished she could see his expression, but the room was too dark. Ah, well, there would be tomorrow—all their tomorrows—to talk of love. Right now she wanted more tangible proof.

"I'm cold, too," she whispered demurely, her hand stealing out from beneath the quilts to run tentatively up his thigh. "Won't you warm me up?"

"Ah, God, Cathy, you're still drunk," he groaned. Cathy smiled in the darkness. Yes, she was drunk. Drunk on the heady nectar of his love. Her hand moved higher, her fingers running teasingly along the hard bulge in his breeches. He started to pull back, then stopped. A low growl sounded deep in his throat and his hand came down to cover hers, pressing her fingers against him.

"I want you." His voice sounded strangled. Cathy's fingers curled against the soft velvet, kneading, probing. She touched the hard round-ness of a button, freeing first it, then its fellow. Her cool little fingers slid inside to delicately stroke his hot flesh.

"Ah, God," he groaned, coming down beside her on the bed. His arms went around her and he strained her body against his hard length. The thick quilts were between them and Jon kicked them aside impatiently, his mouth twisting across hers with searing need. Cathy twined her own arms tightly around his neck, returning his kiss with abandon, sobbing endearments against his mouth. She could feel the tremors that racked his corded limbs as they pressed her to him.

Through the thin silk of her nightdress, Jon's fingers burned on her breasts and thighs and belly. Cathy writhed under his caresses, thrilling to his touch. Her own hands came away from his neck to tug at his shirt. The buttons popped, al-lowing her access to his furred, muscular chest. She pulled her mouth away from his, pressing wanton kisses on his body. His breath rattled in his throat as though he was dying.

Jon sat up suddenly, and Cathy could have screamed at the removal of his warm flesh.

"Darling?" she questioned huskily, moving to kneel behind him where he sat on the edge of the bed, her soft arms sliding around his waist.

"I have to take off my damned boots," he gritted,

tugging at the offending footgear.

Cathy chuckled softly, the sound seductive. She pressed her breasts tightly against the hard muscles of his back, and he groaned, his hand leaving what he was doing to pull her head around for a brief, burning kiss. Then, dropping his boots to the floor one at a time, he stood up, stripping off his clothes with hands that shook. Cathy stayed where she was, kneeling on the edge of the bed, watching him boldly. In the flickering firelight his flesh looked orangey-bronze, as hard and pagan as any savage's. Cathy admired the bulging muscles of his arms and thighs through half-closed lids, reveling in his strength. When at last he was naked, her eyes swept him with a long, desirous look that made him catch his breath. With every pore of her body she was aware of his maleness and his passion.

"Wanton," he murmured, coming to her and pulling her nightgown over her head with a swift movement, leaving her as naked as he. She pressed against him uninhibitedly, loving the rasp of his body hair against her soft breasts, the heat and hardness of him. He bore her backwards, his knee parting her thighs as they came to rest on the softness of the mattress.

When he possessed her, Cathy felt throbbing burning ecstasy. She arched against him, grinding her softness to his strength, sobbing her need against his mouth. He was gasping, his heart beating so hard that it sounded like a drum being pounded between them. He took her to the edge of rapture once, and then again. When at last he was still, his mouth pressed warmly against the curve of her neck and his hand gently stroking her hair, she felt as if she had died and gone to heaven. Her fingers came up to touch his mouth wonderingly, and then before she could tell him of her joy she fell asleep.

Jon slept too, but not as deeply as Cathy. He awoke just as the sun was peeping over the horizon, the first of its rays slanting into the room, to find his arms wrapped tightly around her naked body. Jon ran a lazy hand over her silken skin, then when that brought no response he propped himself up on one elbow, staring down at the sleeping loveliness of her face.

His eyes touched tenderly on the dark lashes that lay in long, feathery crescents against her delicately tinted cheeks, her small nose, the lovely, seductive curve of her rose-colored mouth. He admired the fine-boned curve of her jaw, her slender neck, the strawberries-and-cream perfection of her breasts. The quilts were still twisted about their feet, and the slenderness of her waist, the rounded turn of her hip, her long, lissome legs were all laid bare to his appreciative gaze. He thought of the incredible bliss she had given him in the night, and marveled at the depth of his passion. Never before in his life had he experienced anything like it.

A stray sunbeam touched a curling lock of her

hair, bringing it to vibrant, shimmering life. Jon picked up the strand, testing its silken texture with his fingers, lifting it to his nose to inhale its sweet fragrance, pressing it reverently to his lips. He froze in the act. He was behaving like some besotted half-wit! Last night the devouring love he felt for her had blinded him to everything but her beauty and his need. Daylight, with its accompanying return to sanity, had come not a moment too soon. Jon thanked God that Cathy had slept through his awakening. If she had not, he would have confessed his love, imploring her on bended knees if necessary to return it. God, how she would have enjoyed that! Her revenge would have been complete.

Jon got off the bed hastily, gathering up his discarded clothes from where they had fallen. A scowl furrowed his brow. He needed time to think before facing Cathy again. They could not go on as they were. At least, he could not. Not bothering to do more than pull on his breeches, he let himself quietly out of the room.

The day was well-advanced when Cathy awoke, the sun high up in the sky. She stirred sleepily, missing the warmth that had curled around her in the night. Her eyes blinked open, and she pressed her face lovingly to the indentation in the pillow next to hers. Jon must already have gone out to the fields. What a slug-a-bed he must think her! And what a shameless hussy, she thought, blushing as she remembered her boldness of the night.

Jon loved her. The thought rang with a clarion purity through the otherwise confusing memories of last night. Could she doubt it, remembering his wild lovemaking? Slowly a frown marred her features as less welcome memories began to intrude. He had taken her more than once, last night. The first time was in the carriage on the way home from the ball. With sickening detail, Jon's brutal rape of her body replayed itself in her mind. God, how could he have done such a thing? If he loved her? Had he actually said that he loved her, or had she only imagined it because she wanted it so much? She concentrated, trying to remember. A deep, painful blush crept up over her face to the very roots of her hair as the events of the night came back to her. God, she had acted like a bitch in heat, practically begging him to make love to her! She remembered the way she had touched him, had pressed wanton kisses all over his body, and wanted to die.

He didn't love her. He couldn't. Not after the bestial, disgusting way he had taken her in the carriage! The champagne she had consumed had combined with her desperate need to make the words up out of thin air! God, how he must be laughing at her! How he must despise her! Or worse, maybe he just didn't care. Maybe such nights were so common to him that he wouldn't even give her behavior a second thought.

A discreet knock at the door interrupted her agonized musings. She took a deep breath, willing herself to be calm.

"Yes?"

"About time you woke up, Miss Cathy," Martha scolded good-humoredly, opening the door. "Master John told me to let you sleep, but enough's enough. Master Cray is making such a to-do that you'd think he was about to starve!"

"You've seen Jon this morning!" Cathy said with as much coolness as she could muster.

"Yes, and a fine feather he looked to be in, too. You must have stirred his blood for him, last night!"

In spite of herself, Cathy could feel a blush stealing across her cheeks. There was no doubt that she had, as Martha put it, stirred his blood! Humiliation rose like bile in her throat, and Martha's amused chuckles didn't help.

"Was he going out to the fields?" She had to know how much time she had to prepare for her next meeting with him. Martha's eyes widened with surprise.

"Why, no, lovey, he said he had to go to Atlanta on business. He said he'd be gone about a week. Didn't he tell you!" Martha sounded suddenly concerned, as if she was beginning to suspect that something was not quite right. Cathy swallowed, and did her best to produce a bright smile.

"Oh, yes, of course he did. I just forgot, for a moment," she lied. "Did you say Cray was hungry? Poor little boy! Bring him here, please, and I'll see what I can do about it."

Cathy went through the rest of the day like a zombie. She smiled, she played with Cray, she made all the right responses while one thought pounded repeatedly in her brain: Jon cared so little for her, thought so little of what had happened between them the night before, that he could take off to Atlanta for a week without a word, without even saying good-bye! Dear God, the thought hurt! Cathy had never felt so totally forsaken in her life.

Late that afternoon as she played with Cray in the rose garden she heard a carriage roll up the drive. What now, she thought dismally, and prepared herself for a gossip session with a catty neighbor. Some pretty probing questions were likely to be directed at herself, she realized with a blush. Last night had been a disaster on all fronts.

"You've got a visitor, miss," Petersham came out to tell her, sounding vaguely disapproving. Cathy looked at him, puzzled by his tone.

"Who is it?"

"A gentleman, miss. He wouldn't give his name."

Which accounted for Petersham's disapproval, Cathy reflected. She hoped fervently that it wasn't Paul Harrison come to apologize for his behavior of last night, or, worse, to pursue their acquaintance. Cathy carried Cray with her as she followed Petersham back into the house, hurriedly smoothing her hair as Petersham indicated the parlor.

"I put him in there, Miss Cathy. If you need me, I'll be within call."

Really, did he expect the man to attack her in her own house? Cathy frowned at him impatiently, then pushed open the parlor door. A nattily dressed, silver haired gentleman stood with his back to her.

He turned slowly as Cathy opened the door. Cathy recognized him as soon as he moved. A glad cry rose in her throat, and she practically ran across the room to embrace him.

"Papa! Oh, Papa, I'm so glad you're here!"

Seventeen

"Are you sure you're doing the right thing, Miss Cathy?" Martha sounded deeply troubled as she poured steaming cans of hot water into the ornate bath.

"Yes, Martha, I'm sure." Cathy's reply was clipped. Inwardly she wished she was really as certain as she claimed to be. Part of her longed to tuck Cray under one arm and her portmanteau under the other and fly back to Woodham—and Jon—as if her feet had suddenly sprouted wings. But that was the soft, weak, feminine part. With the rest of her—her pride, her self-respect, her common sense—she knew that the time had come to cut her losses. Jon did not love her—his behavior had made that more than clear. It was folly—no, madness—to stay with a man who sooner or later would take her heart and break it into millions of tiny pieces. She had to get away while she still had the strength of will to do so—and before she had another infant growing under her skirt. Now that the ice had been broken and he was once again taking her to bed, it would not be long before she found herself with child a second time. And the bonds that bound her to Jon would be stronger than ever. Even now, she could only hope that his seed from those last two encounters had not taken.

The thought of Jon's reaction to her leave-taking made Cathy swallow nervously. But luckily she wouldn't be around to see or hear it, she thought, shifting Cray to a more comfortable position as he nursed. By the time Jon returned to Woodham, the "Unicorn" would be well out to sea. He had said he'd be gone for a week, and two days had already passed. Two more would see the "Unicorn" on her way to England.

Her father's presence was providential. Without Sir Thomas she would never have been able to arrange passage in the time available to her. But Sir Thomas had already reserved one cabin on the "Unicorn," and with his influence it was easy to arrange for two more.

Something about her father's attitude puzzled Cathy. He acted worried, guilty almost, and he went to great pains to assure himself that both she and Cray had not been harmed. He had even questioned Martha as to how they had fared, and when the woman told him roundly that Captain Hale treated both his wife and new son with the utmost kindness Sir Thomas became thoughtful, even morose. When Cathy had announced her intention of leaving Woodham while her husband was still away, Sir Thomas had seemed almost reluctant to help her. He had only relented when she had broken down and cried on his shoulder.

429

But finally, she had gotten her own way as she always did with him. And here she was, in a luxurious cabin aboard the English ship "Unicorn," her son at her breast, her nanny to care for them both, and under the protection of her father. Why then did she feel so miserable?

"Lovey, won't you change your mind before it's too late?" Martha's words broke into her thoughts. Cathy stirred restlessly in the chair by the bed, one hand joggling Cray's diaper-clad bottom as she stretched her aching back.

"No, Martha, I won't." Cathy was tired of the endless discussion and her voice reflected it. "It's best that we go back to England for a number of reasons you know nothing about."

This attempt to quell Martha failed abysmally, as Cathy should have known it would. Instead of being silenced, Martha merely shifted the focus of her attack.

"You'll break the poor man's heart, lovey. He's that daft about you."

Cathy slanted Martha a reproachful look, then deliberately shifted her attention back to Cray, whose grip on her nipple was lessening as he struggled with sleep. A fond smile curved her mouth as she watched his silent battle. As long as her son lived she would never be able to forget his father, she thought a trifle sadly. The two were so alike, even in Cray's infancy, that it was uncanny.

"Captain Hale's a fine man, Miss Cathy. You'll be hard put to it to find another to match him, or his care of you."

Cathy was unable to stop herself from responding to this.

"Captain Hale kidnapped me, raped me, and got me with child. He then deserted me, and only came back because he wanted revenge for some fancied wrong. If that's what you call his care of me, you can have it. I think I'll be better off without it."

"He's your husband, lovey, whether you like it or not. In the eyes of God and the eyes of the law. It's not right, you taking his son and leaving him."

"Oh, hush, Martha, for Gods sake!" Cathy cried angrily. The shrillness of her voice caused Cray's blue eyes to open wide with alarm. The small replica of Jon's face crinkled ominously, and Cathy got hurriedly to her feet as Cray let out a frightened yell.

"Hush, my darling, mommy wasn't fussing. Shh, now, that's my good boy," she crooned into the black curls that lay against her shoulder as she walked him back and forth. At Martha she cast a burning glare, as if to say, "Now see what you've done." The woman looked unrepentant. Her face was set in stolid lines as she laid out soap and towels for Cathy's bath.

Finally Cray's sobs quieted to gulping sniffles, and then these too ceased. Cathy crossed with him to the bunk. If she moved very carefully and was very quiet she might be able to put the child down without waking him. He had been fractious all day, and she was worn out with tending him. She could only surmise that the change in his surroundings had not agreed with him, as Martha had pointed out earlier with gloomy relish.

Cathy positioned Cray on his stomach close to the wall side of the bunk, then covered him with the tiny hand-crocheted blanket that she had brought with them from Woodham. Dear as the child was to her, she welcomed his periods of sleep. The bath water steamed invitingly, and she longed to climb in and soothe her stiff muscles with a long, luxurious soak.

Martha was thankfully silent as she helped Cathy to undress. Cathy knew that this unaccustomed forbearance was not due to anything she had said or done. Martha was just reluctant to disturb Cray's rest. Sooner or later the woman would start again with her recriminations. They would undoubtedly be thrown at her head incessantly until the "Unicorn" was at sea.

The water, as she slid into it, felt wonderful. Cathy sank to her chin, breathing deeply of the soft honeysuckle fragrance and blowing idly on the bubbles. She closed her eyes, determined to enjoy the first moments of peace and quiet she had had all day. A dark, hawkish face appeared on the screen of her closed lids. Cathy opened them immediately. She would not allow herself to think of Jon.

Taking the bath sponge in one hand and the soap in the other, she worked up a vigorous lather on the skin of her arms and legs. One long tendril escaped from the mass on top of her head, and she tucked it up impatiently. Finally she scrubbed at her face, and then rinsed the soap away. Martha was ready with a towel as Cathy climbed out.

Cathy was wrapping the towel around herself when the door to the cabin was kicked open with such force that it bounced back on its hinges. Cathy gasped, clutching the towel to her, and turned startled eyes on the door. Martha was doing the same, and little Cray, his sleep disturbed, blinked once before starting to cry.

Her consternation was such that Cathy had no thought even for Cray. Surveying her grimly from the open doorway was Jon. Water dripped from the brim of his hat and his clothes were soaked, and looking beyond him Cathy saw that rain was falling steadily, making the already dark night look even darker. His mouth was set in an uncompromisingly straight line, and his eyes blazed at her accusingly.

"Good evening, Cathy," he said mockingly when she only gaped at him. "I'm glad to see you've fared so well in my absence." His glance raked her scantily clad, still damp body from head to toes.

In her return, Cathy swiftly inspected him. He was dressed for riding in dark breeches, caped coat that swirled around his knees, tall boots and a wide-brimmed hat. From the looks of him he had just ridden in from Atlanta, found her gone, and somehow traced her to the "Unicorn." Cathy swallowed, her throat suddenly dry. All her plans, her preparations might have been for naught. Then she pursed her lips thoughtfully. This was an English ship, and her father was nearby. Jon could not force her to go with him.

While Cathy stared at Jon as if frozen in place, Martha gathered her wits and crossed the cabin to pick up Cray. The baby's cries stilled as Martha rocked him comfortingly. Jon flicked a glance toward his son and the nursemaid.

"Martha, would you take Cray elsewhere, if you please? I would like to have a word with my wife."

"Yes, sir." Martha sounded subdued, and Cathy guessed that the woman found Jon almost as intimidating as she did. But such thoughts were rudely shattered when Martha turned a brief, triumphant look on her before sliding from the cabin. When the two were gone, Jon closed the door very softly, then shed his wet hat and coat with almost casual movements. The dampness of the night had pushed his black hair into deep waves, and he raked a hand through it impatiently before leaning back against the closed door, his arms folded over his chest.

"Suppose you explain to me just what the sweet hell you think you're doing here." His voice was still mild, but his eyes were leaping with anger. Cathy wanted to drop her own before that burning gaze. Instead she wrapped the towel more securely around her body, tilted her chin, and returned his look coldly.

"I'm leaving you. I should think that was obvious."

"So you're leaving me, are you? Just like that, without a word, while I'm away earning a living for you and your son? Our son." The gray eyes burned brightly at her. Cathy met them steadily.

"Yes."

"Like hell." His shoulders came away from the door, and he crossed the floor toward her in two swift strides, his hands clamping hurtfully down over her slender bare shoulders. Cathy held her ground, forcing herself to look up into that menacing face with a calmness she was far from feeling. His long fingers bit deeply into her soft flesh.

"You're not leaving me." The words were ground out from between clenched teeth. That telltale muscle was throbbing warningly in his jaw. His big body was tense with anger, his face dark with it. He looked as if he could easily do her an injury.

"You can't stop me. Even if you were to carry me bodily off this ship, I'd find another sooner or later. You can't keep me locked in, or watch me all the time."

Her calm response seemed to infuriate him. He shook her, letting her feel the strength in his hands. Cathy's hair tumbled down and the towel slipped. She caught the edge of it, holding it in front of her. He stopped shaking her, his eyes running over her nearly naked body almost savagely.

"Why? Have I beaten you, mistreated you in any way?" Cathy could tell he was holding on to his temper with an iron rein. She looked at him derisively. He had the grace to flush.

"You're angry about the other night." It was a statement, not a question. Cathy refused to answer, shifting her gaze so that she was staring stonily over his shoulder. His hands slid down to her upper arms, tightened.

"I'm sorry about that. Like you, I'd had too much to drink. Anyway, you can't deny that you deliberately provoked me. You'd been teasing me for months, since even before Cray was born. What kind of response did you expect?"

"Not rape!" Cathy snapped, then wished she had been coldly dignified instead.

"All right, I'm sorry. It won't happen again, I promise. What else can I say?"

"Not a thing." Cathy pulled away from him as she spoke, and clutching the towel around her went to pull her wrapper from the trunk. She kept her back to him as she slid into it, but she could feel his eyes burning into her.

"Goddamn it, you're not leaving me!" His voice cracked like a whip behind her. Cathy whirled to face him, golden hair flying, blue eyes flashing.

"Oh, yes, I am," she hissed at him, tying the belt to her wrapper then clenching her fists. "And you can't stop me!"

"The hell I can't."

"The hell you can't!" Cathy was suddenly as enraged as he was. "You don't own me, you know. And there is such a thing as divorce. Although there really isn't much point. You've made this marriage such a hell that I'm not likely to repeat it!"

Jon drew in his breath sharply, his eyes darkening as if he'd been punched in the stomach. Cathy took perverse pleasure in knowing that she'd somehow managed to hurt him. He took a step toward her, then stopped. A thin white line appeared at each corner of his mouth.

"You want me to beg you, don't you?" he asked savagely. "That's what you've wanted all along, to have me groveling at your feet. All right, you bitch, you win. I'm begging you: don't do this."

The look he turned on her was hating. Cathy stared at him, feeling her mouth go slack with amazement. He was begging her. . . . Her proud pirate captain was actually begging her not to leave him! Hope began to beat suffocatingly in her breast. Was it possible . . . ? She had to be sure.

"Why do you want me to stay, Jon?" she asked softly, her eyes never leaving his. Angry red color seeped up under the flesh of his cheekbones. His eyes glared at her.

"God, you want your pound of flesh, don't you?" he demanded ferociously. "All right, I'll give it to you. I love you, goddamn it. So go ahead and laugh."

"Say that again." Cathy could feel the corners of her mouth quivering up into a smile. He saw it too, and his face tightened almost fiendishly. Cathy didn't care. She was beginning to feel wildly, deliriously happy. She couldn't believe it. He'd said he loved her, and from the fierceness of him he meant it.

"So you think it's funny, do you, bitch?" he growled, reaching for her and pulling her hard against him. "We'll see how hard you laugh after this!"

His mouth was deliberately ungentle over hers, his arms around her like iron bands. The force of his kiss threatened to snap her spine. Cathy trembled in his hold, her arms sliding up to twine around his neck, hugging him tightly.

"I love you too, you dolt," she murmured into the warm strength of his neck when he at last allowed her to draw breath. He went very still against her, his hands freezing in their caressing movements. After a moment he caught her by the arms, holding her out at arm's length so that he could look down into her face. Cathy smiled up at him mistily.

"What did you say?" His voice sounded hard, suspicious. His eyes were leaping with strange wild lights.

"I said I love you. If you weren't so stubborn and suspicious, you'd have known it months ago."

His eyes began to blaze, their hot depths searing her.

"If this is some kind of game you're playing. . . ." He broke off, his teeth snapping together warningly. Cathy shook her head at him, her eyes warm and tender on his tense face.

"Is it so hard to believe?" she asked, gently teasing. "Of course, you can be a bully and a brute and you're jealous and you have a vile temper, but there's no accounting for tastes, after all."

He closed his eyes, pulling her to him with shaking hands. She felt his mouth on her hair, and slid her arms around his waist, holding him tightly. He was murmuring love words, promises, endearments to the top of her head. They were all a low jumble of pure happiness to Cathy. She snuggled against his hard muscles, her mouth adoring his silk-covered chest, pulling his shirt out from the waistband of his breeches with hands that were not quite steady. She touched his warm flesh, ran her hands over the muscles of his back, her sensitive fingertips feeling the ridges of the scars he would carry with him to his grave. Her hands stroked lovingly, then stilled. He couldn't still believe. . . .

"Darling, you believe me now, don't you?" she whispered, pulling back from him a little so that he could hear her. He had to bend his head to catch her words.

"About what?" he smiled when she repeated her words. Cathy leaned back in the warm circle of his arms, studying his face lovingly. His eyes glowed at her, his expression gentler than she had ever seen it. She had tamed an eagle, she thought, intoxicated by the look and feel and smell of him, taught a fierce gray timber wolf to feed from her hand. The sensation was indescribable, the smile she returned to him dazzling. She was tempted to let all the unanswered questions slide until later, but she wanted to be sure that all the unhappiness was behind them.

"About what happened to you in prison," she persisted softly. The muscles in the arms holding her tensed, the old guarded look returned to his eyes. Her heart was in her eyes as she watched these changes, and after a moment he relaxed with an effort and smiled down at her, although his face was still somewhat strained.

"You don't have to find excuses for what you did," he said steadily, his eyes burning with the flames of passion. "I deserved it, I know. What I did to you—kidnap, rape, forcing you to be my mistress—was unforgivable. If you love me now, that's all that matters. We'll never speak of what's past again."

Cathy uttered a sound that hovered somewhere between a laugh and a cry.

"But, Jon, darling, I promise you that I had nothing to do with it! I didn't even know you were in prison, I swear. The 'Lady Chester' sailed for England the day after you escaped! How could I have known?"

"After I escaped?" he repeated disbelievingly, his black brows drawing together in a frown. "What are you talking about?"

"After we were married," Cathy reminded him patiently, but accompanied the words with a reproachful look. "You escaped. You can't possibly have forgotten!"

"My love, after we were married, and your father very properly knocked me unconscious for daring to snarl at you, I was in no condition to escape anywhere. I spent the voyage in the 'Lady Chester's' brig. When she docked in Portsmouth, I was taken in chains to London and thrown into Newgate Prison. A couple of days later I was informed that I had been sentenced to death for the crime of piracy without even the courtesy of being allowed to be present at my own trial. If not for my men, I would even now be rotting in a limestone pit in the prison yard. The only escape I made was in London, that night I came to your aunt's house."

"But I thought. . . ." Cathy's mind was in a whirl. How could this be? Before she could get her thoughts sorted a hard knock sounded at the door. Jon's arms tightened around her, his eyes questioning.

"Are you expecting a guest?"

"No, of course not. It's probably Martha—or my father."

"Ah, yes. Your father. I have something I want to discuss with him."

This speech was decidedly odd coming from a man who had only met her father once under unfavorable circumstances. There was something here that she did not understand. Cathy's face puckered in a puzzled frown as she went to open the door.

"Daughter, I need to talk to you. There's something you should know. . . ." Sir Thomas's voice trailed off as his eyes went past Cathy to touch on the tall man who was regarding him coolly from the other side of the room.

"Hale. I want you to know I would have sent for you. That's what I was coming to tell Cathy."

"Papa, what are you talking about? Why would you have sent for Jon?" Cathy asked, bewildered, as she stood back to let her father enter. Sir Thomas ignored her as Jon's eyes bore into his.

"It was a lie, wasn't it? She had nothing to do with it, knew nothing about it."

441

"Yes." Sir Thomas's face was ashen, his eyes almost pleading with the implacable figure before him. "She knew nothing."

"Good God, man, I might have killed her!" The words were hissed from between clenched teeth.

"I know." Sir Thomas sounded very tired suddenly. "I was almost out of my mind when she disappeared. I'd just been informed that you had managed to escape, and I knew you had her. I thought. . . . God, what I thought! But you didn't harm her, and I thank God for it."

"You should. It was touch and go. I wanted to, but I couldn't. But. . . ."

"For goodness' sake, will one of you please tell me what this is all about? Papa? Jon?" Cathy looked from one to the other of them. Their cryptic conversation could have been in Greek for all the sense it made to her.

Both men looked at her, small and fragile-seeming in the dim lamplight, long golden hair swirling about her blue silk-clad form, a frown marring her lovely brow. Jon's eyes softened, glowed. Cathy smiled at him, a small intimate smile that she was barely conscious of. Sir Thomas watched them both, his eyes deeply troubled.

"I've done you a wrong, daughter." Sir Thomas said heavily. "But please believe that at the time I thought I was acting in your best interests."

He paused, seeming to search for the necessary words. Cathy stared at him, faint suspicion crystallizing into a certainty. Jon crossed the room to stand behind her, his arms sliding around her waist as he pressed her back against him. Cathy's eyes never left her father as she leaned back against the hard wall of her husband's chest.

"Jon didn't escape on the 'Lady Chester,' did he, Papa? You lied to me." She knew it was true even as she said it. The slight inclination of her father's head was unnecessary confirmation.

"Tell me, Papa." The words were quiet. Cathy could feel tears pricking at the backs of her eyes as Sir Thomas described in a halting voice how he had had Jon imprisoned in England, arranged for his trial and his subsequent death sentence. When he came to the part about the beatings he had ordered and paid for while telling Jon that they were Cathy's doing, she let out a little shocked cry. Jon's arms tightened around her waist, and she could feel his lips in her hair. Sir Thomas looked wretched.

"And then, when I finally traced you to Charleston, I found my daughter looking physically well, although she was emotionally upset," Sir Thomas concluded, addressing his remarks to Jon over Cathy's head. "I managed to glean enough information from her to conclude that she felt herself to be unloved. After seeing how well you had treated her under the circumstances, I knew that that wasn't the case at all, so I agreed to help her leave you while intending to get in touch with you and tell you the truth. I thought that you would take it from there. But from what I've seen tonight, you've already managed to get things straightened out without me.

I deeply regret any pain I may have caused either of you, and I hope that you'll find it in your hearts to forgive me."

His tired blue eyes rested on Cathy sorrowfully as he finished, and she could not bring herself to ignore their silent appeal. She pulled away from Jon's hold and crossed the room to her father, putting a gentle hand on his arm and reaching up to press a soft kiss to his cheek.

"Of course we forgive you, Papa. I know you only did it for me." She slanted a pleading look over her shoulder at Jon, who stiffened, then sighed and very slowly crossed the room to extend a hand to Sir Thomas. The older man grasped it eagerly, and Cathy nearly cried herself when she saw the suspicious moisture glistening in his eyes.

"I suppose we'll have to learn to tolerate each other," Jon said dryly, extricating his hand finally from Sir Thomas's rather frenzied hold. "You're the father of my wife, the grandfather of my son. And as I intend keeping them both, and even adding to the fold, we'll likely be seeing quite a bit of each other. If you can stomach a reformed pirate for a son-in-law, I guess I can live with a devious Earl for a father-in-law."

Jon smiled as he spoke, and Sir Thomas fairly beamed in return.

"I'm proud to have you in the family," said Sir Thomas. He hugged his daughter, shook hands with Jon again, and took himself off. As the door closed behind him Jon leaned against it, looking at Cathy with glowing eyes.

"Well, my love?" he asked softly. She flew across the room to him, burying her face against his shirt front. His arms went around her, holding her close.

"You must have hated me, Jon," she murmured. He smiled a little, pressing his face into her bright hair, savoring its softness, the sweet smell he always associated with it.

"I did—but only because I loved you so much I couldn't bear to think that you would do such a thing to me. I was just beginning to think you cared for me, you see, when everything blew up in my face."

"Cared for you?" Cathy laughed with a slight catch in her voice. "By that time I'd been head over heels in love with you for weeks. I would have told you, but I was so afraid that you didn't love me. I thought you just wanted me for . . . for. . . ." She broke off, her face blushing rosily. Jon held her a little away from him so that he could see her expression. He grinned at her heightened color.

"You were right," he told her wickedly. "I did want you for . . . for. . . . I still do. But I also love you more than I ever thought I could love anything or anyone in my life. And if you let me, I'll spend the rest of my life proving it."

These last words were said very quietly, and Cathy practically melted at their tenderness. She smiled at him lovingly, going up on her toes to touch her mouth to his. Jon's arms tightened gently around her, his mouth parting over hers.

He kissed her hotly, but with a new reverence that thrilled Cathy to her toes. When she finally pulled back from him to catch her breath, she was trembling, her cheeks rosy and her eyes languorous with love. He continued to press kisses over the silken flesh of her throat, his mouth trailing down the deep plunge neckline of her wrapper to burn in the valley between her breasts. Cathy held him to her, tenderly stroking his black head. He loved her, and she loved him. Nothing could ever go wrong between them again.

"Darling, what you said to my father about adding to the fold—did you mean it? I—I know you weren't too happy when I told you about Cray . . ." she broke off as he raised his head to look at her.

"Sweetheart, you can't think I didn't want Cray, can you? I love you. I'll love any children you give me. I was just so afraid of losing you. . . . I was afraid you would die. I couldn't stand the thought. That's why I said what I did, when you told me about the baby."

"Oh, Jon," she sighed, pressing herself against his rapidly hardening muscles and running her hands caressingly across his broad shoulders. "Will we have many children?"

"Dozens," he breathed, swinging her up in his arms to hold her cradled against his chest, his eyes burning hotly as they met hers. "At least two score. I'm making a project of it. And I suggest that we'd better begin work right away if we hope to meet our goal."

"Here?" Cathy asked faintly even as she melted against him. "But, darling, shouldn't we go home first? I. . . ."

"Right now all I can think of is how much I want to make love to you," he said against her ear, his mouth doing funny things to her insides as it nibbled and nuzzled. "We can go home tomorrow."

And they did.

Center Point Publishing
Brooks Road • PO Box 1
Thorndike ME 04986-0001 USA

**(207) 568-3717
US & Canada:
1 800 929-9108**